The Other Mrs.

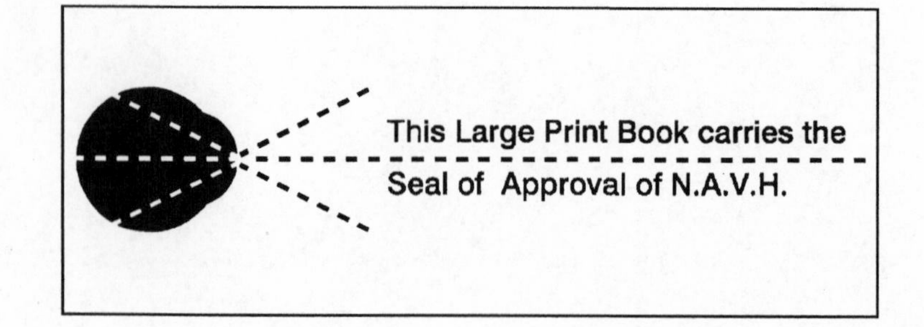
This Large Print Book carries the
Seal of Approval of N.A.V.H.

The Other Mrs.

Mary Kubica

THORNDIKE PRESS
A part of Gale, a Cengage Company

This is a work of fiction. Names, characters, places, and incidents are either the product of the author's imagination or are used fictitiously. Any resemblance to actual persons, living or dead, businesses, companies, events, or locales is entirely coincidental.

Thorndike Press® Large Print Core.
The text of this Large Print edition is unabridged.
Other aspects of the book may vary from the original edition.
Set in 16 pt. Plantin.

**LIBRARY OF CONGRESS CIP DATA ON FILE.
CATALOGUING IN PUBLICATION FOR THIS BOOK
IS AVAILABLE FROM THE LIBRARY OF CONGRESS**

ISBN-13: 978-1-4328-7631-9 (hardcover alk. paper)

Published in 2020 by arrangement with Harlequin Books S.A.

Printed in Mexico
Print Number: 01 Print Year: 2020

For Michelle and Sara

Sadie

There's something off about the house. Something that nags at me, makes me feel uneasy, though I don't know what it is that makes me feel this way. On the surface, it's perfectly idyllic, gray with a large covered porch, one that runs the full width of the house. It's boxy and big, a foursquare farmhouse with windows aligned in rows, symmetrical in a way I find eye-pleasing. The street itself is charming, sloped and tree-covered, each home as lovely and well kept as the next.

On the surface, there's nothing not to like. But I know better than to take things at face value. It doesn't help that the day, like the house, is gray. If the sun were out maybe I'd feel differently.

"That one," I say to Will, pointing at it because it's identical to the one in the picture that was given to Will from the executor of the estate. He'd flown in last week, to Portland, to take care of the official paperwork. Then he'd flown back, so we could drive here together. He hadn't had time to see the house then.

Will pauses, bringing the car to rest in the street. He and I lean forward in our seats at exactly the same time, taking it in, as do the boys in the back seat. No one speaks, not at first, not until Tate blurts out that the house is *gigantic* — transposing his soft and his hard *g*'s as seven-year-olds have a tendency to do — and Will laughs, overjoyed that someone besides him can see the advantage of our move to Maine.

The house is not gigantic, not really, but in comparison to a 1,200-square-foot condo, it is, especially when it comes with its own yard. Tate has never had his own yard before.

Will gently steps on the gas, easing the car into the driveway. Once in Park, we climb out — some more quickly than others, though the dogs are the quickest of all — stretching our legs, grateful, if for nothing else, to be done with the long drive. The air outside is different than what I'm used to, infused with the scent of damp earth, salty ocean and the woodsy terrain. It smells nothing like home. The street is quiet in a way I don't like. An eerie quiet, an unsettling quiet, and at once I'm reminded of the notion that there's safety in numbers. That bad things are less likely to happen among crowds. There's a misconception that rural living is better, safer than urban living, and yet it's simply not true. Not when you take into account the disproportionate number of people living in cities, the inadequate health care system in rural parts.

I watch Will walk toward the porch steps, the dogs running along beside him, passing him up. He's not reluctant like me. He struts as much as he walks, anxious to get inside and check things out. I feel resentful because of it, because I didn't want to come.

At the base of the steps he hesitates, aware only then that I'm not coming. He turns toward me, standing still next to the car, and asks, "Everything all right?" I don't answer because I'm not sure if everything is all right.

Tate goes dashing after Will, but fourteen-year-old Otto hovers like me, also reluctant. We've always been so much alike.

"Sadie," Will says, modifying his question, asking this time, "are you coming?" He tells me it's cold out, a fact of which I was unaware because of my focus on other things, like how the trees around the house tower high enough to block the light. And how dangerously slick the steep street must be when it snows. A man stands up at the top of the hill, on his lawn with a rake in hand. He's stopped raking and stands perched, watching me, I think. I raise a hand and wave, the neighborly thing to do. He doesn't wave back. He turns away, goes back to raking. My gaze goes back to Will, who says nothing of the man. Surely he saw him as well as I did.

"Come on," Will says instead. He turns and climbs the steps with Tate beside him. "Let's go inside," he decides. At the front door, Will reaches into his pocket and pulls out the house keys. He knocks first, but he doesn't wait to be let in. As Will unlocks the door and pushes it open, Otto moves away from me, leaving me behind. I go, too, only because I don't want to be left alone outside.

Inside we discover that the house is old, with things like mahogany paneling, heavy drapery, tin ceilings, brown-and-forest-green walls. It smells musty. It's dark, dreary.

We crowd together in the entryway and assess the home, a traditional floor plan with the closed-in rooms. The furnishings are formal and unwelcoming.

My attention gets lost on the curved legs

of the dining room table. On the tarnished candelabra that sits on top of it. On the yellowing chair pads. I hardly see her standing at the top of the stairs. Were it not for the slightest bit of movement caught out of the corner of my eye, I might never have seen her. But there she stands, a morose figure dressed in black. Black jeans, a black shirt, bare feet. Her hair is black, long with bangs that slant sideways across her face. Her eyes are outlined in a thick slash of black eyeliner. Everything black, aside from the white lettering on her shirt, which reads, *I want to die.* The septum of her nose is pierced. Her skin, in contrast to everything else, is white, pallid, ghostlike. She's thin.

Tate sees her, too. At this, he moves from Will to me, hiding behind me, burrowing his face into my backside. It's not like Tate to be scared. It's not like me to be scared, and yet I'm well aware that the hairs on the nape of my neck now stand on end.

"Hello," I say, my voice weak.

Will now sees her, too. His eyes go to her; he says her name. He starts climbing the steps to her, and they creak under his feet, protesting our arrival. "Imogen," he says with arms wide, expecting, I think, that she'll fold herself into them and let him hold her. But she doesn't because she's sixteen and standing before her is a man she hardly knows. I can't fault her for this. And yet the brooding, melancholic girl was not what I'd imagined when we discovered we were given guardianship of a child.

Her voice is acidic when she speaks, quiet — she doesn't ever raise her voice; she doesn't need to. The muted tone is much more unsettling than if she screamed. "Stay the fuck away from me," she says coolly.

She glowers down over the stair banister. My hands involuntarily move behind me and to Tate's ears. Will stops where he is. He lowers his arms. Will has seen her before, just last week when he came and met with the executor of the estate. It was then that he signed the papers and took physical possession of her, though arrangements had been made for her to stay with a friend while Will, the boys and I drove here.

The girl asks, her voice angry, "Why'd you have to come?"

Will tries to tell her — the answer is easy, for were it not for us, she'd likely have entered the foster care system until she turned eighteen, unless she was granted emancipation, which seemed unlikely at her age — but an answer is not what she wants. She turns away from him, disappearing into one of the second-story rooms where we hear her futzing angrily with things. Will makes a move to follow, but I say to him, "Give her time," and he does.

This girl is not the same as the little girl Will had shown us in the photograph. A happy-go-lucky freckled brunette of about six years old. This girl is different, much changed. The years have not been kind to her. She comes with the house, just another thing that's been left to us in the will, mixed in with the house and the heirlooms, what assets remain in the bank. She's sixteen, nearly able to be on her own — a moot point that I tried arguing, for certainly she had a friend or some other acquaintance who could take her in until she turned eighteen — but Will said no. With Alice dead, we were all that remained, her only family, though she and I were meeting just now for the first time. *She needs to be with family,* Will told me at the time, days ago only, though it feels like weeks. *A family who will love and care for her. She's all alone, Sadie.* My maternal instinct had kicked in then, thinking of this orphaned child all alone in the world, with no one but us.

I hadn't wanted to come. I'd argued that she should come to us. But there was so much more to consider, and so we came anyway, despite my reservations.

I wonder now, and not for the first time this week, what kind of disastrous effect this change will have on our family. It can't possibly be the fresh start Will so auspiciously believes it to be.

SADIE

Seven Weeks Later . . .

The siren woke us at some point in the middle of the night. I heard the scream of it. I saw the dazzling lights that streamed in the bedroom window as Will grabbed his glasses from the bedside table and sat up abruptly in bed, adjusting them on the bridge of his nose.

"What's that?" he asked, holding his breath, disoriented and confused, and I told him it was a siren. We sat hushed for a minute, listening as the wail drifted farther away, quieting down but never going completely silent. We could hear it still, stopped somewhere just down the street from our home.

"What do you think happened?" Will asked, and I thought only of the elderly couple on the block, the man who pushed his wife in a wheelchair up and down the street, though he could barely walk. They were both white-haired, wrinkled, his back curved like the hunchback of Notre Dame. He always looked tired to me, like maybe she was the one who should be doing the pushing. It didn't help that our street was steep, a decline to the ocean below.

"The Nilssons," Will and I said at the same time, and if there was a lack of empathy in our voices it's because this is what is expected of older people. They get injured, sick; they die.

"What time is it?" I asked Will, but by then he'd returned his glasses to the bedside table and said to me, "I don't know," as he pressed in closely and folded an arm around my waistline, and I felt the subconscious pull of my body from his.

We fell back asleep that way, forgetting altogether about the siren that had snatched us from our dreams.

In the morning I shower and get dressed, still tired from a fitful night. The boys are in the kitchen, eating breakfast. I hear the commotion downstairs as I step uneasily from the bedroom, a stranger in the home because of Imogen. Because Imogen has a way of making us feel unwelcome, even after all this time.

I start to make my way down the hall.

Imogen's door is open a crack. She's inside, which strikes me as odd because her door is never open when she's inside. She doesn't know that it's open, that I'm in the hallway watching her. Her back is to me and she's leaned into a mirror, tracing the lines of black eyeliner above her eyes.

I peer through the crevice and into Imogen's room. The walls are dark, tacked with images of artists and bands who look very much like her, with the long black hair and the black eyes, dressed in all black. A black gauzy thing hangs above her bed, a canopy of sorts. The bed is unmade, a dark gray pintuck duvet lying on the floor. The blackout curtains are pulled taut, keeping the light out. I think of vampires.

Imogen finishes with the eyeliner. She snaps the cap on it, turns too fast and sees me before I have a chance to retreat. "What the fuck do you want?" she asks, the anger and the vulgarity of her question taking my breath away, though I don't know why. It's not as if it's the first time she's spoken to me this way. You'd think I might be used to it by now. Imogen scuttles so quickly to the door that at first I think she's going to hit me, which she hasn't ever done, but the speed of her movement and the look on her face make me think she might. I involuntarily flinch, moving backward, and instead, she slams the door shut on me. I'm grateful for this, for getting the door slammed in my face as opposed to getting hit. The door misses my nose by an inch.

My heart thumps inside my chest. I stand in the hallway, breathless. I clear my voice, try to recover from the shock of it. I step closer, rap my knuckles on the wood and say, "I'm leaving for the ferry in a few minutes. If you want a ride," knowing she won't accept my offer. My voice is tumultuous in a way that I despise. Imogen doesn't answer.

I turn and follow the scent of breakfast downstairs. Will is by the stove when I come down. He stands, flipping pancakes in an apron, while singing one of those songs from the jaunty CDs Tate likes to listen to, something far too merry for seven fifteen in the morning.

He stops when he sees me. "You okay?" he asks.

"Fine," I say, voice strained.

The dogs circle Will's feet, hoping he'll drop something. They're big dogs and the kitchen is small. There isn't enough room for four of us in here, let alone six. I call to the dogs and, when they come, send them into the backyard to play.

Will smiles at me when I return and offers me a plate. I opt only for coffee, telling Otto to hurry up and finish. He sits at the kitchen table, hunched over his pancakes, shoulders slumped forward to make himself appear small. His lack of confidence worries me, though I tell myself that this is normal for fourteen. Every child goes through this, but I wonder if they do.

Imogen stomps through the kitchen. There are tears up the thighs and in the knees of her black jeans. Her boots are black leather combat boots, with nearly a two-inch heel. Even without the boots, she's taller than me. Raven skulls dangle from her ears. Her shirt reads, *Normal people suck.* Tate, at the table, tries to sound it out, as he does all of Imogen's graphic T-shirts. He's a good reader, but she doesn't stand still long enough for him to get a look at it. Imogen reaches for a cabinet pull. She yanks open the door, scanning the inside of the cabinet before slamming it shut.

"What are you looking for?" Will asks, always eager to please, but Imogen finds it then in the form of a Kit Kat bar, which she tears open and bites into.

"I made breakfast," Will says, but Imogen, blue eyes drifting past Otto and Tate at the kitchen table, seeing the third, vacant place setting set for her, says only, "Good for you."

She turns and leaves the room. We hear her boots stomp across the wooden floors. We hear the front door open and close, and only then, when she's gone, can I breathe.

I help myself to coffee, filling a travel mug before making an effort to stretch past Will for my things: the keys and a bag that sit on the countertop just out of reach. He leans in to kiss me before I go. I don't mean to, and yet it's instinctive when I hesitate, when I draw back from his kiss.

"You okay?" Will asks again, looking at me curiously, and I blame a bout of nausea for my hesitation. It's not entirely untrue. It's been months now since the affair, and yet his hands are still like sandpaper when he touches me and, as he does, I can't help but wonder where those hands have been before they were on me.

A fresh start, he'd said, one of the many reasons we find ourselves transported to this home in Maine, which belonged to Will's only sister, Alice, before she died. Alice had suffered for years from fibromyalgia before the symptoms got the best of her and she decided to end her life. The pain of fibromyalgia is deep. It's diffused throughout the body and often accompanied by incapacitating exhaustion and fatigue. From what I've heard and seen, the pain is intense — a sometimes stabbing, sometimes throbbing pain — worse in the morning than later in the day, but never going completely away. It's a silent disease because no one can see pain. And yet it's debilitating.

There was only one thing Alice could do to counter the pain and fatigue, and that was to head into the home's attic with a rope and step stool. But not before first meeting with a lawyer and preparing a will, leaving her house and everything inside of it to Will. Leaving her child to Will.

Sixteen-year-old Imogen spends her days doing only God knows what. School, presumably, for part of it at least, because we only get truancy calls on occasion. But how she spends the rest of the day I don't know. When Will or I ask, she either ignores us or she has something smart to say: that she's off fighting crime, promoting world peace, saving the fucking whales. *Fuck* is one of her favorite words. She uses it often.

Suicide can leave survivors like Imogen feeling angry and resentful, rejected, abandoned, full of rage. I've tried to be understanding. It's getting hard to do.

Growing up, Will and Alice were close, but they grew apart over the years. He was rattled by her death, but he didn't exactly grieve. In truth, I think he felt more guilty than anything: that he did a negligent job of keeping in touch, that he wasn't involved in Imogen's life and that he never grasped the gravity of Alice's disease. He feels he let them down.

At first, when we'd learned of our inheritance, I suggested to Will that we sell the home, bring Imogen to Chicago to live with us, but after what happened in Chicago — not just the affair alone, but all of it, *everything* — it was our chance to make a new beginning, a fresh start. Or so Will said.

We've been here less than two months, so that we're still getting the lay of the land, though we found jobs quickly, Will and me, he working as an adjunct professor teaching human ecology two days a week, over on the mainland.

As one of only two physicians on the island, they practically paid me to come.

I press my lips to Will's mouth this time, my ticket to leave.

"I'll see you tonight," I say, calling again to Otto to hurry up or we'll be late. I grab my things from the countertop and tell him I'll be in the car waiting. "Two minutes," I say, knowing he'll stretch two to five or six as he always does.

I kiss little Tate goodbye before I go. He

stands on his chair, wraps his sticky arms around my neck and screams into an ear, "I love you, Mommy," and somewhere inside of me my heart skips a beat because I know that at least one of them still loves me.

My car sits on the driveway beside Will's sedan. Though we have a garage attached to the house, it's overrun with boxes that we have yet to unpack.

The car is cold when I arrive, covered in a thin layer of frost that has settled on the windows overnight. I unlock the door with my key fob. The headlights blink; a light turns on inside.

I reach for the door handle. But before I can give it a tug, I catch sight of something on the window that stops me. There are lines streaked through the frost on the driver's side. They've started to liquefy in the warmth of the morning's sunlight, softening at their edges. But still, they're there. I step closer. As I do, I see that the lines are not lines at all, but letters traced into the frost on the window, coming together to form a single word: *Die.*

A hand shoots to my mouth. I don't have to think hard to know who left this message for me to find. Imogen doesn't want us here. She wants us to leave.

I've tried to be understanding because of how awful the situation must be for her. Her life has been upended. She lost her mother and now must share her home with people she doesn't know. But that doesn't justify threatening me. Because Imogen doesn't mince words. She means just what she said. She wants me to die.

I make my way back up the porch steps and call through the front door for Will.

"What is it?" he asks, making his way from the kitchen. "Did you forget something?" he asks as he cocks his head to the side, taking in my keys, my bag, my coffee. I didn't forget something.

"You have to see this," I say, whispering now so the boys don't hear.

Will follows me barefoot out the front door, though the concrete is bitterly cold. Three feet from the car I point at it, the word inscribed in the frost of the window. "You see it?" I ask, turning my eyes to Will's. He sees it. I can tell as much in his expression, in the way it turns instantly distressed, mirroring mine.

"Shit," he says because he, like me, knows who left that there. He rubs at his forehead, thinking this through. "I'll talk to her," he says, and I ask defensively, "What good will that do?"

We've talked to Imogen many times over the last few weeks. We've discussed the language she uses, especially around Tate; the need for a curfew; more. Though talking *at* would be a more fitting term than talking *to* because it isn't a conversation we have. It's a lecture. She stands while Will or I speak. She listens, maybe. She rarely replies. She takes nothing to heart and then she leaves.

Will's voice is quiet when he speaks. "We don't know for certain that she left this here," he says softly, floating an idea by me, one I'd rather not consider. "Isn't it possible," Will asks, "that someone left that message for Otto?"

"You think someone left a death threat on my window for our fourteen-year-old child?" I ask, in case Will has somehow misconstrued the meaning of that word *Die*.

"It's possible, isn't it?" he asks, and though I know that it is, I tell him, "No." I say it with more conviction in my voice than I feel, because I don't want to believe it. "Not again," I insist. "We left all that behind when we moved."

But did we? It isn't entirely outside the realm of possibility that someone is being mean to Otto. That someone's bullying him. It's happened before. It can happen again.

I say to Will, "Maybe we should call the police."

But Will shakes his head. "Not until we know who did this. If it's Imogen, is that really a reason to involve the police? She's just an angry girl, Sadie. She's grieving, lashing out. She'd never do anything to hurt any of us."

"Wouldn't she?" I ask, far less sure than Will. Imogen has become another point of contention in our marriage. She and Will are related by blood; there's a connection there that I don't have.

When Will doesn't reply, I go on, arguing, "No matter who the intended recipient, Will, it's still a *death* threat. That's a very serious thing."

"I know, I know," he says, glancing over his shoulder to be sure Otto isn't on his way out. He speaks quickly, says, "But if we get the police involved, Sadie, it will draw attention to Otto. Unwanted attention. The kids will look at him differently, if they don't already. He won't stand a chance. Let me call the school first. Speak to his teacher, the principal, make sure Otto isn't having trouble with anyone. I know you're worried," he says, voice softening as he reaches out, runs a comforting hand along my arm. "I'm worried, too," he says. "But can we do that first," he asks, "before calling the police? And can I at least have a conversation with Imogen before we just assume this was her?"

This is Will. Always the voice of reason in our marriage.

"Fine," I tell him, relenting, admitting that he might be right. I hate to think of Otto as an outcast in a new school, of him being bullied like this.

But I also can't stand to consider the animosity Imogen has toward us. We have to get to the bottom of this without making things worse. "But if it happens again, if anything like this happens again," I say, pulling my hand from my bag, "we go to the police."

"Deal," Will agrees, and he kisses me on the forehead. "We'll get this taken care of," he says, "before it has a chance to go too far."

"Do you promise?" I ask, wishing Will could snap his fingers and make everything better, just like that.

"I promise," he says as I watch him skip back up the stairs and inside the house, disappearing behind the door. I scribble my hand through the letters. I wipe my hands on the thighs of my pants before letting myself into the cold car. I start the engine and blast the defrost, watching as it takes the last traces of the message away, though it'll stay with me all day.

The minutes on the car's dash pass by, two and then three. I stare at the front door, waiting for it to open back up, for Otto to appear this time, slogging to the car with an unreadable expression on his face that gives no indication of what's going on inside his mind. Because that's the only face he makes these days.

They say that parents should know these things — what our kids are thinking — but we don't. Not always. We can never really know what anyone else is thinking.

And yet when children make poor choices, parents are the first to be blamed.

How didn't they know? critics often ask. *How did they overlook the warning signs?*

Why weren't they paying attention to what their kids were doing? — which is a favorite of mine because it implies we weren't.

But I was.

Before, Otto was quiet and introverted. He liked to draw, cartoons mostly, with a fondness for anime, the hip characters with their wild hair and their larger-than-life eyes. He named them, the images in his sketch pad — and had a dream to one day create his own graphic novel based on the adventures of Asa and Ken.

Before, Otto had only a couple of friends — exactly two — but those that he had called me *ma'am.* When they came for dinner, they brought their dishes to the kitchen sink. They left their shoes by the front door. Otto's friends were kind. They were polite.

Otto did well in school. He wasn't a straight A student, but *average* was good enough for him and Will and me. His grades fell in the B/C range. He did his homework and turned it in on time. He never slept through class. His teachers liked him, and only ever had one complaint: they'd like to see Otto participate more.

I didn't overlook the warning signs because there were none to overlook.

I stare at the house now, waiting for Otto to come. After four minutes, my eyes give up on the front door. As they do, something out the car window catches my eye. Mr. Nilsson pushing Mrs. Nilsson in her wheelchair, down the street. The slope is steep; it takes great effort to hang on to the rubbery handles of the wheelchair. He walks slowly, more on the heels of his feet, as if they are car brakes and he's riding the brakes all the way down the street.

Not yet seven twenty in the morning, and they're both completely done up, him in twill slacks and a sweater, her in some sort of knit set where everything is a light pink. Her hair is curled, tightly woven and set with spray, and I think of him, scrupulously wrapping each lock of hair around a roller and securing the pin. Poppy is her name, I think. His might be Charles. Or George.

Right before our home, Mr. Nilsson makes a diagonal turn, going to the opposite side of the street from ours.

As he does, his eyes remain on the rear of my car where the exhaust comes out in clouds.

All at once the sound of last night's siren returns to me, the waning bellow of it as it passed by our home and disappeared somewhere down the street.

A dull pain forms in the pit of my stomach, but I don't know why.

Sadie

The drive from the ferry dock to the medical clinic is short, only a handful of blocks. It takes less than five minutes from the time I drop Otto off until I pull up to the humble, low-slung blue building that was once a house.

From the front, it still resembles a house, though the back opens up far wider than any home ever would, attaching to a low-cost independent living center for senior citizens with easy access to our medical services. Long ago someone donated their home for the clinic. Years later, the independent living center was an addition.

The state of Maine is home to some four thousand islands. I didn't know this before we arrived. There's a dearth of doctors on the more rural of them, such as this one. Many of the older physicians are in the process of retiring, leaving vacancies that prove difficult to fill.

The isolation of island living isn't for everyone, present company included. There's something unsettling in knowing that when the last ferry leaves for the night, we're quite literally trapped. Even in daylight, the island is rocky around its edges, overcome with tall pines that make it suffocating and small. When winter comes, as it soon will, the harsh weather will shut much of the island down, and the bay around us may freeze, trapping us here.

Will and I got our house for free. We got a tax credit for me to work at the clinic. I said no to the idea, but Will said yes, though it wasn't the money we needed. My background is in emergency medicine. I'm not board-certified in general practice, though I have a temporary license while I go through the process of becoming fully licensed in Maine.

Inside, the blue building no longer resembles a house. Walls have been put up and knocked down to create a reception desk, exam rooms, a lobby. There's a smell to the building, something heavy and damp. It clings to me even after I leave. Will smells it, too. It doesn't help that Emma, the receptionist, is a smoker, consuming about a pack a day of cigarettes. Though she smokes outside, she hangs her coat on the same rack as mine. The smell roves from coat to coat.

Will looks curiously at me some nights after I've come home. He asks, *Have you been smoking?* I might as well be for the smell of nicotine and tobacco that follows me home.

Of course not, I've told him. *You know I don't smoke,* and then I tell him about Emma.

Leave your coat out. I'll wash it, Will has told me countless times. I do and he washes it, but it makes no difference because the next day it happens all over again.

Today I step into the clinic to find Joyce, the head nurse, and Emma waiting for me.

"You're late," Joyce says, but if I am, I'm only a minute late. Joyce must be sixty-five years old, close to retirement, and a bit of a shrew. She's been here far longer than either Emma or me, which makes her top dog at the clinic, in her mind at least. "Didn't they teach you punctuality where you came from?" she asks.

I've found that the minds of the people are as small as the island itself.

I step past her and start my day.

Hours later, I'm with a patient when I see Will's face surface on my cell phone, five feet away. It's silenced. I can't hear the phone's ring, though Will's name appears above the picture of him: the attractive, chiseled face, the bright hazel eyes. He's handsome, in a take-your-breath-away way, and I think that it's the eyes. Or maybe the fact that at forty, he could still pass for twenty-five. Will wears his dark hair long, swept back into a low bun that's growing in popularity these days, giving off an intellectual, hipster vibe that his students seem to like.

I ignore the image of Will on my phone and attend to my patient, a forty-three-year-old woman presenting with a fever, chest pain, a cough. Undoubtedly bronchitis. But still, I press my stethoscope to her lungs for a listen.

I practiced emergency medicine for years before coming here. There, at a state-of-the-art teaching hospital in the heart of Chicago, I went into each shift without any idea of what I might see, every patient coming in in distress. The victims of multiple-vehicle collisions, women hemorrhaging excessively following a home birth, three-hundred-pound men in the midst of a psychotic break. It was tense and dramatic. There, in a constant state of high alert, I felt alive.

Here, it is different. Here, every day I

know what I will see, the same rotation of bronchitis, diarrhea and warts.

When I finally get the chance to call Will back, there's a hitch to his voice. "Sadie," he says, and, from the way that he says it, I know that something is wrong. He stops there, my mind engineering scenarios to make up for that which he doesn't say. It settles on Otto and the way I left him at the ferry terminal this morning. I got him there just in time, a minute or two before the ferry would leave. I said goodbye, my car idling a hundred feet from the waiting boat, watching as Otto moped off for another day of school.

It was then that my eyes caught sight of Imogen, standing at the edge of the pier with her friends. Imogen is a beautiful girl. There's no rebutting that. Her skin is naturally fair; she doesn't need to cover it in talcum powder, as her friends must do, to make herself look white. The piercing through her nose has taken some getting used to. Her eyes, in contrast to the skin, are an icy blue, her former brunette showing through the unkempt eyebrows. Imogen eschews the dark, bold lipstick the other girls like her wear, but instead wears a tasteful rosy beige. It's actually quite lovely.

Otto has never lived in such close proximity to a girl before. His curiosity has gotten the better of him. The two of them don't talk much, no more than Imogen and I speak. She won't ride with us to the ferry dock; she doesn't speak to him at school. As far as I know, she doesn't acknowledge him on the commute there. Their interactions are brief. Otto at the kitchen table working on math homework last night, for example, and Imogen passing through, seeing his binder, noting the teacher's name on the front of it, commenting: *Mr. Jansen is a fucking douche.*

Otto had just stared back wide-eyed in reply. The word *fuck* is not yet in his repertoire. But I imagine it's only a matter of time.

This morning, Imogen and her friends were standing at the edge of the pier, smoking cigarettes. The smoke encircled their heads, loitering, white in the frosty air. I watched as Imogen brought a cigarette to her mouth, inhaled deeply with the expertise of someone who'd done this before, who knew what she was doing. She held it in and then exhaled slowly and, as she did, I was certain her eyes came to me.

Did she see me sitting there in my car, watching her?

Or was she just staring vacantly into space?

I'd been so busy watching Imogen that, now that I think back on it, I never saw Otto board the ferry. I only assumed he would.

"It's Otto," I say aloud now, at the same time that Will says, "It wasn't the Nilssons," and at first I don't know what he means by that. What does Otto have to do with the elderly couple who lives down the street?

"What about the Nilssons?" I ask, but my mind has trouble going there, because — at the sudden realization that I didn't see Otto board the ferry — all I can think about is Otto in the single seat across from the principal's office with handcuffs on his wrists, a police officer standing three feet away, watching him. On the corner of the principal's desk, an evidence bag, though what was inside, I couldn't yet see.

Mr. and Mrs. Foust, the principal had said to us that day and, for the first time in my life, I attempted some clout. *Doctor,* I said to him, face deadpan as Will and I stood behind Otto, Will dropping a hand to Otto's shoulder to let him know that whatever he'd done, we were there for him.

I wasn't sure if it was my imagination, but I was quite certain I saw the police officer smirk.

"The siren last night," Will explains now over the phone, bringing me back to the present. That was before, I remind myself, and this is now. What happened to Otto in Chicago is in the past. Over and done with. "It wasn't the Nilssons after all. The Nilssons are perfectly fine. It was Morgan."

"Morgan Baines?" I ask, though I'm not sure why. There isn't another Morgan on our block, as far as I know. Morgan Baines is a neighbor, one I've never spoken to but Will has. She and her family live just up the street from us in a foursquare farmhouse not unlike our own, Morgan, her husband and their little girl. Because they lived at the top of the hill, Will and I often speculated that their views of the sea were splendid, three hundred sixty degrees of our little island and the ocean that walls us in.

And then one day Will slipped and told me they were. The views. Splendid.

I tried not to feel insecure. I told myself that Will wouldn't have admitted to being inside her home if there was something going on between them. But Will has a past with women; he has a history. A year ago I would have said Will would never cheat on me. But I couldn't put anything past him now.

"Yes, Sadie," Will says. "Morgan Baines," and only then do I make out her face, though I've not seen her up close before.

Only from a distance. Long hair, the color of milk chocolate, and bangs, the type that hang too long, that spend their time wedged behind an ear.

"What happened?" I ask as I find a place to sit, and, "Is everything all right?" I wonder if Morgan is diabetic, if she's asthmatic, if she has an autoimmune condition that would trigger a middle-of-the-night visit to the emergency room. There are only two physicians here, myself and my colleague, Dr. Sanders. Last night she was on call, not me.

There are no EMTs on the island, only police officers who know how to drive an ambulance and are minimally trained in lifesaving measures. There are no hospitals as well, and so a rescue boat would have been called in from the mainland to meet the ambulance down by the dock to cart Morgan away for treatment, while another waited on shore for the third leg of her commute.

I think of the amount of time that would have taken in sum. What I've heard is that the system works like a well-oiled machine and yet it's nearly three miles to the mainland. Those rescue boats can only go so fast and are dependent on the cooperation of the sea.

But this is catastrophic thinking only, my mind ruminating on worst-case scenarios.

"Is she all right, Will?" I ask again because in all this time, Will has said nothing.

"No, Sadie," he says, as if I should somehow know that everything is not all right. There's a pointedness about his reply. A brevity, and then he says no more.

"Well, what happened?" I urge, and he takes a deep breath and tells me.

"She's dead," he says.

And if my response is apathetic, it's only because death and dying are a part of my everyday routine. I've seen every unspeakable thing there is to see, and I didn't know Morgan Baines at all. We'd had no interaction aside from a onetime wave out my window as I drove slowly by her home and she stood there, thrusting the bangs behind an ear before returning the gesture. I'd thought about it long after, overanalyzing as I have a tendency to do. I wondered about that look on her face. If it was meant for me or if she was scowling at something else.

"Dead?" I ask now. "Dead how?" And as Will begins to cry on the other end of the line, he says, "She was murdered, they say."

"They? Who's they?" I ask.

"The people, Sadie," he says. "Everyone. It's all anyone's talking about in town," and as I open the door to the exam room and step into the hall, I find that it's true. That patients in the waiting room are in the thick of a conversation about the murder, and they look at me with tears in their eyes and ask if I heard the news.

"A murder! On our island!" someone gasps. A hush falls over the room and, as the door opens and a man steps in, an older woman screams. It's a patient only, and yet with news like this, it's hard not to think the worst of everyone. It's hard not to give in to fear.

CAMILLE

I'm not going to tell you everything. Just the things I think you should know.

I met him on the street. The corner of some city street, where it crosses beneath the "L" tracks. It was gritty, grungy there. The buildings, the tracks didn't let the light in. Parked cars, steel girders, orange construction cones filled the road. The people, they were ordinary Chicago people. Just your everyday eclectic mix of hipsters and steampunk, hobos, trixies, the social elite.

I was walking. I didn't know where I was going. All around, the city buzzed. Air-conditioning units dripped from up above; a bum begged for cash. A street preacher stood on the curb, foaming at the mouth, telling us we're all hell-bound.

I passed a guy on the street. I was going the other way. I didn't know who he was, but I knew his type. The kind of rich former prep school kid who never fraternized with the trashy public school kids like me. Now he was all grown up, working in the Financial District, shopping at Whole Foods. He's what you'd call a *chad,* though his name was probably something else like Luke, Miles, Brad. Something smug, uptight, overused. Mundane. He gave me a nod and a smile, one that said women easily fell for his charms. But not me.

I turned away, kept walking, didn't give him the satisfaction of smiling back.

I felt his eyes follow me from behind.

I spied my reflection in a storefront window. My hair, long, straight, with bangs. Rust-colored, stretching halfway down my back, over the shoulders of an arctic-blue tee that matched my eyes.

I saw what that chad was looking at.

I ran a hand through my hair. I didn't look half bad.

Overhead, the "L" thundered past. It was loud. But not loud enough to tune out the street preacher. Adulterers, whores, blasphemers, gluttons. We were all doomed.

The day was hot. Not just summer but the dog days of it. Eighty or ninety degrees out. Everything smelled rancid, like sewage. The smell of garbage gagged me as I passed an alley. The hot air trapped the smell so there was no escaping it, just as there was no escaping the heat.

I was looking up, watching the "L," getting my bearings. I wondered what time it was. I knew every clock in the city. The Peacock clock, Father Time, Marshall Field's. Four clocks on the Wrigley Building, so that it didn't matter which way you came at it from, you could still see a clock. But there were no clocks there, on the corner where I was at.

I didn't see the stoplight before me go red. I didn't see the cab come hustling past, racing another cab to snatch up a fare down the street. I stepped right into the street with both feet.

I felt him first. I felt the grip of his hand tighten on my wrist like a pipe wrench so that I couldn't move.

In an instant, I fell in love with that hand — warm, capable, decisive. Protective. His fingers were thick; his hands big with clean, short nails. There was a tiny tattoo, a glyph on the skin between his fingers and thumb. Something small and pointy, like a mountain peak. For a minute, that was all I saw. That inky mountain peak.

His grip was powerful and swift. In one stroke, he stopped me. A second later, the cab raced past, not six inches from my feet. I felt the rush of it on my face. The wind off the car pushed me away, and then sucked me back in as it passed. I saw a flash of colors only; I felt the breeze. I didn't see the cab shoot past, not until it was speeding off down the street. Only then did I know how close I came to being roadkill.

Overhead, the "L" screeched to a stop on the tracks.

I looked down. There was his hand. My eyes went up his wrist, his arm; they went to his eyes. His eyes were wide, his eyebrows pulled together in concern. He was worried about me. No one ever worried about me.

The light turned green, but we didn't move. We didn't speak. All around, people stepped past us while we stood in the way, blocking them. A minute went by. Two. Still, he didn't let go of my wrist. His hand was warm, tacky. It was humid outside. So hot it was hard to breathe. There was no fresh air. My thighs were moist with sweat. They stuck to my jeans, made the arctic-blue tee cling to me.

When we finally spoke, we spoke at the same time. *That was close.*

We laughed together, released a synchronous sigh.

I could feel my heart pound inside of me. It had nothing to do with the cab.

I bought him coffee. It sounds so unimaginative after the fact, doesn't it? So cliché.

But that was all I could come up with in a pinch.

Let me buy you a coffee, I said. *Repay you for saving my life.*

I fluttered my eyelashes at him. Put a hand on his chest. Gave him a smile.

Only then did I see that he already had a coffee. There in his other hand sat some iced froufrou drink. Our eyes went to it at the same time. We sniggered. He lobbed it into a trash can, said, *Pretend you didn't just see that.*

A coffee would be nice, he said. When he smiled, he smiled with his eyes.

He told me his name was Will. There was a stutter when he said it, so that it came out *Wi-Will.* He was nervous, shy around girls, shy around me. I liked that about him.

I took his hand into mine, said, *It's nice to meet you, Wi-Will.*

We sat in a booth, side by side. We drank our coffees. We talked; we laughed.

That night there was a party, one of those rooftop venues with a city view. An engagement party for Sadie's friends, Jack and Emily. She was the one who was invited, not me. I don't think Emily liked me much, but I planned to go anyway, just the same as Cinderella went to the royal ball. I had a dress picked out, one I took from Sadie's closet. It fit me to a T, though she was bigger than me, Sadie with her broad shoulders and her thick hips. She had no business wearing that dress. I was doing her a favor.

I had a bad habit of shopping in Sadie's closet. Once, when I was there, all alone or so I thought, I heard the jiggle of keys in the front door lock. I slipped out of the room, into the living room, arriving only a second before she did. There stood my darling roommate, hands on her hips, looking quizzically at me.

You look like you've been up to no good, she said. I didn't say one way or the other whether I'd been being good. It wasn't often that I was good. Sadie was the rule follower, not me.

That dress wasn't the only thing I took from her. I also used her credit card to buy new shoes, metallic wedge sandals with a crisscross strap.

I said to Will that day in the coffee shop about the engagement party: *We don't even know each other. But I'd be an idiot not to ask. Come with me?*

I'd be honored, he said, making eyes at me in the café booth. He sat close, his elbow brushing against mine.

He'd come to the party.

I gave him the address, told him I'd meet him inside.

We parted ways beneath the "L" tracks. I watched him walk away until he got swallowed up in pedestrian traffic. Even then, I still watched.

I couldn't wait to see him that night.

But as luck would have it, I didn't make it to the party after all. Fate had other plans that night.

But Sadie was there. Sadie, who had been invited to Jack and Emily's engagement party. She was out of this world. He went right up to her, fawned all over her, forgot about me.

I'd made it easy on her, inviting him to that party. I always made things easy for Sadie.

If it wasn't for me, they never would've met. He was mine before he was hers.

She forgets that all the time.

Sadie

There isn't much to our street, just like any of the other inland streets that lie braided throughout the island. There's nothing more than a handful of shingled cottages and farmhouses bisected by patches of trees.

The island itself is home to less than a thousand. We live on the more populous part, in walking distance of the ferry, where there's a partial view of the mainland from our steeply sloped street, the size of it shrunken by distance. And yet the sight of it brings comfort to me.

There is a world out there that I can see, even if I'm no longer a part of it.

I drive slowly up the incline. The evergreens have lost their needles now, the birch trees their leaves. They're strewn about the street, crunching beneath the car's tires as I drive. Soon they will be buried by snow.

Salty sea air enters the window, open just a crack. There's a chill to the air, the last lingering traces of fall before winter arrives full bore.

It's after six o'clock in the evening. The sky is dark.

Up above me, across the street and two doors down from my own home, there is a flurry of activity going on at the Baineses' home. Three unmarked cars are parked outside, and I imagine forensic technicians inside, collecting evidence, fingerprinting, photographing the crime scene.

The street looks suddenly different to me.

There is a police car in my own driveway as I pull up. I park beside it, a Ford Crown Victoria, and climb slowly out. I reach into the back seat to gather my things. I make my way to the front door, looking warily around to be sure that I'm alone. There's the greatest sense of unease. It's hard not to let my imagination get the best of me, to imagine a killer hiding among the bushes watching me.

But the street is silent. There are no people around that I can see. My neighbors have gone inside, mistakenly believing they're safer inside their own homes — which Morgan Baines must have thought, too, before she was killed in hers.

I press my keys into the front door. Will leaps to his feet when I enter. His jeans are slouchy, baggy in the knees, his shirt partly tucked. His long hair hangs loose.

"There's an officer here," he says briskly, though I see this for myself, the officer sitting there on the arm of the sofa. "He's investigating the murder," Will says, practically choking on that word. *Murder.*

Will's eyes are weary and red; he's been crying. He reaches into a pocket and pulls out a tissue. He dabs his eyes with it. Will is the more thin-skinned of us, the more sensitive. Will cries at movies. He cries when watching the evening news.

He cried when I found out he'd been sleeping with another woman, though he tried in vain to deny it.

There is no other woman, Sadie, he said as he fell to his knees all those months ago before me and cried his eyes out, pleading his innocence.

To his point I never saw the woman herself, but the signs of her were everywhere.

I blamed myself for it. I should have seen it coming. After all, I was never Will's first choice for a wife. We've been trying hard to get past it. *Forgive and forget,* they say, but it's easier said than done.

"He has some questions for us," Will says now, and I ask, "Questions?" looking toward the officer, a man in his fifties or sixties with receding hair and pitted skin. A small tract of hair grows above the upper lip, a would-be mustache, brownish gray like the hair on his head.

"Dr. Foust," he says, meeting my eye. He extends a hand and tells me his name is Berg. Officer Berg, and I say that I am Sadie Foust.

Officer Berg looks troubled, a bit shell-shocked even. I gather that his typical calls are complaints of dogs leaving their feces in neighbors' yards; doors left unlocked at the American Legion; the ever-popular 911 hang-up calls. Not this. Not murder.

There are only a handful of patrolmen on the island, Officer Berg being one of them. Oftentimes they meet the ferry down by the dock to be sure everyone boards and departs without any problems, not that there ever are. Not this time of year anyway, though I've heard the change we'll see come summer, when tourists abound. But for now, it's peaceful and quiet. The only people on the boat are the daily commuters who paddle across the bay for school and work.

"What kind of questions?" I ask. Otto sits slouched in a chair in the corner of the room. He fidgets with the fringe of a throw pillow, and I watch as strands of blue come loose in his hands. His eyes look weary. I worry about the stress this is causing him, having to hear from a police officer that a neighbor was murdered. I wonder if he's scared because of it. I know I am. The very idea is unfathomable. A murder so close to our own home. I shudder to think about what went on in the Baineses' home last night.

I glance around the first floor, looking for Imogen, for Tate. As if he knows what I'm thinking, Will says to me, "Imogen isn't home from school yet," and Officer Berg, taking interest in this, asks, "No?"

School ends at two thirty. The commute is long, but still, Otto is home most days by three thirty or four. The clock on the fireplace mantel reads ten after six.

"No," Will tells the officer, "but she'll be home soon. Any minute," he says, citing some tutoring session that Will and I know she didn't have. The officer tells us that he'll need to speak with Imogen, too, and Will says, "Of course." If she isn't home soon, he offers to drive her to the public safety building tonight. It's a catchall building, where a couple of police officers double as EMTs and first responders in the case of fire. If our home went up in flames, Officer Berg would just as likely appear at my door in a fire truck. If Will or I had a heart attack, he'd come in the ambulance.

Only seven-year-old Tate has been spared from the police officer's interrogation. "Tate is outside," Will tells me, seeing the way my eyes look for him. "He's playing with the dogs," he says, and I hear them then, the dogs barking.

I give Will a look, one that wonders how smart it is to leave Tate alone outside when there was a murderer on our street just last night. I stray toward a rear-facing window to find Tate, in a sweatshirt and jeans, a wool hat thrust down over his head. He's having a go with the dogs and a ball. He lobs the ball as far as he can — laughing as he does so — and the girls dash after it, arguing over which will be the one to carry it back to Tate's waiting hand.

Outside, there's evidence of a fire in the backyard firepit. The fire is dying down now, only embers and smoke. There's no longer a flame.

It's far enough away from Tate and the dogs that I don't worry.

Officer Berg sees the smoldering fire, too, and asks if we have a permit for it.

"A permit?" Will asks. "For the fire?" When Officer Berg says yes, Will goes on to explain that our son Tate had come home from school begging for s'mores. They'd read a book about them, *S is for S'mores,* and the rest of the day, Tate had a craving for them.

"The only way we did s'mores back in Chicago was in the toaster oven. This was just a quick treat," Will says. "Completely harmless."

"Around here," Officer Berg tells him, uninterested in Tate's craving, "you need a permit for any open fire."

Will apologizes, blames ignorance, and the officer shrugs. "Next time you'll know," he says, forgiving us this one transgression. There are bigger issues at hand.

"Can I be excused?" Otto asks, saying he has homework to do, and I see this discomfort in his eyes. This is a lot for a fourteen-year-old boy to handle. Though much older than Tate, Otto is still a child. We forget that sometimes. I pat him on the shoulder. I lean in close to him and say, "We're safe here, Otto. I want you to know that," because I don't want him to be scared. "Your dad and I are here to protect you," I tell him.

Otto meets my eyes. I wonder if he believes me when I'm not so sure myself. Are we safe here?

"You can go," the officer tells him and, as he leaves, I find my way to the other arm of the sofa, Officer Berg and I bisected by a velvet sofa the color of marigolds, the furniture left behind in the home all midcentury, and not, unfortunately, midcentury modern. It's just old.

"You know why I'm here?" the officer asks, and I tell him that Will and I heard the siren late last night. That I know Mrs. Baines was murdered.

"Yes, ma'am," he says, and I ask how she was murdered, though the details of her death have not yet been released. They're waiting, he says, until the family has been notified.

"Mr. Baines doesn't know?" I ask, but all he'll say is that Mr. Baines was traveling for business. The first thought that crosses my mind is that, in cases like this, it's always the husband. Mr. Baines, wherever he is, has done this, I think.

Berg tells us how the little Baines girl was the one who found Mrs. Baines dead. She called 911 and told the operator that Morgan wouldn't wake up. I sharply inhale, trying not to imagine all the things that poor little girl might have seen.

"How old is she?" I ask, and Berg replies, "Six years old."

A hand rises to my mouth. "Oh, how awful," I say, and I can't imagine it, Tate finding either Will or me dead.

"She and Tate are in school together," Will declares, looking at Officer Berg and then me. They share the same teacher. They share the same peers. The island school serves children in grades kindergarten through fifth while the rest, those in middle school and beyond, have to be ferried to the mainland for their education. Only fifty-some students go to the elementary school. Nineteen in Tate's classroom because his first grade is combined with the kindergarten class.

"Where is the little girl now?" I ask, and he tells me that she's with family while they try to connect with Jeffrey, traveling for business in Tokyo. The fact that he was out of the country doesn't make Jeffrey Baines any less culpable in my mind. He could have hired someone to carry out the task.

"The poor thing," I say, imagining years' worth of therapy in the child's future.

"What can we do to help?" I ask Officer Berg, and he tells me he's been speaking to residents along the street, asking them questions. "What kind of questions?" I ask.

"Can you tell me, Dr. Foust, where you were last night around eleven o'clock?" the officer asks. In other words, do I have an alibi for the time the homicide occurred?

Last night Will and I watched TV together, after we'd put Tate to bed. We'd lain on different sides of the room, him spread out on the sofa, me curled up on the love seat as we do. Our allocated seats. Shortly after we'd gotten situated and turned on the TV, Will brought me a glass of cabernet from the bottle I'd opened the night before.

I watched him for a while from my own seat, remembering that it wasn't so long ago that I would have found it impossible to sit this far away from Will, on separate sofas. I thought fondly of the days that he would have handed me the wine with a lengthy kiss to the lips, another hand feeling me up as he did so, and I would have found myself easily wiled by the persuasive kiss and the persuasive hands and those eyes. Those eyes! And then one thing would have led to the next and, soon after, we would have giggled like teenagers as we tried to hastily and noiselessly make love on the sofa, ears tuned in to the creaks of the floorboards above us, the rasp of box springs, footsteps on the stairs, to be sure the boys still slept. There was a magnanimity about Will's touch, something that once made me feel giddy and light-headed, drunk without a drop to drink. I couldn't get enough of him. He was intoxicating.

But then I found the cigarette, a Marlboro Silver with lipstick the color of strawberries along its filter. I found that first, followed shortly after by charges for hotel rooms on our credit card statement, a pair of panties in our bedroom that I knew weren't mine. I realized at once that Will was magnanimous and intoxicating to someone other than me.

I didn't smoke. I didn't wear lipstick. And I was far too sensible to leave my underwear lying around someone else's home.

Will just looked at me when I shoved the credit card statement under his nose, when I asked him outright about the hotel charges on our bill. He appeared so taken aback that he'd been caught that he didn't have the wherewithal to manufacture a lie.

Last night, after I'd finished that first glass of wine, Will offered to top me off and I said yes, liking the way the wine made me feel weightless and calm. The next thing I remember was the siren rousing me from sleep.

I must have fallen asleep on the love seat. Will must have helped me to bed.

"Dr. Foust?" the officer asks.

"Will and I were here," I tell him. "Watching TV. The evening news and then *The Late Show.* The one with Stephen Colbert," I say as Officer Berg transcribes my words onto a tablet with his stylus. "Isn't that right, Will?" I ask, and Will nods his head and confirms that I am right. It was *The Late Show.* The one with Stephen Colbert.

"And after *The Late Show*?" the officer asks, and I say only that after *The Late Show* we went to bed.

"Is that right, sir?" Officer Berg asks.

"That's right," Will says. "It was late," he tells the officer. "After *The Late Show,* Sadie and I went to bed. She had to work in the morning and I, well," he says, "I was tired. It was late," he says again, and if he notices the redundancy, he doesn't show it.

"What time was that?" Officer Berg asks.

"Must've been around twelve thirty," I say because even though I don't know for sure, I can do the math. He makes note of this, moving on, asking, "Have you seen anything out of the ordinary over the last few days?"

"Such as?" I inquire, and he shrugs, suggesting, "Anything unusual. Anything at all. Strangers lurking about. Cars you don't recognize, cruising by, surveilling the neighborhood."

But I shake my head and say, "We're new here, Officer. We don't know many people."

But then I remember that Will knows people. That when I'm at work all day, Will has been making friends.

"There was one thing," Will says, speaking up all of a sudden. The officer and I turn to him at the same time.

"What's that?" asks Officer Berg.

But just as soon as he's said it, Will tries to renege. He shakes his head. "Never mind," he says. "I shouldn't have brought it up. I'm sure it means nothing, just an accident on my part."

"Why don't you let me decide," Officer Berg says.

Will explains, "There was a day not so long ago, a couple of weeks maybe. I'd taken Tate to school and headed out on a few errands. I wasn't gone long, a couple of hours, tops. But when I came home, something was off."

"How so?"

"Well, the garage door was up, for one. I would've bet my life I put it down. And then, when I came inside, I was nearly knocked over by the smell of gas. It was so potent. Thank God the dogs were okay. Lord only knows how long they'd been breathing it in. It didn't take long to find the source. It was coming from the stove."

"The stove?" I ask. I tell Will, "You didn't tell me this." My voice is flat, composed, but inside I feel anything but.

Will's voice is conciliatory. "I didn't want

you to worry for nothing. I opened the doors and windows. I aired the house out." He shrugs and says, "It probably wasn't even worth mentioning, Sadie. I shouldn't have brought it up. It had been a busy morning. I was making French toast. Tate and I were running late. I must have left the burner on in a mad scramble to get out the door on time. The pilot light must have blown out."

Officer Berg dismisses this as an accident. He turns to me now. "But not you, Doctor?" he asks. "You haven't noticed anything out of the ordinary?" I tell him no.

"How did Mrs. Baines seem the last time you spoke to her, Doctor?" Officer Berg asks me now. "Was she . . . ?" he begins, but I stop him there and explain that I don't know Morgan Baines. That we've never met.

"I've been busy since we arrived," I say, apologizing, though there's really no need to. "I just never found the time to stop by and introduce myself," I tell him, thinking — though I don't dare say it; that would be insensitive — that Morgan Baines also never found the time to stop by and introduce herself to me.

"Sadie's schedule is fast and furious," Will interjects, so that the officer doesn't judge me for not making friends with the neighbors. I'm grateful for this. "She works long shifts, nearly every day of the week, it seems. My own schedule is the opposite. I teach only three courses, which overlap with Tate's school schedule. It's intentional. When he's here, I'm here. Sadie's the breadwinner," Will admits with no indignity, no shame. "I'm the stay-at-home dad. We never wanted our children to be raised by a nanny," he says, which was something we came up with long ago, before Otto was born. It was a personal choice. From a financial standpoint, it made sense that Will would be the one to stay home. I made more money than him, though we never talked about things like that. Will did his part; I did mine.

"I spoke to Morgan just a couple of days ago," he says, answering the officer's question for me. "She seemed fine, well enough at least. Their hot water heater was on the fritz. She was waiting on a repairman to see if it could be fixed. I tried to fix it myself. I'm handy enough," he says, "just not that handy.

"Do you have any leads?" Will asks, changing topics. "Any signs of forced entry, any suspects?"

Officer Berg flips through his tablet and tells Will that he can't reveal too much just yet. "But," he tells Will, "what I can say is Mrs. Baines was killed between the hours of ten and two last night," and there, on the arm of the sofa, I sit up straighter, staring out the window. Though the Baineses' home is just out of view from where I sit, I can't help but think about how last night as we were here, drinking wine and watching TV, she was there — just beyond my viewpoint — being murdered.

But that's not all.

Because every night at eight thirty in the evening, the last ferry leaves. Which means that the killer spent the night among us, here on the island.

Officer Berg stands up quickly, startling me. I gasp, my hand going to my heart.

"Everything all right, Doctor?" he asks, gazing down at me, trembling.

"Fine," I tell him. "Just fine."

He runs his hands down the thighs of his pants, straightening them. "I suppose we're all a bit jumpy today," he tells me, and I nod my head and agree.

"Anything Sadie and I can do," Will tells Officer Berg as he walks him to the front door. I rise from my seat and follow along. "Anything at all, please let us know. We're here to help."

Berg tips his hat at Will, a sign of gratitude.

"I appreciate that. As you can imagine, the entirety of the island is on edge, people fearful for their lives. This kind of thing doesn't bode well for tourism either. No one wants to visit when there's a murderer on the loose. We'd like to get this wrapped up as quickly as we can. Anything you hear, anything you see . . ." he says, voice drifting, and Will says, "I understand."

The murder of Morgan Baines is bad for business.

Officer Berg says his goodbyes. He hands Will a business card. He's about to leave, but before he does, he has one last inquiry.

"How's the house treating you?" he asks off topic, and Will replies that it's been all right.

"It's dated and, as dated things go, has issues. Drafty windows, a faulty furnace that we'll need to replace."

The officer grimaces. "A furnace isn't cheap. That'll run you a few grand."

Will tells him he knows.

"Shame about Alice," Officer Berg says then, meeting Will's eye. Will echoes his sentiment.

It isn't often that I broach the subject of Alice with Will. But there are things I find myself wanting to know, like what Alice was like, and if she and I would have gotten along if we'd ever had the chance to meet. I imagine that she was antisocial — though I'd never say that to Will. But I think that the pain of fibromyalgia would have kept her at home, away from any sort of social life.

"I never would have pegged her for the suicide type," Officer Berg says then and, as he does, I get the sense that my instinct was wrong.

"What does that mean?" Will asks, a hint of defensiveness in his voice.

"Oh, I don't know," Officer Berg says, though clearly he does because he goes on to tell us how Alice, a regular at Friday night bingo, was affable and jolly when he saw her. How she had a smile that could light up a room. "I guess I just never understood how a person like that winds up taking their own life."

The space between us fills with silence, tension. I don't think he meant anything by it; the man is a bit socially awkward. Still, Will looks hurt. He says nothing. I'm the one to speak. "She suffered from fibromyalgia," I say, realizing Officer Berg must not know this, or maybe he's one of those people who think it's more of a mental disorder than a medical one. Fibromyalgia is highly misunderstood. People believe it's made up, that it isn't real. There is no cure, and, on the surface, a person appears to be fine; there's no test that can be used to diagnose fibromyalgia. Because of this, the diagnosis is based on symptoms alone — in other words, widespread pain that can't otherwise be explained. For this reason, a large portion of physicians themselves question the credibility of the condition, often suggesting patients see a psychiatrist for treatment instead. It makes me sad to think about, Alice in so much pain and no one believing it.

"Yes, of course," Officer Berg says. "It's such a terrible thing. She must have really been hurting to do what she did," he says, and again, my eyes go to Will. I know that Officer Berg doesn't mean to be rude; in his own awkward way, he's offering his sympathy.

"I liked Alice a lot," he says. "She was a lovely lady."

"Indeed she was," Will says, and again Officer Berg mumbles, "Such a shame," before he says a final goodbye and goes.

Once he's gone, Will heads quietly to the kitchen to start dinner. I let him go, watching out the narrow pane of glass alongside the door as Officer Berg pulls his Crown Vic from our drive. He heads uphill, about to join his cohort at the Baineses' home, or so I think.

But then he doesn't go to the Baineses' home. Instead he pulls his car to the end of the drive across the street from theirs, at the home of the Nilssons. Officer Berg steps out. He leaves the car running, red taillights bright against the darkness of night. I watch as Berg places something inside a mailbox and closes the door. He returns to his car, disappearing over the crest of the hill.

Camille

I disappeared that night after Will and Sadie met. I was full of anger, of self-loathing.

But I couldn't stay away from Will forever. I thought about him all the time. He was there every time I so much as blinked.

Eventually, I sought him out. A little internet surfing told me where he lived, where he worked. I looked for him. I found what I was looking for. Though by then he was older, grayer, with kids, while in all those years, I hadn't changed much. My gene pool was apparently a good one. Age couldn't touch me. My hair was still the color of rust, my eyes an electric blue. My skin had yet to betray me.

I put on a dress, a black off-the-shoulder dress. I put on makeup, perfume. I put on jewelry. I did my hair.

I followed him for days, showed up where he least expected to see me.

Remember me? I asked, cornering him in

a deli. I stood too close. I grasped him by the elbow. I called him by name. Because there's nothing that excites us more than the sound of our own name. It's the sweetest sound in the world to us. *Corner of Madison and Wabash. Fifteen years ago. You saved my life, Will.*

It didn't take but a moment for him to remember. His face lit up.

Time had taken its toll on him. The strain of marriage, of parenting, of a job, a mortgage. This Will was a burned-out version of the Will I met.

It was nothing I couldn't fix.

He just needed to forget for a while that he had a wife and kids.

I could help him with that.

I gave him a wide smile. I took him by the hand.

If it wasn't for you, I said, leaning in to whisper the words in his ear, *I'd be dead.*

There was a spark in his eyes. His cheeks flushed. His eyes swept me up and down, landing near my lips.

He smiled, said, *How could I ever forget?*

He lightened up; he laughed. *What are you doing here?*

I tossed my hair over a shoulder, said, *I was outside, just passing by. I thought I saw you through the window.*

He touched the ends of my hair, said it looked nice.

And that dress, he said, followed it up with a long, low whistle.

He wasn't looking at my lips anymore. Now he was looking at my thighs.

I knew where I wanted this conversation to go. As I often did, I got my way. It wasn't instantaneous, no. It took some power of persuasion, which comes naturally to me. Rule number one: reciprocity. I do something for you, you do something for me in return.

I wiped the mustard from his lip. I saw that his drink was empty. I reached for the cup, refilled it at the soda fountain.

You didn't have to do that, he said as I sat back down, slid his Pepsi across the table, made certain our hands touched as I did. *I could have gotten it myself.*

I smiled and said, *I know I didn't have to. I wanted to, Will.*

And just like that, he owed me something.

There's also likability. I can be extremely likable when I want to be. I know just what to say, what to do, how to be charming. The trick is to ask open-ended questions, to get people to talk about themselves. It makes them feel like the most interesting person in the world.

There's also the importance of touch. Compliance is so much easier to achieve with a single touch to the arm, the shoulder, the thigh.

Add that to the fact that his and Sadie's marriage read more like a guidebook on abstinence, from what I'd seen. Will needed something only I could give to him.

He didn't say yes at first. He grinned sheepishly instead, turning red. He said he had a meeting, somewhere else he needed to be.

I can't, he said. But I convinced him he could. Because not fifteen minutes later, we were slipping down an adjacent alleyway. There in that alley, he leaned me against a building. He eased his hand under the hem of the dress, pressed his mouth to mine.

Not here, I said, thinking only of him. I'd be fine doing that there. But he had a marriage, a reputation. I had neither. *Let's go somewhere,* I said into his ear.

There was a hotel he knew, half a block away. Not the Ritz, but it would do. We raced up the stairs, into the room.

There, he threw me on the bed, had his way with me. When we were done, we lay in bed, breathing heavy, trying to catch our breath.

Will was the first to speak. *That was just . . .*

He was tongue-tied when we were through, but radiant, beaming.

He tried again. *That was amazing. You,* he said, kneeling over me, hands on either side of my head, eyes on mine, *are amazing.*

I winked, said, *You're not so bad yourself.*

He stared at me awhile. I'd never been looked at like that by a man, like he couldn't get enough of me. He said that he needed this, more than I'd ever know. An escape from reality. My timing, he said, was impeccable. He'd been having a shitty day, a shitty week.

This was perfect.

You, he said, drinking me in with his eyes, *are perfect.*

He listed for me the reasons why. My heart swelled as he did, though it was all skin-deep: my hair, my smile, my eyes.

And then, like that, I was kissing him again.

He pushed himself from bed when he was through. I lay there, watched as he slipped back into a dress shirt and jeans. *You're leaving so soon?* I asked.

He stood there at the end of the bed, watching me.

He was apologetic. *I have a meeting. I'm going to be late as it is. You stay as long as you'd like,* he said. *Take a nap, get some rest,* as if that was some consolation prize. Sleeping alone in a cheap hotel.

He leaned over me before he left. He kissed my forehead, stroked my hair. He gazed into my eyes, said, *I'll see you soon.* It wasn't a question. It was a promise.

I smiled, said, *Of course you will. You're stuck with me, Will. I won't ever let you go,* and he smiled and said that was exactly what he wanted to hear.

I tried not to be jealous as he left. I wasn't the jealous type. Not until I met Will, and then I was, though I never felt guilty for what happened between Will and me. He was mine. Sadie took him from me. I didn't owe her a thing.

If anything, she owed me.

SADIE

Two times I circle the house. I make sure all the doors and windows are locked. I do it once, and then, because I can't be sure I got them all, I do it again. I pull the blinds, the curtains closed, wondering if it would be prudent to have a security system installed in the home.

This evening, as promised, Will drove Imogen to the public safety building to speak with Officer Berg. I hoped Will would come home with news about the murder — something to settle me — but there was nothing to report. The police weren't any closer to solving the crime. I've seen statistics on murders. Something like one-third or more of murders become cold case files, leaving police departments mired in unsolved crimes. It's an epidemic.

The number of murderers walking among us every day is frightening.

They can be anywhere and we'd never know.

According to Will, Imogen had nothing to offer Officer Berg about last night. She was asleep, as I knew she'd been. When asked if she'd seen anything out of the ordinary over the last few weeks, she turned stiff and gray and said, "My mom hanging from the end of a fucking noose." Officer Berg had no more questions for her after that.

As I contemplate a third go-round of the windows and doors, Will calls to me from the top of the stairs, asks if I'm coming to bed anytime soon. I tell him yes, I'm coming, as I give the front door a final tug. I leave on a living room lamp to give the pretense we're awake.

I climb the stairs and settle into bed beside Will. But I can't sleep. All night, I find myself lying in bed, thinking about what Officer Berg said, how the little Baines girl was the one to find Morgan dead. I wonder how well Tate knows this little girl. Tate and she are in class together, but that doesn't mean they're friends.

I find that I'm unable to shake from my mind the image of the six-year-old girl standing over her mother's lifeless body. I wonder if she was scared. If she screamed. If the killer lurked nearby, getting off on the sound of her scream. I wonder how long she waited for the ambulance to arrive, and if, in that time, she feared for her own life. I think of her, alone, finding her mother dead in the same way that Imogen found her own mother dead. Not the same, no. Suicide and murder are two very different things. But still, it's unfathomable for me to think what these girls have seen in their short lives.

Beside me, Will sleeps like a rock. But not me. Because as I lie there unsleeping I start to wonder if the killer is still on the island with us, or if he's gone by now.

I slip from bed at the thought of it, my heart gaining speed. I have to be sure the kids are okay. The dogs, on their own beds in the corner of the room, take note and follow along. I tell them to hush as Will rolls over in bed, pulling the sheet with him.

On the wooden floors, my bare feet are cold. But it's too dark to feel around for slippers. I leave them behind. I step out of the bedroom, moving down the narrow hall.

I go to Tate's room first. There, in the doorway, I pause. Tate sleeps with the bedroom door open, a night-light plugged in to keep monsters at bay. His small body is set in the middle of the bed, a stuffed Chihuahua held tightly between his arms. Peacefully he sleeps, his own dreams uninterrupted by thoughts of murder and death, unlike mine. I wonder what he dreams of. Maybe puppy dogs and ice cream.

I wonder what Tate knows of death. I wonder what I knew of death when I was seven years old, if I knew much of anything.

I move on to Otto's room. There's a roof outside Otto's window, a single-story slate roof that hangs over the front porch. A series of climbable columns hold it upright. Getting in or out wouldn't be such a difficult task in the middle of the night.

My feet instinctively pick up pace as I cross the hall, telling myself Otto is safe, that certainly an intruder wouldn't climb to the second floor to get in. But in that moment, I can't be so sure. I turn the handle and press the door silently open, terrified of what I'll find on the other side. The window open, the bed empty. But it's not the case. Otto is here. Otto is fine.

I stand in the doorway, watching for a while. I take a step closer for a better look, holding my breath so I don't wake him. He looks peaceful, though his blanket has been kicked to the end of the bed and his pillow tossed to the floor. His head lies flat on the mattress. I reach for the blanket and draw it over him, remembering when he was young and would ask me to sleep with him. When

I did, he'd toss a heavy arm across my neck and hold me that way, not letting go the entire night. He's grown up too fast. I wish for it back.

I go to Imogen's room next. I set my hand on the handle and sluggishly turn, careful not to make any noise. But the handle doesn't turn. The door is locked from the inside. I can't check on her.

I turn away from the door and inch down the stairs. The dogs follow on my heels, but I move far too slowly for their liking. At some point, they bypass me and dash down the rest of the steps, cutting through the foyer for the back door. Their nails click-clack on the wooden floors like typewriter keys.

I pause before the front door and glance out the sidelight window. From this angle, I catch a glimpse of the Baineses' house. There's activity going on even at this late hour. Light floods the inside of it, a handful of people milling about inside. Police on a quest. I wonder what they'll find.

The dogs whine at me from the kitchen, stealing my attention away from the window. They want to go outside. I follow them, opening the sliding glass door, and they go rushing out. They make a beeline for the corner of the yard, where they've recently begun digging divots in the grass. The incessant digging has become their latest compulsion and also my pet peeve. I clap my hands together to get them to stop.

I brew myself a cup of tea and sit down at the kitchen table. I look around for things to do. There's no point in going back to bed because I know I won't sleep. There's nothing worse than lying in bed, restless, worrying about things I can't do anything about.

On the edge of the table sits a book Will has been reading, a true crime novel with a bookmark thrust in the center of it.

I take the book into the living room, turn on a lamp and settle myself on Alice's marigold sofa to read. I spread an afghan over my lap. I open the book. By accident Will's bookmark comes tumbling out, falling to the floor beside my feet.

"Shit," I say, reaching down for the bookmark, feeling guilty that I've lost Will's page.

But the guilt only lasts so long before it's replaced with something else. Jealousy? Anger? Empathy? Or maybe surprise. Because the bookmark isn't the only thing that's fallen out of the pages of the book. Because there's also a photo of Erin, Will's first fiancée, the woman he was supposed to marry instead of me.

My gasp is audible. My hand comes to a

stop inches above her face, my heart hastening.

Why is Will hiding a photograph of Erin inside this book? Why does Will still have this photograph at all?

The photo is old, twenty years maybe. Erin looks to be about eighteen or nineteen in it. Her hair is wild, her smile carefree. I stare at the picture, into Erin's eyes. There's a pang of jealousy because of how beautiful she is. How magnetic.

But how can I be jealous of a woman who is dead?

Will and I had been dating for over a month before he mentioned her name. We were still in that completely smitten stage, when everything felt noteworthy and important. We'd talk on the phone for hours. I didn't have much to say about my past, and so, instead, I told him about my future, about all the things I planned to one day do. Will's future was undecided when we met, and so he told me about his past. About his childhood dog. About his stepfather's diagnosis with cancer, the fact that his mother has been married three times. And he told me about Erin, the woman he was supposed to marry, a woman he was engaged to for months before she died. Will cried openly when he told me about her.

He held nothing back, and I loved him for it because of his great capacity to love.

In all my life, I didn't think I'd ever seen a grown man cry.

At the time, the sadness of Will losing a fiancée only attracted me to him more. Will was broken, like a butterfly without wings. I wanted to be the one to heal him.

It's been years since her name has come up. It's not as if we talk about her. But every now and then another Erin is mentioned and it gives us pause. The name alone carries so much weight. But why Will would dig this photograph out of God knows where and carry it around with him is beyond me. Why now, after all this time?

My hand grazes the photograph but I don't have it in me to pick it up. Not yet. I've only seen one other photograph of Erin before, one that Will showed to me years ago at my request. He didn't want to, but I insisted. I wanted to know what she looked like. When I asked to see a picture, he showed me with circumspection. He wasn't sure how I'd react. I tried to be poker-faced about it, but there was no denying the sharp pains I felt inside. She was breathtaking.

I knew in that instant: Will only loved me because she was gone. I was his second pick.

I brush my finger against Erin's fair skin

now. I can't be jealous. I simply can't. And I can't be mad. It would be insensitive of me to ask him to throw it away. But here I am, after all these years, feeling like I'm playing second fiddle to the memory of a woman who's dead.

I reach for the photo and hold it in my hand this time. I won't let myself be a coward. I stare at her. There's something so childish about her face, so audacious and raw, that I feel the greatest need to scold her for whatever it is she's thinking as she makes a pouty face at the camera, one that is as provocative as it is bold.

I jam the picture and the bookmark somewhere back inside the book, rise from the sofa and bring the book to the kitchen table. I leave it there, having suddenly lost the desire to read.

The dogs have begun to bark. I can't leave them outside barking in the middle of the night. I open the slider and call to them, but they don't come.

I'm forced outside into the backyard to get their attention. The patio is freezing cold on my bare feet. But that discomfort is secondary to what I feel inside as I get taken in, swallowed by the darkness. The kitchen light fades quickly behind me as the December night closes in.

I can see nothing. If someone was there, standing in the darkness of our yard, I wouldn't know. An unwanted thought comes pummeling into me then. My saliva catches in my throat and I choke.

Dogs have adaptations that people don't have. They can see much better than humans in the dark. It makes me wonder what the dogs see that I can't see, what they're barking at.

I hiss out into the night, calling quietly for the girls. It's the middle of the night; I don't want to shout. But I'm too scared to go any farther outside than I already am.

How do I know that Morgan Baines's killer isn't there?

How do I know that the dogs aren't barking because there's a murderer in my yard?

Backlit by the kitchen light, I'm a fish in a fishbowl.

I can see nothing. But whoever is there — if anyone is there — can easily see me.

Without thinking it through, I take a step suddenly back. The fear is overwhelming. There's the greatest need to run back into the kitchen, close and lock the door behind myself, pull the drapes shut. But would the dogs be able to fend off a killer all on their own?

And then the dogs suddenly stop their

barking and I'm not sure what terrifies me more, the barking or the silence.

My heart pounds harder. My skin prickles, a tingling sensation that runs up and down my arms. My imagination goes wild, wondering what horrible thing is standing in my yard.

I can't stand here waiting to find out. I clap my hands, call to the dogs again. I hurry inside for their biscuits and shake the box frantically. This time, by the grace of God, they come. I open the box, spill a half dozen treats on the kitchen floor before closing and locking the slider, pulling the drapes tightly closed.

Back upstairs, I check again on the boys. They're just as I left them.

But Imogen's door, this time as I pass by, is open an inch. It's no longer closed. It's no longer locked. The hallway is narrow and dark with just enough light that I'm not blind. A faint glow from the lamp in the living room rises up to me. It helps me see.

My eyes go to that one-inch gap between Imogen's door and the frame. It wasn't like that the last time I was here. Imogen's room, like Otto's, faces onto the street. I go to her door and press on it, easing it open another inch or two, just enough so that I can see inside. She's lying there, on her bed, with her back to me. If she's faking sleep, she does so quite well. Her breathing is rhythmic and deep. I see the rise and fall of the sheet. Her curtains are open, moonlight streaming into the room. The window, like the door, is open an inch. The room is icy cold, but I don't risk stepping inside to close it.

Back in our bedroom, I shake Will awake. I won't tell Will about Imogen because there's nothing really to say. For all I know, she was up using the bathroom. She got hot and opened her window. These are not crimes, though other questions nag at the back of my mind.

Why didn't I hear a toilet flush?

Why didn't I notice the chill from the bedroom the first time I passed by?

"What is it? What's wrong?" Will asks, half-asleep.

As he rubs at his eyes, I say, "I think there's something in the backyard."

"Like what?" he asks, clearing his throat, his eyes drowsy and his voice heavy with sleep.

I wait a beat before I tell him. "I don't know," I say, leaning into him as I say it. "Maybe a person."

"A person?" Will asks, sitting quickly upright, and I tell him about what just happened, how there was something — or someone — in the backyard that spooked the dogs. My voice is tremulous when I speak. Will notices. "Did you see a person?" he asks, but I tell him no, that I didn't see anything at all. That I only knew something was there. A gut instinct.

Will says compassionately, his hand reassuringly stroking mine, "You're really shaken up about it, aren't you?"

He wraps both hands around mine, feeling the way they tremble in his. I tell him that I am. I think that he's going to get out of bed and go see for himself if there's someone in our backyard. But instead he makes me second-guess myself. It isn't intentional and he isn't trying to patronize me. Rather, he's the voice of reason as he asks, "But what about a coyote? A raccoon or a skunk? Are you sure it wasn't just some animals that got the dogs worked up?"

It sounds so simple, so obvious as he says it. I wonder if he's right. It would explain why the dogs were so upset. Perhaps they sniffed out some wildlife roaming around our backyard. They're hunters. Naturally they would have wanted to get at whatever was there. It's the far more logical thing to believe than that there was a killer traipsing through our backyard. What would a killer want with us?

I shrug in the darkness. "Maybe," I say, feeling foolish, but not entirely so. There was a murder just across the street from us last night and the murderer hasn't been found. It's not so irrational to believe he's still nearby.

Will tells me obligingly, "We could mention it to Officer Berg anyway in the morning. Ask him to look into it. If nothing else, ask if coyotes are a problem around here. It would be good to know anyway, to make sure we keep an eye on the dogs."

I feel grateful he humors me. But I tell him no. "I'm sure you're right," I say, crawling back into bed beside him, knowing I still won't sleep. "It probably was a coyote. I'm sorry I woke you. Go back to bed," I say, and he does, wrapping a heavy arm around me, protecting me from whatever lies on the other side of our door.

Sadie

I come to when Will says my name. I must have spaced out.

He's there beside me, giving me a look. A Will look, fraught with worry. "Where'd you go?" he asks, as I look around, get my bearings. A sudden headache has nearly gotten the best of me, making me feel swimmy inside.

I tell him, "I don't know," not remembering what we were talking about before I spaced out.

I look down to see that a button on my shirt has come undone, revealing the black of my bra beneath. I button back up, apologize to him for zoning out in the middle of our conversation. "I'm just tired," I say, rubbing at my eyes, taking in the sight of Will before me, the kitchen around me.

"You look tired," Will agrees, and I feel the agitation brim inside. I glance past Will and into the backyard, expecting to see something out of place. Signs of a trespasser in our yard last night. There's nothing, but still, I prickle anyway, remember what it felt like as I stood in the darkness, pleading for the dogs to come.

The boys are at the table, eating the last of their breakfast. Will stands at the counter, filling a mug that he passes to me. I welcome the coffee into my hands and take a big gulp.

"I didn't sleep well," I say, not wanting to admit the truth, that I didn't sleep at all.

"Want to talk about it?" he asks, though it doesn't seem like something that needs to be said. This is something he should know. A woman was murdered in her home across the street from us two nights ago.

My eyes breeze past Tate at the table, and I tell him no because this isn't a conversation Tate should hear. For as long as we can, I'd like to keep his childhood innocence alive.

"Do you have time for breakfast?" Will asks.

"Not today," I say, looking at the clock, seeing that it's even later than I thought it was. I need to get going. I begin gathering things, my bag and my coat, to go. Will's bag waits for him beside the table, and I wonder if he stuck his true crime novel inside the bag, the book with the photograph of Erin hidden inside. I don't have the courage to tell Will I know about the photograph.

I kiss Tate goodbye. I snatch the earbuds from Otto's ears to tell him to hurry.

I drive to the ferry. Otto and I don't say much on the way there. We used to be closer than we are, but time and circumstance have pulled us apart. How many teenage boys, I ask myself, trying not to take it personally, are close with their mother? Few, if any. But Otto is a sensitive boy, different than the rest.

He leaves the car with only a quick goodbye for me. I watch as he crosses the metal grate bridge and boards the ferry with the other early-morning commuters. His heavy backpack is slung across his back. I don't see Imogen anywhere.

It's seven twenty in the morning. Outside, it's raining. A mob of multicolored umbrellas makes its way down the street that leads to the ferry. Two boys about Otto's age claw their way on board behind him, bypassing Otto in the entranceway, laughing. They're laughing at some inside joke, I assure myself, not at *him,* but my stomach churns just the same, and I think how lonely it must be in Otto's world, an outcast without any friends.

There's plenty of seating inside the ferry where it's warm and dry, but Otto climbs all the way up to the upper deck, standing in the rain without an umbrella. I watch as deckhands raise the gangplank and untie the boat before it ventures off into the foggy sea, stealing Otto from me.

Only then do I see Officer Berg staring at me.

He stands on the other side of the street just outside his Crown Victoria, leaned up against the passenger's side door. In his hands are coffee and a cinnamon roll, just a stone's throw away from the stereotypical doughnut cops are notorious for eating, though slightly more refined. As he waves at me, I get the sense that he's been watching me the entire time, watching as I watch Otto leave.

He tips his hat at me. I wave at him through the car window.

What I usually do at this point in my drive is make a U-turn and go back up the hill the same way I came down. But I can't do that with the officer watching. And it doesn't matter anyway because Officer Berg has abandoned his post and is walking across the street and toward me. He motions with the crank of a hand for me to open my window. I press the button and the window drops down. Beads of rain welcome themselves inside my car, gathering along the interior of the door. Officer Berg doesn't carry an umbrella. Rather, the hood of a rain jacket is thrust over his head. He doesn't appear to be bothered by the rain.

He jams the last bite of his cinnamon roll into his mouth, chases it down with a swig of coffee and says, "Morning, Dr. Foust." He has a kind face for a police officer, lacking the usual flintiness that I think of when I think of the police. There's something endearing about him, a bit of awkwardness and insecurity that I like.

I tell him good morning.

"What a day," he says, and I say, "Quite a doozy."

The rain isn't expected to go on all day. The sun, however, won't make an appearance anytime soon. Where we live, just off the coast of Maine, the climate is tempered by the ocean. The temperatures aren't as bitter as they are in Chicago this time of year, though still it's cold.

What we've heard is that the bay has been known to freeze come wintertime, ferries forced to charge through ice floes to get people to and from the mainland. One winter, supposedly, the ferry got stuck, and passengers were made to walk across yards of ice to get to the shoreline before the Coast Guard came in with a cutter to chop it up.

It's unsettling to think about. A bit suffocating, if I'm being honest, the idea of being trapped on the island, cordoned off from the rest of the world by a giant slab of ice.

"You're up early," Officer Berg says, and I reply, "As are you."

"Duty calls," he says, tapping at his badge. I reply, "Me, too," finger at the ready to hoist the window up so that I can leave. Joyce and Emma are expecting me, and if I'm not there soon, I'll never hear the end of it. Joyce is a stickler for punctuality.

Officer Berg glances at his watch, makes an off hand guess that the clinic opens around eight thirty. I say that it does. He asks, "Have a moment to spare, Dr. Foust?" I tell him a quick one.

I pull my car closer to the curb and put it in Park. Officer Berg rounds the front end of it and lets himself in through the passenger's side door.

Officer Berg cuts straight to the chase. "I finished speaking to your neighbors yesterday, asking them the same questions I asked of you and Mr. Foust," he tells me, and I gather from his tone that this isn't merely an update on the investigation — though what I want is an update on the investigation. I want Officer Berg to tell me that they're ready to make an arrest so I can sleep better at night, knowing Morgan's killer is behind bars.

Early this morning before the kids were up, Will searched online for news about her murder. There was an article detailing how Morgan had been found dead in her home. There were facts in it that were new to Will and me. How, for example, the police found threatening notes in the Baineses' home, though they didn't say what the threats said.

Overnight the police released the little girl's 911 call. It was there online, an audio clip of the six-year-old girl as she fought back tears, telling the operator on the other end of the line, *She won't wake up. Morgan won't wake up.*

In the article, she was never referred to by name, only ever as *the six-year-old girl,* because minors are blessed with a certain anonymity adults don't have.

Will and I lay in bed with the laptop between us, listening to the audio clip three times. It was gut-wrenching to hear. The little girl managed to remain relatively calm and composed as the dispatcher talked her through the next few minutes and sent help, keeping her on the line the entire time.

But there was something about the audio clip that got under my skin, something I couldn't put my finger on. It pestered me nonetheless, and it wasn't until the third go-round that I finally heard it.

She calls her mother Morgan? I'd asked Will, because the little girl didn't say her mother wouldn't wake up. She said Morgan wouldn't wake up. *Why would she do that?* I asked.

Will's reply was immediate.

Morgan is her stepmother, he said. Then he swallowed hard, tried not to cry. *Morgan* was *her stepmother, I mean.*

Oh, I said. I don't know why this mattered. But it seemed it did.

Jeffrey was married before? I asked. It's not always the case, of course. Children are born out of wedlock. But it was worth asking.

Yes, he said, but he said no more. I wondered about Jeffrey's first wife. I wondered who she was, if she lived here on the island with us. Will himself is the product of divorced parents. It's always been a sore subject with him.

How long were Jeffrey and Morgan married? I asked, wondering what else she told him.

Just over a year.

They're newlyweds, I said.

They're nothing anymore, Sadie, Will corrected me again. *He's a widower. She's dead.*

We stopped talking after that. Together, in silence, we read on.

I wonder now, as I sit in my car beside Officer Berg, about signs of forced entry — a broken window, a busted doorjamb — or blood. Was there blood at the scene? Or defensive wounds, maybe, on Morgan's hands? Did she try to fight her intruder off?

Or maybe the little girl saw the attacker or heard her stepmother scream.

I don't ask Officer Berg any of this. It's been over twenty-four hours since the poor woman was killed. The etched lines on his forehead are deeper today than they were before. The pressure of the investigation is weighing on him, and I realize then: he's no closer to solving this crime than he was yesterday. My heart sinks.

Instead I ask, "Has Mr. Baines been located?" and he tells me that he's on his way, though it's a twenty-some-hour trip from Tokyo with layovers at LAX and JFK. He won't be home until tonight.

"Have you found her cell phone? That might give you something to go on?" I ask.

He shakes his head. They've been looking, he says, but so far they can't find her phone. "There are ways to track a missing cell phone, but if the phone is off or the battery is dead, those won't work. Obtaining a warrant for records from a telecommunications company is tedious. It takes time. But we're working on it," he tells me.

Officer Berg shifts in the seat. He turns his body toward mine, knees now pointed in my direction. They bump awkwardly into the gearshift. There are raindrops on his coat and his hair. There's icing on his upper lip.

"You told me yesterday that you and Mrs. Baines never met," he says, and I have trouble snatching my eyes from the icing as I reply, "That's right. We never met."

There was a photograph online of the woman. According to the paper, she was twenty-eight years old, eleven years younger than me. In the photo, she stood surrounded by her family, her happy husband on one side, stepdaughter the other, all of them dolled up in coordinating clothes and wreathed in smiles. She had a beautiful smile, a tad bit gummy if anything, but otherwise lovely.

Officer Berg unzips his rain jacket and reaches inside. He removes his tablet from an interior pocket, where there it stays dry. He taps on the screen, trawling for something. When he finds the spot, he clears his throat and reads my words back to me.

"Yesterday you said, *I just never found the time to stop by and introduce myself.* Do you remember saying that?" he asks, and I tell him I do, though it sounds so flippant now, my words coming back to me this way. A bit merciless, if I'm being honest, seeing as the woman is now dead. I should have tacked on an empathetic addendum, such as, *But I wish I had.* Just a little something so that my words didn't sound so callous.

"The thing is, Dr. Foust," he begins, "you said you didn't know Mrs. Baines, and yet it seems you did," and though his tone is well-disposed, the intent of his words is not.

He's just accused me of lying.

"I beg your pardon?" I ask, taken completely aback.

"It seems you did know Morgan Baines," he says.

The rain is coming down in torrents now, pounding on the roof of the car like mallets on tin cans. I think of Otto all alone on the upper deck of the ferry, getting pelted with rain. A knot forms in my throat because of it. I swallow it away.

I force my window up to keep the rain at bay.

I make sure to meet the officer's eye as I assert, "Unless a onetime wave out the window of a moving vehicle counts as a relationship, Officer Berg, I didn't know Morgan Baines. What makes you think that I did?" I ask, and he explains again, at great length this time, how he canvassed the entire street, spoke to all the neighbors, asked them the same questions he asked Will and me. When he came to the home of George and Poppy Nilsson, they invited him into their kitchen for tea and ginger cookies. He tells me that he asked the Nilssons what they were doing the night Morgan died, same as he did Will and me. I wait to hear their reply, thinking Officer Berg is about to tell me how the older couple sat in their living room that night, watching out the window as a killer slipped from the cover of darkness and into the Baineses' home.

But instead he says, "As you can expect, at eighty-some years old, George and Poppy were asleep," and I release my withheld breath. The Nilssons didn't see a thing.

"I don't understand, Officer," I say, glancing at the time on the car's dash, knowing I'll need to leave soon. "If the Nilssons were asleep, then . . . *what*?"

Because clearly if they were asleep, then they saw and heard nothing.

"I also asked the Nilssons if they'd seen

anything out of the ordinary over the last few days. Strangers lurking about, unfamiliar cars parked along the street."

"Yes, yes," I say, nodding my head quickly because he also asked this question of Will and me. "And?" I ask, trying to hurry things along so that I can get on to work.

"Well, it just so happens that they did see something out of the ordinary. Something they haven't seen before. Which is saying a lot, seeing as they've lived half their lives on that street." And then he taps away at that tablet screen to find his interview with Mr. and Mrs. Nilsson.

He goes on to describe for me an afternoon just last week. It was Friday, the first of December. It was a clear day, the sky painted blue, not a cloud to be seen. The temperatures were cool, crisp, but nothing a heavy sweater or a light jacket wouldn't fix. George and Poppy had gone for an afternoon walk, Officer Berg says, and were headed back up the steep incline of our street. Once they reached the top, George stopped to catch his breath, pausing before the Baineses' home.

Officer Berg goes on to tell me how there Mr. Nilsson rearranged the blanket on Poppy's lap so that she didn't catch a draft. As he did, something caught his attention.

It was the sound of women hollering at one another, though what they were hollering about he wasn't sure.

"Oh, how awful," I say, and he says it was because poor George was really shaken up about it. He'd never heard anything like that before. And that's saying a lot for a man his age.

"But what does this have to do with me?" I ask, and he reaches again for the tablet.

"George and Poppy stayed there in the street for a moment only, but that's all it took before the women stepped out from the shade of a tree and into view and George could see for himself who they were."

"Who?" I ask, slightly breathless, and he waits a beat before he replies.

"It was Mrs. Baines," he says, "and you."

And then, from some recording app on his device, he plays for me the testimonial of Mr. Nilsson, which states, "She was fighting with the new doctor lady on the street. The both of them were hooting and hollering, mad as a hornet. Before I could intercede, the doctor lady grabbed a handful of Ms. Morgan's hair right out of her head and left with it in her fist. Poppy and I turned and walked quickly home. Didn't want her to think we were snooping or she might do the same thing to us."

Officer Berg stops it there and turns to me, asking, "Does this sound to you like an altercation between two women who'd never met?"

But I'm speechless.

I can't reply.

Why would George Nilsson say such an awful thing about me?

Officer Berg doesn't give me a chance to speak. He goes on without me.

He asks, "Is it often, Dr. Foust, that you swipe handfuls of hair from women you don't know?"

The answer, of course, is no. Though still I can't find my voice to speak.

He decides, "I'll take your silence as a no."

His hand falls to the door and he pushes it open against the weight of the wind. "I'll leave you to it," he says, "so that you can get on with your day."

"I never spoke to Morgan Baines" is what I manage to say just then before he leaves, though the words that emerge are limp.

He shrugs. "All right, then," he says, stepping back out into the rain.

He never said if he believed me.

He didn't need to.

Mouse

Once upon a time there was a girl named Mouse. It wasn't her real name, but for as long as the girl could remember, her father had called her that.

The girl didn't know why her father called her Mouse. She didn't ask. She worried that if she brought attention to it, he might stop using the nickname, and she didn't want him to do that. The girl liked that her father called her Mouse, because it was something special between her father and her, even if she didn't know why.

Mouse spent a lot of time thinking about it. She had ideas about why her father called her by that nickname. For one, she had a soft spot for cheese. Sometimes, when she pulled strands of mozzarella from her string cheese and laid them on her tongue to eat, she thought that maybe that was the reason he called her Mouse, because of how much she liked cheese.

She wondered if her father thought she looked like a mouse. If, maybe, there were whiskers that grew along her upper lip, ones so small even she couldn't see them, though her father could somehow see them. Mouse would go to the bathroom, climb up on the sink, press in closely to the mirror so she could search for whiskers. She even brought a magnifying glass along with her once, held it between her lip and her reflection, but she didn't see any whiskers there.

Maybe, she decided, it had nothing to do with whiskers, but something to do with her brown hair, her big ears, her big teeth.

But Mouse wasn't sure. Sometimes she thought it had to do with the way she looked, and then other times she thought it had nothing to do with the way she looked, but was something else instead, like the Salerno Butter Cookies she and her father ate after dinner sometimes. Maybe it was because of those cookies that he called her Mouse.

Mouse loved her Salerno Butter Cookies more than any other kind of cookie, even more than homemade. She'd stack them up on her pinkie, slide her finger through the center hole, gnaw her way down the side of the stack just like a mouse gnawing its way through wood.

Mouse ate her cookies at the dinner table. But one night, when her father had his back turned, taking the dishes to the sink to wash, she slipped an extra few in her pockets for a late-night snack, in case she or her teddy bear got hungry.

Mouse excused herself from the table, tried sneaking up to her bedroom with the cookies in her pockets, though she knew that crammed there in her pockets, the cookies would quickly turn to crumbs. To Mouse, it didn't matter. The crumbs would taste just as good as the cookie had.

But her father caught her red-handed trying to make off with the cookies. He didn't scold her. He hardly ever scolded her. There wasn't a need for Mouse to be scolded. Instead he teased her for hoarding food, storing it somewhere in that bedroom of hers like mice store food in the walls of people's homes.

But somehow Mouse didn't think that was why he called her Mouse.

Because by then, she already was Mouse.

Mouse had a vivid imagination. She loved to make stories up. She never wrote them down on paper, but put them in her head where no one else could see. In her stories, there was a girl named Mouse who could do anything she wanted to, even cartwheels on the moon if that was what she wanted to do because Mouse didn't need silly things like oxygen or gravity. She was afraid of nothing because she was immortal. No matter what she did, no harm could come to imaginary Mouse.

Mouse loved to draw. Her bedroom walls were covered in pictures of her father and her, her and her teddy bears. Mouse spent her days playing pretend. Her bedroom, the only one on the second floor of the old home, was full of dolls, toys and stuffed animals. Each animal had a name. Her favorite was a stuffed brown bear named Mr. Bear. Mouse had a dollhouse, a toy kitchen set with pretend pots and pans and crates of plastic food. She had a tea set. Mouse loved to set her dolls and animals in a circle on her floor, on the edge of her striped rag rug, and serve them each a tiny mug of tea and a plastic doughnut. She would find a book on her shelf and read it aloud to her friends before tucking them into bed.

But sometimes Mouse didn't play with her animals and dolls.

Sometimes she stood on her bed and pretended the floor around her was hot lava oozing from the volcano at the other end of the room. She couldn't step on the floor for risk of death. Those days, Mouse would scramble from her bed to a desk, climbing to safety. She'd tread precariously across the top of the small white desk — the legs of it wobbling beneath her, threatening to break. Mouse wasn't a big girl but the desk was old, fragile. It wasn't meant to hold a six-year-old child.

But it didn't matter because soon enough Mouse was clambering into a laundry basket full of dirty clothes on the bedroom floor. As she did, she took extra care not to step on the floor, breathing a sigh of relief when she was safely inside the basket. Because even though the basket was on the floor, it was safe. The basket couldn't get swallowed up by lava, because it was made of titanium, and Mouse knew that titanium wouldn't melt. She was a smart girl, smarter than any other girl her age that she knew.

Inside the laundry basket, the girl rode the waves of the volcano until the lava itself cooled and crusted over, and the land was safe enough to walk on again. Only then did she venture out of the basket and go back to playing along the edge of the rag rug with Mr. Bear and her dolls.

Sometimes Mouse thought that that, her tendency to disappear to her bedroom — *quiet as a church mouse,* as her father put it

— and play all day, was the reason he called her Mouse.

It was hard to say.

But one thing was certain.

Mouse loved that name until the day Fake Mom arrived. And then she no longer did.

Sadie

I'm sitting on the floor in the lobby of the clinic. Before me is an activity table, the kind meant to keep kids entertained while they wait. The dark carpet beneath me is thin and cheap. It's unraveling in spots, with stains that blend into the nylon so you wouldn't see them unless you were as close to it as I am.

I'm cross-legged on the floor, sitting on the side of the activity table that faces a shape sorter. I watch on as my hand drops a heart-shaped block into the appropriate opening.

There's a girl on the other side of the table. At first glance, she looks to be about four years old. She wears a pair of crooked pigtails. Strands of blond hair have come loose from the elastics. They fall to her face, hang into her eyes where she leaves them be, not bothering to shove them away. Her sweatshirt is red. Her shoes don't match.

One is a black patent leather Mary Jane and the other a black ballet flat. An easy enough mistake to make.

My own legs have begun to ache. I unknot them, find a different position to sit in, one better suited for a thirty-nine-year-old woman. The waiting room chair catches my eye, but I can't rise from the floor and leave, not yet, because the little girl across the table is watching me expectantly.

"Go," she says, grinning oddly, and I ask, "Go where?" though my voice is strangled when I speak. I clear my throat, try again.

"Go where?" I ask, this time sounding more like myself.

On the floor, my body is stiff. My legs hurt. My head hurts. I'm hot. I didn't catch a wink of sleep last night and am paying for it today. I'm tired and disoriented. This morning's conversation with Officer Berg has rattled my nerves, made a bad day even worse.

"Go," the girl says again. When I stare at her, doing nothing, she says, "It's your turn," pronouncing none of the *r*'s, but turning them to *w*'s instead.

"My turn?" I ask, taken aback, and she says to me, "Yeah. You're the red, remember?" Except she doesn't say *red.* She says *wed. Wed, wemember?*

I shake my head. I must not have been paying attention because I don't remember. Because I don't know what she's talking about until she points it out for me, the red beads at the top of the roller-coaster table, the ones that go up and down the red wire hills, around the red corkscrew turns.

"Oh," I say, reaching out to touch the red wooden beads before me. "Okay. What should I do with the red?" I ask the girl, her nose oozing snot, eyes a bit glazed over as if febrile, and I don't have to think hard to know why she's here. She's my patient. She's come to see me. She coughs hard, forgetting to cover her mouth. The little ones always do.

"You do it like this," she says as she takes her dirty, germy hand and grasps a train of yellow beads with it, driving the beads over the yellow hill and around the yellow corkscrew turns.

"You do it like that," she says when the beads finally reach the other end and she lets go of them. Her hands fall to her hips as she stares at me, again expectantly.

I smile at the girl as I start to move the red beads.

But before they've gone far, I hear *"Dr. Foust"* hissed at me from behind. It's a woman's voice, clearly annoyed. "What are you doing down there, Dr. Foust?"

I turn to see Joyce standing behind me. Her posture is straight, her expression firm. She tells me that my eleven o'clock appointment is here, waiting for me in exam room three. I rise slowly to standing, shake out my stiff legs. I have no idea why I thought it would be a good idea to get down on the ground and play with the little girl. I tell her I have to get back to work. I say that maybe we can play again later and she smiles shyly at me. She wasn't shy before but she's shy now. She's changed, and I think it has something to do with my height. Now that I'm standing, I'm no longer three feet tall like her. I'm different.

She rushes to her mama's side, wraps her arms around her mother's knees.

I say to her mother, "What a sweet girl," and her mother thanks me for playing with her.

Around me, the waiting room is crawling with patients. I follow Joyce through the lobby doors and down the hall. But once there, I head the other way from the exam room, going to the kitchen instead, where I help myself to a sip of water from the watercooler, taking a moment to catch my breath. I'm tired. I'm hungry. My head still hurts.

Joyce follows me into the kitchen. She gives me this look, like I have some nerve to drink water at a time like this, when we have a patient waiting. I can see it in her eyes every time she looks at me: Joyce doesn't like me. I don't know why Joyce doesn't like me. There's nothing I've done that would make her not like me. I tell myself it has nothing to do with what happened back in Chicago, that there's no way she can know about that. No, that stayed there, because I resigned. It was the only way a claim of negligence didn't end my medical career. But whether I'd practice emergency medicine again, I didn't know. It was a blot on my confidence, if not my résumé.

I tell Joyce that I'll be right there, but she stands watching in teal blue scrubs and nursing clogs, with her hands on her hips. She pouts, and only then do I take note of the clock on the wall behind her where red numbers inform me that it's one fifteen in the afternoon.

"Oh," I say, though that can't be. I couldn't possibly have fallen that far behind schedule. My bedside manner is decent enough — I've been known to go on a tad too long with patients — but not like this.

I glance down at my watch, sure that it's slow, that my watch is to blame for my falling behind schedule. But the time on my watch mirrors the time on the clock.

I feel a frustration start to well inside of me. Emma has mistakenly scheduled too many patients in not enough time, so that I'll spend the rest of the day scrambling to catch up and we'll pay for it, the whole lot of us, Joyce, Emma, the patients and me. But mainly me.

It's a short drive home. The entirety of the island is only about a mile by a mile and a half wide — which means that on a bad day such as this, I don't have time to decompress before I arrive home. I drive slowly, taking my time, needing an extra lap around the block to catch my breath before I pull into my own driveway.

This far north in the world, night falls early. The sun begins to set at just past four o'clock, leaving us with only nine hours of daylight this time of year, the rest of the day various shades of twilight and dark. The sky is dark now.

I don't know most of my neighbors. Some I've seen in passing, but most I've never seen because it's late fall, early winter, the time of year people have a tendency to hide indoors. The home next door to ours is a summer property only, someone's second home. It's unoccupied this time of year. The owners — Will learned and told to me — move to the mainland as soon as fall comes, leaving their home abandoned for Old Man Winter. Which makes me think now that a home like that could be vulnerable to break-ins, making for an easy place for a killer to hide.

As I go by it, the house is dark as it always is until just after seven o'clock when a light flicks on. The light is set on a timer. It goes off near midnight. The timer is meant to serve as a deterrent for burglars and yet is so predictable, it's not.

I go on. I bypass my own home and head up the hill. The Baineses' house is dark as I drive past. Across the street, at the home of the Nilssons, a light is on, the soft glow of it just barely breaking through the periphery of the heavy drapes. I pause before the home, car idling, my eyes set on the picture window in front. There's a car in the drive, Mr. Nilsson's rusty sedan. Puffs of smoke spew from the chimney and into the winter night. Someone is home.

I have half a mind to pull into the drive, park the car, knock on the front door and ask about what Officer Berg told me. How Mr. Nilsson claimed he saw me arguing with Morgan in the days before she died.

But I also have enough self-awareness to know that if I do, it might come off as brash — threatening even — and that's not the message I want to send.

I make my way around the block before going home.

Moments later, I stand alone in the kitchen, peeking beneath the lid of a skillet to see what Will's cooking tonight. Pork chops. It smells divine.

I stand, with my shoes still on my feet, a bag slung across me. The bag is heavy. The strap burrows deeply into my skin, though I hardly feel the weight of it because it's my stomach that hurts the most. I'm hungry, completely famished, my day getting away from me so that I never had time for lunch.

Without a word, Will slips silently into the kitchen and curls up behind me. He nestles his chin onto my shoulder. He slips his warm hands beneath the waistline of my shirt, wrapping them around me. A single thumb sweeps up and down my navel, strumming me like a guitar. I feel myself tense up at Will's touch. "How was your day?" he asks.

I think back to the days when Will's arms around me made me feel safe, invulnerable and loved. For a moment, I want nothing more than to turn and face him, to unload about the dreary workday; the run-in with Officer Berg. I know just exactly what would happen if I did. Will would stroke my hair before lifting the heavy workbag from my shoulder and setting it to the ground. He'd say something empathetic, like *That sounds rough,* as he poured me a glass of wine. He wouldn't attempt to fix things for me as other men might do. Instead, he'd lead me to the single spindle-back chair pressed against a kitchen wall and hand me the wine. He'd drop to the kitchen floor before me and remove my shoes, massage my feet. And he'd listen.

But I don't tell Will about my day because I can't. Because there on the countertop sits his true crime novel, and in an instant, last night comes tumbling back to me all over again. From where I stand, I see the edge of Erin's photograph jutting out from the pages of the book, just a couple of millimeters of blue trim, and even though I can't see it, I still imagine the blue eyes, blond hair, rounded shoulders. The willowy woman who stands with her hands on her hips, pouting at the camera, baiting whoever's on the other side of it.

"What's wrong?" Will asks, and though I hesitate — thinking I might just say *nothing* and leave the room, too exhausted for this conversation right now, I say, "I started reading your book last night. When I couldn't sleep," motioning to it there on the countertop.

Will doesn't pick up the innuendo. He draws away from me and begins tending to dinner while asking, "Oh yeah? What do you think of it so far?" with his side now turned toward me.

"Well," I say, hesitating. "I didn't actually have a chance to read it. I opened it up and Erin's picture fell out," feeling shame-faced for admitting this, as if I've done something wrong.

Only then does he put the tongs down and turn to me.

"Sadie," he says, reaching for me, and I say, "It's fine, really it is," trying my hardest to be diplomatic because, for heaven's sake, Erin is *dead.* I can't be outwardly angry or jealous that Will's been carrying her photograph around after all this time. That just wouldn't feel right. Besides, there's no reason for me to be concerned. I, too, had a high school sweetheart once. We broke up when he went off to college. He didn't die, but we severed ties just the same. I never think of him. If I were to pass him on the street, I wouldn't know.

Will married *me,* I remind myself. He has

children *with me.*

I look down at my hand. It doesn't matter that the ring I wear once belonged to her. As a family heirloom, Will's mother refused to let Erin be buried with it. He was honest when he gave it to me. He came clean, told me what the ring had been through and where it had been. I promised, at the time, to wear the ring in both his grandmother's and in Erin's honor.

"It's just," I say, staring at the book as if I can see straight through the cover to what's inside, "I never knew you carried her picture around with you. That you still thought about her."

"I don't. I didn't. Listen," he says, reaching for my hands. I don't pull back, though that's exactly what I want to do. I want to be hurt. I *am* hurt. But I try to be compassionate. "Yes, I have a photograph of her still. I came across it in some of my stuff when I was unpacking. I didn't know what to do with it, so I stuck it in the book. But it's not what you think. It's just that, I realized recently that it will be twenty years next month. Twenty years since Erin died. That's all. I don't think about her, hardly ever, Sadie. But it got me thinking, and not in a mournful way. More in a *holy shit, twenty years* sort of way." He pauses, runs his hands through his hair, thinks his next words through before he speaks.

"Twenty years ago, I was a different man. I wasn't even a man," he says. "I was a boy. The odds that Erin and I would have actually gone through with it and gotten married aren't great. Sooner or later we would have realized how dumb we were. How naive. What we had was just young love between two stupid kids. What you and I have," he says, tapping my chest and then his in turn, and I have to look away because his stare is so intense it gets inside of me. "This, Sadie. This is marriage."

And then he draws me in and wraps his arms around me and, for just this once, I let him.

He presses his lips to my ear and whispers, "Whether you believe me or not, there are times I thank God it happened this way because if it didn't, I might have never met you."

There's nothing to say to that. It's not as if I, too, can say that I'm glad she's dead. What kind of person would that make me?

After a minute, I pull back. Will goes back to the stove. He reaches for the tongs, flips over the pork chops in the frying pan. I tell him that I'm running upstairs to change.

In the living room, Tate sits playing with

Legos on the nicked-up coffee table. I say hello and he rises from the floor and squeezes me tight, calling out, "Mommy's home!" He asks me to play with him, and I promise, "After dinner. Mommy's going to go change."

But before I can go, he pulls on my hand, calling out, "Statue game, statue game."

I don't know what he means by this, *statue game.* But I'm too tired for him to be pulling on me. He doesn't mean for it to be, but his tugging is rough. It hurts my hand.

"Tate," I say, "be gentle," as I withdraw my hand from his and see him pout.

"I want to play the statue game," he whines, but instead I say, "We'll do Legos. After dinner. I promise," seeing the castle he's already begun to create, complete with a tower and gatehouse. It's impressive. A mini figure sits at the top of the tower, keeping watch over the land, while three more figures stand on the coffee table, ready to attack.

"You did that all by yourself?" I ask, and Tate tells me he did, beaming proudly as I disappear up the stairs to change.

It's dim in the house. Aside from the shortage of windows and, therefore, a scarcity of natural lighting, the house is coated with a dated wooden paneling, which makes everything dark. Gloomy. It does nothing to bolster our moods, especially on days like this, which are depressing enough as is.

Upstairs, I find Otto's bedroom door pulled to. He's there, inside, as he always is, listening to music and doing homework. I rap on the door and call out a quick hello. He says back, "Hi." I wonder how Otto's commute was to school, if he wore wet clothes all day from the rain-drenched ferry ride to the school bus waiting on the other side, if he sat with anyone at lunch. I could ask him, but the truth is I'd rather not know the answer. As they say, ignorance is bliss.

Imogen's door is open a smidge. I peek in, but she's not there.

I head to Will's and my bedroom. There I stare at my tired reflection in the floor-length mirror, the weary eyes, the poplin shirt, the skirt. My makeup has nearly worn away. My skin is washed out, more gray than anything else, or maybe it's just the lighting. Crow's-feet sneak from the edges of my eyes. My laugh lines become more prominent each day. The joys of aging.

I'm pleased to see my hair starting to grow back to its usual length after an impulsive chop, one of those regrettable haircuts I hated. All I'd ever gotten were the dead ends trimmed. But then one day my long-time stylist went and sheared off four inches or more. I stared at her aghast when she was through, eyeing the clumps of hair on her salon floor.

What? she'd asked, as wide-eyed as me. *That's what you said you wanted, Sadie.*

I told her it was fine. *It's hair. It grows back.*

I didn't want her to feel bad for what she'd done. And it is only hair. It does grow back.

But if we hadn't moved when we did, I would have been on the hunt for a new stylist.

I yank the high heels from my feet and stare at the blisters on my skin. I step from my skirt, tossing it into the laundry basket. After sinking my feet into a pair of warm socks, my legs into a pair of comfy pajama pants, I head back downstairs, checking the thermostat on the way down. This old home is either icy cold or burning hot, but never anything in between. The furnace can no longer distribute heat properly. I turn the heat up a notch.

Will is still in the kitchen when I arrive, putting away the rest of the dinner prep. He slips the flour and cornstarch in a cabinet, sets the dirty skillet in the sink.

He calls the boys for dinner. Moments

later, we sit at the kitchen table to eat. Will has served the pork chops with a side of spinach couscous tonight, his culinary skills easily trumping mine.

"Where's Imogen?" I ask, and Will tells me she's with a friend, studying for a Spanish quiz. She'll be home by seven. I roll my eyes, mutter, "Don't hold your breath." Because Imogen rarely, if ever, does as she says. Only sometimes does she eat dinner with us. When she does, she saunters into the kitchen five minutes later than the rest of us because she can. Because we're not going to nag her about it. She knows that if she wants to eat the dinner Will's made, she eats with us, or she doesn't eat at all. Though still, when she does eat with us, she comes late and leaves early to exercise her autonomy.

Tonight, however, she's a no-show, and I wonder if she's really studying with a friend, or if she's doing something else, like hanging out at the abandoned military fortification at the far end of the island where kids have been rumored to drink, do drugs, have sex.

I put it out of my mind for now. Instead I ask Otto about his day. He shrugs and says, "Okay, I guess."

Will asks, "How was the science test?"

inquiring about things like static and kinetic friction, and asking him, "Did you remember what they mean?"

Otto says he did, he thinks. Will reaches over, ruffles his hair and says, "Atta boy. The studying helped." I watch as a dark thatch of hair falls into Otto's eyes. His hair has grown too long so that it's shaggy and unkempt. It hides his eyes. Otto's eyes are hazel like Will's, and can turn on a dime from a warm brown to a sky blue, though I can't see which tonight.

Dinner conversation consists mostly of Tate's day at school, though half the class was apparently absent because half of the parents have the good sense not to send their children to school when there is a murderer on the loose. Though Tate doesn't know this.

I watch as Otto, across from me, slices through the pork chop with a steak knife. There's a crudeness about the way he holds the knife, about the way he cuts his meat with it. The pork is succulent. It's cooked to perfection; my own knife slices right through. But still, Otto goes after his full tilt, as if it's overcooked, tough and rubbery, nearly impossible to get through with the serrated knife edge, which it's not.

There's something about the knife in his

hand that makes me lose my appetite.

"Aren't you hungry?" Will asks, seeing that I'm not eating. I don't answer his question. I reach for my fork instead. I set a bite of pork in my mouth. The memories come rushing back to me, and I find that I can hardly chew.

But still I do chew because Will is watching me, as is Tate. Tate, who doesn't like pork chops, though we have a three-bite rule in our home. Three bites and then you can be through. He's only had one.

But Otto, on the other hand, eats voraciously, sawing through the meat like a lumberjack with a log.

I'd never thought much about knives before. They were just part of the flatware. Not until the day Will and I walked into the principal's office at Otto's public high school in Chicago and there he sat in a chair, back to us, handcuffs on his wrists. It was alarming to see, my son with his hands bound behind him like a common criminal. Will had received a call from the principal that there was a problem at school, something we needed to discuss. I cut short my shift in the ER. As I drove to the school alone with plans to meet Will there, my mind went to a failing grade, or the overlooked signs of a learning disability we didn't yet know about. Perhaps Otto was dyslexic. The idea of Otto struggling with something, with anything, saddened me. I wanted to help.

I walked straight past the police cruiser parked outside. I didn't think anything of it.

But then, at the sight of Otto there in the chair in handcuffs, the mama bear in me reared up at once. I don't think I've ever been so angry in my entire life. *Take those off of him this minute,* I demanded. *You have no right,* I said, but whether the police officer did or didn't, I didn't know. He stood just feet shy of Otto, looking down on the boy whose eyes sat glued to the floor, head slumped forward, arms awkwardly tethered together behind him so that he couldn't sit all the way back. Otto looked so small in the chair. Helpless and frail. At fourteen, he had yet to experience the same growth spurt that other boys his age already had. He stood a head shorter than most of them, and twice as thin. Though Will and I were right there with him, he was alone. Completely alone. Anyone could see that. It made my heart break for him.

The school principal sat on the other side of a large desk, looking grim.

Mr. and Mrs. Foust, he said, rising to his feet and extending a hand in greeting, a hand which Will and I both ignored.

Doctor, I amended. The police officer smirked.

The evidence bag on the corner of the principal's desk, I soon learned, contained a knife. And not just any knife, but an eight-inch chef's knife from Will's prized set, stolen that morning from the block of them that sat on the corner of the kitchen counter.

The principal explained to Will and me that Otto brought the knife to school, hidden in his backpack. *Fortunately,* the principal said, one of the students saw and had the good sense to inform a teacher and the local police were called in to apprehend Otto before any damage could be done.

As the principal spoke, I could think only one thing. How humiliating it would have been for Otto to be handcuffed in front of his peers. To be removed from his classroom by the local police. Because never once did I think it was possible that Otto brought a knife to school or that he threatened children with it. This was a mistake only. A horrible mistake for which Will and I would seek retribution for our son and his marred reputation.

Otto was quiet, kind. Not ostentatiously happy, but happy. He had friends, a handful only, but friends nonetheless. He was always very rule-abiding, never once getting into trouble at school. There had never been a detention, a note sent home, a phone call with a teacher. There was no need for any of these things. And so, I easily reasoned, there was no way Otto had done something as delinquent as bring a knife to school.

Upon closer examination of the knife itself, Will recognized it as his own. He tried to downplay the situation — *It's a popular knife set. I bet many people have it* — and yet no one could dispute the look of recognition that crossed his face, the look of shock and horror.

There in the principal's office, Otto began to cry.

What did you think you were doing? Will asked him gently, a hand on Otto's shoulder, massaging it. *You're better than that, buddy,* he said. *You're smarter than that.*

By then, they were both crying. I was the only one whose eyes remained dry.

Otto confessed to us then in not quite so many words, his voice hard to hear at times through the gasping sobs, that, the previous spring, he'd become the target of teenage bullying. He thought it would go away on its own, but the situation had only become more exacerbated when he returned to school that August.

What Otto told us was that some of the more popular boys in school claimed he was making eyes at another kid in his class. A boy. Rumors circulated quickly, and before long, not a day went by that Otto wasn't called a homo, a queer, a fairy, a fag. *Stupid faggot,* they'd say. *Die, faggot, die.*

Otto went on and on, rambling off the epithets his classmates used. Only when Otto paused for breath did the principal ask who, specifically, said these things, and whether there were witnesses to Otto's claims or if this was simply a matter of *he said, she said,* so to speak.

There was the clear sense that the principal didn't believe him.

Otto went on. He told us how the smack talk was only part of it. Because there was also the physical abuse, the threats. Being cornered in the boys' bathroom or shoved into lockers. The cyberbullying. The photos they'd taken of him, heinously photoshopped to their liking, and shared far and wide.

This broke my heart and made me angry with good reason. I wanted to find the boys who had done this to Otto and wring their little necks. My blood pressure spiked. There was a pounding in my head, my chest, as my hand fell to the back of Otto's chair to steady myself. *What will happen to those boys?* I'd asked, demanding, *Certainly they'll be punished for what they've done. They can't get away with this.*

His reply was limp. *If Otto would tell us who did this, I could talk to them,* he said. A look crossed Otto's face. He would never tell on these kids because if he did, life would suddenly be even more insufferable than it already was.

Why didn't you tell us? Will asked, dropping down beside Otto so that he could look him straight in the eye.

Otto looked at him, head shaking, and asserted, *I'm not gay, Dad,* as if it would matter if he were. *I'm not gay,* he maintained, losing any lingering traces of composure.

But that wasn't the question Will had asked because things like that — sexual orientation — didn't matter to Will or me.

Why didn't you tell us you were being bullied? Will clarified then, and that was when Otto said he did. He did tell. He told me.

In that moment, my heart sank so low it slipped right out of me.

Violence throughout the city was on a rise. That meant more and more patients showing up in my emergency room with bloodied bodies and gunshot wounds. My everyday routine started to resemble the sensationalist portrayal of ERs you see on TV, and not merely all fevers and broken bones. Add to that the fact that we'd been understaffed. Back in those days, my twelve-hour shifts looked more like fifteen, and it was a constant marathon during which there was little time to empty my bladder or eat. I was in a fog when I was home, tired and sleep-deprived. I forgot things. A dental cleaning, to pick up a gallon of milk on the way home from work.

Had Otto told me he was being bullied and I'd dismissed it?

Or had I been so lost in thought that I didn't hear him at all?

Will's eyes had turned to mine then, inquiring in that single incredulous stare whether I had known. I shrugged my shoulders and shook my head, made him believe that Otto hadn't told me. Because maybe he had and maybe he hadn't. I didn't know.

What made you think it was okay to take a knife to school? Will had asked Otto then, and I tried to imagine the logic that went through his mind that morning when deciding to take the knife. Would there be legal recourse for what he had done, or would a slap on the wrist suffice? How could I possibly stand to send him back to the classroom when this was through?

What did you think you were going to do with it, buddy? Will asked, meaning the knife, and I braced myself, not sure I was ready to hear his reply.

Otto gazed over a shoulder at me then and whispered, his voice breathy from crying, *It was Mom's idea.* I blanched at his words, turning all shades of white because of the preposterousness of the statement. A bald-faced lie. *It was Mom's idea to take the knife to school. To scare them with,* Otto lied, his eyes dropping to the floor while Will, the police officer and I watched on. *She's the one who put it in my backpack,* he said under his breath, and I gasped, knowing immediately why he said it. I was the one who always had his back. We're cut from the same cloth, Otto and me. He's a mama's boy; he's always been. He thought I would protect him from this, that if I could take the blame for what he'd done, he'd get off scot-free. But he didn't pause to think of the ramifications it might have on my reputation, on my career, on me.

I was heartbroken for Otto. But now I was also angry.

Until that moment, I didn't know he was being picked on at school. And far be it from me to suggest he bring a knife, *a knife!,* to school to threaten teenage boys with, much less slip it inside his backpack.

How did he possibly think anyone would fall for that lie?

That's ridiculous, Otto, I breathed out as all eyes in the room moved in unison to mine. *How could you say that?* I asked, my own eyes starting to well with tears. I pressed a finger to his chest. I whispered, *You did this, Otto. You,* and he winced in the chair as if he'd been slapped. He turned his back to me and once again began to cry.

Soon after, we took Otto home, having been informed that there would be an expulsion hearing before the board to see if Otto could return to school. We didn't wait for an answer. I could never send Otto back there again.

Later that night, Will asked me in private, *Don't you think you were too harsh on him?*

And there it was. The first rift in our marriage.

Until that moment, there'd been no breaches in our relationship, no gaps, none that I knew about at least. Will and I were like diamonds, I thought, able to withstand the crushing pressures of marriage and family life.

I felt sorry for the way things had unfolded in the principal's office. There was an awful pain in the pit of my stomach knowing that

Otto had been enduring the bullying and abuse for so long and we didn't know. I felt sad it had come to this, that my son thought taking a knife to school was his only option. But I was angry that he tried to lay the blame for it on me.

I told Will no, I didn't think I was too harsh on Otto, and he said, *He's just a boy, Sadie. He made a mistake.*

But some mistakes, I soon came to learn, couldn't so easily be forgiven. Because it wasn't two weeks later that I discovered Will was having an affair, that he'd been having an affair for quite some time.

Next came the news of Alice's death. I wasn't sure, but Will was. It was time to leave.

Happenstance, he called it.

Everything happens for a reason, he said.

Will promised me we could be happy in Maine, that we just needed to leave behind everything that happened in Chicago and start fresh, though of course it struck me as ironic that our happiness came at Alice's expense.

As we sit now at the table, eating the last of our dinner, I find myself staring out the dark window above the kitchen sink. Thinking about Imogen and the Baines family, about Officer Berg's accusation this morning, I wonder if we can ever be happy here, or if bad luck is destined to follow us wherever we go.

CAMILLE

After that first time together, my meetups with Will became a regular thing. There were other hotel rooms, ones that became more fancy the more I begged. I didn't like the hotels he first took me to. They were dank, dingy, cheap. The rooms had stuffy smells to them. The sheets were scratchy and thin. They had stains on them. I heard people on the other side of the walls; they heard me.

I deserved more than that. I was too good for budget hotels, for the criticism of a minimally paid staff. I was special and deserved to be treated as such. Will should have known that by then. I dropped a hint one afternoon.

I've always dreamed of seeing the inside of the Waldorf, I said.

The Waldorf? he asked, standing before me, laughing at my suggestion. We were deep in the alcove of an apartment complex where no one could see us. We never talked about his marriage. It was one of those things that's just there. One of those things you don't want to believe is there, like death, aliens, malaria.

The Waldorf Astoria? he asked when I suggested it. *You know that's like four hundred dollars a night, maybe more.*

I asked, pouting, *Am I not worth that to you?*

As it turned out, I was. Because within an hour's time, we had a room on the tenth floor, champagne compliments of room service.

There's nothing, Will said as he opened the door to the lavish hotel suite and let me in, *that I wouldn't do for you.*

In the room, there was a fireplace, a terrace, a mini bar, a fancy bathtub where I could soak, staring out at the views of the city from the luxury of a bubble bath.

The hotel staff referred to us as Mr. and Mrs. Foust.

Enjoy your stay, Mr. and Mrs. Foust.

I imagined a world where I was Mrs. Foust. Where I lived in Will's home with him, where I carried and raised his babies. It was a good life.

But I didn't ever want to be mistaken for Sadie. I was so much better than Sadie.

Will meant what he said: that there was

nothing he wouldn't do for me. He proved it time and again. He showered me with sweet nothings. He wrote me love notes. He bought me things.

When no one was there, he brought me to his home. It was far different than the gloomy apartment where Sadie and I used to live, that two-bedroom in Uptown where drunks and bums hung around, accosting us for money when we stepped outside, not that we had any to spare. Even if I did, I wasn't about to share. I'm not known for my generosity. But Sadie was, always digging away in her purse, and they clung to her, the drunks and the bums did, like lice to hair.

They tried the same with me. I told them to fuck off.

Inside Will and Sadie's home, I ran my hands across the arm of a leather sofa, fondled glass vases and candelabras and such, all clearly expensive. The Sadie I once knew could never afford these things. A doctor's salary came with all the perks.

Will led the way to the bedroom. I followed along.

There was a picture of Sadie and him on a bedside table, a wedding picture. It was charming, really. In the picture, they were standing in the center of a street. They were sharply in focus while the rest of the picture gradually blurred. The trees canopied over them, full of springtime blooms. They weren't facing the camera, smiling cheesy grins at some photographer's request like most brides and grooms do. Instead, they were leaned into each other, kissing. Her eyes were closed, while his watched her. He stared at her like she was the most beautiful woman in the world. His hand was wrapped around the small of her back, hers pressed to his chest. There was a spray of rice in the air. For prosperity, fertility and good fortune.

Will caught me looking at the picture.

To save face I said, *Your wife's pretty,* as if I'd never seen her before. But Sadie was a far cry from pretty. She was ordinary at best.

He wore a hangdog look, said, *I think so.*

I told myself he had to say that. That it wouldn't be right for him to say anything else.

But he didn't mean it.

He came to me, ran his hands through my hair, kissed me deeply. *You're beautiful,* he said, the superlative form of pretty, which meant I was prettier than her.

Will led me to the bed, tossed pillows to the ground.

Don't you think your wife will mind? I asked

as I sat on the edge of the bed.

I have little moral compass. I'm sure that much is clear. I didn't mind. But I thought maybe he did.

Will's smile was mischievous. He came to me, slipped a hand up my skirt, said, *I hope she does.*

We didn't talk about his wife anymore after that.

What I'd come to learn was that Will was a ladies' man before he got married. A philanderer, the kind of man who thought he'd never settle down.

As they say, old habits die hard. It was something Sadie tried to keep in check.

But, try as we might, we can't change people. So she kept a tight rein on him instead, same as she once did me. Long ago, my lighters, my smokes would disappear if she found them, locks would change when I'd forget to close the apartment door behind myself. She was quite the disciplinarian, quite the despot.

I could see in his eyes the way she enfeebled him, the way she emasculated him.

I, on the other hand, made him feel like a man.

Sadie

It's seven thirty. Imogen still isn't home. Will doesn't seem worried, not even when I press him on it, asking who she's studying with and where the friend lives.

"I know you want to believe the best in her, Will. But come on," I say to him. "We both know she's not studying Spanish."

Will shrugs and tells me, "She's just being a teenager, Sadie."

"A delinquent teenager," I retort, my face expressionless. Otto, at fourteen, is a teenager, too. But it's a school night and he's at home with us as he should be.

Will wipes down the table from dinner and tosses the dirty dishrag into the sink. He turns to me, smiling his magnanimous smile, and says, "I was a delinquent teenager once, and look how I turned out. She'll be fine," as Otto comes into the room with his geometry folder.

Will and Otto spread out at the kitchen

table to work on homework. Tate turns on the living room TV and settles in, snuggled up under an afghan, to watch a cartoon.

I carry my glass of wine upstairs. A long soak in a warm bath is what I have in mind. But at the top of the steps, I find myself drawn not to the master bathroom, but instead to Imogen's room.

It's dark when I enter. I press my palm against the door, opening it wide. I ignore a sign on the door that tells me to keep out. I let myself into the room, feeling the wall for a light switch and turning it on. The room becomes visible and I discover a jumble of dark clothing strewn across the floor, enough of it that I have to move it to avoid stepping on it.

The room smells of incense. The box of sticks lies there on Imogen's desk beside a coiled snake–shaped holder. The sticks go inside the snake's mouth, the smell still potent enough that I wonder if she was here, after school, burning incense in her room before she disappeared to wherever she is. The desk is wooden and old. Imogen has carved words into the wood with the sharp edge of some sort of blade. They're not nice words. Indeed, they're angry words. *Fuck you. I hate u.*

I take a swig of my wine before setting the

glass on the desktop. I trace my finger across the wooden trenches, wondering if this is the same handwriting that was left on my car window. I wish, in retrospect, that I had thought to take a photo of my car window before blasting that word away with the defrost. Then I could compare the handwriting, see if the shape of the letters is the same. Then I'd know.

This is the first time I've stepped all the way inside Imogen's room. I didn't come with the intent of snooping. But this is my family's home now. It feels within my right to snoop. Will wouldn't like it. I just barely make out his and Otto's muffled voices coming from the kitchen. They have no idea where I am.

I look inside the desk drawers first. It's just what you'd expect to find in a desk drawer. Pens, paper, paper clips. I stand on the desk chair, running my hands blindly along the bookshelf above the desk, coming up with only a palmful of dust. I ease myself back down to the floor.

I leave my wine where it is. I go to the bedside table, pull on the drawer knob. I sift through random things. A child's rosary, wadded up tissues, a bookmark. A condom. I reach for the condom, hold it in my hand a moment, debate whether to tell Will.

Imogen is sixteen. Sixteen-year-olds, these days, have sex. But a condom at least tells me Imogen is being smart about the choices she makes. She's being safe. I can't fault her for that. If we were on better terms I'd have a conversation with her, woman to woman. But we're not. Regardless, an appointment with a gynecologist isn't out of the question now that she's of a certain age. That might be a better way to handle things.

I put the condom back. Then I find a photograph.

It's a photograph of a man, I can tell, from the body shape and what's left of the hair, that which hasn't been scuffed off in apparent anger. But the man's face, on the other hand, has been obliterated like a scratch-off lottery ticket, scored with the edge of a coin. I wonder who the man is. I wonder how Imogen knows him, and what made Imogen so angry that she felt the need to do *this.*

I drop to my hands and knees beside the bed. I look beneath, before foraging in the pockets of the misplaced clothing. I rise to my feet and go to the closet, sliding the door open. I reach in, feeling blindly for the light string and giving it a pull.

I don't want Will to know I'm nosing around in Imogen's room. I hold my breath, listen for noises coming from downstairs, but all that I hear is Tate's cartoon on the TV, the sound of his innocent laugh. If only he'd stay this age forever. Will and Otto are quiet and I envision them folded over notebooks on the kitchen table, lost in thought.

Not so long after what happened with Otto, I read an article about how to best snoop in your teen's room, the places to look. Not the obvious spots like desk drawers, but instead: secret pockets in the lining of coats; inside the electrical sockets; in false-bottomed soda cans. What we were to look for wasn't so obvious either, but rather cleaning supplies, plastic bags, over-the-counter medicine — all of which were easily misused by teens. I never actually snooped through Otto's room. I didn't need to. What happened with him was one and done. Otto had learned his lesson. We talked about it. It would never happen again.

But Imogen is a closed book to me. She hardly speaks, not more than a sentence at best, and even that is never forthcoming. I know nothing about her, about who she's having sex with (and does she have sex here, in this room, when Will and I are gone, or does she sneak out the bedroom window at night?), about those girls she smokes cigarettes with, about what she does in these missing hours that she's not with us. Will and I should have a better handle on these things. We shouldn't be so uninformed. It's irresponsible that we are, but every time I've broached the subject with Will — who is Imogen *really*? — he puts me off, saying that we can't push too hard. That she'll open up to us when she's ready.

I can't wait anymore.

I search the closet. I find the letter in the pocket of a charcoal sweatshirt. It really isn't hard to find. I check the shoeboxes first, the back corners of the closet where only dust resides. And then on to the clothing. It's on the fourth or fifth try that my hand folds around something and I pull it out of a pocket to see. It's paper, folded many, many times so that it's small, no more than an inch tall by an inch wide, and thick.

I bring it out of the closet. I gently unfold it.

Please don't be mad is scrawled on the page, the ink pale like maybe the sweatshirt was run through the washing machine with it. But it's there and visible, written in print, far more masculine than my own spidery script, which leads me to believe it was written by a man's hand, which I could have guessed anyway from the content of the note. *You know as well as I do how hard this is for me. It's nothing you did. It doesn't mean*

I don't love you. But I can't keep living this double life.

From downstairs, the front door suddenly opens. The door slams closed.

Imogen is home.

Inside my chest, my heart begins to hammer.

Will's voice greets her, more cordial than I wish he would be. He asks if she's hungry, if she wants him to warm her up some dinner — which goes against the rules we laid down for her, that she eats dinner with us or she doesn't eat our dinner at all. I wish Will wouldn't be so obliging, but it's the way Will is, always eager to please. Imogen's replies are short, brute — *no, no* — as her voice drifts toward the steps.

I react, moving quickly. I refold the note and jam it back into the sweatshirt pocket, tousling the clothes into place. I pull the string light and slide the door closed, hurrying from the room, remembering at the last minute to turn the bedroom light off, to pull the door closed just so, as it was when I found it, open a smidge.

I don't have time to double-check that everything is as I found it. I pray that it is.

Our paths cross in the stairwell and I offer a tight smile but say nothing.

Mouse

Once upon a time there was an old house. Everything about the house was old: the windows, the appliances, and especially the steps in the house were old. Because any-time anyone walked on them, they groaned like old people sometimes groan.

Mouse wasn't sure why the steps did that. She knew a lot of things, but she didn't know anything about how treads and risers rubbed together, grinding against nails and screws on the other side, somewhere below the steps where she couldn't see. All she knew was that the steps made a noise, all of them did, but especially the last step, which made the most noise of all.

Mouse thought she knew something about those steps that no one else did. She thought it hurt for them to be stepped on, and that was the reason they groaned and pulled back from underfoot whenever she did — though Mouse only weighed forty-six pounds and couldn't hurt a fly if she tried.

It made Mouse think of the old people across the street, the ones who moved like everything hurt, who groaned just like the stairs sometimes groaned.

Mouse was sensitive in a way other people weren't. It worried her to walk on that last stair. And so, just as she was careful not to step on caterpillars and roly-polies when she walked down the street, Mouse took extra care to step over that last tread, though she was a little girl and her stride was not wide.

Her father tried to fix the stairs. He was always getting worked up about them, swearing under his breath about the incessant, infuriating squeak.

Then why don't you just step over it? the girl asked her father because Mouse's father was a tall man, his stride much wider than hers. He could have easily walked right over that last stair without putting weight on it. But he was also an impatient man, the kind who always wanted things *just so.*

Her father wasn't cut out for doing chores around the house. He was much better suited for sitting behind a desk, drinking coffee, jabbering into the phone. Mouse would sit on the other side of the door when he did that and listen. She wasn't allowed to interrupt, but if she stayed real quiet, she could hear what he had to say, the way his voice changed when he was on that phone with a customer.

Mouse's father was a handsome man. He had hair that was a dark chestnut brown. His eyes were big, round, always watching. He was quiet most of the time, except for when he walked, because he was a big man and his footsteps were heavy. Mouse could hear him coming from a mile away.

He was a good father. He took Mouse outside and played catch with her. He taught her things about bird nests and how the rabbits hid their babies in holes in the ground. Mouse's father always knew where they were, and he'd go to the holes, lift up the clumps of grass and fur on top, and let Mouse take a peek.

One day, when he'd had enough of that squeaky stair, Mouse's father gathered his toolbox from the garage and climbed the steps. With a hammer, he drove nails into the tread, clamping it down to the wood on the other side. Then he grabbed a handful of finishing nails. He tapped them into the tread, reattaching it to the riser beneath.

He stood back proudly to examine his handiwork.

But Mouse's father had never been much

of a handyman.

He should have known that no matter what he did, he would never be able to fix the step. Because even after all his hard work, the stair continued to make noise.

In time, Mouse came to depend on that sound. She would lie in bed, staring up at the light that hung from her ceiling, heart beating hard, unable to sleep.

There she would listen for that last step to bellow out a warning for her, letting her know someone was coming up the stairs for her room, giving her a head start to hide.

SADIE

I watch from bed as Will changes out of his clothes and into a pair of pajama pants, dropping his clothes into the hamper on the floor. He stands for a second at the window, looking out onto the street beneath.

"What is it?" I ask, sitting upright in bed. Something has caught Will's eye and drawn him there, to the window. He stands, contemplatively.

The boys are both asleep, the house remarkably quiet.

"There's a light on," Will tells me, and I ask, "Where?"

He says, "Morgan's house."

This doesn't surprise me. As far as I know, the house is still a crime scene. I'd have to imagine it takes days for forensics to process things before some bioremediation service gets called in to scrub blood and other bodily fluids from inside the home. Soon Will and I will watch on as people in yellow splash suits with some sort of breathing apparatus affixed to their heads move in and out, taking bloodstained items away.

I wonder again about the violence that happened there that night, about the bloodshed.

How many bloodstained items will they have to take away?

"There's a car in the drive," Will tells me. But before I have a chance to reply, he says, "Jeffrey's car. He must be home from Tokyo."

He stands motionless before the window for another minute or two. I rise from bed, leaving the warmth of the blankets. The house is cold tonight. I go to the window and stand beside Will, our elbows touching. I look out, see the same thing he sees. A shadowy SUV parked in the driveway beside a police cruiser, both of them illuminated by a porch light.

As we watch on, the front door of the home opens. An officer steps out first, then ushers Jeffrey through the door. Jeffrey must be a foot taller than the policeman. He pauses in the open doorway for a last look inside. In his hands, he carries luggage. He steps from the home, passing the officer by. The officer closes the door and locks it behind them. The officer has met him here,

I think, and kept an eye on the crime scene while Mr. Baines packed up a few personal things.

Under his breath Will murmurs, "This is all so surreal."

I lay a hand on his arm, the closest I come to consoling him. "It's awful," I say because it is. No one, but especially not a young woman, should have to die like this.

"You heard about the memorial service?" Will asks me, though his eyes don't stray from the window.

"What memorial service?" I ask, because I didn't hear about a memorial service.

"There's a memorial service," Will tells me. "Tomorrow. For Morgan. At the Methodist church." There are two churches on the island. The other one is Catholic. "I overheard people talking about it at school pickup. I checked and found the obituary online, the notice of the memorial service. I assume there will be a funeral eventually but . . ." he says, leaving that there, and I easily deduce that the body is still being held by the morgue and will be until the investigation is through. Formalities like a funeral and a wake will have to wait until the murderer is caught. In the interim, a memorial service will have to do.

Tomorrow I work. But depending on what

time the memorial service is, I can go with Will after. I know he'll want to go. Will and Morgan were friends, after all, and, though our relationship has been rocky of late, it would be lonely for him, I think, walking into that memorial service all alone. I can do this for him. And besides, selfishly I'd like to get a good look at Jeffrey Baines up close.

"I work until six tomorrow," I say. "We'll go together. As soon as I finish up. Maybe Otto can keep an eye on Tate," I say. It would be a quick trip. I can't imagine us staying long. We'd pay our respects and then leave.

"We're not going to the memorial service," Will says. His words are conclusive.

I'm taken aback, because this isn't what I expect him to say. "Why not?" I ask.

"It feels presumptuous to go. You didn't know her at all, and I didn't know her that well." I start to explain that a memorial service isn't exactly the type of thing that one needs an invitation to attend, but I stop because I can see Will has already made up his mind.

I ask instead, "Do you think he did it?" I keep my eyes trained to Jeffrey Baines on the other side of the window. I have to crane my neck a bit to see, as the Baineses' house isn't directly across the street. I watch as Jeffrey and the officer exchange words in the driveway, before parting ways and heading for their own cars.

When Will doesn't answer my question, I hear myself mutter, "It's always the husband."

This time, his reply is quick. "He was out of the country, Sadie. Why would you think he had anything to do with this?"

I tell him, "Just because he was out of the country doesn't mean he couldn't have paid someone else to kill his wife." Because, on the contrary, being out of the country at the time of his wife's murder provided him with the perfect alibi.

Will must see the logic in this. There's a small, almost imperceptible nod of the head before he asks, backtracking, "What's that supposed to mean anyway, about it always being the husband?"

I shrug and tell him I don't know. "It's just, if you watch the news long enough, that's the way it seems to be. Unhappy husbands kill their wives."

My gaze stays on the window, watching as, on the other side of the street, Jeffrey Baines pops the trunk of his SUV and tosses the luggage in. His posture is vertical. There's something supercilious about the way he stands.

He doesn't sag at the shoulders, he doesn't convulse and sob like men who have lost their wives are supposed to do.

As far as I can tell, he doesn't shed a single tear.

CAMILLE

I was addicted. I couldn't get enough of him. I watched him, I mirrored him. I followed his routine. I knew where his boys went to school, which coffee shops he patronized, what he ate for lunch. I'd go there, get the same thing. Sit at the same table after he'd left. Forge conversations with him in my mind. Pretend we were together when we weren't.

I thought of him all day, I thought of him all night. If I'd have had my way, he'd be with me all the time. But I couldn't be that woman. That obsessed, hung-up woman. I had to keep my cool.

I worked hard to make sure our run-ins seemed more like chance encounters than what they were. Take, for example, the time we crossed paths in Old Town. I stepped from a building to find him on the other side of it, surrounded by pedestrian traffic. Another cog in the machine.

I called to him. He took a look, smiled. He came to me.

What are you doing here? What's this place? he asked of the building behind me. His embrace was swift. Blink and you might miss it.

I looked at the building behind me, read the sign. I told him, *Buddhist meditation.*

Buddhist meditation? he asked. His laugh was light. *I learn something new about you every day.* He said, *I never took you for the meditation type.*

I wasn't. I'm not. I hadn't come for Buddhist meditation, but for him. Days before, I'd gotten a peek at his calendar, saw a reservation for lunch at a restaurant three doors down. I chose any old building nearby, waited in the foyer for him to pass by. I stepped from the building when I saw him, called to him and he came.

A chance encounter that was anything but.

Some days I found myself standing outside his home. I'd be there when he left for work, hidden by the chaos of the city. Just another face in the crowd. I'd watch as he pushed his way through the building's glass door, as he blended in with the rush of commuters on the street.

From his building, Will would walk three blocks. There, he'd slip down the subway steps, catch the Red Line north to Howard, where he'd transfer to the Purple Line — as would I, twenty paces behind.

If only he'd have turned and looked, he would have seen me there.

The college campus where Will worked was ostentatious. White brick buildings sat covered with ivy, beside glitzy archways. It was thick with people, students with backpacks on, racing to class.

One morning I followed Will down a sidewalk. I kept just the right distance, close but not too close. I didn't want to lose him, but I couldn't risk being seen. Most people aren't patient enough for this kind of pursuit. The trick is to fit in, to look like everyone else. And so that was what I did.

All at once, a voice called for him. *Hey, Professor Foust!*

I looked up. It was a girl, a woman, who stood nearly as tall as him, her coat fitted and tight. There was a beanie on her head, flashy, red. Strands of unnatural blond fell from beneath the hat, draped across her shoulders and back. Her jeans were tight, too, hugging her curves before meeting with the shaft of a tall brown boot.

Will and she stood closely. In the center, their bodies nearly touched.

I couldn't hear what they were saying. But

the tones of their voices, the body language said it all. Her hand brushed against his arm. He said something to her and they both doubled over in laughter. She had her hand on his arm. I heard her then. She said to him, *Stop it, Professor. You're killing me.* She couldn't stop laughing. He watched her laugh. It wasn't the hideous way most people laugh, mouths wide, nostrils flaring. There was something delicate about it. Something graceful and lovely.

He leaned in close, whispered into her ear. As he did, the green-eyed monster grabbed ahold of me.

There's a saying. *Keep your friends close and your enemies closer.* Which is why I took the time to get to know her. Her name was Carrie Laemmer, a second-year pre-law student with aspirations of becoming an environmental lawyer. She was in Will's class, that one in the front row whose hand shot up every time he asked a question. The one who lingered after class, who bantered about poaching and human encroachment as if they were something worth discussing. The one who stood too close when they thought they were alone, who leaned in, who confessed, *Such a damn tragedy about the mountain gorilla,* wanting him to console her.

One afternoon I caught her as she was making her way out of the lecture hall.

I brushed up beside her, said, *That class. It's killing me.*

I carried the class textbook in my hands, the one I spent forty bucks on just to make believe I was in the same class as her, just another student in Professor Foust's global public health course.

I'm in over my head, I told her. *I can't keep up. But you,* I said, praising her to high heaven. I told her how smart she was. How there was nothing she didn't know.

How do you do it? I asked. *You must study all the time.*

Not really, she said, beaming. She shrugged, told me, *I don't know. This stuff just comes easily for me. Some people say I must have a photographic memory.*

You're Carrie, aren't you? Carrie Laemmer? I asked, letting it go to her head, this idea that she was somebody special, that she was *known.*

She reached out a hand. I took it, told her I could really use some help if she had time. Carrie agreed to tutor me, for a fee. We met twice. There, in some little tea shop just off campus where we drank herbal tea, I learned that she was from the suburbs of Boston.

She described it for me, this place where she grew up: the narrow streets, the ocean views, the charming buildings. She told me about her family, her older brothers, both collegiate swimmers for some top-ranked college, though she, oddly enough, couldn't swim. But there were many things she could do, all of which she listed for me. She was a runner, a mountain climber, a downhill skier. She spoke three languages and had an uncanny ability to touch her tongue to her nose. She showed me.

She spoke with a classic Boston accent. People loved to hear it. Just the sound of her voice drew people to her. It lured them in. It didn't matter what she had to say. It was the accent they liked.

She let that go to her head, as she let many things go to her head.

Carrie's favorite color was red. She knit the beanie herself. She painted landscapes, wrote poetry. Wished her name was something like Wren or Meadow or Clover. She was your quintessential right-brain type, an idealist, a wishful thinker.

I saw Will and her together many times after that. The odds of running into someone on a campus that size are small. Which is how I knew that she sought him out, that she knew where he'd be and when. She put herself there, made him think it was kismet that made them keep running into each other instead of what it really was. A trap.

I'm not insecure. I don't have an inferiority complex. She was no prettier than me, no better. This was plain and simple jealousy.

Everyone gets jealous. Babies get jealous, dogs do, too. Dogs are territorial, the way they stand guard on their toys, their beds, their owners. They don't let anyone touch what's theirs. They get angry and aggressive when you do. They snarl, they bite. They maul people in their sleep. Anything to protect their belongings.

I didn't have a choice about what happened next. I had to protect what was mine.

Sadie

Later that night, I awaken from a dream. I come slowly to, and find Will sitting in the slipcovered chair in the corner of the room, hiding among the shadows. I just barely make out the outline of him, the blackened curve of his silhouette and the faint glow off the whites of his eyes as he sits there, watching me. I lie in bed awhile, too drowsy and disoriented to ask him what he's doing, to suggest that he come back to bed with me.

I stretch in bed. I roll over, onto my other side, dragging the blanket with me, turning my back toward Will in the chair. He'll come to bed when he's ready.

I fold myself into the fetal position. I pull my knees into me, press them into my abdomen. I brush against something in the bed. Will's dense memory foam pillow, I assume, but soon feel the swell of a vertebrae, the convexity of a shoulder blade instead. Beside me, Will is shirtless, his skin clammy and warm to the touch. His hair falls sideways, down his neck, pooling on the mattress.

Will is in bed with me. Will is not in the chair in the corner of the room.

Someone else is here.

Someone else is watching us sleep.

I bolt upright in bed. My eyes fight to adjust to the blackness of the room. My heart is in my throat. I can hardly speak. "Who's there?" I ask, but there's a bulge in my throat and all that comes out is a gasp.

I reach a hand to the bedside table, make an effort to turn the knob on the lamp. But before I can, her voice comes to me, quietly and measured, the words chosen carefully.

"I wouldn't do that if I was you."

Imogen rises from the chair. She comes to me, sets herself gingerly on the edge of my bed.

"What are you doing here? Do you need something?" I ask, trying not to let on to my own state of alarm. But it can't so easily be disguised. My panic is transparent. There should be relief in seeing that it's Imogen — not an intruder, but one of our own — but there's no relief in it. Imogen doesn't belong in my bedroom this late at night, lingering in the darkness.

I search Imogen with my eyes, looking for

a reason as to why she's here. Looking for a weapon, though the thought alone makes me sick, the idea of Imogen sneaking into our room with the intent of hurting us.

"Is something wrong?" I ask. "Something you want to talk about?"

Always a heavy sleeper, Will doesn't budge.

"You had no right," she scolds, quietly seething, "to come into my room."

There's a sudden tightness in my chest.

My gut instinct is to lie.

"I wasn't in your room, Imogen," I whisper back, and it's in my best interest now to keep quiet because I don't want Will to know that I was there. That instead of bathing, I went through the drawers in Imogen's bedroom, the pockets of her clothing. An invasion of privacy, Will would say, not taking kindly to my searching through her things.

"You're a liar." Imogen speaks through her teeth now, as I swear, "I'm not. Honestly, Imogen. I wasn't in your room."

Her next words come as a punch to the gut. "Then what was your wine doing there?" she asks. My face flames and I know that I've been caught. I picture it, clear as day, setting the glass of cabernet on the desktop as I canvassed her room.

And then later, fleeing in a hurry, leaving the wine behind.

How could I have been so stupid?

"Oh," I say, straining for a lie. But a lie doesn't come. Not a credible enough one to share anyway, and so I don't try. I've never been a very good liar.

"If you ever," she begins. But it's also where she ends, words cutting off abruptly, leaving it for me to figure out what comes next.

Imogen rises from the edge of the bed. Her sudden height gives her an advantage. She towers over me, stealing the breath from my lungs. Imogen isn't a big girl. She's thin, but she has great height, which must have come from her father's side since Alice was petite. She's taller than I ever realized now that she's standing so closely beside me. She leans down and breathes into my ear, "Stay the fuck out of my room," giving me a slight shove for good measure.

And then she goes. She steals away from the bedroom, her feet noiseless on the wooden floors as they must have been when she let herself into our room.

I lie in bed, sleepless and alert, listening vigilantly for her to return.

How long it goes on this way, I don't

know, until eventually I give in to my drowsiness and slip back to my dream.

SADIE

I go during my lunch break. I try to be subtle about it, slipping out the door when I think no one is watching. But Joyce spots me anyway and asks, "Taking off on us again?" with an edge to her voice that suggests she doesn't approve of me leaving.

"I'm just grabbing a quick lunch," I tell her, though I'm not sure why I lie when the truth might have been better.

Joyce asks, "When can we expect you back?" and I tell her, "In an hour."

She grunts at that and says, "I'll see it when I believe it," which is by no means a fair assessment of me — that I let my lunch breaks drag on longer than the allotted hour. But there's no point in arguing. I go anyway, still anxious about finding Imogen in our bedroom last night. She must have known as soon as she found my wineglass that I'd been in her room. She could have come right then and told me. But she didn't. Instead she waited hours, until I was dead asleep, to tell me. She wanted to scare me. That was her intent.

Imogen isn't some ingenuous child. She's quite cunning.

I find my car in the parking lot and drive. I tried to talk myself out of going to the memorial service. At first I thought that there was really no reason to go, other than my desire to see Jeffrey Baines. We've lived in our home for a little while now, and in that time, I've never gotten a good look at the man. But I can't shake the idea that he killed his wife. For my safety and the safety of my family, I need to know who he is. I need to know who my neighbors are. I need to know if we're safe with this man living just across the street from us.

The Methodist church is white with a tall steeple, a sharply honed spire. Four modest stained glass windows line each side of the building. The church is small, your archetypical, provincial church. Matching evergreen wreaths hang from nails on the double doors, adorned with red bows. The scene is charming. The small lot is jammed with cars. I park on the street, follow others inside the building.

The memorial service is being held in the fellowship hall. Ten or fifteen round tables fill the space, covered in white linens. There's a banquet table at the front of the room and, on it, trays of cookies.

I walk with purpose; I have as much right to be here as anyone else, no matter what Will said. A woman I've never seen before reaches out to shake my hand as I step into the room. She thanks me for coming. There's a handkerchief crumpled in her hand. She's been crying. She tells me she is Morgan's mother. She asks who I am. "Sadie," I say, "a neighbor," followed with deference by, "I'm so sorry for your loss."

The woman is older than me by twenty or thirty years. Her hair is gray, her skin a road map of wrinkles. She's trim, dressed in a black dress that goes just past her knees. Her hand is cold and, as she shakes mine, I feel the handkerchief press between our hands. "It was sweet of you," she says, "to come. It makes me happy, knowing my Morgan had friends."

I blanch at that because of course we weren't friends. But that's something her grieving mother needn't know. "She was a lovely woman," I say for lack of anything better to say.

Jeffrey stands five feet back, speaking with an older couple. Truth be told, he looks bored. He displays none of the same grief that Morgan's mother openly displays. He doesn't cry. It's a masculine thing, not crying. That I understand. And grief can manifest itself in many ways, aside from crying. Anger, disbelief. But I see none of this in Jeffrey as he pats the old man on the back, unleashes a laugh.

I've never been this close to him before. I've never gotten a good look at him until now. Jeffrey is a polished man, tall and refined, with a suave thatch of dark hair that combs up and backward. His features are dark, his eyes hidden behind a pair of bold, thick-rimmed glasses. His suit is black. It's been tailored for him. He's quite handsome.

The older couple moves on. I tell Morgan's mother once more how sorry I am and step past her. I move to Jeffrey. He takes my hand into his. His handshake is firm, his hand tepid. "Jeffrey Baines," he says, holding my stare, and I tell him who I am, how my husband and I live with our family just across the street from him.

"Of course," Jeffrey says, though I doubt he's ever paid attention to the goings-on across the street. He strikes me as one of those savvy businessmen who know how to work a room, adept at the fine art of schmoozing. On the surface, he's charming.

But under, there's more that I can't see.

He tells me, "Morgan was thrilled to have new blood on the street. She would have appreciated your being here, Sandy," he says, and I correct him and say, "Sadie."

"Yes, that's right. Sadie," he says, trying it on for size. He's self-deprecating as a means of apology. "I was never any good with names," he says as he lets go of my hand and I draw it back, folding my hands together before me.

"Most people aren't," I tell him. "This must be a very hard time for you," I say, rather than the standard *I'm so sorry for your loss.* That feels commonplace, a sentiment that's being echoed over and over again around the room. "Your daughter. She must be devastated," I say, my body language trying its best to be sympathetic. I drop my head, furrow my eyebrows. "I can't imagine what she must be going through."

But Jeffrey's response is unexpected. "I'm afraid she and Morgan were never close" is what he says. "The upshot of divorce, I suppose," he tells me, making light of it, deemphasizing the fact that his daughter and wife didn't get along. "No woman would ever outshine her mother," he says, and I reply, "Oh," because I can think of nothing else to say.

If Will and I were ever to divorce and he

to remarry, I'd hope the boys would love me more than their stepmother. And yet Morgan was murdered. She's dead. The little girl found her. The nonchalance surprises me. "Is she here?" I ask. "Your daughter."

He tells me no. His daughter is in school. It's odd, the fact that she's at school while her stepmother is being mourned.

My surprise is visible.

He explains, "She was sick earlier this year. Pneumonia that landed her in the hospital on IV antibiotics. Her mother and I would hate for her to miss any more school."

I'm not sure his explanation makes it better.

"It's so hard to get caught up" is all I can come up with in a pinch.

Jeffrey thanks me for coming. He says, "Help yourself to cookies," before looking past me to the next in line.

I go to the cookie table. I help myself to one and find a table to sit. It's awkward sitting alone in a room where nearly no one is alone. Everyone has come with someone else. Everyone but me. I wish that Will were here. He should have come. Many of the people in the room cry, quiet, suppressed cries. Only Morgan's mother is unreserved about her grief.

Two women brush up behind me just then. They ask if the vacant seats at the table are being saved. "No," I tell them. "Please, help yourself," and they do.

One of the women asks, "Were you a friend of Morgan?" She has to lean in toward me because it's loud in the room.

A wave of relief washes over me. I'm no longer alone.

I say, "Neighbors. And you?" as I scoot my folding chair closer. They've left empty seats between themselves and me, which is socially appropriate. And yet it makes it hard to hear.

One of the women tells me that they're old friends of Patty's, Morgan's mother. They tell me their names — Karen and Susan — and I tell them mine.

"Poor Patty is just a wreck," Karen says, "as you can imagine."

I tell her how unfathomable this all is. We sigh and discuss how children are supposed to lose their parents first and not the other way around. The way it's happened with Morgan goes against the natural order of things. I think of Otto and Tate, if anything bad were to ever happen to either of them. I can't imagine a world in which Will and I don't die first. I don't want to imagine a world like that, where they're gone and I'm left behind.

"And not just once, but twice," Susan says. The other nods grimly. I bob my head along with them, but I don't know what they mean by this. I'm only half listening. My attention is focused on Jeffrey Baines and the way he greets mourners as they come by. There's a smile on his face as he receives people, reaching that warm hand out to shake theirs. The smile is unbecoming for the occasion. His wife was just murdered. He shouldn't be smiling. If nothing else, he should make an effort to appear sad.

I start to wonder if Jeffrey and Morgan argued, or if it was indifference that did them in. Indifference, a sentiment even worse than hate. I wonder if she did something to upset him, or if he simply wanted her dead, the dissolution of their marriage without a nasty battle. Or maybe it was about money. A life insurance policy to be paid out.

"Patty was never the same after that," Susan is saying.

My eyes go to her as Karen replies, "I don't know what she'll do now, how she'll get through. Losing one child is bad enough, but losing *two*?"

"It's unthinkable," Susan says. She reaches into her handbag for a tissue. She's begun to cry. She reminisces on how distraught Patty was the first time this happened, how weeks went by that she couldn't get out of bed. How she lost weight because of it, far too much for a woman who doesn't have any extra weight to spare. I look at the woman, Patty, standing at the head of the receiving line. She is gaunt.

"This will ruin —" Karen begins, but before she can finish, a woman sweeps in through the door, making her way toward Jeffrey. As she does, the smile disappears from his face.

"Oh," I hear Karen say under her breath. "Oh my. Susan. Look who's here."

We all look. The woman is tall like Jeffrey. She's thin, dressed shamelessly in red while nearly everyone else in the room is in dark or muted tones. Her hair is long and dark. It falls down her back over a red top that's floral and drapey and has a notched neckline that reveals a hint of cleavage. Her pants are tight. Over her arm hangs a winter coat. She stops just short of Jeffrey and says something to him. He attempts to take her by the arm, to lead her from the room, but she'll have no part of that. She pulls sharply back. He leans into her, says something quietly. She puts her hands on her hips, takes on a defensive posture. Pouts.

"Who's that?" I ask, unable to take my eyes off the woman.

They tell me. This is Courtney. Jeffrey's first wife.

"I can't believe that she would show up here, of all places," Susan says.

"Maybe she just wanted to pay her respects," Karen suggests.

Susan harrumphs. "Highly doubtful."

"I take it the marriage didn't end on friendly terms," I say, though it doesn't need to be said. What marriage ends amicably?

The ladies exchange a look before they tell me. "I thought it was common knowledge," Susan says. "I thought everyone knew."

"Knew what?" I ask, and they shift seats, getting rid of the empty one in between, and tell me how Jeffrey was married to Courtney when he and Morgan met. That their marriage started as an affair. Morgan was his mistress, they confess, whispering that word, *mistress,* as if it's dirty. A bad word. Jeffrey and Morgan worked together; she was his administrative assistant. His secretary, as cliché as that sounds. "They met, they fell in love," Susan says.

The way Morgan's mother told it to them,

Jeffrey and his then-wife, Courtney, had been at each other's throats for a long time. Morgan wasn't the one to break up their marriage. It was already broken. Their marriage had always been volatile: two like-minded people who constantly clashed. What Morgan told her in the early days of their affair was that Jeffrey and Courtney could both be stubborn and hotheaded. Overwhelmingly type A. Morgan's demeanor, on the other hand, was the better fit for Jeffrey.

I turn back to Jeffrey and his ex. The exchange is heated and brief. She says something curt, then turns and leaves.

I think that's it then. That's all.

I watch as Jeffrey turns to the next in line. He forces a smile and reaches out his hand.

The ladies beside me go back to their gossip. I listen in, but my eyes stay on Jeffrey. Susan and Karen are talking about Morgan and Jeffrey. About their marriage. True love, I hear, though from the expression on his face — detached, dispassionate — I don't see it. But maybe this is a form of self-preservation. He'll cry later, in private, once the rest of us are gone.

"There's no stopping true love," Karen says.

A thought runs through my mind just

then. There is one way to stop it.

Susan asks if anyone wants more cookies. Karen says yes. Susan leaves and returns with a plate of them for us to share. They return to their conversation about Patty, decide to start up a meal train for her to be sure she eats. If no one is cooking for her, it's liable, in her grief, that Patty won't eat. This worries them. Karen thinks aloud about what she'll make. She has a potpie recipe she's been wanting to try, but she also knows that Patty is quite keen on lasagna.

Only I am still watching as Jeffrey, a minute later, excuses himself and slips from the room.

I push my chair back and stand. The legs of the chair skid across the floor and the ladies look sharply at me, surprised by my sudden movement.

"Any idea where the restroom is?" I ask, incanting, "Nature calls." Karen tells me.

The hallway is relatively quiet. Though not a large building by any means, there are a handful of halls, which lessen in people the farther I go. I turn left and right, the halls becoming vacant before I come to a dead end. I find myself backtracking to where I began.

The lobby, when I reach it, is empty.

Everyone is inside the fellowship hall.

There are two doors before me. One for the sanctuary, and one to go outside.

I draw open the doors to the sanctuary by an inch or two, just enough to see inside. The sanctuary is small, poorly lit, cast in shadows. The only light comes from the four stained glass windows on either side of the room. A cross hangs above the pulpit, looking out at the columns of rigid pews.

I think that the sanctuary is empty. I don't see them at first. I'm about to leave, thinking they're outside, considering the possibility that they're not together at all. That she's left the building and he's in the restroom.

But then it's the movement I see. Her hands rise up sharply as she shoves him.

They're tucked in the far corner of the room. Courtney has Jeffrey backed against a wall. He reaches out to stroke her hair, but she pushes him away again, hard enough that this time, he cradles his hand against himself as if injured.

The ex-wife slaps Jeffrey across the face just then. I flinch, drawing back from the doorway like I'm the one who's been hit. His head turns sharply to the right, then comes back to center. I hold my breath and it's only because she raises her voice then that I hear her, these words louder than all the rest. "I'm not sorry for what I did," she confesses. "She took everything from me, Jeff. Every damn thing, and she left me with nothing. You can't blame me for trying to take back what's mine."

She waits a beat before she adds on, "I'm not sorry she's dead."

Jeffrey grabs ahold of her wrist. Their eyes bore into each other. Their mouths move, but they're quiet now, voices muted. I can't hear what they say. But I can imagine, and what I imagine is hateful and barbed.

I take a careful step into the room. I hold my breath, sharpen my focus, try desperately to home in on what they say. At first, I just barely make out phrases like *won't tell* and *never know.* A fan has kicked on in the room. Their voices are muted by the sound of blowing air. It doesn't go on long, thirty seconds maybe. Thirty seconds of the conversation I miss. But then the fan quiets down, and their voices rise. Their words come back to me.

"What you did," he breathes out, shaking his head.

"I wasn't thinking," she admits. "My temper got the best of me, Jeff. I was angry," she says. "You can't blame me for being angry."

She's crying now, but it's more whimpering than anything, a soft cry that produces no tears. It's manipulative. She's trying to elicit sympathy.

I can't tear my eyes away.

He's quiet for a minute. They're both quiet.

He says to her, voice light as a feather, "I've always hated to see you cry."

He softens. They both do.

He strokes her hair for a second time. This time, she leans into his touch. She doesn't push him away. She steps closer to him. His arms encircle the small of her back. He draws her in to him. She wraps her arms around his neck, her head falling to his shoulder. For an instant, she's demure. They stand at nearly the same height. I can't help but watch as they embrace. Because what was savage and cutthroat only seconds ago is now somehow strangely sweet.

The ping of my phone startles me. I pull sharply back, dropping the door. It clicks loudly shut, and for a split second, my knees lock. A deer in headlights.

I hear movement on the other side of the sanctuary door.

They're coming.

I get ahold of myself.

I walk quickly through the double church doors and outside into the bitter December day. When my feet reach the church steps, I begin to run.

I can't let Jeffrey or his ex-wife know it was me.

I dash for my car parked on the street. I open the door and quickly get in, eyes locked on the church doors to see if anyone has followed me out. I lock the car doors, grateful for the mechanical click that says I'm tucked safely inside.

Only then do I peer down at my phone screen.

It's a text message from Joyce. I check the time on my phone. It's been over an hour since I left. Sixty-four minutes, to be precise. Joyce is counting them all.

You're late, she says. Your patients are waiting for you.

My eyes rise back up to the church doors to see Jeffrey Baines's ex-wife, not twenty seconds later, step circumspectly outside. She looks left and then right before jogging down the church steps, pressing the plackets of a black-and-white houndstooth coat together to stave off the cold.

My eyes follow her to her car, a red Jeep parked just down the street. She tugs open the door and slides inside, slamming the door shut behind herself.

I glance back at the church to see Jeffrey

standing in the open doorway, watching as she leaves.

SADIE

There's a cargo van in the drive when I get home that night. I pull up beside it, park my car behind Will's. I read the lettering on the van, relieved Will is having the furnace replaced.

I go to the front door. The house is at first quiet when I step in. The furnace is kept in the dingy basement. The men are down there.

I see only Tate, at the coffee table with his Legos. He waves at me and I step out of my shoes, leaving them by the door. I go to Tate and give him a kiss on the head.

"How was your —" I begin, but before I get the rest of the words out, the sound of angry voices rises through the floorboards to us, though I can't make out what they say.

Tate and I exchange a look, and I tell him, "I'll be right back." When he makes an effort to follow, I say firmly, "Stay here," not knowing what I'll find in the basement when I go down.

I step carefully down the roughened wooden steps to see what's the matter. I'm nervous as I do, thinking only of some strange man in our home. Some strange man who neither Will nor I know.

My next thought is: How do we know that this furnace man is not a murderer? It doesn't feel far-fetched, considering what's happened to Morgan.

The basement is sparse. The walls and the floor are concrete. It's harshly lit, only a series of bare bulbs.

As I approach the bottom step, I'm afraid of what I'll find. The furnace man hurting Will. My heartbeats pick up speed. I curse myself for not having thought to bring something down to protect myself with. To protect Will. But my purse is still with me, and inside it, my phone. That's something. I could call for help if need be. I reach inside, take ahold of my phone in my hand.

My feet reach the final step. I cautiously turn. It's not as I expect.

Will has the furnace man pressed into the basement wall. He stands inches from him in a way that can only be viewed as threatening. Will doesn't hold him there — it's not physical, not yet — but from his proximity to the man, it's apparent he can't leave. The man, in contrast, stands complaisantly back as Will calls him a parasite, an opportunist. Will is red in the face because of it, the veins of his neck enlarged.

He steps somehow even closer to the man so that the man flinches. Will stabs a finger into his chest. A second later he grabs the man by the shirt collar and chides, "I should call the BBB and report you. Just because you're the only fucking furnace —"

"Will!" I say sternly then. It's so unlike Will to be profane. It's also so unlike Will to be physical. I've never seen this side of Will.

"Stop it, Will," I demand, asking, "What in the world's gotten into you?"

Will stands down, only because I am here. His eyes drop to the ground. He doesn't have to tell me what's happened. I know by context clues. This man is the only furnace man on the island. Because of it, his prices are high. Will doesn't like that. But that's no excuse.

As Will takes a step back, the furnace man quickly gathers up his tools and flees.

We don't speak, we don't mention it again all night.

The next morning, I wrap the towel around myself as I step from the shower. Will stands staring at his reflection in the fogged-up mirror above the sink. The silver along the edge of it is tarnished by time. The bathroom, like everything else in the house, is suffocating and small.

I stare at Will staring at his own reflection in the mirror. He catches me. Our eyes meet. "How long do you think you'll keep ignoring me like this?" he asks, referring to our silence in the aftermath of his blowup with the furnace man. In the end, the man had left without doing a thing and so the house is still uncomfortable. The furnace has begun to rattle, too. Soon it will be dead.

I've been waiting for Will to apologize for his behavior or at least acknowledge that it was wrong. I understand why he'd have been upset. What I don't understand is the overreaction. Will's response was over the top, completely irrational, and so unlike Will.

But what Will is expecting, I think, is that I'll just sweep it under the rug and move on.

Instead I say, "I've never seen you like that, over a silly little thing like the cost of a furnace."

Will is visibly hurt by my words. He draws in a breath, says woundedly, "You know how hard I try to take care of this family, Sadie.

This family means everything to me. I won't let anyone take advantage of us like that."

When he says it like this, I see it differently. And soon I am the one apologizing.

He does so much to care for us. I should only be thankful that Will had done his research, that he wasn't willing to let the furnace man price-gouge us like that. Will was protecting our finances, our family. That's money that could otherwise be spent on groceries, on the kids' college education funds. I'm so grateful he had both the knowledge and the intrepidity to protect it. If it'd been me, I would have unknowingly thrown hundreds of dollars away.

"You're right," I tell him. "You're absolutely right. I'm so sorry," I say.

"It's okay," he says, and I can see in his demeanor that he forgives me. "Let's just forget it happened," and like that, it's forgotten.

Will still doesn't know that I went to the memorial service yesterday. I can't bring myself to tell him because he thought we shouldn't go. I don't want him to be mad that I went.

But I can't stop thinking about the strange exchange I witnessed in the church sanctuary, between Jeffrey and his ex-wife. I wish I could talk to Will about it, tell him what I saw.

After she left the memorial service, I followed the ex-wife in my car. I did a U-turn in the street, tailing the red Jeep by thirty feet as she drove the three blocks to the ferry. If Courtney knew I was there, following her, there was no reaction. I sat, idling in the street for ten minutes or so. She sat in her car, on the phone the whole while.

When the ferry arrived, she pulled her car onto the ship. Moments later, she disappeared out to sea. She was gone. And yet she stayed with me, in my mind. She's with me still. I can't stop thinking about her. About Jeffrey. About their altercation, about their embrace.

I'm also thinking about Imogen. About her silhouette in the corner of my bedroom at night.

Will runs his fingers through his hair, his version of a comb. I hear his voice, talking over the sound of the bathroom fan. He's telling me that this evening he's taking Tate to a Legos event at the public library. They're going with another boy from school, one of Tate's playdate buddies. Him and his mother. Jessica is her name, one Will casually drops in the middle of the conversation, and it's the casualness of it, the familiarity of her name, that rubs me the wrong way, makes me forget for just this moment about Jeffrey and his ex, about Imogen.

For years, Will has been the scheduler of playdates for our boys. Before, it never bothered me. If anything, I felt grateful Will picked up the task in my absence. After school, the boys' classmates and their mothers would come around to the condo when I was at work. What I imagined was the boys disappearing down the hall to play while Will and some woman I didn't know sat around my kitchen table, hobnobbing about the other mothers at the elementary school.

I never saw these women. I never wondered what they looked like. But everything is different since the affair. Now I find myself overthinking these things.

"Just the four of you?" I ask.

He tells me yes, just the four of them. "But there will be other people there, Sadie," he says, trying to be reassuring, and yet it comes off as sarcastic. "It's not like it's a private event, just for us."

"Of course," I say. "What will you be doing there?" I ask, lightening my tone, trying not to sound like a harpy, because I know how much Tate loves Legos.

Will tells me that they'll be building something from those tiny bricks I find scattered all over the house, erecting rides and machines that move. "Tate can't wait. And besides," he says, turning away from the mirror to face me, "it might do Otto, Imogen and you some good, a few hours alone. *Bonding time,*" he calls it, and I harrumph at that, knowing there will be no bonding between Otto, Imogen and me tonight.

I step past him. I move from the bathroom and into the adjoining bedroom. Will follows along. He sits on the edge of the bed, pulling on a pair of socks as I get dressed.

The days are getting colder. The coldness leaks into the clinic through the door and windows. The walls are porous, the doors to the clinic always opening and closing. Every time a patient walks in or out, the cold air comes with them.

I dig into a heaping pile of laundry, searching for a brown cardigan, one of those versatile things that go with nearly everything. The sweater isn't mine. It belonged to Alice. It was in the home when we arrived. The sweater is well loved, worn, which is half the reason I like it. It's slightly misshapen, covered in pills, with a wide, ribbed shawl collar and big apron pockets I can sink my hands into. Four faux shell buttons line the front of it. It's close-fitting because

Alice was smaller than me.

"Have you seen my sweater?" I ask.

"What sweater?" Will asks.

"The brown one," I say. "The cardigan. The one that was Alice's."

Will says he hasn't seen it. He doesn't like the sweater. He always thought it was odd that I laid claim to the sweater in the first place. *Where'd you get that?* he asked the first time I appeared with it on.

The closet. Upstairs, I said. *It must have been your sister's.*

Really? he asked. *You don't think that's kind of — I don't know — morbid? Wearing a dead person's clothes?*

But before I could respond, Tate was asking what *morbid* meant and I left the room to avoid that conversation, leaving it to Will to explain.

Now I find another sweater in the laundry to wear, and slip it over the blouse. Will sits, watching until I'm through getting dressed. Then he rises from the bed and comes to me. He wraps his arms around my waist and tells me not to worry about *Jessica.* He leans in, whispers into my ear, "She doesn't stand a chance next to you," making a poor attempt at humor, telling me that Jessica is a hag, that she bathes infrequently, that half of her teeth are missing, that spit comes flying out of her mouth when she talks.

I force a smile. "She sounds lovely," I say. Though still I wonder why they have to drive together, why they can't just meet at the library.

Will leans farther into me, breathes into my ear, "Maybe after the Legos event, after the kids are in bed, you and I can have some bonding time, too." And then he kisses me.

Will and I haven't been intimate since the affair. Because every time he touches me, all I can think of is *her* and I bristle as a result, nipping any suggestion of intimacy in the bud. I couldn't stake my life on it, but I was sure she was a student, some eighteen- or nineteen-year-old girl. She wore lipstick, that I knew. Hot-pink lipstick and underwear that was flimsy and small, leaving it in my bedroom when she left, which meant that she had the audacity to not only sleep with a married man but to parade around sans underwear. Two things I would never do.

I often wondered if she called him *Professor,* or if to her, he was always *Will.* Or maybe *Professor Foust,* but I doubted that somehow. That seemed far too formal for a man you're sleeping with, even if he is twenty years your senior, a father of two with traces of gray in his hair.

I thought a lot about audacious young women. About what one might look like. Pixie cuts came to mind, as did low-cut blouses, midriff bared; shorts so short the pockets hung out from below. Fishnet stockings, combat boots. Dyed hair.

But maybe I was wrong about that. Maybe she was a self-deprecating young woman, shy, lacking in self-respect. Maybe the marginal attention of a married man was all she had going for her, or maybe she and Will had a connection that went beyond sex and to a like-minded desire to save the world.

In which case, I think she did call him *Professor Foust.*

I never asked Will what she looked like. I did, and at the same time didn't, want to know. In the end, I decided that ignorance is bliss and never asked. He would have just lied anyway and told me there wasn't another woman. That it was only me.

If it wasn't for the boys, our marriage may have ended in divorce after the affair. I'd suggested it once, that maybe Will and I would be better off if we got a divorce, that the boys would be better off.

"God, no," Will told me when I'd suggested it. "No, Sadie, no. You said that would never happen to us. That we'd be together forever, that you would never let me go."

If I said that, I didn't remember. Either way, that's the type of ridiculous nonsense people say when they're falling *in* love; it doesn't pass muster in a marriage.

There's a small part of me that blamed myself for the affair. That believed I'd been the one to push Will into the arms of another woman, because of who I am. I blamed my career, which requires that I be detached. That detachment, the absence of an emotional involvement, works its way into our marriage at times. Intimacy and vulnerability aren't my strong suit, nor have they ever been. Will thought he could change me. Turns out he was wrong.

Sadie

When I pull into the clinic parking lot, I'm grateful to find it empty. Joyce and Emma will be here soon, but for now it's only me. My tires skid on the pavement as I make a sharp left turn into my spot, searching the adjacent street for signs of high beams.

I step from the car and make my way across the parking lot. This early in the day, the world is asphyxiated by fog. The air around me is murky, like soup. I can't see what's five feet in front of me. My lungs are heavy, and suddenly I don't know for certain if I'm alone or if there's someone out there in the fog, watching me. Standing just beyond those five feet where I can't see. A chill creeps up my spine and I shiver.

I find myself jogging to the door, plunging the key into the lock to let myself in. I push the door closed behind me, and turn the dead bolt before making my way inside. I move down the narrow hall and to the reception area, Emma's domain.

Before I arrived, there was another doctor in my place, a long-time resident of the island who went on maternity leave and never came back. Joyce and Emma often stand and pass baby photos around and lament how much they miss having Amanda here. They hold me responsible for her leave, as if it's my fault she had that baby and decided to give motherhood a go.

What I've come to discover is that the island residents don't take well to newcomers. Not unless you're a child like Tate or gregarious like Will. It takes a rare breed to choose to live on an island, isolated from the rest of the world. Many of the residents who aren't retired have simply chosen seclusion as a way of life. They're self-reliant, autonomous, and also insular, moody, obstinate and aloof. Many are artists. The town is littered with pottery shops and galleries because of them, making it cultured but also pretentious.

That said, community is important because of the isolation that comes with island living. The difference between them and me is that they chose to be here.

I run a hand along the wall, feeling for the light switch. The lights above me come to life with a hum. There, on the wall before me, sits a large dry-erase calendar, Dr. Sanders's and my work schedule. Emma's brainchild. The schedule is arbitrary and irregular; Dr. Sanders and I are not slated to work the same days from week to week. If there's any method to the madness, I can't see it.

I go to the calendar. The ink is smudged, but still I see what it is that I'm looking for. My name, *Foust,* written under the date December first. The same day Mr. Nilsson supposedly saw Morgan Baines and me arguing. The same day Mr. Nilsson says I savagely tore a handful of hair from the woman's head.

According to Emma's calendar, on December first I was scheduled to work a shift that spanned nine hours, from eight in the morning to five that night. In which case, I was here at the clinic when Mr. Nilsson swears I was outside the Baineses' home. I find my phone in my bag and snap a photo of it for proof.

I sit down at the L-shaped desk. There are notes stuck to it. A reminder for Emma to order more printer ink. For Dr. Sanders to call a patient back with test results. One of our patients is missing her doll. Her mother's phone number is on the desk, with a request to call if the doll is found. The computer password is there, too.

I revive the computer. Our files are stored on medical software. I don't know for certain that Mr. Nilsson is a patient of the clinic, but nearly everyone on this island is.

There are any number of eye disorders that affect the elderly, from presbyopia to cataracts and glaucoma, all the way to macular degeneration, one of the leading causes of blindness in older adults. It's possible Mr. Nilsson suffers from one of these, and that's the reason he thought he saw me with Mrs. Baines. Because he couldn't see. Or maybe he's begun to exhibit the early signs of Alzheimer's disease and was confused.

I open the computer program. I search for the medical records of George Nilsson, and sure enough, they're there. I'm quite certain this violates HIPAA laws, and yet I do it regardless, even though I'm not Mr. Nilsson's physician.

I scan his medical records. I come to discover that he's diabetic. That he takes insulin. His cholesterol is high; he takes statins to keep it in check. His pulse and blood pressure are fine for a man his age, though he suffers from kyphosis, which I already knew. Mr. Nilsson is a hunchback. It's painful and disfiguring, an offshoot of osteoporosis seen far more often in women than men.

None of this interests me.

What I find surprising is that Mr. Nilsson's vision is fine. Dr. Sanders notes no concerns about Mr. Nilsson's cognitive abilities. As far as I can tell, he's of sound mind. His mental facilities aren't failing him and he's not going blind, which takes me right back to where I began.

Why did Mr. Nilsson lie?

I close the program. I move the mouse to the internet, double clicking. It opens before me. I type in a name, Courtney Baines, and only as I press Enter does it occur to me to wonder if she's still a Baines or if, after the divorce, she reverted to a maiden name. Or maybe she's remarried. But there's no time to find out.

From down the hall, the back door opens. I have just enough time to X out of the internet and step back from the desk before Joyce appears.

"Dr. Foust," she says, far too much animosity in her tone for eight o'clock in the morning. "You're here," she tells me as if this is something I don't already know. "The door was locked. I didn't think anyone was here."

"I'm here," I say, more perky than I mean

to be. "Wanted to get a head start on the day," I explain, realizing she's as easily put off when I'm early as when I'm late. I can do no right in her eyes.

MOUSE

Once upon a time there was a woman. Her name was Fake Mom. That wasn't her real name, of course, but that was what Mouse called her, though only ever behind her back.

Fake Mom was pretty. She had nice skin, long brown hair and a big, easy smile. She wore nice clothes, like collared shirts and sparkly tops, which she'd tuck into the waistband of her jeans so that it didn't look sloppy like when Mouse wore jeans. She always looked put together in a way that Mouse did not. She always looked nice.

Mouse and her father didn't wear nice clothes except for when it was Christmas or when her father was going to work. Mouse didn't think nice clothes were comfortable. They made it hard to move. They made her arms and legs feel stiff.

Mouse didn't know about Fake Mom until the night she arrived. Her father had never mentioned her and so Mouse got to thinking he probably met Fake Mom that very day he brought her home. But Mouse didn't ask and her father didn't say.

The night she arrived, Mouse's father came into the house the same way he always did when he'd been gone. Mouse's father usually worked from their home, in the room they called his *office.* He had another office, in a big building somewhere else that Mouse saw once, but he didn't go there every day like other dads she knew did when they went to work. Instead he stayed home, in the room with the door closed, talking to customers nearly all day on the phone.

But sometimes he had to go to his other office, like he had the day he brought Fake Mom home with him. And sometimes he had to go away. Then he'd be gone for days.

The night that Fake Mom came home, he stepped into the house alone. He set his briefcase beside the door, hung his coat on the hook. He thanked the older couple across the street for keeping an eye on her. He walked them to the door with Mouse trailing behind.

Mouse and her father watched them make their way slowly across the street and back home. It looked like it was hard. It looked like it hurt. Mouse didn't think that she ever wanted to get old.

When they were gone, her father shut the door. He turned to Mouse. He told her he had a surprise for her, that she should close her eyes.

Mouse was sure her surprise was a puppy, the one she had been begging for since the day they walked past it in the pet shop window, big and fluffy and white. Her father had said no at the time, that a puppy was *too much work,* but maybe he had changed his mind. He did that sometimes when she really wanted something. Because Mouse was a good girl. He didn't spoil her, but he did like knowing she was happy. And a puppy would make her very, very happy.

Mouse pressed her hands to her eyes. For whatever reason, she held her breath. She listened intently for the sound of yaps and whimpers coming from the other end of the room where her father was standing. But there were no yaps or whimpers.

What she heard instead was the sound of the front door opening and then closing again. Mouse knew why. Her father had gone outside, back to his car to collect the puppy. Because it wasn't like the puppy was hiding in his briefcase. It was still in the car, where he had left it so he could surprise her with it.

As she waited, a grin spread across Mouse's face. Her knees shook in excitement. She could hardly contain herself.

Mouse heard the door close, her father clear his voice.

He was eager when he spoke. He said to Mouse, *Open your eyes,* and before she ever laid eyes on him, she knew that he was smiling, too.

Mouse's eyes flung open, and without meaning to, her hand shot to her mouth. She gasped, because it wasn't a puppy she saw standing before her in her own living room.

It was a woman.

The woman's thin hand was holding Mouse's father's hand, fingers spliced together in that same way Mouse had seen men and women do it on TV. The woman was smiling widely at Mouse, her mouth big and beautiful. She said hello to the girl, her voice somehow as pretty as her face was. Mouse said nothing back.

The woman let go of Mouse's father's hand. She came forward, bent down to the girl's height. The woman extended that same thin hand to Mouse, but Mouse didn't know what to do with it, so she just stared down at the bony hand, doing nothing.

Mouse noticed then how the air was different that night, more dense, harder to breathe.

Her father told her, *Now go on. Don't be rude. Say hello. Shake her hand,* and Mouse did, mumbling a feeble hello and slipping her tiny hand inside the woman's hand.

Mouse's father turned and hurried back outside. The woman followed behind.

Mouse watched on silently, staring through the window as her father unloaded bags of the woman's things from his trunk. So many things, Mouse didn't know what to make of it all.

When they came back inside, the woman slipped a candy bar out from the inside of her purse and handed it to the girl. *Your father says chocolate is your favorite,* she said, and it was, second only to Salerno Butter Cookies. But chocolate was a sorry consolation prize for a puppy. She would have rather had a puppy. But she knew better than to say that.

Mouse thought about asking the woman when she was going to leave. But she knew better than to ask that, too, and so she took the candy bar from the woman's hand. She held it in her sweaty hands, feeling it go limp in her grip as the chocolate started to melt. She didn't eat it. She wasn't hungry, though she hadn't had dinner yet. She had no appetite.

Among the woman's many belongings was a dog crate. That got the girl's attention. It was a good-size cage. Right away, Mouse tried to imagine what kind of dog it might hold: a collie or a basset hound or a beagle. She stared out the window as her father continued to bring things in, wondering when the dog would come.

Where's your dog? the girl asked after her father had finished unloading the car and come back inside, locking up behind himself.

But the woman shook her head and told the girl sadly that she didn't have a dog anymore, that her dog had just very recently died.

Then why do you have a dog crate? she asked, but her father said, *That's enough, Mouse. Don't be rude,* because they could both see that talking about the dead dog made the woman sad.

Mouse? the woman asked, and if Mouse didn't know any better, she'd have thought the woman laughed. *That's some nickname for a little girl.* But that was all she said. *Some nickname.* She didn't say if she liked it or not.

They ate dinner and watched TV from the sofa, but instead of sharing the sofa with her father, as she always did, Mouse sat in a chair on the other side of the room, from which she could hardly see the TV. It didn't matter anyway; she didn't like what they were watching. Mouse and her father always watched sports, but instead they had on some show where grown-ups talked too much and said stuff that made the woman and her father laugh, but not Mouse. Mouse didn't laugh. Because it wasn't funny.

All the while, the woman sat on the sofa by Mouse's father instead. When Mouse dared to look over, they were sitting close, holding hands like they had when she first arrived. It made Mouse feel strange inside. She tried not to look, but her eyes kept going back there, to their hands.

When the woman excused herself to go clean up for bed, her father leaned in close and told the girl that it would be nice for her to call this woman *Mom.* He said he knew it might be strange for a while. That if she didn't want to, it was okay. But maybe she could work her way up to it in time, her father suggested.

The girl always tried to do everything she could to please her father because she loved him very much. She didn't want to call this strange woman *Mom* — not now, not ever — but she knew better than to argue with her father. It would hurt his feelings if she did, and she didn't ever want to hurt his feelings.

The girl already had a mother, and this was not her.

But if her father wanted her to, she would call his woman *Mom.* To her face anyway and to her father's face. But in her own head, she would call this woman *Fake Mom.* That was what the girl decided.

Mouse was a smart girl. She liked to read. She knew things that other girls her age didn't know, like why bananas are curved, and that slugs have four noses, and that the ostrich is the world's biggest bird.

Mouse loved animals. She always wanted a puppy, but she never got a puppy. Instead she got something else. Because after Fake Mom arrived, her father let her pick out a guinea pig. He did it because he thought it would make her happy.

They went to the pet store together. The minute she laid eyes on her guinea pig, Mouse was in love. It wasn't the same as a puppy, but it was something special still. Mouse's father thought that they should name him Bert after his favorite baseball player, Bert Campaneris, and Mouse said yes to that because she didn't have another name in mind. And because she wanted to make her father happy.

Mouse's father bought her a book about guinea pigs, too. The night she brought Bert home, Mouse climbed into bed, under the covers, and read the book from end to end. She wanted to be *informed.* Mouse learned things about guinea pigs that she never knew, like what they eat and what every single squeak and squeal means.

She learned that guinea pigs aren't related to pigs at all, and they don't come from the country of Guinea, but from somewhere high in the Andes Mountains, which are in South America. She asked her father for a map, to see where South America was. He dug one out of an old *National Geographic* magazine in the basement, one that had been Mouse's grandfather's magazine. Her father had tried to throw the magazines away when her grandfather died, but Mouse wouldn't let him. She thought they were fascinating.

Mouse put the map on her bedroom wall with Scotch tape. She stood on her bed and found the Andes Mountains on that map, drew a big circle around them with a purple pen. She pointed at the circle on her map, and told her guinea pig — in his cage on the floor beside her bed — that was where he came from, though she knew her guinea pig hadn't come from the Andes Mountains at all. He had come from a pet store.

Fake Mom was always calling Bert a *pig.* Unlike Mouse, she didn't read the book on guinea pigs. She didn't understand that Bert was a rodent, not a pig, that he wasn't even related to pigs. She didn't know that he only got that name because he squeaked like a pig, and because once upon a time someone thought that he looked like a pig — though he didn't. Not at all. That someone, in Mouse's opinion, was wrong.

Mouse stood in the living room and told Fake Mom all that. She didn't mean to sound like a know-it-all. But Mouse knew a lot of things. She knew big words, and could find faraway places on a map, and could say a few words in French and Chinese. Sometimes she got so excited she couldn't help sharing it all. Because she didn't know what a girl her age was supposed to know and not know, and so she just said what she knew.

This was one of those times.

But this time when she did, Fake Mom blinked hard. She stared at Mouse, saying nothing, with a frown on her face and a deep wrinkle forming between her eyes as wide as a river.

But Mouse's father said something.

He ruffled Mouse's hair, beamed proudly at her and asked if there was anything in the whole wide world that she didn't know. Mouse smiled back and she shrugged. There were things she didn't know, of course. She didn't know where babies came from, and why there were bullies at school, and why people died. But she didn't say that because she knew her father didn't really want to know. He was being *rhetorical,* which was another one of those big words she knew.

Mouse's father looked at Fake Mom and asked, *She's really something, isn't she?*

Fake Mom said, *She sure is. She's unbelievable.* But Fake Mom didn't smile the same way her father had. Not a fake smile, not any kind of smile. Mouse wasn't sure what to make of that word *unbelievable,* because *unbelievable* could mean different things.

The moment passed. Mouse thought the whole conversation about rodents and pigs was through.

But later that night, when her father wasn't looking, Fake Mom got down into Mouse's face and told her if she ever made her look stupid again in front of her father, there would be *hell to pay.* Fake Mom's face got all red. She bared her teeth like a dog does when it's mad. A vein stuck out of her forehead. It throbbed. Fake Mom spit when she spoke, like she was so mad she couldn't stop herself from spitting. Like she was spitting mad. She spit on Mouse's face but Mouse didn't dare raise a hand to wipe it away.

Mouse tried to take a step back, away from Fake Mom. But Fake Mom was holding on too tightly to Mouse's wrist. Mouse couldn't get away because Fake Mom wouldn't let go.

They heard Mouse's father coming down the hallway. Fake Mom let go of Mouse's wrist quickly. She stood straight up, fluffed her hair, ran her hands over her shirt to smooth it down. Her face went back to its normal shade, and on her lips came a smile. And not just any smile, but one that was radiant. She went to Mouse's father, leaned in close and kissed him.

How are my favorite ladies doing? he asked, as he kissed her back. Fake Mom said they were fine. Mouse mumbled something along the same lines, though no one heard because they were too busy kissing.

Mouse told her real mom about Fake Mom. She sat down across from her on the edge of the red rag rug and poured them both cups of pretend tea. There, as they drank their tea and nibbled cookies, she told her how she didn't like Fake Mom much. How sometimes Fake Mom made Mouse feel like a stranger in her own home. How being in the same room with Fake Mom gave Mouse a tummy ache. Mouse's real mom told her not to worry. She told her that Mouse was a good girl and that only good things happened to good girls. *I'll never let anything bad happen to you,* her real mom said.

Mouse knew how much her father liked Fake Mom. She could see it in the way he looked at her how happy she made him. It made Mouse feel sick to her stomach because Fake Mom brought out a kind of happy that Mouse never could, even though they were happy before Fake Mom came.

If her father liked having Fake Mom around, she might stay forever. Mouse didn't want that to happen. Because Fake Mom made her uncomfortable sometimes, and other times scared.

Now when Mouse wrote stories in her head, she started making up stories about bad things happening to an imaginary woman named Fake Mom. Sometimes she fell down those squeaky steps and hit her head. Sometimes she got buried in one of the rabbit holes beneath the clumps of fur and hair and couldn't get out.

And sometimes she was just gone, and Mouse didn't care how or why.

SADIE

That evening, there's a bite to the air. The temperatures are plunging quickly. I pull my car from the parking lot and head home, remembering that Will and Tate are off playing with Legos tonight. The idea of it concerns me, of Will not being around to act as a buffer between Imogen and me.

I try not to let it get the best of me as I drive home. I am a big girl; I can take care of this myself. And besides, Will and I are Imogen's guardians. It's our legal obligation to take care of her until she turns eighteen. If I want to search through her things, it's very much in my right to do so. That said, there are questions I have that I'd like answers to. Namely, who is the man in the photograph that had his face scratched off at Imogen's hand? Is he the same man who wrote the note to Imogen, the one I found in the pocket of her sweatshirt? A Dear John note, I took it to be. His reference to a *double life* leads me to believe that Imogen was the other woman. That he was married, maybe, and broke her heart. But who is he?

I pull into the drive and put the car in Park. I look around before I step from the safety of the locked car, to be sure that I'm alone. But it's dark out, nearly black. Can I really be sure?

I move quickly from the car. I scurry into the safety of my home, where I close and lock the door behind myself. I tug on it twice, to be sure it's closed tight.

I move into the kitchen. A casserole awaits me on the stovetop when I step inside, a piece of foil folded over the top of it to keep it warm. A Post-it note on top. *XO,* it reads. Signed, *Will.*

The dogs are the only ones waiting in the kitchen for me, staring at me with their matching snaggleteeth, begging to be let outside. I open the back door for them. They make a beeline to the corner of the yard to dig.

I climb the creaky steps to find Imogen's bedroom door closed, the lock on it undoubtedly turned so that I couldn't get in if I wanted to. Except that when I look, there's a new lock on the door, a whole system — complete with padlock — that slips over the door handle. The door now locks from the outside in. Imogen must have installed this herself, to keep me out.

Rock bands the likes of Korn and Drowning Pool lash out over the Bluetooth speaker, volume turned all the way up so that there's no misinterpreting the songs' lyrics, dead bodies a recurring theme. The profanity is atrocious, hate spewing through the speakers and into our home. But Tate isn't around to hear it, and so this time, I let it be.

I go to Otto's door, rap lightly and call out, over the sound of Imogen's noise, "I'm home."

He opens the door for me. I look at Otto, seeing the way that he looks more and more like Will each day. Now that he's older, the angles of his face are sharp. There is no more baby fat to soften the edges. He's getting taller all the time, finally enjoying that growth spurt that has for so long bypassed him, keeping him small while the other boys in school grew tall. If not now, then soon he'll rival their height. Otto is handsome like Will. In no time at all, he'll be making girls swoon. He just doesn't know it yet.

"How was your day?" I ask him, and he shrugs and says, "Fine. I guess."

It's an indecisive reply. I take it as an opportunity. "You guess?" I ask, wanting more:

to know how his day really went, if he's getting along with the other kids at school, if he likes his teachers, if he's making friends. When he says nothing, I prod. "On a scale of one to ten, how would you rate it?" It's silly, one of those things doctors say when they're trying to gauge a patient's pain. Otto shrugs again and tells me his day was a six, which ranks as moderate, decent, an okay day.

"Homework?" I ask.

"Some."

"Need any help?"

He shakes his head. He can do it himself.

As I make my way to Will's and my bedroom to change, I catch sight of a light drifting from beneath the doorway that leads to the third-floor attic. The light in the attic is on, which it never is, because it's where Alice killed herself. I asked the boys never to go up there. I didn't think it was a place any of us needed to be.

The boys know that Alice gave us the house. They don't know how she died. They don't know that one day, Alice slipped a noose around her neck, securing the other end of it to the ceiling's support beam, stepping from the stool. What I know as a physician is that, after the noose tightened around her neck and she was suspended, supported only by her jaw and her neck, she would have struggled for air against the weight of her own body. It would have taken minutes for her to lose consciousness. It would have been extremely painful. And even when she finally did lose consciousness, her body would have continued to thrash about, taking much longer for her to die, up to twenty minutes, if not more. Not a pleasant way to go.

It's hard for Will to talk about Alice. This I can understand. After my father passed, it was hard for me to talk about him. My memory isn't the best. But what sticks with me most is when I was around eleven years old, when my father and I lived just outside of Chicago and he worked for a department store in the city. Dad rode the train downtown every day back then. I was old enough to keep watch over myself by then, a latchkey kid. I went to school and I came home. No one had to tell me to do my homework. I was responsible enough for that. I made and ate my own dinner. I did my dishes. I went to bed at a reasonable time. Most nights, Dad would have a beer or two on the train ride home, stopping at the bar after he'd departed the train, not getting home until after I was asleep. I'd hear him, stumbling around the house, knocking things over, and the next morning there'd be a mess for me to clean.

I put myself through college. I lived alone, in a single dorm followed by a small apartment. I tried living with a roommate once. It didn't work for me. The roommate I had was careless and irresponsible, among other things. She was also manipulative, a complete kleptomaniac.

She took phone messages for me that I never received. She made a mess of our apartment. She ate my food. She stole money from my wallet, checks from my checkbook. She used my credit card to buy herself things. She denied doing it, of course, but I'd look at my bank statements later and find checks made out to places like hair salons, department stores, *cash.* When I asked the bank to produce the processed checks for me, I could clearly see that the handwriting on them was not mine.

I could have pressed charges. For whatever reason, I chose not to.

She wore my clothes without asking. She brought them back wrinkled and dirty, sometimes stained, reeking of cigarette smoke. I'd find them hanging in my closet like that. When I asked her about it, she'd gaze at my filthy clothing and say, *You think I actually wore that ugly shirt of yours?*

Because on top of everything else, she was mean.

I put a lock on my bedroom door. That didn't stop her.

Somehow, she still found a way in. I'd come home from a night out to find my door open, my things rifled through.

I didn't want to live like that.

I offered to move out, to let her keep our place. She was angry to the point of being combative. Something about her scared me. She couldn't afford the unit all on her own, she told me, seething. She got in my face, told me I was crazy, that I was a psychopath.

I held my ground. I didn't flinch.

I said calmly, *I could say the same about you.*

In the end, she was the one to leave. That was best, seeing as I'd recently met Will, and needed a place where we could hang out. Even after, I had my suspicions that she was still letting herself in, going through my things. She'd given me her key back, but that didn't mean she hadn't taken it to the hardware store first and made a copy of it to keep. In time I had the locks changed. That, I told myself, would have to stop her. If I thought she was still coming in, it was only my paranoia speaking.

Still, that wasn't the end of her. Because I

saw her some six months ago or so, when I passed her on the street, not far from Will's and my home. She looked the same to me, strutting her stuff down Harrison, just as arrogant as she'd always been. I ducked away when I saw her, slipped down another street.

It was just after graduation when Will and I met, at the engagement party of a friend. Will and I have different versions of the time we met. What I know is that he came up to me at the party, handsome and gregarious as ever, thrust out a hand and said, *Hey there. I think I've seen you before.*

What I remember is feeling awkward and insecure that night, the awkwardness abating ever so slightly with the cheesy pickup line. He hadn't, of course, seen me before. It was a come-on, and it worked. We spent the rest of the night intertwined on the dance floor, my insecurities lessening the more I had to drink.

We'd been dating only a couple of months when Will suggested he move into my apartment with me. Why he was single, I didn't know. Why he chose me over all the other beautiful women in the city of Chicago, I also didn't know. But for whatever reason, he insisted he couldn't stand to be away from me. He wanted to be with me all the time. It was a romantic notion — no one had ever made me feel as desired as Will did back then — but it made sense financially, too. I was finishing up my residency and Will his PhD. Only one of us was earning an income, albeit a small one, most of which went to repay med school debt. But still, I didn't mind covering the rent. I liked having Will with me all the time. I could do that for him.

Not long after, Will and I got married. Shortly after that, Dad died, taken from this world of his own volition. Cirrhosis of the liver.

We had Otto. And then, years later, Tate. And now I find myself living in Maine.

To say I wasn't completely bowled over when word arrived that Will's sister had left us a home and child would be a lie. Will always knew about the fibromyalgia, but we learned about the suicide from the executor of the estate. I didn't think any good could come from our moving to Maine, but Will disagreed.

The months before had been merciless and unsparing. First, Otto's expulsion, followed immediately by the discovery of Will's affair. It wasn't days after that that a patient of mine died on the table. I'd had patients die before, but this one nearly wrecked me.

He'd had a pericardiocentesis done, a relatively safe and routine procedure where fluid is aspirated from the sac that surrounds a person's heart. When I looked back at my medical notes, the procedure was well warranted. The patient was suffering from a condition known as cardiac tamponade, where the accumulation of fluid puts excessive pressure on the heart, stopping it from functioning properly. Cardiac tamponade can be lethal unless some of the fluid is drained. I'd done the procedure before, many times. There'd never been a problem.

But this time, I didn't do the procedure. Because, according to my colleagues, I walked out of the room just as the patient went into cardiac arrest, forcing a resident to perform the pericardiocentesis without me. The patient on the table was dying, and without the procedure he would have died.

But the procedure was done incorrectly. The needle punctured the patient's heart so that he died anyhow.

They found me later, upstairs on the hospital's rooftop, perched on the edge of the fourteen-story building, legs dangling over the edge, where some claimed I was about to jump.

But I wasn't suicidal. Things were bad,

but they weren't that bad. I blamed Otto's expulsion and the affair for it, for wreaking havoc on my emotions and mind. *A nervous breakdown,* claimed the rumors circulating throughout the hospital. The buzz was that I had had a nervous breakdown in the ER, marched myself up to the fourteenth floor, prepared to jump. I'd blacked out is what happened. When all was said and done, I didn't remember any of it. It's a period of my life that's gone. What I remember is examining my patient, and then coming to in a different room — except by then I was the one spread out on a table, hidden beneath a sheet. When I later heard that my patient died at the hands of a less experienced doctor, I cried. I'm not one to cry. But that time, I couldn't keep it inside.

The triggers of a nervous breakdown were there: a period of stress that hadn't been dealt with, feeling disoriented, worthless, unable to sleep.

The next day, the head of the department put me on forced medical leave. He subtly suggested a psych eval. I said thanks, but no thanks. Instead, I chose to resign. I couldn't go back there ever again.

When we arrived in Maine, Will and I found the foursquare farmhouse in quite a state. The step stool was still in the attic along with three feet of rope, snipped at the end while the rest remained bound to some sort of exposed support beam that cut across the ceiling. Anything within reach of Alice's thrashing body had been knocked over, implying death hadn't been a breeze.

I make my way to the attic door and pull it open. From up above, a light glows. I climb the steps two at a time as, beneath my feet, they creak. The attic is an unfinished space, complete with wooden beams, a plank cork flooring, wads of fluffy pink insulation scattered here and there like clouds. The light comes from a single exposed bulb on the ceiling, which someone, whoever was here, has forgotten to turn off. A string dangles beneath. A chimney, wrapped in exposed brick, runs through the center of the room, venting outside. There's a window that faces onto the street. It's so dark outside tonight, there's nothing to see.

Sheets of paper catch my eye. They're on the floor with a pencil, one I recognize right away as one of Otto's graphite drawing pencils. The ones Will and I got for him, the ones he never lets Tate use. They're expensive and also Otto's prized possession, though I haven't seen him use them in months. Since all that happened in Chicago with him, he hasn't been drawing.

I'm stricken with two things: disappointment, for one, that Otto would disobey me and come into the attic when I said not to. But also relief that Otto is drawing again, the first step, perhaps, in a return to normalcy.

Maybe Will is right. Maybe if we give it time, we can find happiness here.

I make my way to the sheets of paper. They're on the floor. The window is open an inch, crisp December air coming in, making the paper move. I bend at the knees to retrieve it, expecting to see the big anime eyes of Asa and Ken staring back at me. The characters from Otto's graphic novel, his work-in-progress. The barbed lines of hair, the sad, disproportionate eyes.

The pencil, sitting inches from the paper, is cracked in half. The end of it is worn down and blunt, which isn't like Otto. He's always taken such great care of these pencils. I reach for that, too, and stand upright, before looking at the image before me. When I do, I gasp, a hand going involuntarily to my mouth.

It's not Asa and Ken I see.

Instead angry, incomplete lines that stop and go. Something dismembered on the page, a body, I assume. A round object at the end of the sheet that I take for a head;

the long, limb-like shapes for arms and legs. At the top of the drawing are stars, a crescent-shaped moon. Night. There's another figure on the page, a woman, by the looks of it, from the long scraggly hair, the lines that jut out of her circular head. In her hand, she holds something with a keen edge that drips with something else, blood, I can only assume, though the drawing is in black and white. No telling red. The eyes of this figure are mad, while the decapitated head nearby cries, big shaded blobs of tears that tear a hole in the page.

I suck in my breath and hold it there. A pain settles in my chest. My arms and legs go momentarily numb.

The same image is replicated on all three sheets of paper. There's nothing different about them, nothing that I can see.

The drawings are Otto's, I tell myself at first because Otto is the artist in the family. The only one of us who draws.

But this is far too primitive, far too rudimentary to be Otto's. Otto can draw much better than this.

But Tate is a happy boy. An obedient boy. He wouldn't have come into the attic if I told him not to. And besides, Tate doesn't draw such violent, murderous images. He could never visualize such things, much less depict them on paper. Tate doesn't know what murder is. He doesn't know that people die.

I go back to Otto.

These drawings belong to Otto.

Unless, I think, drawing in a deep breath and holding it there, they belong to Imogen? Because Imogen is an angry girl. Imogen knows what murder is; she knows that people die. She's seen it with her own eyes. But what would she be doing with Otto's pencils and paper?

I close the window and turn my back to it. There's a vintage dollhouse on the opposite wall. It catches my eye. I first found it the same day we arrived, thinking it might have belonged to Imogen when she was a child. It's a charming green cottage with four rooms, an expansive attic, a slender staircase running up the center of it. The details of it are impeccable. Miniature window boxes and curtains, tiny lamps and chandeliers, bedding, a parlor table, even a green doghouse to match the home, complete with a miniature dog. That first day, I dusted the house out of respect for Alice, laid the family in their beds to sleep until there might be grandchildren to play with it. It wasn't the type of thing Tate would use.

I go to it now, certain I'll find the family fast asleep where I left them. Except that I don't. Because someone has been up here in the attic, coloring pictures, opening windows, meddling with things. Because things in the dollhouse are not how I put them.

Inside the dollhouse, I see that the little girl has risen from bed. She no longer lies in the second-floor bedroom's canopy bed but is on the floor of the room. The father is no longer in his bed either; he's disappeared. I glance around, finding him nowhere. Only the mother is there, sleeping soundly in the sleigh bed on the first floor.

At the foot of the bed lies a miniature knife, no bigger than the pad of a thumb.

There's a box beside the dollhouse, chock-full of accessories. The lid of it is closed, but the latch is unfastened. I open it up and have a look, searching inside the box for the father, but finding him nowhere. I give up my search.

I pull the string and the attic goes black.

As I travel down the steps with a bad feeling in the pit of my stomach, it dawns on me: the house is quiet. Imogen has turned her offensive music off. When I reach the second-story landing, I see her standing in her doorway, backlit by the bedroom light.

Her eyes are accusatory. She doesn't ask, and yet I read it in her expression. She wants to know what I was doing in the attic. "There was a light on," I explain, waiting a beat before I ask, "Was it you? Were you up there, Imogen?"

She snorts. "You're an idiot if you think I'd ever go back up there," she says.

I mull that over. She could be lying. Imogen strikes me as a masterful liar.

She leans against the door frame, crosses her arms.

"Do you know, Sadie," she says, looking pleased with herself, and I realize that she's never called me by name before, "what a person looks like when they die?"

Suffice to say, I do. I've seen plenty of fatalities in my life.

But the question, on Imogen's tongue, leaves me at a loss for words.

Imogen doesn't want an answer. It's for shock value; she's trying to intimidate me. She goes on to describe in disturbing detail the way Alice looked the day she found her, hanging in the attic from a rope. Imogen had been at school that day. She took the ferry home as usual, came into a quiet house to discover what Alice had done.

"There were claw marks on her neck," she says, raking her own violet fingernails down her pale neckline. "Her fucking tongue was purple. It got stuck, hanging out of her mouth, clamped between her teeth like this," she says as she sticks her own tongue out at me and bites down. Hard.

I've seen victims of strangulation before. I know how the capillaries on the face break, how the eyes become bloodshot from the accumulation of blood behind them. As an emergency medicine physician, I've been trained to look for this in victims of domestic violence, for signs of strangulation. But I imagine that, for a sixteen-year-old girl, seeing your mother in this state would be traumatizing.

"She nearly bit the fucking thing off," Imogen says about Alice's tongue. She begins to laugh then, this ill-timed, uncontrollable laugh that gets to me. Imogen stands three feet away, devoid of emotion other than this unseemly gleeful display. "Want to see?" she asks, though I don't know what she means by this.

"See what?" I ask carefully, and she says, "What she did with her tongue."

I don't want to see. But she shows me anyway, a photograph of her dead mother. It's there on her cell phone. She forces the phone into my hands. The color drains from my face.

Before the police arrived that dreadful day, Imogen had the audacity to take a picture on her phone.

Alice, dressed in a pale pink tunic sweater and leggings, hangs from a noose. Her head is tilted, the rope boring into her neck. Her body is limp, arms at her sides, legs unbending. Storage boxes surround her, ones that were once piled two or three high but now lie on their sides, contents falling out. A lamp is on the ground, colored glass scattered at random. A telescope — once used to stare at the sky out through the attic window, perhaps — is also on its side, everything, presumably, knocked violently over as Alice died. The step stool she used to climb up into the gallows stands four feet away, upright.

I think of what Alice must have gone through as she climbed the three steps to her death, as she slipped her head into the knot. The ceilings of the attic are not high. Alice would have had to measure the rope in advance, to be certain that when she stepped off the stool, her feet would not touch the ground. She dropped by only a couple of inches at best. The fall was small; her neck wouldn't have broken from the height, which means that death was painful and slow. The evidence of that is there, in the picture. The broken lamp, the claw marks, the nearly severed tongue.

"Why'd you take this?" I ask, trying to remain calm. I don't want to give her what she wants.

She shrugs her shoulders, asks, with a blatant disregard for her mother's life, "Why the hell not?"

I hide my shock as Imogen takes the phone and turns slowly from me. She goes back into her room, leaving me shaken. I pray that Otto, in his own room just next door, has his earbuds in. I pray that he didn't hear that awful exchange.

I retreat to the bedroom where I change into my pajamas and stand at the window, waiting for Will to come home. I stare into the home next door. There's a light on inside, the very same light that goes on at seven and off near midnight each night. No one lives in that home this time of year and I think of it, empty on the inside, for months on end. What's to keep a person from letting themselves inside?

When a car pulls into the drive, I can't help but watch. The inside of the car becomes flooded with light as the door opens. Tate and his friend are buckled in the back seat, Will in the front beside a woman who is most definitely not a toothless hag but rather a shadowy brunette whom I can't fully see.

Tate is bubbly, bouncy, when they step inside the house. He runs up the stairs to greet me. He proudly announces, "You came to see me at school today!" as he bursts through the bedroom door in his *Star Wars* hoodie and a pair of knit pants. These pants, like all the others, are too short for him, exposing ankles. Will and I can't keep up. There's a hole in the toe of his sock.

Will, half a step behind him, turns to me and asks, "You did?"

But I shake my head at Will. "I didn't," I say, not knowing what Tate means by this. My eyes go to Tate's, and I say, "I was at work today, Tate. I wasn't at your school."

"Yes, you were," he says, on the verge of getting upset. I play along, only to appease him.

"Well, what was I doing?" I ask him. "What did I say?"

"You didn't say anything," he says, and I ask, "Don't you think if I was at your school today, I would have said something to you?"

Tate explains that I stood on the other side of the playground fence, watching the kids at recess. I asked what I had on, and he tells me my black coat and my black hat, which is exactly what I would be wearing. It's what he's used to seeing me in, but there's hardly a woman in town who doesn't wear a black coat and hat.

"I think maybe that was someone else's mommy, Tate," I say, but he just stares, saying nothing.

I find the idea of any woman standing on the periphery of the playground watching kids play a bit unnerving. I wonder how secure the school is, especially when the kids are at recess. How many teachers are on recess duty? Is the fence locked, or can anyone open the gate and step right in? The school seems easy enough to contain when the kids are indoors, but outdoors is a different matter.

Will ruffles his hair, says to him, "I think it's about time we get that vision of yours checked."

I reroute the conversation. "What's this you've got?" I ask. In his hands Tate proudly totes a mini figure he assembled himself at the library event. He shows it to me, before climbing onto the bed to kiss me good-night at Will's request. Will ushers him to his own bedroom, where he reads Tate a story and tucks him into bed snug as a bug in a rug. On the way back to our bedroom, Will stops by Otto's and Imogen's bedrooms to say good-night.

"You didn't eat the casserole," Will says seconds later after he returns to our bedroom. He's concerned, and I tell him I wasn't hungry. "You feeling okay?" he asks, running a warm hand the length of my hair, and I shake my head and tell him no. I think what it would feel like to lean into him. To let his strong arms envelop me. To be vulnerable for once, to fall to pieces before him and let him pick them up.

"How safe is Tate's elementary school?" I ask instead.

He assures me it's safe. "It was probably just some mother dropping off a forgotten lunch," he says. "It's not like Tate is the most observant kid, Sadie. I'm the only dad at school pickup, and still, every day he has trouble finding me in the crowd."

"You're sure?" I ask, trying not to let my imagination get the best of me. Besides, there's something less disconcerting about it because she was a woman. If she had been a man, watching kids play on a playground, I would already be perusing the internet by now, trying to determine how many registered sex offenders live on the island with us.

He tells me, "I'm sure."

I slide the drawings I found in the attic to him. He takes a look at them and believes right away that they're Otto's. Unlike me, Will seems sure. "Why not Imogen?" I ask, wishing they could belong to Imogen.

"Because Otto," he tells me unquestioningly, "is our artist. Remember Occam's razor," he says, reminding me of the belief that states the easiest explanation is most often right.

"But why?" I ask, meaning why would Otto draw like this.

At first he denies the gravity of the situation, saying, "It's a form of self-expression, Sadie. This is natural for a child in pain."

But that alone is disconcerting. Because it's not natural for a child to be in pain.

"You think he's being bullied?" I ask, but Will only shrugs his shoulders and says he doesn't know. But he'll call the school in the morning. He'll find out.

"We need to talk to Otto about this," I tell him, but Will says, "Let me do some investigating first. The more we know, the better prepared we'll be."

I say okay. I trust his instinct.

I tell him, "I think it would be good for Imogen to speak with someone."

"What do you mean?" he asks, taken aback, though I'm not sure why. Will isn't averse to therapy, though she's his niece by blood, not mine. This is for him to decide.

"Like a psychiatrist?" he asks.

I tell him yes. "She's getting worse. She must be harboring so much inside of her. Anger. Grief. I think it would be good for her to speak with someone," I say, telling him about our conversation this evening, though I don't tell him what I saw on Imogen's phone. He doesn't need to know I saw a picture of his dead sister. I say only that Imogen described for me in detail what Alice looked like when she found her.

"Sounds to me like she's opening up to you, Sadie," he says. But I have a hard time believing it. I tell him therapy would be better, with someone trained to deal with suicide survivors. Not me.

"Will?" I ask, my mind going elsewhere, to a thought I had earlier tonight as I stared out the window toward the home next door.

"What?" he asks.

"The vacant house next door. Do you think the police searched it when they were canvassing the neighborhood?"

The look he gives me is confused. "I don't know," he says. "Why do you ask?"

"Just seems an empty home would be an easy place for a killer to hide."

"Sadie," he says in a way that's both patronizing and reassuring at the same time.

"I'm sure there isn't a killer living next door to us."

"How can you be so sure?" I ask.

"We'd know, wouldn't we? Something would look off. Lights on, windows broken. We'd hear something. But that house hasn't changed in all the time we've been here."

I let myself believe him because it's the only way I'll ever be able to sleep tonight.

CAMILLE

There were nights I went to Will's condo that I stood alone in the street, watching from outside. But Will and Sadie lived up too high. It was hard to see inside from the street.

And so one night I helped myself to the fire escape.

I dressed in all black, scrambled up six flights like a cat burglar in the night.

On the sixth floor, I sat on the steel platform, just outside his kitchen window. I looked in, but it was dark inside their home, the dead of night, hard to see much of anything. And so I sat awhile, wishing Will would wake up, that he would come to me.

I lit up a smoke while I waited. I flicked the lighter awhile, watched the flame burst from the end of the wick. I dragged my finger through the flame, wanting it to hurt, but it didn't hurt. I just wanted to feel something, anything, pain. All I felt was empty inside. I let the flame burn for a while. I let the lighter get all heated up. I pressed it to my palm and held it there before drawing it away, smiling at my handiwork.

An angry round burn on the palm of my hand smiled back at me.

I got to my feet. I wiggled my sleeping legs to get the blood back to flowing. Pins and needles stabbed at me.

The city around me was bedazzling. There were lights everywhere. In the distance, streets buzzed, buildings gleamed.

I stayed there all night. Will never came for me. Because our life together wasn't always sunshine and rainbows. We had good days, we had bad.

There were days we were a match made in heaven. There were days we were incompatible, completely out of sync.

Our time spent together, no matter how good or bad it may have been, came with the realization that he would never know me as he knew Sadie. Because what the other woman gets is another woman's table scraps, never the full meal.

Moments with Will were hidden, rushed. I learned to steal my time wisely with Will, to make moments happen. I went to him in his classroom once, let myself inside the room when it was empty, took him by surprise. He was standing at his desk when I came in. I closed and locked the door behind myself, went to him. I hitched my dress up to my waistline, shimmied onto his desk, parted my legs. Let him see for himself that I had nothing on underneath.

Will stared down there a moment too long, eyes wide, mouth agape.

You can't be serious, Will said. *You want to do this here?* he asked.

Of course I do, I told him.

Right here? he asked again, bearing down on the desk to be sure it could hold the both of us.

Is that a problem, Professor? I asked, spreading my legs wider.

There was a twinkle to his eye. He grinned like the Cheshire cat.

No, he said to me. *It's not a problem.*

I bounded from the desktop when we were through, let the dress fall back down my thighs, said my goodbyes. I tried not to think about where he would go from there. It's not easy being the other woman. The only thing there is for us is disdain, never sympathy. No one feels sorry for us. Instead they judge. We're written off as selfish, scheming, shrewd, when all we're guilty of is falling in love. People forget we're human, that we have feelings, too.

Sometimes when Will pressed his lips to mine, it was magnetic and electric, a current that charged through both of us. His kiss was often impassioned, fiery, but sometimes not. Sometimes it was cold and I would think that was it, the end of our affair. I was wrong. Because that's the way it is with relationships sometimes. They ebb and they flow.

One day I found myself speaking to a shrink about it. I was sitting on a swivel chair. The room I was in was tall with floor-to-ceiling windows. Heavy gray drapes bordered the windows, stretched from ceiling to floor. There was a vase of flowers on a coffee table between us, oversized like everything else in the room. Next to the vase were two glasses of water, one for her and one for me.

My eyes circled the room, went searching for a clock. Instead they found shelves of books on mental illness, emotional intelligence, mind games; graduate school diplomas.

Tell me, the shrink said, *what's been happening.*

That was where the conversation began.

I shifted in the chair, adjusted my shirt.

I cleared my throat, fought for my voice.

Everything all right? the shrink asked, watching as I shifted in the chair, as if getting comfortable in my own skin.

I told her everything was all right. I wasn't shy. I never am. I kicked my feet up on an ottoman, told the woman before me, *I've been sleeping with a married man.*

She was heavier set, one of those women who carry the weight in their face.

There was no change in expression other than a slight lift to the left eyebrow. Her brows were thick, heavy.

Her lips parted. *Oh?* she asked, showing no emotion at what I'd said. *Tell me about him. How did you meet?*

I told her everything there was to tell about Will. I smiled as I did, reliving each moment, one at a time. The day we met beneath the tracks. His hand on my wrist, saving my life. Coffee in the coffee shop. Us leaned up against a building, Will's voice in my ear, his hand on my thigh.

But then my mood turned sour. I reached for a tissue, blotted my eyes. I went on, telling her how hard it was being that other woman. How lonely. How I didn't have the promise of daily contact. No check-in phone calls, no late-night confessions as we drifted to sleep. There was no one to talk to about my feelings. Alone, I tried not to ruminate on it. But there are only so many times you can be called by another woman's name and not get a complex.

She encouraged me to end the affair.

But he says he loves me, I told her.

A man who is willing to cheat on his wife, she said, *will often make promises to you that he can't keep. When he tells you he loves you, it's a form of entrapment. Cheating spouses are masters at manipulation,* she said. *He may tell you things to keep you from ending the affair. He has both a wife and a lover on the side. He has no incentive to change.*

It wasn't her intent, but I found relief in that.

Will had no reason to leave me.

Will would never leave me.

Sadie

I lay there half-asleep, shaken from a dream. In the dream, I was lying in a bed that wasn't mine, staring up at a ceiling that was also not mine. The ceiling above me was a trey ceiling with a fan that dropped from the center of it. The blades of the fan were shaped like palm leaves. I'd never seen it before. The bed sagged in the middle so that there was a trench my body slipped easily into, making it hard to move. I lay in the strange bed, trapped in the crevasse.

It happened so fast there wasn't time to wonder where I was, to worry about it, only to realize that I was not in my own bed. I reached a hand across either side of it, feeling for Will. But the bed was empty other than me. My own body was cocooned in a blanket beneath the quilt and I lay there, watching the inert fan above me, illuminated only by a streak of moonlight that came through the window. It was hot in the bed. I wished that the fan would move, that it would send a rush of air to my body to cool me off.

And then suddenly I was no longer in the bed. I was standing beside it, watching myself sleep. The room around me became distorted. The colors began to fade. All at once, everything was monochrome. The walls of the room warped to odd shapes, trapezoids and parallelograms. It was no longer square.

I felt a headache coming on.

In my dream, I forced my eyes closed to stop the room from changing shapes.

When I opened them again, I was in my own bed with an image of Morgan Baines in my mind. I'd been dreaming about her. I can't remember the details of it, but I know for certain that she was there.

Before he left the bedroom a while ago, Will kissed me. He offered to drive the boys to school so that I could sleep in. *You had trouble sleeping last night,* he said, and I wasn't sure if it was a question or a statement. I didn't have trouble sleeping per se, but my dreams were so vivid I must have tossed and turned in my sleep.

Will kissed me on the head. He wished me a good day and he left.

Downstairs now I hear the rustle of breakfast being served, of backpacks being packed. The front door opens and they're gone. Only then do I sit upright in bed. As I do, I see my nightgown lying at the end of it, no longer on me.

I rise to my feet, the covers sliding from my body. I discover that I'm naked. The realization of it startles me. My hand goes inadvertently to my chest. I'm not averse to sleeping nude. It was the way Will and I often slept before the boys started toddling into our room when they were young. But it's not something I've often done since. The idea of sleeping naked when there are kids in my home embarrasses me. What if Otto had seen me like this? Or worse yet, Imogen?

The thought of Imogen suddenly gives me pause, because I heard Will and the boys leave. But I never heard Imogen leave.

I tell myself that Will wouldn't leave before she did. He would have made sure she was gone first, headed to school. Imogen doesn't always make her comings and goings known, which tells me now that she's not here, that she slipped out quietly long before Will and the boys did.

There's dried sweat beneath my arms and between my legs, a result of the inequitable heat in the old home. I remember how hot

I was in my dream. I must have whipped off the nightgown unconsciously.

I find clothes in the dresser drawer, running tights and a long-sleeved shirt that I slip on. As I do, another thought comes to me, about Imogen. What if, like me, Will only assumed she'd gone to school, because of her tendency to slip in and out unnoticed?

My fear of Imogen colors my judgment and I find myself wondering: Is she still home? Are Imogen and I the only ones here?

I cautiously leave the bedroom. Imogen's door is closed, the padlock on the new locking mechanism securely fastened, which tells me she's not there in her room. Because she couldn't lock it if she was inside.

The purpose of the lock: to keep me out. It seems like an innocuous enough thing, but at second glance, I wonder if it would as easily lock someone in as lock someone out.

I call out to Imogen as I make my way down the steps, just to be sure. Downstairs, her shoes and her backpack are gone, as is her jacket.

Will has left breakfast for me on the counter and an empty mug for coffee. I fill the coffee mug and take it and my crepes to the table to eat. Only there do I see that

Will has left his book behind, the true crime novel. He's finished it, I assume, and left it for me to read.

I reach for the book and slide it toward myself. But it isn't the book that I'm thinking about. Not really. It's the photograph inside, that of his former fiancée. I take the book into my hands, take a deep breath and leaf through the pages, expecting Erin's photo to fall out.

When it doesn't, I leaf through again, a second and a third time.

I set the book down. I look up and sigh.

Will has taken the photograph. He's taken the photograph and left the book for me.

Where has Will put the photograph?

I can't ask Will. To bring Erin up again would be in poor taste. I can't possibly nag him over and over again about his dead fiancée. She was long gone before I arrived. But the fact that he hangs on to her photograph after all these years is hard to stomach.

Will grew up on the Atlantic coast, not far from where we now live. He transferred colleges during his sophomore and junior years, leaving the East Coast for a school in Chicago. Between Erin's death and his stepfather's, Will told me, he couldn't stand to stay out east anymore. He had to leave.

Shortly after he did, his mother married for the third time (far too soon, in Will's opinion; she's the kind of woman who can't ever be alone) and moved south. His brother joined the Peace Corps and now lives in Cameroon. Then Alice died. Will doesn't have family on the East Coast anymore.

Erin and Will were high school sweethearts. He never used that term when he told me about her because it was too sentimental, too endearing. But they were. High school sweethearts. Erin was nineteen when she died; he'd just turned twenty. They'd been together since they were fifteen and sixteen. The way Will tells it, Erin, home from college for Christmas break — Will went to community college those first two years — had been missing overnight by the time her body was found. She was supposed to pick him up at six for dinner, but she never showed. By six thirty Will was getting worried. Near seven, he called her parents, her friends in quick succession. No one knew where she was.

Around eight o'clock, Erin's parents made a call to the police. But Erin had only been gone two hours at that point and the police weren't quick to issue a search. It was winter. It had snowed and the roads were slick. Accidents were plenty. The police had their work cut out for them that night. In the meantime, the police suggested Will and her parents keep calling around, checking out any place Erin was liable to be — which was ridiculous since a winter weather warning had been issued, urging drivers to stay off the roads that night.

The route Erin often took to Will's was hilly and meandering, covered in a thin layer of ice and snow that wrapped around a large pond. It was off the beaten path, a scenic route best avoided when the weather took a turn for the worse as it had that night.

But Erin was always foolhardy, not the type, according to Will, that you could tell what to do.

At just thirty-two degrees, the pond where they later found her hadn't had a chance to freeze through. It couldn't bear the weight of the car when Erin hit a patch of ice and went soaring off the road.

That night, Will looked everywhere for Erin. The gym, the library, the studio where she danced. He drove every route he could possibly think of to get from Erin's house to his. But it was dark out, and the pond was only a black abyss.

It wasn't until early morning that a jogger spied the car's fender sticking out of the ice and snow. Erin's parents were notified first.

By the time Will heard the news, more than twelve hours had passed since she hadn't shown up for their date. Her parents were devastated, as was a little sister, only nine years old when she died. As was Will.

I push the book away from me. I don't have the stomach to read it because I can't see the book without thinking of the photo that was once tucked inside.

Where is he keeping Erin's photograph? I wonder, but at the same time comes another thought: *Why do I care?*

Will married me. We have children together.

He loves me.

I leave my breakfast dishes where they are. I step from the kitchen, slip into a windproof jacket that hangs from a hallway hook. I need to go for a run, to blow off steam.

I head out onto the street. The skies this morning are gray, the ground moist from an early rainfall that's drifted somewhere out to sea. I see the rain in the distance. Streaks of it hover beneath the base of the clouds. The world looks hopeless and bleak. By the end of the day, forecasters predict the rain will turn to snow.

I jog down the street. It's a rare day off work. What I have in mind for it is a jog followed by a quiet morning alone. Otto and

Tate have gone to school, Will to work. Will has no doubt caught the ferry by now, getting shuttled to the mainland. There he'll catch a bus to campus, where he'll rivet nineteen-year-olds about alternative energy sources and bioremediation for half the day, before gathering Tate from school and coming home.

I jog down the hill. I take the street that follows the perimeter of the island, moving past oceanfront properties. They're not lavish, not by any means. Rather, they're well-worn, lived in for generations, easily a hundred years old. Breezy cottages, rough around the edges, hidden amid the ample trees. It's a five-mile loop around the island. The landscape isn't manicured. It's far more rural than that, with long stretches of backwoods and public beaches that are not only rugged and seaweed-swept, but eerily vacant this time of year.

I run fast. I have so much on my mind. I find myself thinking about Imogen, about Erin; about Jeffrey Baines and his ex-wife hiding in the church's sanctuary. What were they talking about, I wonder, and where is Erin's photograph? Has Will hidden it from me, or is he using it as a bookmark in his next novel? Is it something as auspicious as that?

I pass cliffs that inhabit the east side of the island. They're precarious and steep, jutting out and over the Atlantic. I try not to think about Erin. As I watch, the ocean's waves come crashing furiously into the rocks. All at once, a flock of migrating birds moves past me in a deranged mass as they do this time of year. The sudden movement of them startles me and I scream. Dozens, if not hundreds, of black birds pulsate as if one, and then flee.

The ocean is tempestuous this morning. The wind blows across it, sending the waves crashing to shore. Angry whitecaps assail the rocky shoreline, throwing upward a ten- or twenty-foot spray.

I imagine the waters this time of year are icy, the depth of the ocean deep.

I pause in my run to stretch. I reach down to touch my toes, loosening my hamstrings. The world around me is so quiet it's unsettling. The only sound I hear is that of the wind slipping around me, whispering into my ear.

All at once I'm startled by words that get carried to me on the jet stream.

I hate you. You're a loser. Die, die, die.

I jolt upright, scanning the horizon for the source of the noise.

But I see nothing, no one. And yet I can't

shake the idea that someone is out there, that someone is watching me. A chill goes dashing up my spine. My hands start to shake.

I call out a feeble "Hello?" but no one replies.

I look around, see nothing in the distance. No one hiding behind the corners of homes or the trunks of trees. The beach is without people, the windows and doors of the homes shut tight as they should be on a day like this.

It's my imagination only. No one is here. No one is speaking to me.

What I hear is the rustle of the wind.

My mind has mistaken the wind for words.

I continue on my run. By the time I reach the fringes of town — a quintessential *small town* with the Methodist church, an inn, a post office, and a handful of places to eat, including a seasonal ice cream shop, boarded up with panels of plywood this time of year — it's begun to rain. What starts as a drizzle soon comes down in sheets. I run as fast as my legs will carry me, ducking into a café to wait the storm out.

I swing open the door and scurry in, dripping wet. I've never been here before. This café is rustic and provincial, the kind of place where old men spend the day, drinking coffee, grumbling about local politics and weather.

The café door doesn't have a chance to close before I overhear a woman ask, "Did anyone go to the memorial service for Morgan?"

This woman sits on a wobbly, broken-spindled chair in the center of the restaurant, eating from a plate of bacon and eggs. "Poor Jeffrey," she says, shaking her head mournfully. "He must be devastated." She reaches for a carton of creamer and douses her coffee with it.

"It's all so awful," another woman replies. They sit, a troop of middle-aged women at a long laminated table beside the window of the restaurant. "So unspeakable," the same woman says.

I tell the hostess I need a table for one, by the window. A waitress stops by and asks what she can get for me, and I tell her coffee, please.

The ladies at the table go on. I listen.

"I heard them talking about it on the news this morning," someone says.

"What did they say?" another asks.

"Police have been speaking to a person of interest."

Jeffrey, I tell myself, is the person of interest.

"I heard she got stabbed," I overhear just then, and my stomach lurches at the words. My hand falls to my own abdomen, thinking what it would feel like when the knife punctured the skin, when it slipped inside her organs.

The next voice is incredulous. "How do they know *that*?" the woman asks, slamming her mug too hard to the table, and the ladies leap, including me. "Police haven't released any information yet."

The first voice again. "Well, now they have. That's what the coroner said. The coroner said she was stabbed."

"Five times, they said on the news. Once in the chest, twice in the back and the face."

"The face?" someone asks, aghast. My hand rises up to my cheek, feeling the insubstantiality of it. The thin skin, the hard bones. Nowhere for the blade of the knife to go. "How awful."

The women wonder aloud what it would feel like to be stabbed. If Morgan felt the pain straightaway or not until the first signs of blood. Or maybe it happened so fast, a woman guesses, the repeated thrust in and out of her, that she didn't have time to feel a thing because she was already dead.

What I know as a physician is that if the weapon hit a major artery on the way in, Morgan Baines would have passed mercifully quick. But if it didn't, though she may have been incapacitated, death by exsanguination, *bleeding out,* would have taken longer. And, once the shock of it wore off, it would have been painful.

For her sake, I hope Morgan's assailant hit a major artery. I hope it was quick.

"There were no signs of forced entry. No broken windows. No busted door."

"Maybe Morgan opened the door for him."

"Maybe she never locked it in the first place," someone chirps. "Maybe she was expecting him," she says, and a discussion follows about how most murder victims know their assailant. Someone quotes a statistic, saying how random crime is relatively rare. "Getting stabbed in the face. That sounds personal to me."

My mind goes to the ex, Courtney. Courtney had reason to want Morgan dead. I think of her proclamation. *I'm not sorry for what I did!* What did she mean by that?

"The killer must have known Jeffrey was gone," one of the ladies speculates.

"Jeffrey travels often. From what I hear, he's almost always gone. If it isn't Tokyo then it's Frankfurt or Toronto."

"Maybe Morgan was seeing someone else. Maybe she had a boyfriend."

The incredulous voice returns just then. "It's all hearsay. All rumor," she says, admonishing the other women for gossiping this way about a dead woman.

Someone quickly contradicts. "Pamela," the woman says, tone antagonistic. "It's not hearsay. It was on *the news.*"

"They said on the news that Morgan had a boyfriend?" Pamela asks.

"Well, no. Not that. But they said that she was stabbed."

I wonder if Will knows any of this.

"A knife, they said," and I find this omniscient *they* starting to wear on my nerves. Who is *they*? "That's what they said was the murder weapon. Can you imagine?" the woman asks, as she latches down on the handle of a butter knife and hoists it indecorously over her head, makes believe she's stabbing the woman next to her with the blunt edge of the knife. The ladies admonish her. "Jackie," they say, "stop it. What in the world's gotten into you? A woman was killed."

"That's what they say," the woman named Jackie continues. "Just stating the facts, ladies. According to coroner reports, it was a boning knife by the shape and length of the wound. Narrow and curved. About six inches long. Though that's just speculation because Morgan's killer didn't leave it behind. He took it with him. Took it with him and probably tossed it out to sea."

Sitting there in the café, I imagine the angry, tempestuous waves I saw on my run. I think of all the people who ride the ferry to and from the mainland day after day after day, sitting at the top of it with over three miles of seawater with which to dispose of a murder weapon.

So much latitude, so much leeway. Everyone so wrapped up in themselves, not paying attention to what others around them are doing.

The current of the Atlantic sweeps upward along the coast and toward Nova Scotia. From there it's Europe-bound. There's little chance a knife would wash ashore on the coast of Maine if the killer tossed it out to sea.

I leave my coffee where it is when I go. I didn't drink a drop of it.

CAMILLE

I've always hated the ocean. But somehow I convinced myself to follow him there because wherever Will was was where I wanted to be.

I found a place to stay, an empty house near his. The house was teensy, tiny, pathetic, with sheets that hung from furniture, making everything ghostlike.

I walked through the inside of the house, looked everything over. I sat on their chairs, I lay on the beds just like Goldilocks. One was too big, too small, but one was just right.

I opened and closed dresser drawers, saw nearly nothing inside, forgotten things only, like socks, dental floss, toothpicks.

I turned the faucets. Nothing came out. The pipes were empty, the toilet was, too. The cupboards, the refrigerator were nearly bare. The only thing there was a box of baking soda. The house was cold.

In that house, my existential crises were frequent. I found myself stuck inside, killing time, wondering why. I was trapped in darkness, feeling like I didn't exist, feeling like I shouldn't exist. I thought that maybe I'd be better off dead. I thought about ways to end my life. It wouldn't be the first time. I'd tried before, would have done it, too, if I hadn't been interrupted. It's only a matter of time until I try again.

Some nights I left that house, stood in the street watching Will through the window of his own home. Most nights, the porch light was on, a beacon for Sadie when she wasn't there. It pissed me off. He loved Sadie more than he loved me. I hated Sadie for it. I screamed at her. I wanted to kill her, I wanted her dead. But it wasn't as easy as that.

As I stood in the street, I watched smoke come gushing from the chimney and into the night, gray against the navy sky. There were lamps on inside the home. A yellow glow filled the window, where the curtains were parted in a perfect V.

Everything about it read like a damn greeting card.

One night, I stood watching through that window. For a second, I closed my eyes. I imagined myself on the other side of it with him. In my mind, I grappled with his sweater. He tugged at my hair. He pressed his mouth to mine. It was wild and fierce. He bit my lip. I tasted blood.

But then the rev of a car engine roused me. I opened my eyes, saw the car come chugging up the street. *The Little Engine That Could.* I stepped out of the way, dropped down into the ditch where the driver wouldn't see me lurking in the shadows.

The car passed slowly by. Puffs of smoke sputtered from the back end of it. *I think I can, I think I can.*

I watched as Will knelt in the room inside his house. He wore a sweater that night, gray, the kind with a half zip. He wore jeans, he wore shoes. He was playing with his kid, the little one, on their knees in the middle of the room. The stupid kid, he was smiling. He was happy as a damn clam.

He took the kid by the hand. Together, they rose from the floor, went to the window. They stood, looking out into the night. I could see them, but they couldn't see me. I could see everything on the inside because of how dark it was outside. The fire in the fireplace. The vase on the mantel; the painting on the wall.

They were waiting for Sadie to come home.

I told myself he wasn't trying to ditch me when he came to this island. He had no choice but to go. Just like a larva has no choice but to turn into a flea.

Just then another car came passing by, but this time I didn't move.

I tried not to be a nuisance. But some days I couldn't help myself. I left messages on Sadie's car window; I sat on the hood of her car, chain-smoked my way through a pack of cigarettes before some old hag tried to tell me I couldn't smoke there, that I had to smoke somewhere else. I didn't like being told what to do. I told her, *This is a free country. I can smoke wherever the hell I want.* I called her things, a biddy, an old bag. She threatened to tell on me.

I let myself into their home one day when no one was there. Getting inside was easy. If you watch anyone long enough, you know. The passwords, the PINs — they're all the same. And they're all there in the paperwork that gets tossed in the trash. Someone's birth date, the last four digits of a Social Security number on a tax form, a pay stub.

I hid out of sight, watched Will's car as it pulled away before I went to the garage keypad, plugged some code in. I got it on the third try.

From there, the door to the house unlocked. I turned the knob, let myself in.

The dogs didn't bark when I stepped inside. Some guard dogs they are. They scurried over, sniffed my hand. They licked me. I petted their heads, told them to go lie down, and they did.

I stepped out of my shoes, made my way around the kitchen first, tinkering with things, touching things. I was hungry. I opened the refrigerator door, found something inside, sat at the table to eat.

I pretended this was my home. I kicked my feet up on another chair, reached for a days-old newspaper. I sat awhile, reading obsolete headlines as I ate.

I glanced across the table, imagined Will eating with me, imagined I wasn't alone.

How was your day? I asked Will, but before he could reply, the phone rang. The sound of it was unexpected. I startled, bounding from my chair to answer the phone, feeling aggrieved that someone would call in the middle of Will's and my dinner together.

I lifted the receiver from the cradle, pressed it to my ear.

Hello? I asked. It was an old rotary phone. The kind no one in the world still used.

Is this Mrs. Foust? he asked. The voice belonged to a man. He was chipper.

I didn't miss a beat. *This is she,* I said, leaning my back against the countertop, grinning. *This is Sadie Foust,* I said.

He was from the cable company, calling to see if Will and I wanted to upgrade our cable package. His voice was persuasive, friendly. He asked questions. He called me by name.

Well, not my name exactly.

But still.

How is your current package treating you, Mrs. Foust? Are you happy with your choice of channels?

I told him I was not. That the selection was quite slim.

Do you find yourself ever wishing for the hottest premium channels, Mrs. Foust, or your husband the MLB Network?

I told him I did. That I wished for that all of the time. That I longed to watch movies on HBO or Showtime. *They're not part of our current package, are they, sir?*

Unfortunately, no, they're not, Mrs. Foust, he told me. *But we can change all that. We can change it right now over the phone. This is a great time to upgrade, Mrs. Foust.*

His offer was hard to refuse. I couldn't say no.

I set the phone back into its cradle. I left my casserole where it was. I ran my hands over the countertop. I opened and closed drawers, fiddled with the knobs of the gas range.

I turned the dial, bypassed the ignition valve.

It didn't take long for the smell of gas to reach my nose.

I moved to the living room, laid my fingers on photographs, sat on the sofa, played the piano.

I turned and headed toward the stairs, where I gripped the handrail, climbed the steps up. The steps were wooden, sunken in the middle. They were old, as old as the house was old.

I moved down the hall, looked in each room.

It didn't take long to figure out which bedroom was his.

The bed was wide. A pair of his pants was draped over the edge of a laundry basket. Inside were his shirts, his socks, her bras. I thumbed the lace of her bra, dropped it back in the basket, dug through until I found a sweater. It was brown wool, a cardigan, ugly and worn, but warm. I slipped my arms into it, ran my fingers along the ribbed trim, touched the buttons.

I sank my hands into the big apron pockets, did a little spin.

I went to Sadie's dresser, where her jewelry hung from a stand. I draped a necklace over my neck, slipped a bracelet over my wrist. I slid open a drawer, found makeup there. I watched on in the attached mirror as I patted my nose with her powder puff, as I swept her blush across my cheeks.

Don't you look lovely, Mrs. Foust, I said to my reflection, though I'd always been so much prettier than Sadie. But even so, if I wanted to, I could do my hair like hers, I could dress like her, pass myself off as Mrs. Foust. Persuade others to believe that I was Will's wife, his chosen one. If I wanted to.

I went to the bed, grabbed ahold of the top sheet and pulled it back. The sheets were soft, gray, the kind with a high thread count, no doubt expensive.

I ran my hands over the sheets, I fingered the hem. I sat on the edge of the bed. I couldn't help myself; I had to get inside. I slipped my feet under the sheets, moved down beneath the covers. I lay on my side, closed my eyes awhile. Pretended Will was beside me in bed.

I was gone before he came back. He never knew I was there.

■ ■ ■ ■

I was there at the pier when he came. The day was dingy, gray. The clouds sank from the sky, they fell to street level, like smog. Everyone and everything was blurred because of it. Everyone was gray.

There were people outside just for the hell of it. As if they liked this, the dreary cold. They stood, staring at the ocean, watching a dot at sea that may or may not have been the ferry. It moved in, getting closer, leaving small boats behind. They rolled back and forth in the ship's wake.

The wind cut through me like a knife. I stood with my ticket in hand, holed up behind the ticket booth, waiting for Will to come. I spotted him as he made his way down the street for the dock.

His smile was electric. My heart beat hard.

But he wasn't smiling at me.

He was smiling at the hoi polloi, making small talk with the commoners.

I waited behind the ticket booth, watched him take his place at the end of the line. I waited, then fell in line behind him, a handful of people between us.

I draped a hood over my head. With sunglasses, I hid my eyes.

The ferry was the last of us to arrive. We paraded across the bridge, prisoners on a death march. There were holes in the bridge, one of those you see straight through to the churning water below. I saw seaweed. I smelled fish.

Will went up the steps to the upper deck. I sat where I could watch him without being seen. I couldn't take my eyes off him. I watched as he stood at the stern of the ship; as he gripped the guardrail; as he stared at the shoreline as it slipped from view.

The water beneath us was briny and brown. Ducks circled the boat.

I watched the whole time. Will stood like a ship's figurehead, Poseidon, god of the sea, keeping watch over the ocean. My eyes orbited his body, traced the shape of his silhouette. They circled his windblown hair, rounded his broad shoulder, slipped down an arm, counted each fingertip. They followed the seam of his jeans from his thighs to his feet. Dropped beneath the soles of his shoes, went up the other side, the same way they came down. Feet to thighs to fingers. I ran my hands through his hair. Remembered what it felt like when his hair got tangled up in the webs of my hands.

Twenty minutes or so, it went on this way.

The shore came closer. Buildings got

larger. All the while, they were there, blocks on the horizon. But all of a sudden, they were big and gray like everything else that day.

When the ferry docked, I followed Will from the boat and across a pier. Somewhere on the other side of it, we hopped a bus. I dug in my bag, happy to see I had a Metra card.

I climbed aboard. I found a seat behind him.

The bus clomped along, shuttling us across town.

It wasn't long before we arrived. Another college campus. More buildings covered in brick. I fell back into my usual routine, following Will as he walked, mirroring him, keeping twenty paces behind all the time.

I watched as he made his way to a building. I climbed the steps thirty seconds after he did. I followed him to a classroom, stood in the hallway and listened to him speak. His voice, it was easy on the ears. Like a babbling brook, the exhilarating rush of a waterfall. It excited and subdued me all at the same time, made me weak in the knees.

Will got all fired up, aroused, talking about population density, about people living in overcrowded conditions, drinking dirty water. I pressed my back to the wall and listened. Not to his words, those meant nothing to me, but to the sound of his voice.

There in the hallway, I closed my eyes, made believe every word out of his mouth was a secret message meant just for me.

When people came tumbling out, they were loud, raucous.

I stepped in when the room was empty.

He stood at the front of the room. A wave of relief washed over him when he saw me.

He was happy to see me. He was smiling, this full-out smile that he tried to hide but couldn't. The corners of his lips turned up on their own.

I can't believe it, he said, coming to me, scooping me up into his arms. *I can't believe you're here. What are you doing here?* he asked.

I told him, *I came to see you. I missed you.*

He asked, *How did you know where to find me?*

I said with a wink, *I followed you here. I think you have a stalker, Professor Foust.*

Sadie

I jog home from the coffee shop. The temperatures have dropped even more than before. The rain has turned to sleet, striking me in the eyes so that I stare only at the concrete as I run. It comes down heavy and thick, sticking to my clothing. Before long, this sleet will be snow.

As I approach our house, I hear the sound of a car engine idling nearby, up the hill, ahead of me. I lift my eyes in time to see a Crown Victoria parked at the end of the Nilssons' drive. The engine is running, exhaust fumes drifting past the red taillights and into the cold air. There's a man standing beside the Nilssons' mailbox. On a day such as this, no one should be outside.

I slow down my pace, put a hand to my brow to repel the sleet. My view of the man is obstructed because of the weather and the distance. But it doesn't matter. I know who it is; I've watched this same scene before.

There, not fifty yards from where I stand, is Officer Berg. He hovers behind the rear of his Crown Victoria, with an item in hand. He looks around to be sure no one's watching before forcing it into the Nilssons' mailbox. I manage to slip behind a tree just in time.

Officer Berg has done this before, the same day he interrogated Will and me in our home. I watched after he left, as he drove to the Nilssons' mailbox and left something there that day, too.

It's the circumspection that piques my interest the most. What is he leaving in the Nilsson mailbox that he doesn't want anyone else to know about?

Berg closes the receptacle door and climbs back into his car. He pulls away, over the crest of the hill. Curiosity gets the best of me. I know I shouldn't and yet I do. I push the wet hair from my face, jog up the street. I reach in and take the item from the mailbox with none of the circumspection Officer Berg had.

Nearby, under the canopy of a tree, I see that it's an unmarked envelope, sealed shut, with a sheaf of paper packed inside. I hold the envelope up to the negligible light. I can't be certain, but I'm quite sure it's a wad of cash.

The rev of a car engine in the distance startles me. I thrust the envelope back in the mailbox and walk quickly home.

It's midmorning, but for as dreary as it is outside, it might as well be the middle of the night. I hurry inside my home, closing and locking the door behind myself. The dogs come running to greet me and I'm grateful for their company.

I turn away from the window. In the foyer, I trip over something. It's a toy, one of Tate's toys, which, upon closer inspection, is a doll. I think nothing of it, the fact that it's a doll. We're not into gender-specific toys in our home. If Tate wants to play with a doll over Transformers, so be it. But it's the placement of it that upsets me, lying in the middle of the foyer so that someone might trip. I kick it aside, taking my anxiety out on the poor doll.

I call Will but he's in the middle of a lecture. When he finally gets a chance to call me back, I tell him about the coroner report, about the boning knife. But Will already knows because he read about it once he reached the mainland this morning.

"It's horrible," he says, and together we chew over how tragic and unthinkable the whole thing is.

"Are we safe here?" I ask Will, and when he hesitates — because how can either of us know if we're safe? — I say decisively, "I think that we should leave."

Before he can argue, I say, "Imogen would come with us, of course."

What I don't say is that on our turf, we'd have the upper hand. I'd feel a sense of control over Imogen that I don't feel now.

"Leave and go where?" Will asks, but it seems so obvious to me, the way that our fresh start isn't so fresh after all. Our stay in Maine has been stormy, to say the least. If anything, our lives have gotten worse since being here.

"Home," I tell him, but he only asks, "Where is home anymore, Sadie?" and at those words, my heart aches.

Our Chicago condo, the one where Will and I spent our entire married lives until now, is gone, sold to a couple of millennials. My job at the hospital is gone, too, no doubt replaced with some young recent med school grad. Otto can never return to his public school, nor Tate to his, not because of anything he did, but because he's guilty by association. They'd both need to go to some private school, and on Will's salary alone — assuming he could even get his old job back — that would never work.

When I say nothing, Will says, "Let's talk about this when I get home," and I say okay. I end the call and make my way into the kitchen to start the teakettle. As I cross into the kitchen, I see our knives and am stricken with a morbid curiosity to see for myself what a boning knife is, what one looks like, to hold it in my hand. Will has a set of knives he keeps in a wooden block on the counter, just out of reach of Tate's inquisitive hands.

I go to the block. I don't know what a boning knife is, but an internet search tells me I'm looking for an arched blade with a very sharp point, five to nine inches long. I yank on the handles of the knives, pulling them out in turn to examine their blades. It doesn't take long to see that there's no knife matching the description in the block. Furthermore, I see that one space on the wooden block is empty. This set of twenty-one knives only contains twenty. One knife is gone.

My imagination gets the best of me. I try to stay calm, sensible, remembering again about Occam's razor. Maybe some other knife belongs here. Maybe Will doesn't own a boning knife. Maybe the missing knife is in the sink, though I look and it's not.

Maybe Will lost that knife long ago, or it got placed in the cutlery drawer by mistake. I pull open the drawer, rifle through Alice's modest collection of knives — steak and dinner knives mostly, a paring knife, one with a serrated edge — but it's not there.

I think of Imogen in our bedroom at night. You hear stories about children murdering their parents in the middle of the night. It happens; it's not that far-fetched. And Imogen is a hostile girl, a damaged girl. I don't know that I'd put it past her to take that knife to threaten me with, or worse.

I turn and step from the kitchen. I climb the steps to the second floor, my slick hand gripping the banister. I go to her room, planning to search it as I did the other night, but my plan is quickly derailed when I come to her door and realize there's no getting in without the padlock key.

I curse, shaking on the door handle. I try another call to Will to tell him about the missing knife, but he's on his way home now, likely on the ferry, where reception is spotty. My call doesn't go through. I put my phone away, relieved to know that he'll be home soon.

I find something to keep myself busy. I dust the house. I strip the sheets from the beds. I start to gather them in a pile to lug down to the laundry room.

In our bedroom, I tug on the fitted sheet. As I do, something black comes skidding out from my side of the bed, something that had been wedged between the mattress and the bed frame for some time. As the object slews halfway across the bedroom floor, my first instinct is to think it's the remote control for the bedroom TV we rarely use. I go to pick it up. As I do, I realize that it's not a remote, but rather a phone, one which is neither Will's nor mine. I turn it over in my hands. There's nothing discernible about it. It's simply a phone, an older generation iPhone. Perhaps Alice's, I think, noting that the phone is not-surprisingly dead. Alice herself has been dead for quite some time. Of course the phone would be dead, too.

Back downstairs in a drawer full of gadgets, I find a charger that fits. I plug it into an outlet in the living room wall, stretching the phone to the fireplace mantel.

I go back to straightening the house until Will arrives soon after with Tate in tow. I greet them in the foyer, and Will sees it in my eyes straightaway: something is wrong.

Both he and Tate are wet with snow. It's on their coats, on their hair, melting quickly. Tate stomps it from his feet, creating a puddle on the wood. He's trying to tell me a story about something that happened at school today, something he learned. He starts to sing a song but I'm not listening, and neither is Will.

"Take your shoes off," Will tells him, before helping Tate out of his coat. He hangs it from the hook in the darkened foyer, and it occurs to me that I should turn on a light, but I don't.

"Do you like it, Mommy?" Tate asks about the song. "Days of the week, days of the week, days of the week," he sings in tune to *The Addams Family* theme song, clapping twice between each line. Though I hear him, I don't reply. "Do you like it?" he asks, louder this time, nearly screaming.

I nod my head, but I'm just barely listening. I hear his song, but my mind can't process it because all I'm thinking about is the missing knife.

Tate doesn't like the brush-off. His posture shifts; he throws his arms across himself and begins to pout.

Will turns to me, wrapping his arms around me. It feels good, being held.

"I've looked into home security systems," he tells me, returning to the conversation we started on the phone earlier today, about whether or not we're safe here. "I set up an appointment to have one installed. And let's give Officer Berg a chance to get to the bottom of this, before we cut and run. This is our home, Sadie. Whether we like it or not, for now this is our home. We have to make do."

I pull back from his embrace. He's trying to be reassuring. But I don't feel reassured. I meet his eye, and ask, "But what if a security system can't protect us?"

His look is quizzical. "What do you mean?" he asks.

"What if there's a threat inside our home?"

"You mean as if someone got past the security system?" he asks, assuring me that we could keep the house armed at all times, that these things are monitored twenty-four hours a day. If the alarm was triggered, help would be on its way almost instantly.

"It's not an intruder I'm thinking about," I say. "It's Imogen."

Will shakes his head, disbelieving. "Imogen?" he asks, and I say yes. "You can't possibly think —" he begins, but I interrupt him.

"Our *k-n-i-f-e,*" I tell him, spelling the word out for Tate's benefit. Tate can spell, but not well enough. "Our boning *k-n-i-f-e* isn't here. I can't find it," I say, admitting in a forced whisper, "She scares me, Will."

I think about her in our bedroom the other night, watching us sleep. The strange exchange we had in the hallway. The photograph of her dead mother that she carries around on her phone. These are abnormal behaviors.

And then there's the padlock on her bedroom door. "There's something in there she doesn't want us to find," I say, finally admitting to him that I was in there the other day, before the lock was installed. I tell him about the picture I found with the man's face scratched off, the Dear John note, the condoms. "She's been sleeping with someone," I tell him. "A married man, I think," based on the content of the note.

Will doesn't say much to this. He's more disappointed that I would violate her privacy by snooping through her room. What he does say, however, is that there's nothing criminal about sleeping with a married man. "She's sixteen," Will reminds me. "Sixteen-year-olds do stupid things all the time. You know why she put that lock on the door?" Will asks, saying before I can reply, "She's a teenager, Sadie. That's why. She doesn't want people coming into her room. How would you feel if she went snooping through your stuff?" he asks.

"It wouldn't matter," I tell him. "I have

nothing to hide. But Imogen is an angry girl with a short fuse, Will," I argue. "She worries me."

"Try putting yourself in her shoes, Sadie. You don't think you'd be angry?" he asks, and of course I'd be grieving and uncomfortable — my mother dead by her own hand, me forced to live with people I don't know — but would I be *angry*? "We have no idea what Imogen saw that day," he asserts. "If we'd seen what she must have seen, we'd be on a short fuse, too. You can't unsee that.

"Besides," Will tells me, coming back to the knife, "I used the boning knife just the other day to skin chicken for a casserole. You're all worked up for nothing, Sadie," he says, asking if I checked the dishwasher for the knife. I didn't. I didn't even think to look in the dishwasher.

But it doesn't matter right now, because my mind has moved on from the knife and to the picture on Imogen's cell phone. The one of Alice dead. I know exactly what Imogen saw the day her mother died, though I'm reluctant to tell Will because the last thing he needs to see is what Alice went through. And yet I tell him anyway because it isn't right, it isn't *normal,* for Imogen to have taken a picture of Alice postmortem and for her to be carrying it around. What is she doing with it anyway? Showing her friends?

I look away from Will. I confess to him that I do know what Imogen saw. "Imogen took a picture that day before the coroner took Alice away. She showed it to me," I say.

Will grows suddenly silent for a moment. He swallows hard.

"She took a picture?" he asks after some time. I nod. "What did she look like?" he asks, meaning Alice.

I'm generally nondescript. "Well, she was *d-e-a-d,*" I tell him, treading lightly. "But she looked peaceful," I lie. I don't tell him about claw marks, the severed tongue. I don't tell him about the state of the attic, the toppled storage boxes, the broken lamp, the pitchpoled telescope. But I re-create them in my mind, imagining Alice's thrashing body knocking into these things, toppling them, as her oxygen supply was siphoned off.

As I dredge up the images of them, something gets under my skin. Because I picture the boxes and the lamp overturned, and yet the step stool — the one Alice used to raise herself up to the height of the noose — stood upright. I remember that now.

How could the very thing that Alice would have needed to kick away to go through with the suicide not be overturned?

Even more, the stool was out of reach of Alice's body. Which makes me think someone else yanked it from beneath her feet.

In which case, was it even a suicide? Or was it murder?

I turn white. A hand goes to my mouth. "What's wrong?" Will asks. "Everything all right?" I shake my head, tell him no, I don't think so.

"I just realized something," I say, and he asks with urgency, "What?"

"The picture of Alice. On Imogen's phone," I say.

"What about it?" he asks.

"The police hadn't come yet when Imogen took the picture. It was only Imogen," I say, wondering how much time lapsed in between her arriving home and calling the police. Was it enough time for Imogen to stage a suicide? Imogen is tall, but she's not heavily built. I can't imagine she'd have had the strength to haul Alice to the third floor — even if Alice was drugged and unconscious, unable to fight back — to hoist her up and into the noose. Not alone. Someone would have had to help her. I consider the friends she smokes with while waiting for the ferry to arrive. Clad in all black, rebellious and oppositional, full of self-loathing. Would they have helped?

"In the picture, Will, the step stool we found in the attic. The one Alice would have had to use to do what she did. Everything else was knocked over. But the stool remained upright. And it was too far away for Alice to reach. If she'd been alone, the stool would have been knocked over, and it would have been much closer to her feet."

He shakes his head. "What are you getting at?" he asks, and I see a change come over him. His posture shifts. Ruts form between his eyes. He frowns at me. He knows what I'm suggesting.

"How can we know for certain," I ask, "that it was a *s-u-i-c-i-d-e*? There was no investigation. But there was also no note. Don't people who *k-i-l-l* themselves usually leave a note? Officer Berg said it himself, remember? He told us he never pegged Alice for the type."

"How would Berg know," Will asks angrily, "if Alice was the suicide type?" It isn't like Will to get angry. But this is his sister we're talking about. His niece. His flesh and blood.

"I don't trust Imogen," I admit. "She scares me," I say again.

"Listen to yourself, Sadie," Will says. "First you accuse Imogen of taking our knife. Now you're saying she killed Alice." Will is too worked up to spell the words out, though he mouths them for Tate's benefit. "You're all over the place. I know she hasn't exactly been welcoming, but she's done nothing to lead me to believe she's capable of murder," he says, seemingly having already forgotten about the writing on my car window just the other day. *Die.*

"Are you really suggesting that this was a murder made to look like a suicide?" he asks, disbelieving.

Before I can reply, Tate again begs, "Please, Mommy, play with me." My eyes drop to his, and they look so sad, my heart aches.

"All right, Tate," I tell him, feeling guilty that Will and I are going on like this, ignoring him. "What do you want to play?" I ask him, voice softening though my insides are still in a tizzy. "Do you want to play charades, or a board game?"

He tugs hard on my hand and is chanting, "Statue game, statue game!"

The wrenching on my hand has begun to hurt. It's wearing on my nerves, because not only is he pulling on my hand, hurting me, but he's trying to turn my body, to make it go ways it doesn't want to go. It's subliminal, the way I yank my hand suddenly away, holding it above my head, out of reach of his. I don't mean to do it. But there's an immediacy to it. So much so that Tate flinches like he's been slapped.

"Please, Mommy," Tate begs, eyes suddenly sad as he stands before me and leaps for my hand. I try to be patient, I really do, but my mind is whirling in a dozen different directions and I don't know what Tate means by this statue game. He's begun to cry. Not a real cry but crocodile tears, which wear on me even more.

That's when I catch sight of the doll I kicked aside over an hour ago. Her limp body is pressed against the wall. "Put your toys away and then we'll play," I tell him, and he asks, "What toys?"

"Your doll, Tate," I say, losing patience. "Right there," I tell him, motioning to the floppy doll with her frizzy hair and marble-like eyes. She lies on her side, dress torn along a seam, one shoe missing.

Tate's look is leery. "It's not *mine,*" he says, as if this is something I should know. But of course it's his — it's not like any of the rest of us still play with toys — and my first thought is that Tate is embarrassed for having been caught playing with a doll.

"Put it away," I say, and Tate comes back with a quintessential childish reply.

"You put *your* doll away," he says, hands on hips, tongue thrust out at me. It startles me. It's not like Tate to act this way. Tate is my good boy, the kind and obedient one. I wonder what's gotten into him.

But before I can answer, Will does so for me. "Tate," he says, voice stern. "Do as your mother says and put your toy away. Right now," he says, "or your mother won't play with you."

Having no choice, Tate picks the doll up by a single leg and carries her upside down to his bedroom. Through the floors, I hear the thump of her plastic head hitting the hardwood.

When he returns, Tate chants, "Statue game, statue game," over and over again until I'm forced to admit that I don't know what this statue game is. That I've never played it before, that I've never heard of it.

It's then that he snaps and calls me a liar. "Mommy is a liar!" is what he screams, taking my breath away. He says, "Yes, you do!" as his crocodile tears turn to real tears. "You do know what it is, you liar."

I should reprimand him, I know. But I'm speechless and stunned. For the next few seconds, I can't find the words to speak as

Tate scampers from the room, bare feet sliding on the wooden floors. Before I can catch my breath, he's gone. In the next room, I hear his body drop to the ground. He's thrown himself down somewhere, as limp as the doll. I do nothing.

Will steps closer, his hand brushing the hair from my eyes. I close my eyes and lean into his touch. "Maybe a warm bath would help you relax?" he suggests, and it's only then that I remember I haven't showered today. That instead I'm wet through from the run in the rain. My clothes, my hair have yet to completely dry. There's a smell to me. It's not a good one.

"Take your time," Will tells me. "Tate and I will be fine. I'll take care of this," he says, and I feel grateful for that. That Will will clean up this mess I've made with Tate. By the time I return from my bath, everything will be as good as new.

On the way upstairs I call back to Tate that we'll play something just as soon as I'm through. "Okay, buddy?" I ask, leaning over the banister where I see him, body thrown across the arm of the sofa, tears seeping into the marigold fabric. If he hears me, he makes no reply.

Beneath my feet, the steps creak. Upstairs in the hall, I find the sheets stripped from the beds, just where I left them. I'll replace them later, put them back on the beds just as dirty as they were when I took them off.

The darkness of the outside world seeps into the home, making it hard to believe it's not the middle of the night. I flip a light in the hallway on, but then just as quickly turn it off, on the off chance that someone is standing in the street, staring through the windows at Will, Tate and me.

Mouse

Not long after they brought Bert the guinea pig home, he started getting fat. So fat that he could barely move. He spent his days laid out, flat on his big belly like a parachute. Her father and Fake Mom told Mouse she was feeding him too many carrots. That was why he was getting fat. But Mouse couldn't help herself. Bert loved those carrots. He made a squealing sound every time Mouse brought him some. Even though she knew she shouldn't, she kept on feeding him the carrots.

But then one day, Bert gave birth to babies. That was how Mouse knew that Bert wasn't a boy after all, but that he was a girl, because she knew enough to know that boys don't have babies. Those babies must have already been inside Bert when they got her from the pet store. Mouse wasn't sure how to take care of guinea pig babies, but it didn't matter because none of those babies survived. Not a single one.

Mouse cried. She didn't like to see anything get hurt. She didn't like to see anything die.

Mouse told her real mom what happened to Bert's babies. She told her what those babies looked like when they were born and how hard it was for Bert to get those babies out of her insides. She asked her mother how those babies got inside of Bert, but Mouse's real mom didn't say. She asked her father, too. He told her he'd tell her another day, when she was older. But Mouse didn't want to know another day. She wanted to know that day.

Fake Mom told her that it was probably Bert's fault those babies died, because Bert didn't take care of them like a good mom should. But Mouse's father said to her in private that it wasn't really Bert's fault, because Bert probably just didn't know any better because she had never been a mom before. And sometimes these things happen for no reason at all.

They scooped up what was left of the babies and buried them in one big hole in the backyard. Mouse laid a carrot on top, just in case they would have liked carrots as much as Bert liked carrots.

But Mouse saw the look on Fake Mom's

face. She was happy those babies were dead. Mouse thought that maybe Fake Mom had something to do with Bert's babies dying. Because she didn't like having one rodent in the house, let alone five or six. She said that to Mouse all the time.

Mouse couldn't help but think that it was Fake Mom who made Bert's babies die, rather than Bert. But she didn't dare say this because she guessed there'd be hell to pay for that, too.

Mouse learned a lot about animals from watching them through her bedroom window. She'd sit on the window seat and stare out into the trees that surrounded her house. There were lots of trees in the yard, which meant lots of animals. Because, as Mouse knew from the books she read, the trees had things that animals needed, like shelter and food. The trees made the animals come. Mouse was thankful for the trees.

Mouse learned how the animals got along with one another. She learned what they ate. She learned that they all had a way of protecting themselves from the mean animals who wanted to hurt them. The rabbits, for example, ran real fast. They also had a way of snaking around the yard, never going in a straight line, which made it hard for the neighbor's cat to catch up with them. Mouse played that out in her bedroom sometimes. She ran in a zigzag, leaping from desk to bed, pretending that someone or something was coming at her from behind and she was trying to get away.

Other animals, Mouse saw, used camouflage. They blended right into their surroundings. Brown squirrels on brown trees, white rabbits in white snow. Mouse tried that, too. She dressed in her red-and-pink-striped shirt, lay on her rag rug, which was also red and striped. There she made believe she was invisible on account of her camouflage, that if someone came into the room they'd step right on her because they couldn't see her lying here.

Other animals played dead or fought back. Still others came out only at night so they wouldn't be seen. Mouse never saw those animals. She was asleep when they came out. But in the morning, Mouse would see their tracks across the snow or dirt. That's how she'd know they'd been there.

Mouse tried that, too. She tried to be nocturnal.

She left her bedroom, and tiptoed around her house when she thought her father and Fake Mom were asleep. Her father and Fake

Mom slept in her father's room on the first floor. Mouse didn't like how Fake Mom slept in her father's bed. Because that was her father's bed, not Fake Mom's. Fake Mom should get her own bed, in her own bedroom, in her own house. That's what Mouse thought.

But the night Mouse was nocturnal, Fake Mom was not asleep in her father's bed. That's how she knew that Fake Mom didn't always sleep, that sometimes she was nocturnal, too. Because sometimes she stood at the kitchen counter with not one light on, talking to herself, though never anything sensible, but just a bunch of poppycock. Mouse said nothing at all when she found Fake Mom awake like that, but quietly turned and tiptoed back the way she came from and went to sleep.

Of all the animals, Mouse liked the birds the best, because there were so many different kinds of birds. Mouse liked that they mainly all got along, all except for the hawk who tried to eat the rest of them, which she didn't think was nice.

But Mouse also thought that was kind of how people are, how they mainly get along except for a few who try to hurt everyone else.

Mouse decided that she didn't like the

hawk, because the hawk was ruthless and sneaky and mean. It didn't care what it ate, even if it was baby birds. Especially, sometimes, if it was baby birds because they didn't have it in them to fight back. They were an easy target. The hawk had good eyesight, too. Even when you didn't think it was watching, it was, like it had eyes on the back of its head.

In time Mouse came to think of Fake Mom a little bit like that hawk. Because she started picking on Mouse more and more when her father went to his other office, or when he was talking on the phone behind the closed door. Fake Mom knew that Mouse was like one of those baby birds who couldn't defend herself in the same way a mom or dad bird could. It wasn't as if Fake Mom tried to eat Mouse like the hawks tried to eat the baby birds. This was different, more subtle. Bumping Mouse with her elbow when she passed by. Stealing the last of the Salerno Butter Cookies from Mouse's plate. Saying, at every chance she could, how much she hated mice. How mice are dirty little rodents.

Mouse and her father spent a lot of time together before Fake Mom arrived. He taught her how to play catch, how to throw a curveball, how to slide into second base with a pop-up slide. They watched old black-and-white movies together. They played games, *Monopoly* and card games and chess. They even had their very own made-up game that didn't have a name, just one of those things they came up with on a rainy afternoon. They'd stand in the living room, spin in circles until they were both dizzy. When they stopped, they froze in place, holding whatever silly position they landed in. The first to move was the loser, which was usually Mouse's father because he moved on purpose so that Mouse could win, same as he did with *Monopoly* and chess.

Mouse and her father liked to go camping. When the weather was nice they'd load their tent and supplies into the back of her father's car and drive into the woods. There, Mouse would help her father pitch the tent and gather sticks for a campfire. They'd roast marshmallows over the fire. Mouse liked it best when they were crispy and brown on the outside, but mushy and white inside.

But Fake Mom didn't like for Mouse and her father to go camping. Because when they did, they were gone all night. Fake Mom didn't like to be left alone. She wanted Mouse's father home with her. When she saw Mouse and her father in the garage, gathering up the tent and the sleeping bags, she'd press in close to him in that way that made Mouse uncomfortable. She'd lay her hand on Mouse's dad's chest and nuzzle her nose into his neck like she was smelling it. Fake Mom would hug and kiss him, and tell Mouse's father how lonely she was when he was away, how she got scared at night when she was the only one home.

Mouse's father would put the tent away, tell Mouse, *Another time.* But Mouse was a smart girl. She knew that *Another time* really meant *Never.*

SADIE

I step into an exam room to find Officer Berg waiting for me.

He isn't sitting on the exam table when I come in, as other patients would do. Instead, he ambles around the room, tinkering with things. He lifts the lids off the sundry jars, steps on the foot pedal of the stainless-steel garbage.

As I watch, he helps himself to a pair of latex gloves, and I say, "Those aren't free, you know."

Officer Berg stuffs the gloves back into the cardboard box, saying, "You caught me," as he goes on to explain how his grandson likes to make balloons with them.

"You're not feeling well, Officer?" I ask as I close the door behind myself and reach for his file, only to find the plastic box where we leave them empty. My question is rhetorical, it seems. It comes to me quite quickly then that Officer Berg is feeling fine. That he doesn't have an appointment, but that he's here to speak with me.

This isn't an exam but rather an interrogation.

"I thought we could finish our conversation," he says. He looks more tired today than he did before, the last time I saw him, when he was already tired. His skin is raw from the winter weather, windblown and red. I think that it's from all that time spent outdoors, watching the ferry come and go.

There have been more police than usual around the island, detectives from the mainland trying to step on Officer Berg's toes. I wonder what he thinks of that. The last time there was a murder on the island it was 1985. It was gory and ghastly and still unsolved. Crimes against property are frequent; crimes against persons rare. Officer Berg doesn't want to end up with another cold case when the investigation is through. He needs to find someone to pin this murder on.

"Which conversation is that?" I ask, as I set myself down on the swivel stool. It's a decision I regret at once because Officer Berg stands two feet above me now. I'm forced to look up to him like a child.

He says, "The one we began in your car the other day," and I feel a glimmer of hope for the first time in days because I now have the evidence on my phone to prove I didn't argue with Morgan Baines the day Mr. Nilsson says I did. I was here at the clinic that day.

I say to Officer Berg, "I told you already, I didn't know Morgan. We never spoke. Isn't it possible that Mr. Nilsson is mistaken? He is getting on in years," I remind him.

"Of course it's possible, Dr. Foust," he begins, but I stop him there. I'm not interested in his theories when I have proof.

"You told me that the incident between Morgan and me happened on December first. A Friday," I say as I retrieve my cell phone from the pocket of my smock. I open the photos app and swipe across each image until I find the one I'm looking for.

"The thing is that on December first," I say when I find it, "I was here at the clinic, working all day. I couldn't have been with Morgan because I can't be in two places at one time, can I?" I ask, my words rightfully smug.

I hand him my phone so he can see for himself what I'm talking about. The photograph of the clinic's dry-erase calendar where Emma has written my name, scheduling me for a nine-hour shift on Friday, December first.

Officer Berg looks it over. There's this moment of hesitation before the realization sets in. He gives in. He nods. He drops to the edge of the exam table, eyes locked on the photograph. He rubs at the deep trenches of his forehead, mouth tugging down at the corners into a frown.

I would feel sorry for him, if he wasn't trying to pin Morgan's murder on me.

"You've looked into her husband, of course," I say, and only then do his eyes rise back up to mine, "and his ex-wife."

"What makes you say that?" he asks. Either he's a good liar or he seriously hasn't considered that Jeffrey Baines killed his wife. I don't know which I find more disconcerting.

"It just seems like that's a good place to start. Domestic violence is a major cause of death for women these days, isn't it, Officer?" I ask.

"More than half of women murdered die at the hands of a romantic partner, yes," he confirms. "If that's what you're asking."

"It is," I say. "Isn't that a good-enough reason to question her husband?"

"Mr. Baines has an alibi. He was out of the country, as you know, at the time of the murder. There's proof of that, Dr. Foust. Video surveillance of Mr. Baines in Tokyo.

His name on the airplane's manifest the following day. Hotel records."

"There are other ways," I say, but he doesn't take the bait. He says instead that in cases of domestic violence, quite often men fight with their fists while women are the first to reach for a weapon.

When I say nothing, he tells me, "Don't you know, Doctor? Women aren't always the victim. They can be the perpetrator as well. Though men are often stigmatized as wife beaters, it works both ways. In fact, new studies suggest that women initiate more than half the violence in volatile relationships. And jealousy is the cause of most homicides in the United States."

I don't know what that's supposed to mean.

"Anyway," he says, "I didn't come to talk about Jeffrey Baines, or his marriage. I came to talk about you, Dr. Foust."

But I don't want to talk about myself.

"Mr. Baines was married before," I say, and he looks skeptically at me and tells me he knows. "Have you considered she might have done this? Jeffrey's ex?"

"I have an idea," he says. "How about if I ask the questions for a change, Dr. Foust, and you answer?"

"I've already answered your question," I

remind him. And besides, I, too, like Jeffrey, had an alibi at the time of Morgan's death. I was at home with Will.

Officer Berg rises from the end of the exam table. "You were with a patient when I arrived this morning. I had a few minutes to visit with Emma at the front desk," he tells me. "Emma used to go to school with my youngest. We go quite a bit back," and he explains in his usual blathering way how Emma and his daughter, Amy, were friends for many years and that he and his wife were in turn friends with Emma's mother and father.

He gets to the point. "I spoke to Emma while you were finishing up with your patient. I wanted to be sure I'd dotted my *i*'s and crossed my *t*'s, and it just so happened that I hadn't. Because when I was speaking to Emma I saw for myself the same thing you just showed me. And I asked Emma about it, Dr. Foust. Just to be sure. Because we all make mistakes, don't we?"

I tell him, "I don't know what you mean."

But I feel my body tense up regardless. My boldness start to wane.

"I wanted to be sure that the schedule hadn't been changed. So I asked Emma about it. It was a long shot, of course, expecting her to remember anything that happened a week or two ago. Except that she did, because that day was unique. Emma's daughter had gotten sick at school and needed to be picked up. Stomach flu," he says. "She'd thrown up at recess. Emma is a single mother, you know; she needed to go. Except that what Emma remembers from that day is it was bedlam here at the clinic. A backlog of patients waiting to be seen. She couldn't leave."

I rise to my feet. "This essentially describes every day here, Officer. We see nearly everyone who lives here on the island. Not to mention that cold and flu season is in full swing. I don't know why this would be unique."

"Because that day, Dr. Foust," he says, "even though your name was on the schedule, you weren't here the whole day. There's this gap in the middle where neither Joyce nor Emma can account for your whereabouts. What Emma remembers is you stepping out for lunch just after noon, and arriving back somewhere in the vicinity of three p.m."

It comes as a swift punch to my gut. "That's a lie," I say, words curt. Because that didn't happen. I swell with anger. Certainly Emma has mixed up her dates. Perhaps it was Thursday, November thirtieth, that her daughter was sick, a day that Dr. Sanders was scheduled to work and not me.

But before I can suggest this to the officer, he says, "Three patients were rescheduled. Four chose to wait. And Emma's daughter? She sat on a chair in the nurse's office until the end of the school day. Because Emma was here, making excuses for your absence."

"That's not what happened," I tell him.

"You have proof to the contrary?" Officer Berg asks, which of course I don't. Nothing concrete.

"You could call the school," I manage to think up just then. "Check with the school nurse to see which day Emma's daughter was sick. Because I'd bet my life on it, Officer. It wasn't December first."

The look he gives me is leery. He says nothing.

"I'm a good doctor" is all I can think in that moment to say. "I've saved many lives, Officer. More than you know," and I think of all those people who would no longer be alive if it wasn't for me. Those with gunshot wounds to vital organs, in diabetic comas and respiratory distress. I say it again. "I'm a good doctor."

"Your work ethic isn't what concerns me,

Doctor," he says. "What I'm trying to get at is that on the afternoon of the first, between the hours of twelve and three, your whereabouts are unaccounted for. You have no alibi. Now, I'm not saying you had anything to do with Morgan's murder or that you are somehow an unfit physician. What I'm saying is that there seems to be some ill will between you and Mrs. Baines, some sort of hostility that needs explaining, as do your lies. It's the cover-up, Dr. Foust, that's often worse than the crime. So why don't you just tell me. Just go on and tell me what happened that afternoon between you and Mrs. Baines," he says.

I cross my arms against my chest. There's nothing to say.

"Let me let you in on a little secret," he says in response to my silence. "This is a small island and stories spread quick. Lots of loose lips."

"I don't know what that has to do with anything."

He says, "Let's just say that yours wouldn't be the first husband who ever had eyes for Mrs. Baines."

And then he offers a flinty stare, waiting for some response, for me to become indignant.

I won't give in.

I swallow hard. I force my hands behind me; they've begun to shake.

"Will and I are happily married. Madly in love," I say, forcing my eyes on his. Will and I were madly in love, once. It's a half-truth, not a lie.

The lie comes next. "Will has never had eyes for any woman but me."

Officer Berg smiles. But it's a tight-lipped smile. A smile that says he knows better than to believe this. "Well," he says, careful with his words. "Mr. Foust is a very lucky man. You're both lucky. Happy marriages these days are a rare bird." He raises his left hand to show me the bare ring finger. "Married twice," he confesses, "divorced twice. No more weddings for me. Anyhow," he says, "maybe I misinterpreted what they said."

My willpower isn't strong. I know I shouldn't and yet I do. I take the bait.

"What who said?" I ask.

He tells me, "The mothers at the school pickup line. They stand in clusters outside the gate, waiting for their kids to be released. They like to talk, to gossip, as I'm sure you know. For most, it's the only adult conversation they have all day until their husbands come home from work."

It strikes me as a very misogynistic thing

to say. That women gossip, that husbands work. I wonder what Officer Berg thinks of Will's and my arrangement. I don't ask. He goes on to say, "It's just that, when I questioned them, they alluded to the fact that your husband and Mrs. Baines were quite — What's the word they used?" he thinks aloud, deciding, "*Chummy.* Yes, that's it. Chummy. He said that they were quite chummy."

My reply is immediate. "You've met him. Will is outgoing, easy to get along with. Everyone likes him. This doesn't surprise me."

"No?" he asks. "Because the details," he tells me, "surprised me a bit. The way these women said they would stand close, their conversations hushed, whispering words so that no one else could hear. One of the women had a picture."

"She took a picture of Will and Morgan?" I interject, incredulous. Not only is she gossiping about my husband, but she's taking photos of him — for what purpose?

"Calm down, Dr. Foust," he says, though it's patronizing the way he says it. On the surface, I am calm, though inside my heart is racing. "She took a picture of her son coming out of school. He'd received the Principal's Award," he explains, finding the photo that this woman shared and showing it to me. Her son stands in the foreground. Maybe ten years old, a mop of flaxen hair that hangs into his eyes, his winter coat unzipped, shoe untied. In his hands he holds a certificate that reads Principal's Award, a big deal in elementary school, though it shouldn't be. Because by the end of the year everyone gets one. But for the kids, it's a big deal. The boy's grin is wide. He's proud of his certificate.

My eyes move to the background. There stand Will and Morgan, just as Officer Berg described. They stand close in a way that makes my stomach churn. He's turned toward her, facing her, his hand on her arm. There's sadness on her face, in her eyes. It's plain to see. His torso is bent at the waist so that he slopes into her by twenty or thirty degrees. His face is only inches from hers. His lips are parted, eyes locked on hers.

He's speaking to her, telling her something.

What was Will telling her when this picture was taken?

What was he saying that he had to be standing so close to say it?

"Looks a little suspect, if you ask me," Officer Berg says, snatching the photograph from me.

"I didn't ask," I think aloud, getting angry, unable to stop the words that come next.

"I saw you," I remember just then. "I saw you put something into the Nilssons' mailbox, Officer. Twice. It was money," I say. An indictment.

Officer Berg remains composed. "How did you know it was money?"

"I was curious," I tell him. "I watched you. After you left, I went to see."

"Mail fraud is a federal crime. It carries a hefty penalty, Dr. Foust. Up to five years in prison, a steep fine."

"But this wasn't mail, was it? Mail goes through the postal service. This didn't. You put it there. Which, in and of itself, is a crime, I believe."

To this, he says nothing.

"What was it, Officer? A kickback, hush money?" Because there seems no other logical explanation why Officer Berg would secretly place an envelope of bills in the Nilssons' mailbox, and all at once, puzzle pieces drop into place.

"Did you pay Mr. Nilsson to lie?" I ask, dismayed. "To say he saw me when he didn't?"

Because without a murderer, Officer Berg needed only a scapegoat, someone to blame for the crime of killing Morgan Baines.

He chose me.

Berg leans against the countertop. He wrings his hands before him. I take a deep breath and gather myself, spinning the conversation in a different direction. "How much does obstruction of justice go for these days?" I ask.

"Pardon me?"

I make sure my question is clear this time. "How much did you pay Mr. Nilsson to lie for you?" I ask.

A beat of silence passes by. All the while he watches me, surprise turning to sadness. "I almost wish that was the case, Doctor," he says, lowering his head. "But no. Unfortunately not. The Nilssons have fallen on hard times. They're nearly broke. Their son got in some trouble, and George and Poppy spent half their savings to help him out. Now there's talk that the city might take their home if George can't find a way to pay his municipal taxes on time. Poor George," he sighs. "But George is a proud man. It'd kill him to ask for help. I keep my donations anonymous, so it doesn't feel like a handout. I'd appreciate it if you didn't say anything," he says.

He takes a step closer to me and says, "Look, Dr. Foust. Between you and me, I don't think you're capable of murder. But the truth is that spouses don't always make the most viable alibis. They're subject to bias; there's a motive to lie. The fact that you and your husband both claim you were at home when Morgan was killed isn't an impenetrable alibi. A prosecutor may see right through that. Add to that witness statements, and we have ourselves a bit of a problem."

I say nothing.

"If you help me, I will do everything I can to help you."

"What do you want from me?" I ask.

He says, "The truth."

But I've already told him the truth. "I've been nothing but honest with you," I say.

"You're certain of that?" he asks.

I tell him I am. He stares awhile.

And then, in time, he tips his hat at me, and he leaves.

SADIE

At night I find it hard to sleep. I spend most of the restless night awake, on alert, waiting for Imogen to creep into the bedroom. Every sound worries me, thinking it's the opening of a bedroom door, footsteps padding across the floor. It's not. It's just the house showing its age: water through pipes, the furnace quickly dying. I try to talk myself down, reminding myself that Imogen only came into our room the one time because of something I'd done. It wasn't unprovoked. I tell myself she wouldn't come again, but that doesn't come close to allaying my concerns.

I'm also thinking about the photograph Officer Berg showed to me. I wonder if, in the photograph, Will was consoling Morgan because she was already sad? Or if Will had said or done something to make her sad?

What power would my husband have over this woman to make her sad?

In time, morning comes. Will goes to start breakfast. I wait upstairs as Imogen, just down the hall, gets ready for school. I hear her moving about before she clomps down the stairs, her feet heavy and embittered, spiteful.

Downstairs, I hear her talking to Will. I move into the upstairs hall to listen. But, try as I might, I can't make out their words.

The front door opens and then slams closed. Imogen is gone.

Will is standing in the kitchen when I come downstairs. The boys are at the table, eating a French toast breakfast that he's made.

"Do you have a second?" Will asks, and I follow him from the room to where we can speak in private. His face is inexpressive, his long hair pulled back into a tidy bun. He leans against a wall; he holds my gaze. "I spoke to Imogen this morning," he tells me, "about your concerns," and it's his word choice that gets on my nerves. *Your,* as in *mine.* Not *our* concerns. I hope he didn't approach the conversation with Imogen that same way. Because then she'd hate me more than she already does.

"I asked her about the photograph you said you saw on her phone. I wanted to see it."

He chooses his words carefully. That's not lost on me. *You said you saw.*

"And?" I ask, sensing his hesitation. He drops his gaze. Imogen has done something, I think. "Did she show you the picture of Alice?" I ask, hoping that Will, too, saw the same thing I saw. The step stool standing vertical, far out of reach of Alice's dangling feet. The half of the night I wasn't kept awake thinking about Will and Morgan, I was thinking about this. How a woman could spring five feet from a stool and land with her head in a noose.

"I looked at her phone," Will says. "I looked through all the pictures. Three thousand of them. There was nothing there like what you described, Sadie," he says.

My blood pressure spikes. I feel hot all of a sudden and angry. "She deleted it," I say rather matter-of-factly. Because of course she did. "It was there, Will. Did you check the recently deleted folder?" I ask him, and he tells me he did check the deleted folder. It wasn't there either.

"Then she permanently deleted it," I say. "Did you ask her about it, Will?"

"I did, Sadie. I asked her what happened to the photograph. She said there never was a photograph. She couldn't believe you'd make something like this up. She was upset.

She thinks you don't like her."

At first I say nothing. I can only stare, struck dumb by his statement. I search Will's eyes.

Does he, too, think I made this up?

Tate calls to Will from the kitchen. He's hungry for more French toast. Will goes to the kitchen. I follow along. "She's lying, you know." Otto, at the table, gives me a look as I say it.

Will dishes another slice of French toast onto Tate's plate. He says nothing. His lack of a reply hits a raw nerve. Because if he doesn't believe Imogen lied, then he's suggesting I did.

"Look," he says, "let me think on this a little while, figure out what to do. I'll see if there is a way to recover deleted photos."

Will hands me my pills and I swallow them with a swig of coffee. He's dressed in a Henley and cargo pants because he teaches today, his workbag packed and waiting by the door for him to go. He's reading a new book these days. It's there, jutting out from his workbag on the floor. A hardcover with a dust jacket, the spine of which is orange.

I wonder if Erin's photograph is inside this book, too.

Tate stares sideways at me from the table.

Though I've tried to apologize, he's still mad at me for what happened the other day with the doll and his game. I decide to pick up a new Lego kit for him today. Legos make everything better.

Otto and I go. He's quieter than usual in the car. I see in his eyes that something is wrong. He knows more than he lets on, about the tension in Will's and my marriage, about Imogen. Of course he does. He's a fourteen-year-old boy. He isn't stupid. "Is everything okay?" I ask. "Anything you want to talk about?"

His reply is short. "Nope," he says, looking away.

I drive him to the dock and drop him off, searching the waterfront for Imogen. She isn't here. The ferry comes and the ferry goes. When Otto is gone, I step from my car and go to the ticket window. I purchase a ticket for the next ferry to the mainland. I get back in my car and wait. When the ferry arrives, not thirty minutes later, I drive onto the vehicle deck and put the car in Park. I turn it off and leave my car there, walking up the steps to the upper deck of the ferry. I sit on a bench and stare at the ocean as we go. It's only eight o'clock. I have nearly the whole day in front of me. Will, off to work, won't know how I've spent my time.

As the ferry makes its way across the bay, a sense of relief washes over me. Our island shrinks in size and becomes just one of many islands off the coast of Maine. As the mainland draws near, a city swells before me, with buildings and people and noise. For now, I push my thoughts of Imogen aside.

The police are looking for a scapegoat only. Officer Berg is trying to pin this murder on me. In order to clear my own name, I need to find out who killed Morgan.

I use my commute time wisely, searching my phone for information on Jeffrey Baines's ex, Courtney, who lives somewhere on the other side of the Atlantic. I don't know this for a fact, but it's easy enough to assume. She doesn't live on the island with us. And I watched the other day, after the memorial service, as she and her red Jeep boarded the ferry and disappeared out to sea.

I type "Courtney Baines" into the web browser. Finding her is almost too easy because, I come to find out, she's the superintendent of the local school district. Her name pops up nearly everywhere. It's all very professional, nothing personal. Superintendent Baines approving salary increases for teachers and staff; Superintendent Baines expressing concern over a string of recent school violence.

I find an address of the administrative building and type it into my map app. It's an eight-minute drive from the ferry terminal. I'll arrive by 8:36 a.m.

The ferry steers into the terminal and docks. I jog down the steps, from the upper deck and to my car. I start the car and, when given the go-ahead, I pull from the ferry.

I head out onto the street and follow my directions toward the school district's administrative building. The city is nothing compared to Chicago. The population is less than a hundred thousand; not one building surpasses fifteen stories tall. But it's a city nonetheless.

Located in the heart of downtown, the administrative building shows its age. I drive into the lot, search for a place to park. I don't know what I'm doing here. I don't know what I'm going to say to Superintendent Baines when we meet.

I make a plan quickly as I weave through the parking lot. I'm a concerned parent. My child is being bullied. It's not so hard to believe.

I step through the first row of cars. As I

do, I spot Courtney Baines's Jeep, the same red Jeep I watched pull from the Methodist church. I go to it, look around to be sure that I'm alone before reaching a hand up to tug on the car's handle. It's locked, of course. No one with any common sense would leave their car unlocked. I cup my hands around my eyes and peer inside, seeing nothing unusual.

I make my way into the administrative building. Once inside, a secretary greets me.

"Good morning," she says, and, "What can we do for you?" speaking in the first-person plural, though there is no *we* here. She's the only one in the room.

When I tell her I'd like to speak to the superintendent, she asks, "Do you have an appointment, ma'am?"

I don't, of course, and so I say, "This will only take a second."

She looks at me, asks, "So you don't have an appointment, then?"

I tell her no.

"I'm so sorry, but the superintendent's schedule is completely booked today. If you'd like to make an appointment for tomorrow, we can get you in." She glances at the computer screen, tells me when the superintendent will be free.

But I don't want to see the superintendent

tomorrow. I'm here now. I want to speak with her today.

"I can't do it tomorrow," I tell this secretary, making up some sob story about my sick mother and how she'll be going in for chemotherapy tomorrow. "If I could just speak with her for three minutes, tops," I say, not sure what I think I'll accomplish in three minutes — or what I think I'll accomplish at all. I just want to speak with the woman. To get a sense of the kind of person she is. Is she the kind of woman who could kill another? That's what I want to know. Would three minutes tell me this?

It doesn't matter. She shakes her head empathetically, says again how sorry she is but the superintendent's schedule is completely booked for the day.

"I can take your phone number," she suggests. She reaches for paper and a pen to jot my information down. But before I can give it to her, a woman's voice — one that's surly and astute — comes through an intercom, beckoning the secretary.

I know this voice. These days, I hear it nearly every time I close my eyes.

I'm not sorry for what I did.

The secretary pushes her chair back and stands. Before she goes, she tells me she'll be right back. She leaves and I'm alone.

My first thought is to go. To just leave. There's no chance I'm getting past the secretary without resorting to desperate measures. Times aren't desperate, not yet. I make my way toward the door. On the wall behind me is a coat hanger, a cast-iron frame with matching pegs. A black-and-white houndstooth coat hangs from it.

I recognize the coat. It belongs to Courtney Baines. It's the same coat she wore the day she slipped out of Morgan's memorial service and hurried to her car.

I take a deep breath. I listen for the sounds of voices, of footsteps. It's quiet, and so I go to the coat. Without thinking, I run my fingers along the wool. I sink my hands into the pockets. Immediately my hand clasps down on something: Courtney Baines's keys.

I stare at the keys in my hand. Five silver keys on a leather keychain.

A door opens behind me. It's immediate and swift. There was never the warning of footsteps.

I spin around with the keys still in my hand. I don't have time to put them back.

"I'm sorry to keep you waiting," the secretary says as she drops back down into her seat. There's a stack of papers in her hands now, and I'm grateful for this, because it's the papers she's looking at, not me.

I step quickly away from the coatrack. I fold the keys into my fist.

"Where were we?" she asks, and I remind her. I leave her a name and a number and ask that the superintendent call me when she has time. Neither the name nor the number belongs to me.

"Thanks for all your help," I say, turning to leave.

It isn't with forethought that I let myself into the Jeep. The thought didn't cross my mind until I was standing beside the car with the keys in my hand. But it would be ludicrous not to act on this. Because what this is is destiny. A series of events outside of my control.

I unlock the driver's door; I get into the car.

I search quickly, looking for nothing in particular, but rather insight into the woman's life. She listens to country music, stockpiles McDonald's napkins, reads *Good Housekeeping* magazine. The latest copy is there on the passenger's seat, mixed up in a pile of mail.

To my great disappointment, there's no evidence of a murderer here.

I put the keys into the ignition. I start the car.

There's a navigation panel on the dashboard. I press the menu button and, when it prompts me to, I direct the system to Home.

Not my home, but Courtney Baines's home.

And just like that I have an address on Brackett Street, less than three miles away.

I have no choice but to go.

Mouse

What Mouse came to learn about Fake Mom was that there were two sides to her, like a coin.

When Mouse's father was around, Fake Mom took an hour in the morning to get dressed, to curl her hair. She wore a pretty hot-pink lipstick and perfume. She made breakfast for Mouse and her father before he went to work. Fake Mom didn't make cereal like Mouse was used to eating, but something else like pancakes, crepes, eggs Benedict. Mouse had never had crepes or eggs Benedict before. The only breakfast her father ever made her was cereal.

When Mouse's father was around, Fake Mom spoke with a voice that was soft, sweet and warm. She called Mouse things like *Sweetie* and *Darling* and *Doll.*

You want powdered sugar on your crepes, Doll? Fake Mom would ask, holding the shaker of it in her hand, ready to douse the crepes with a heap of delicious powdered sugar, the kind that melted in Mouse's mouth. Mouse would shake her head, though she really did want that powdered sugar. But even at six years old, Mouse knew that nice things came with a price sometimes, one she didn't want to pay. She started missing her father's cold cereal, because that never came with a price, only milk and a spoon.

When Mouse's father was around, Fake Mom was kind. But Mouse's father wasn't always around. He had the kind of job where he traveled a lot. When he left on one of his business trips, he was gone for days.

Until that first time he left her with Fake Mom, Mouse had never been alone with her for long. Mouse didn't want to be left alone with her. But she didn't tell her father this because she knew how much her father loved Fake Mom. She didn't want to hurt his feelings.

Instead she held on to his arm as he said his goodbyes. She thought that if she held on real tight, he wouldn't go. Or if he did, that he'd bring her with him. She was small. She could fit in his suitcase. She wouldn't make a peep.

But he didn't do either.

I'll be back in a few days, her father promised her. He didn't tell her exactly how many was a few. He pulled his arm gently away, kissed Mouse on the forehead before he left.

You and I are going to get along just fine, Fake Mom said, stroking Mouse's brown hair with her hand. Mouse stood in the doorway, trying not to cry as Fake Mom's tacky hand tugged on her hairs from her head. She didn't think Fake Mom meant to pull her hair, but maybe she did. And either way, it made Mouse wince. She took a step forward, trying to stop her father before he could leave.

Fake Mom's hand went to Mouse's shoulder and she squeezed real tight, not letting go.

That, Mouse knew, she meant to do.

Mouse carefully raised her eyes to Fake Mom, not sure what she would find when she did. Slanted eyes, an angry stare. That was what she thought she'd see. It was neither, but rather a frightening smile, the kind that made her insides hurt. *If you know what's good for you, you will stop where you are and say goodbye to your father,* Fake Mom ordered. Mouse complied.

They watched as her father's car pulled out of the drive. They stood in the doorway as the car rounded a bend down the street.

It disappeared somewhere Mouse couldn't see. Only then did Fake Mom's grip on Mouse's shoulder lessen slightly.

As soon as he was gone from sight, Fake Mom turned mean.

In the blink of an eye, that soft, sweet, warm voice went cold.

Fake Mom turned away from the door. She slammed it closed with the bottom of her foot. She hollered at Mouse to stop looking for her father, that her father was gone.

He isn't coming back, not anytime soon. You better just deal with it, she said, before telling her to get away from the door.

Fake Mom's eyes moved around the room, looking for some transgression she could get angry about. Any transgression. She found it in Mr. Bear, Mouse's beloved brown bear who sat perched in the corner of the sofa, positioned with the remote control under his tiny furry hand. Mr. Bear was watching TV, just the same as he did every day, all the same shows that Mouse liked to watch.

But Fake Mom didn't want the bear to watch TV. She didn't want the bear anywhere she could see him. She snatched it from the corner of the sofa by a single arm, telling Mouse that she needed to put her *stupid toys* away before she threw them in the trash. She shook the living daylights out of the bear before hurling him to the ground.

Mouse looked at her beloved bear lying on the ground. He looked to Mouse like he was asleep, or maybe he was dead on account of Fake Mom shaking him so much. Even Mouse knew you weren't supposed to do that to a living thing.

Mouse knew she should shut her mouth. She knew she should do as told. But she couldn't stop herself. Without meaning for them to, words came out. *Mr. Bear isn't stupid,* she yelled as she reached for her bear, clutching him to her chest, consoling him. Mouse ran her own hand over the stuffed animal's downy fur and cooed into his ear, *Shhh. It's okay, Mr. Bear.*

Don't you talk back to me, Fake Mom said. *Your father isn't here now, and so you listen to me. I'm in charge. You pick up after yourself when I'm here, you little rodent,* she said. *Do you hear me, Mouse?* she asked right before she started to laugh.

Mouse, she called her mockingly this time. She said how much she hated mice, how they're pests. She told Mouse that they carry feces around on their feet, that they spread germs, that they make people sick.

She asked, *How'd you get a nickname like that, you dirty little rodent?*

But Mouse didn't know, and so Mouse didn't say. That made Fake Mom angry.

Do you hear me? she asked, getting down into Mouse's face. Mouse wasn't a tall girl. She was small, only about three and a half feet tall. She barely reached Fake Mom's waist, right where she tucked those pretty shirts into the waistband of her jeans. *You answer me when I ask you a question,* Fake Mom said, pointing a finger at Mouse's nose, so close that she swatted her. Whether she meant to hit her or not, Mouse didn't know, or maybe it was one of those things that happens accidentally on purpose. But it didn't matter because either way it hurt. It hurt her nose and it hurt her feelings.

I don't know why Daddy calls me that, she said honestly. *He just does.*

Are you being sassy with me, you little rodent? Don't you ever be sassy with me, Fake Mom said, grabbing Mouse by the wrist. She shook her like she had the bear, until Mouse's head and wrist hurt. Mouse tried to tug her arm away, but it only made Fake Mom hold tighter, long fingernails digging into the skin.

When she finally did let go, Mouse saw the red impression of Fake Mom's hand there on hers. There were crescent-shaped indentations in her skin from Fake Mom's fingernails.

Her eyes welled with tears because it hurt, both her head and her hand, but even more, her heart. It made her sad when Fake Mom shook her like that, and also scared. No one had ever talked to or touched Mouse like that, and Mouse didn't like it. It made a drop of pee sneak out from her insides and slide down a leg where it got absorbed in the fabric of her pants.

Fake Mom laughed when she saw Mouse's little quivering lip, the tears pooling in her eyes. She asked, *What are you going to do? Cry like a little baby? Well, isn't that just dandy,* she said. *A sassy little crybaby. How's that for an oxymoron,* she laughed, and though Mouse knew many things, she didn't know that word *oxymoron,* but she knew what *moron* meant because she heard kids call one another that at school. So that was what Mouse thought, that Fake Mom had called her a moron, which wouldn't have even been the meanest thing she did that day.

Fake Mom told Mouse to go somewhere where she couldn't see her, because she was sick of looking at her sassy, crybaby face.

And don't you come back until I tell you you can come back, she said.

Mouse carried her bear sadly up to her bedroom and gently closed the door. She laid Mr. Bear on the bed and hummed a lullaby into his ear. Then she lay down beside him and cried.

Mouse knew even then that she wouldn't tell her father what Fake Mom had said and done. She wouldn't even tell her real mom. It wasn't like her to be a tattletale, but more so, she knew how much her father loved Fake Mom. She could see it in his eyes every time he looked at her. Mouse didn't want his feelings to be hurt. Because he would be sad if he knew what Fake Mom had done, even sadder than Mouse felt. Mouse was an empathetic little girl. She didn't ever want to make anyone sad. Especially her father.

SADIE

I commit the address to memory. I get in my own car and drive to Courtney's home. I parallel park on the street, sliding easily between two cars. I step from my car. I bring Courtney's keys with me.

Ordinarily I wouldn't do something like this. But my back is to a wall.

I knock before attempting to let myself inside. No one comes to the door.

I finger the keys in my hands. It could be any one of them. I try the first key. It doesn't fit.

I glance over my shoulder, seeing a woman and her dog near the end of the park where it meets with the street. The woman is bent at the waist, cleaning the dog's mess from the snow with a plastic bag; she doesn't see me.

I fiddle with the second key. This one fits. The knob turns and the door opens, and I find myself standing in the doorway of

Courtney Baines's home. I step inside; I close the door. The interior of the house is charming. It bursts with character: arched doorways, wall niches and wooden built-ins. But it's also neglected and unloved. There isn't much in the way of *things.* The house is unkempt. Stacks of mail are strewn across the sofa, two empty coffee cups on the wooden floor. A basket of unfolded laundry waits at the base of the stairs. Kids' toys wither in the corner of the room; they haven't been played with in a while.

But there are photographs. They hang from the wall slightly askew, a layer of dust coating the top ledge of them.

I go to the pictures, nearly run my hands through the dust. But then, in the nick of time, I think of fingerprints, of *evidence,* and pull quickly back. I search my coat pockets for a pair of winter gloves and slip them on.

The photographs are of Jeffrey, Courtney and their little girl. This strikes me as odd. If Will and I had gone through with a divorce in the aftermath of his affair, I would have rid my home of photographs of him, so I wouldn't be reminded of him every day.

Not only does Courtney keep family photographs in her home, but there are wedding photographs, too. Romantic scenes of Jeffrey and her kissing. I wonder what this means. If she still has feelings for him. Is she in denial about his affair, the divorce, his remarriage? Does she think there's a chance they might get back together again, or is she only pining for the love they once had?

I wander the halls, looking in bedrooms, in bathrooms, in the kitchen. The home is three narrow floors tall, each room as Spartan as the next. In the child's bedroom, the bed is covered with woodland creatures, deer and squirrels and such. There's a rug on the floor.

Another room is an office with a desk inside. I go to the desk, pull the drawers out at random. I'm not looking for anything in particular. But there are things I see, like felt-tip pens and reams of paper and a box of stationery.

I return downstairs. I open and close the refrigerator door. I peel back a curtain and look outside to be sure no one is coming.

How long do I have until Courtney realizes that her keys are missing?

I sit lightly on the sofa, paying attention not to disturb the careful order of things. I thumb through the mail, keeping it in the same order that it is, in case there's some method to the madness that I can't see. It's bills and junk mail mostly. But there are other things, too, like legal petitions. State of Maine is typed across the envelopes, and that's what makes me peel the flaps back, slide the documents out with my gloved hands.

I was never very good with legalese, but words like *child endangerment* and *immediate physical custody* leap out at me. It takes but a minute to realize Jeffrey and Morgan Baines were attempting to gain full custody of his and Courtney's child.

The thought of someone taking Otto or Tate from me makes me instantly upset. If someone tried to take my children from me, I don't know what I'd do.

But if I know one thing, it's that getting between a woman and her child will never end well.

I slide the documents back into their envelopes, but not before first snapping a photo of them on my phone. I put the mail back how it was. I rise from the sofa and slip back out the front door, done with my search for now. I'm not sure if what I found is enough to suspect Courtney of murder. But it is enough to raise questions.

I drop the keys into a zipped compartment in my bag. I'll dispose of them later.

People lose their keys all the time, don't they? It's not such an unusual thing.

I'm halfway to my car parked on the other side of the street when my cell phone rings. I pull it from my bag and answer the call. "Mrs. Foust?" the caller asks. Not everyone knows that I'm a doctor.

"Yes," I say. "This is she."

The woman on the other end of the line informs me that she's calling from the high school. My mind goes instinctively to Otto. I think of our short exchange as we drove to the dock this morning. Something was bothering him but he wouldn't say what. Was he trying to tell me something?

"I tried calling your husband first," the woman tells me, "but I got his voice mail." I look at my watch. Will is in the middle of a lecture. "I wanted to check on Imogen. Her teachers marked her absent today. Did someone forget to call her in?" this woman asks, and — feeling relieved the call isn't about Otto — I sigh and tell her no, that Imogen must be playing hooky. I won't bother myself with making up lies for Imogen's absence.

Her tone isn't kind. She explains to me that Imogen is required to be in school and that she is quickly closing in on the number of unexcused absences allowed in a school year.

"It's your responsibility, Mrs. Foust, to make sure Imogen is in school," she says. A meeting will be scheduled with Will and me, Imogen, teachers and administrators. An intervention of sorts. If that fails, the school will be forced to follow legal protocol.

I end the call and climb into my car. Before I pull out, I send Imogen a text. *Where are you?* I ask. I don't expect a reply. And yet one comes. *Find me*, it reads.

Imogen is playing games with me.

A series of photos comes next. Headstones, a bleak landscape, a bottle of prescription pills. They're Alice's old pills, used to manage fibromyalgia pain. An antidepressant that doubles as a nerve blocker. Her name is on the label.

I have to get to Imogen before she does something stupid with them, before she makes a careless decision she can't take back. I speed away, forcing the legal documents I found in Courtney's home out of my mind for now. Finding Morgan's killer will have to wait.

Mouse

Fake Mom didn't give Mouse any dinner that night, but Mouse heard her down in the kitchen, making something for herself. She smelled the scent of it coming up to the second floor through the floor vents, slipping under the crack of Mouse's bedroom door. Mouse didn't know what it was, but the smell of it got her tummy rumbling in a good way. She wanted to eat. But she couldn't because Fake Mom never offered to share.

By bedtime, Mouse was hungry. But she knew better than to ask about dinner because Fake Mom told her explicitly that she did not want to see her until she said it was okay. And Fake Mom never said it was okay.

As the sun set and the sky went dark, Mouse tried to ignore the hunger pangs. She heard Fake Mom moving about downstairs for a long time after she had finished eating, doing the dishes, watching TV.

But then the house got quiet.

A door closed, and Fake Mom, Mouse thought, had gone to bed.

Mouse pulled her own door open an inch. She stood just behind the door, holding her breath, making sure that the house stayed quiet. That Fake Mom hadn't only gone in the bedroom to come right back out again. That Fake Mom wasn't trying to trick her into coming down.

Mouse knew she should go to sleep. She tried going to sleep. She wanted to go to sleep.

But she was hungry.

And, even worse than that, she had to use the bathroom, which was downstairs. Mouse had to go really badly. She'd been holding it for a long time, and didn't think she could hold it much longer. She certainly couldn't hold it the whole night. But she also didn't want to have an accident in her bedroom because she was six years old, too old to have accidents in her bedroom.

But Mouse wasn't allowed to leave her bedroom until Fake Mom said she could. So she pressed her legs together real tight and willed the pee to stay inside of her. She used her hand, too, squeezing it into her crotch like a cork, thinking that might hold the pee in.

But in time her stomach hurt too much, because she was both hungry and had to pee.

Mouse coaxed herself into going downstairs. It wasn't easy to do. Mouse wasn't the kind of girl who liked breaking rules. Mouse was the kind of girl who liked to obey the rules, to never get in trouble.

But, she remembered, Fake Mom didn't tell her she had to go to her bedroom. Mouse had decided to do that. What Fake Mom had said was *Go somewhere I can't see you.* If Fake Mom was asleep, Mouse decided, then she wouldn't see Mouse on the first floor, not unless she could see with her eyes closed. In which case, Mouse wasn't breaking any rules.

Mouse opened her bedroom door all the way. It groaned as she did and Mouse felt her insides freeze, wondering if that would be enough to rouse Fake Mom from sleep. She counted to fifty in her head, and then, when the house stayed quiet, no sign of Fake Mom waking up, she went.

Mouse crept down the steps. Across the living room. She tiptoed toward the kitchen. Just shy of the kitchen was a hallway that veered off and toward the room Fake Mom was in. Mouse peeked around the corner, trying to get a glimpse of the door, grateful to find it all the way closed.

Mouse had to pee more than she was hungry. She went toward the bathroom first. But the bathroom was just a few feet away from her father and Fake Mom's room, and that made Mouse scared as heck. She skated her socks to that bathroom door, trying hard not to lift her feet from the floor.

The house was darkish. Not entirely dark, but Mouse had to feel the walls with her fingertips so as not to run into anything. Mouse wasn't afraid of the dark. She was the kind of kid who wasn't afraid of much of anything because she had always felt safe in her home. Or at least she had before Fake Mom arrived. Now she no longer felt safe, though the darkness was the least of her concerns.

Mouse made it to the bathroom.

Inside, she gently closed the door. She left the light switch off, so that it was pitch black in the bathroom. There was no window there, no scant amount of moonlight sneaking in through glass, no night-light.

Mouse felt her way to the toilet. By the grace of God, the lid was already up. She didn't have to risk making noise by lifting it.

Mouse pulled her pants down to her knees. She set herself so slowly on the toilet seat that it made her thighs burn. Mouse tried to control her urine, to let it seep out slowly and inaudibly. But she'd been holding it for so long. She couldn't control the way it came out. And so instead, once the floodgates were open, the urine came rushing out of her in a way that was turbulent and loud. Mouse was sure everyone on the whole block might've heard it, but especially Fake Mom, who was right across the hall in her father's bed.

Mouse's heart started to race. Her hands got all sweaty. Her knees trembled so that, when she was done on the toilet and pulling her pants back up to her bony hips, it made it hard to stand. Her own legs wobbled like the desk legs when she tried to climb over it to avoid the hot lava spewing into her bedroom. They shook beneath her, threatening to break.

With her bladder emptied and her pants pulled up, Mouse stood there in the bathroom for a long while with the lights turned off. She didn't bother washing her hands. But she wanted to make sure the sound of her pee hadn't woken Fake Mom before she left the bathroom. Because if Fake Mom was in the hall, then she would see Mouse.

Mouse counted to three hundred in her

head. Then she counted another three hundred.

Only then did she leave. But Mouse didn't flush the toilet for fear of the noise it would make. She left everything inside the toilet bowl where it was, urine, toilet paper and all.

She opened the bathroom door. She skated back out into the hallway, grateful to find the bedroom door on the other side of the hall still closed tight.

In the kitchen, Mouse helped herself to a few Salerno Butter Cookies from the cabinet, and a glass of milk from the fridge. She rinsed her glass and set it in the dish rack to dry. She gathered her cookie crumbs in her hand and threw them in the trash. Because Fake Mom had also said, *You pick up after yourself when I'm here, you little rodent,* and Mouse wanted to do as she was told. She did it all in silence.

Mouse climbed the steps.

But on the way up, her nose began to tickle.

Poor Mouse had tried so hard to be quiet, to not make any noise. But a sneeze is a reflex, one of those things that happens all on its own. Like breathing and rainbows and full moons. Once it began, there was no stopping it, though Mouse tried. Oh, how Mouse tried. There, on the stairs, she cupped her hands around her nose. She pinched the bridge of her nose. She pushed her tongue all the way up to the roof of her mouth and held her breath and begged God to make it stop. Anything she could think of to stop that sneeze from coming.

But still the sneeze came.

Sadie

The space is typical for a cemetery. I drive along the narrow graveled path and park my car at the chapel. I open the car door as a gust of wind rushes in to greet me. I climb out and walk across the graded land, sliding between headstones and full-grown trees.

The plot where Alice is buried has yet to be covered with grass. It's a fresh grave, filled in with dirt and scattered with snow. There is no headstone, not until the land settles and it can be installed. For now, Alice is identifiable only by a section and lot number.

Imogen sits on her knees on the snowy earth. She hears my footsteps approaching and turns. When she looks at me, I can see that she's been crying. The black eyeliner she so painstakingly applies is smeared across her cheeks. Her eyes are red, swollen. Her lower lip trembles. She bites on it to make it stop. She doesn't want me to see her vulnerable side.

She looks suddenly younger than her sixteen years. But also damaged and angry.

"Took you fucking long enough," she says. Truth be told, there was a moment on the way here that I thought about not coming at all. I put in a call to Will to let him know about the photos Imogen sent to me, but again the call went unanswered. I was headed back to the ferry when my conscience got the better of me and I knew I had to come. The bottle of prescription pills remains closed, lying beside Imogen on the ground.

"What are you doing with those, Imogen?" I ask, and she shrugs nonchalantly.

"Figured they had to be good for something," she says. "They didn't do shit for Mom. But maybe they could help me."

"How many did you take?" I ask.

"None yet," she says, but I'm not sure I believe it. I move cautiously toward her, lean down and snatch the pills from the ground. I open the cap and look inside. There are pills still there. But how many there were to begin with, I don't know.

It's thirty degrees out at best. The wind blows through me. I raise my hood up over my head, plunge my hands into my pockets.

"You'll catch your death out here, Imogen," I say, a poor word choice given the circumstance.

Imogen doesn't wear a coat. She doesn't wear a hat or gloves. Her nose is a brilliant red. Snot drips from the tip of it, running down to her upper lip, where, as I watch, she licks it away with a tongue, reminding me that she is a child. Her cheeks are frosty patches of pink.

"I couldn't be so lucky," she says.

"You don't mean that," I say, but she does. She believes she would be better off dead.

"The school called," I tell her. "They said you're truant again."

She rolls her eyes. "No shit."

"What are you doing here, Imogen?" I ask, though the answer is mostly clear. "You're supposed to be at school."

She shrugs, says, "I didn't feel like going. Besides. You're not my mom. You can't tell me what to do." She wipes at her eyes with a shirtsleeve. Her jeans are black and torn, her shirt a red-and-black button-up, unbuttoned, over a black T-shirt.

She says to me, "You told Will about the picture. You shouldn't have told him." She presses up from the ground and rises to her feet. It strikes me again just how tall Imogen is, tall enough to look down on me.

"Why not?" I ask, and she tells me, "He's

not my fucking father. Besides, that was for your eyes only."

"I didn't know it was a secret," I say. I take a step backward, regaining my personal space. "You didn't ask me not to tell him. If you had, I wouldn't have mentioned it," I lie. She rolls her eyes. She knows I'm lying.

There's a moment of silence. Imogen is quiet, brooding. I wonder what exactly she's brought me here to do. I keep my defenses up. I don't trust her.

"Did you ever know your father?" I ask. I take another step back, bumping into the trunk of a tree. She glares at me. "I was just thinking how tall you are. Your mother wasn't very tall, was she? Will isn't particularly tall. Your height must come from your father's side."

I'm babbling now. I can hear it as well as she.

She claims not to know him. And yet she admits to knowing his name, the name of his wife, that he has three kids. She's seen his house. She describes it for me. She knows that he has an optometry practice. That he wears glasses. That his oldest, Elizabeth, who's fifteen, is just seven months younger than she is. Imogen is smart enough to know what this means.

"He told my mom he wasn't ready to be a

dad." But clearly he was. He just didn't want to be Imogen's dad.

I see it in her expression: the dismissal still stings.

"Thing is," she says, "if my mom wasn't so fucking lonely all the time, she might've wanted to live. If he'd have loved her back, maybe she would have stuck around a while longer. She was so tired of putting on a happy face all the fucking time. Miserable on the inside, but happy out. Nobody believed she was in pain. Even her doctors. They didn't believe her. There was no way for her to prove that she hurt. Nothing to make her feel better. All those fucking naysayers. They're the ones who killed her."

"Fibromyalgia," I tell her. "It's a terribly frustrating thing. I wish I would have known your mother. I might've been able to help."

"Bullshit," she says. "Nobody could help."

"I would have tried. I would have done anything I could to help."

Her laugh is a cackle. "You're not as smart as you want everyone to think. You and me have a little something in common," she says, changing tack.

"Oh yeah?" I ask, disbelieving. "What's that?"

I can't think of one thing Imogen and I would ever have in common.

She comes closer. "You and me," she says, pointing between us, "we're both fucked up."

I swallow against a lump in my throat. She takes a step closer, points her finger at me, stabs me in the chest with it. The bark of the tree presses against my back and I can't move. Her voice is loud now, losing control.

"You think you can come in here and take her place. Sleep in her bed. Wear her fucking clothes. You are not her. You will never be her!" she screams.

"Imogen," I whisper. "I never . . ." I start to say as her head drops into her hands. Imogen begins to sob, her entire body surging like ocean waves. "I would never try to take your mother's place," I say in a muted tone.

The air around us is bitter and bleak. I brace myself as a gust of wind comes rushing past and through me. I watch as Imogen's dyed black hair swirls around her, her skin raw and red instead of its usual pale white.

I go to reach a hand out to her, to pat her arm, to console her. She draws swiftly away from the touch.

She drops her arms. She raises her eyes. She screams at me then, the suddenness of her statement, the emptiness of her eyes startling me. I pull back.

"She couldn't do it. She wanted to. But she just couldn't get herself to do it. She froze up. She looked at me. She was crying. She begged me. *Help me, Imogen,*" she seethes, saliva coming from her mouth, building in the corners of her lips. She leaves it there.

I shake my head, confused. What is she saying? "She wanted you to help with her pain?" I ask. "She wanted you to make the pain go away?"

She shakes her head; she laughs. "You're an idiot," she says.

She composes herself then. She wipes at the spit, stands upright. Looks at me defiantly, more like the Imogen I know now, no longer in pieces.

"No." She continues undaunted. "She didn't want me to help her live. She wanted me to help her *die.*"

My breath leaves me. I think of the step stool, out of reach of Alice's feet.

"What did you do, Imogen?" I force out.

"You have no idea," she says, her tone chilling. "You have no fucking clue what it was like to hear her cry in the middle of the night. Pain so bad at times that she couldn't help but scream. She'd get all excited about some new doctor, some new treatment, only for it to fucking fail again, her hopes dashed. It was hopeless. She wasn't getting any better. She was never going to get any better. No one should have to live like that."

Imogen, with tears dripping from her eyes, starts at the beginning and goes through it again. The day began like any other day. She woke up; she went to school. Most days Alice would be waiting in the foyer when she came home. But that day Alice wasn't there. Imogen called out to her. There was no reply. She started searching the house when a light in the attic lured her to the third floor. There she found her mother standing on the step stool, the noose around her neck. She'd been that way for hours. Alice's knees were shaking in fear, in exhaustion, as she tried in vain to will herself from the stool. She'd left a note. It was lying on the floor. Imogen has it memorized. *You know as well as I do how hard this is for me,* the note read. *It's nothing you did. It doesn't mean I don't love you. But I can't keep living this double life.* Not a Dear John note but Alice's suicide note, which Imogen picked up and slipped into the pocket of her sweatshirt that day. Imogen at first tried to talk her down from the stool. To convince her to stay and live. But Alice was decided. She just couldn't take the plunge. *Help me,*

Imogen, she begged.

Imogen looks straight at me, says, "I yanked that fucking stool from beneath her feet. It wasn't easy. But I closed my eyes and I yanked for dear life. And I ran. I ran faster than I have in my life. I ran to my bedroom. I hid beneath the fucking pillow. And I screamed my head off so I didn't have to hear her die."

I catch my breath. It was not suicide, not exactly, but also not as malevolent as I once believed. It was assisted dying, like those doctors who slip a lethal dose of sleeping pills to a terminal patient to let them die of their own accord.

I've never been that kind of doctor.

My job is to help patients live, not to help them die.

I stare at Imogen openmouthed, thinking: What kind of person could do that? What kind of person could grab ahold of the step stool and pull, knowing full well what the outcome would be?

It would take a certain kind of person to do what Imogen has done. To act on impulse and not think of what comes next. She just as easily could have called for help in that moment that she pulled. She just as easily could have cut down her mother's noose.

Before me she cries; she convulses. I can't

stand to think what she's been through, what she's seen. No sixteen-year-old should ever be put in such a position.

Shame on Alice, I think.

But also: shame on Imogen.

"You did the only thing you knew to do," I lie, saying it only to console her because I think she needs to be consoled. I reach hesitantly for her, and for a split second, she lets me. Only a second.

But as I wrap my arms gingerly around her, scared and just barely touching, it strikes me that I'm holding a murderer, even if the reasons for it were justified in her mind. But she is repentant and grieving now. For the first time Imogen displays an emotion other than anger. I've never seen her like this before.

But then, true to form, as if she can hear the thoughts in my mind, she stands suddenly upright. She swats at her tears with a sleeve. Her eyes are vacant, her face deadpan.

She gives me a sudden shove in the shoulder. There's nothing gentle about it. It's rough, hostile. The spot where her fingertips press violently into the thoracic outlet, that tender place between the collarbone and ribs, stings. I fall a step back, tripping over a rock behind me, as she says, "Get your fucking hands off me or I'll do to you what I did to her."

The rock is large enough that I lose my balance completely and fall to my seat on the wet, snowy earth.

I stifle a gasp. I stare up at her, standing over me, unspeaking. There's nothing to say.

She finds a fallen stick on the ground. She grabs for it, coming at me quickly like she might hit me again. I flinch, throw my hands inadvertently to my head to protect it.

This time, she steps down.

Instead of hitting me, Imogen screams so loudly that I feel the earth beneath me shake, "Leave!" the single word drawn out.

I find my feet. As I walk quickly away, terrified to turn my back to her though I do, I hear her call me a freak for good measure, as if the death threat wasn't enough.

Sadie

I drive home that night, pulling onto our street, heading up the hill. It was hours ago that I left Imogen at the cemetery. It was early afternoon then and now it's night. It's dark outside. Time has gotten away from me. There are two calls on my phone that I've missed, both from Will, wondering where I am. When I see him, I'll tell him how I spent the day. About my conversation with Imogen at the cemetery. But I won't tell him everything because what would he think of me if he knew I stole a woman's keys and broke into her home?

As I drive past the vacant house next door to ours, my eyes go to it. It's dark as it should be; the lights won't turn on for a while still. Snow accumulates on the drive while others have been shoveled clean. It's so obvious no one lives there now.

I'm overcome with a sudden urge to see for myself what's inside that home.

It's not that I think anyone is there now. But my mind can't get past one thing. If someone had come to the island to murder Morgan late at night, there would have been no ferry back to the mainland. He or she would have had to spend the night here with us.

And what better place to stay than a vacant home, where no one would know.

It's not a murderer I'm looking for as I leave my car in my own driveway and sneak across the snow-covered lawn. It's evidence that someone has been here.

I look over my shoulder as I go, wondering if anyone is watching me, if anyone knows I'm here. There are footprints in the snow. I follow them.

The house next door is a cottage. It's small. I go to the door first and knock. I don't expect anyone to answer. But I do it anyway because it would be foolish not to. No one answers the door. And so I press my face to the glass and look in. I see nothing out of the ordinary. Just a living room with furniture draped in plastic.

I make my way around the periphery of the home. I don't know what I'm looking for. But I'm looking for something. A way in, conceivably, and sure enough — after a little searching, a few failed attempts, dwindling hope — it's there.

The window well cover on the back of the home is not secure.

I lift it up and it easily gives. I dust off the snow. I remove the whole thing and set it aside, hands trembling as I do.

I carefully lower myself down into the window well. It's a tight fit. I have to contort my body in an odd way to get to the window. The screen, when I get to it, is torn. Not just a little, but enough for a whole body to get through. I tug on the window behind it, thinking it won't give — surely this can't be so easy — but to my surprise it does.

The window into the basement is unlocked.

What kind of homeowner doesn't secure their home before leaving for the winter?

I press my body through the window, feet first. I climb awkwardly into the dark basement. My head passes through a cobweb as my feet land on concrete. The cobweb sticks to my hair, though it's the least of my concerns. There are so many more things to fear than this. My heart pounds inside of my chest as I glance around the basement to be certain I'm alone.

I don't see anyone. But it's too dark to really know.

I inch across the basement, find the unfinished steps to the first floor. I go slowly, dragging my feet, careful not to make any noise as I climb. At the top of the steps, I set my hand on a door handle. My hand is sweaty, shaking, and suddenly I'm wondering why I thought it was such a good idea to come here. But I've come this far. I can't go back. I have to know.

I turn the knob, press the door open and step onto the first floor.

I'm terrified. I don't know who's here, if anyone is here. I can't call out for fear that someone might hear me. But as I creep around the first floor of the home, the reality is hard to ignore. I see no one, but there are signs of life everywhere. It's dark outside and in; I have to use the flashlight on my phone to see. I discover an indentation in the plastic that covers a living room chair, as if someone sat down there. A piano seat is pulled out, sheet music on the rack. There are crumbs on the coffee table.

The cottage is a single-story home. I make my way down the dark, narrow hall, tiptoeing so I don't make a sound. I hold my breath as I go, taking short, shallow breaths only when I have to, only when the burn of carbon dioxide in my lungs is more than I can bear.

I come to the first room and look inside,

shining my flashlight along the four walls. The room is small, a bedroom that has been converted into a sewing room. A seamstress lives here.

The next room is a small bedroom crammed with ornate antique furniture that's buried beneath plastic. The carpeting is thick, plush. My feet sink into it, and I feel guilty for wearing my shoes inside, as if that's the worst of my infractions. But there's also breaking and entering.

I leave that room and step into the largest bedroom of the three, the master bedroom. The room is spacious in comparison. But that's not the reason my eyes do a double take when I step inside.

The sun has set outside. Only a faint hint of blue creeps in through the windows. The blue hour, it's called, when the residual sunlight takes on a blue tone and turns the world to blue.

I shine my flashlight into the room. I see the ceiling fan, the blades of which are formed into the shape of palm leaves. The ceiling is a trey ceiling. And I've seen it before.

I've dreamed of this room. I dreamed of myself lying in this bed, or a bed similar to this, hot and sweating beneath that fan, in the crevasse that is still in the center of the bed. I stared at the fan, willed it to move, to push a gust of cold air onto my hot body. But it didn't because the next thing I knew I was standing beside the bed watching myself sleep.

This bed, unlike the other furniture in the house, isn't covered with plastic. The plastic that should be on the bed lies in a heap on the floor, on the other side of the bed.

Someone has been sleeping in this bed.

Someone was here.

I don't bother with the basement window well this time. I head straight out the front door. I close it behind myself, the light in the living room flicking on as I leave.

As I run back home, I convince myself that the ceiling, the bed, the fan weren't the very same as they were in my dream. They were similar, yes, but not the same. Dreams have a way of fading fast, and so the true details of it were likely gone before I ever opened my eyes.

And besides, it was dark in that cottage. I didn't get a good look at the ceiling or the fan.

But without a shred of doubt, the plastic was pulled from that bed. The homeowner covered the bed just like all the other furniture in the home. But then someone else removed it.

Once in my own yard, I look at my cell phone. It's dying. The battery percentage hovers at around 2 percent. I put in a call to Officer Berg. He'll be able to search for fingerprints and figure out who's been there. God willing, he'll find Morgan's murderer.

I have a minute or two at best before the phone dies. My call goes to voice mail. I leave a quick message. I ask him to call me. I don't tell him why.

Before I can end the call, my cell phone dies.

I drop the dead phone into my coat pocket. I step across the driveway, moving toward the porch. The house, from the outside, is dark. Will has forgotten to leave the porch light on for me. There are lights on inside, but I can't see the boys from here.

There's a warmness about the house. Heat spews from the vents, gray against the near blackness of night. Outside, it's windy and cold. The snow that's fallen over the last few days blows about, creating snowdrifts on the driveways and streets. The sky is clear. There's no threat of snow tonight but forecasters are going hog wild about a storm that's to arrive late tomorrow. The first substantial storm of the season.

A noise from behind startles me. It's a

grinding noise, something discordant. I'm not ten feet from the porch when I hear it. I spin and at first I don't see him because his body is blocked by a formidable tree. But then he steps forward, away from the tree, and I see him moving slowly, deliberately, a snow shovel dragging behind him and through the street.

The snow shovel is the sound that I hear. Metal on concrete. He holds on to the shaft of the shovel with a gloved hand, scraping the blade across the street. Jeffrey Baines.

Will is in the house making dinner. The kitchen is in the rear of the house. He wouldn't hear me if I screamed.

At the end of our drive, Jeffrey turns and makes his way toward me. There's something bedraggled about him. His hair stands on end. His dark eyes are rheumy and red-rimmed. His glasses are missing. He looks nothing like the suave, affable man I met at the memorial service the other day. Rather, he looks like something the cat dragged in.

My eyes go to the shovel. It's the kind of thing that's versatile. It has dual purposes because not only could he hit me over the head and kill me with it, but he could use it to bury my body.

Does he know I watched him and Courtney at the memorial service? That I was in her home?

I'm stricken with a sudden terror: What if there are security cameras inside her home? One of those fancy new doorbells with the camera to let you know who's at your door when you're not there?

"Jeffrey," I say, inching backward. I try not to let my imagination get the best of me. There could be so many reasons why he's here. So many other reasons than the one I imagine.

"You're home," I say because I've only just realized that his home is no longer a crime scene.

Jeffrey senses my fear. He hears it in my voice; he sees it in my body language. My feet retreat, though it's inappreciable the way that they do. But still, his eyes drop to them. He sees the movement. Like a dog, he can smell my fear.

"I was shoveling my drive. I saw you pull up," he says, and I reply, "Oh," realizing that if he did — if he saw my car pull into the drive fifteen or twenty minutes ago — he may have seen me force my way into the home next door. He may have heard the voice mail I left for Officer Berg.

"Where's your daughter?" I ask.

He says, "She's busy with her toys." As I look across the street, I see a light on in a second-floor window. The shades are open, the bedroom bright. I see the little girl's silhouette as she bounds around the room with a teddy bear on her shoulders, as if giving him a piggyback ride. The little girl is laughing to herself, to her bear. It only adds to my unease. I think of what Jeffrey confessed, about how she and Morgan weren't close.

Is she glad her stepmother is dead? Is she glad to have her father back all to herself?

"I told her I'd be just a minute. Am I keeping you from something?" Jeffrey asks, running a gloved hand through his hair. He wears gloves, but no hat. I wonder why, if he's bundled up to shovel snow, he wears no hat. Do the gloves serve another purpose than keeping his hands warm?

"Will," I tell him, inching backward, "is inside. The boys. I haven't been home all day" is what I say, though it's a pathetic excuse, and I know as I say it that I should have said something more tangible than that, more concrete, more decisive. *Dinner is ready.*

But my reply is wishy-washy at best, and it's Jeffrey instead who is decisive as he says, "Your husband isn't home."

"Of course he's home," I say, but as I turn back to the house, I take in the darkness of our home, the lack of movement, the sudden realization that Will's car isn't in the drive. How did I not realize when I pulled in and parked that Will's car wasn't here? I wasn't paying attention when I got home. I was too caught up in other things to notice.

I sink my hand into my pocket. I'll call Will, find out where he is. I'll beg him to come home.

But the nonresponsive black screen reminds me: my cell phone is dead.

My face must whiten. Jeffrey asks, "Is everything all right, Sadie?" and as tears of panic prick my eyes, I force them back. I swallow against a lump in my throat and say, "Yes, yes, of course. Everything is fine."

I lie and tell him then, "It's been a busy day. It slipped my mind. Will had to pick our son up from a friend's house. He lives just around the block," I say, pointing arbitrarily behind me, hoping Jeffrey might assume it will be a quick trip for Will. There and back in a matter of minutes. He'll be home soon.

I tell Jeffrey, "I better get inside. Get dinner started. It was nice seeing you," though I'm terrified to turn my back to him. But there's no other way. I have to get inside, close the door and lock the dead bolt behind myself. I hear the dogs bark. I see their faces pressed to the windows that flank the front door. But where they are, trapped inside, they can't help me.

I hold my breath as I turn. I grind my teeth, steel myself for the agonizing pain of the square blade against the back of my head.

I've barely moved when a heavy, gloved hand falls to my shoulder.

"There was something I wanted to ask before you go."

The tone of his voice is oppressive as he says it. It's chilling. Between my legs, my pelvic floor weakens. Urine seeps into my underpants. I turn reluctantly back to see the shovel rooted to the ground now. Jeffrey leans on it, uses it for support, tugs on the cuff of his gloves to be sure they're on tight.

"Yes?" I ask, voice quivering.

Headlights veer this way and that through the trees. But they're in the distance, moving away instead of drawing near.

Where is Will?

Jeffrey tells me that he's come to talk to me about his dead wife.

"What about her?" I ask, feeling the way my vocal cords vibrate inside of me.

But as he starts to speak of Morgan, a change becomes him. His stance shifts. He gets choked up speaking about Morgan. It's subtle, a film that covers his eyes, rather than tears that run from his nose and across his cheeks. His eyes glisten in the moonlight, in the glow off the snow.

"There was something wrong with Morgan," he tells me. "Something had her upset. Scared even. She wouldn't say what. Did she tell you?"

It seems so obvious, so transparent. I shouldn't have to be the one to put the idea in his head. But maybe the idea is already there, and he's only being cunning. Sly as a fox. I think he or his ex-wife had something to do with it. The proof is in her house, in her own confession. But how can I admit to eavesdropping on their conversation in the church sanctuary, to breaking into the other woman's house and going through her things?

I shake my head. "Morgan told me nothing."

I don't tell him that I didn't know Morgan well enough for her to tell me why she was upset. I don't tell him that I didn't know Morgan at all. It's easy to see that communication wasn't Jeffrey and Morgan's strong suit because if it was, one would think he'd already know that Morgan and I weren't friends.

I ask, "What makes you think she was

scared?"

"My company has gone global recently. I've spent a great deal of time overseas. It's been difficult, to say the least. The time away from home, yes, but more so the difficulties of learning a new language, culture, of trying to integrate into a foreign country, succeed at my job. I'd been under a lot of pressure. I don't know why I'm telling you all this," he says, apologetically almost. There's a hint of vulnerability there.

I don't know what to say to him, and so I say nothing.

I don't know why he's telling me this either.

Jeffrey goes on. "I guess I'm just trying to say that I was overworked, burned out. Completely overwhelmed with work. I haven't been home much lately. Any time spent at home was often beset with jet lag. But something had Morgan upset. I asked what it was. But she was selfless to a fault. She wouldn't tell me. She said it was nothing. She wouldn't burden me with whatever it was. I asked," he admits, saddened. "But I didn't ask enough."

It strikes me that this isn't the face of a madman I see.

This is the face of a grieving widower.

"I heard on the news that there were

threatening notes," I say.

"There were," he says. "Yes. The police found notes in our home."

"Forgive me for saying this. It's not my business. But your ex-wife. Is it possible she had hard feelings about a new woman in your life?"

"You think Courtney did this? Sent the threats, murdered Morgan." He shakes his head, says decisively, "No. No way. Courtney is the type to fly off the handle, yes. She's rash. She has a temper. She does stupid things."

And then he goes on to tell me about some night Courtney came to the island with the sole intent of stealing her own child. She almost got away with it, because she had keys to the home Jeffrey and Morgan shared since it was once her own home. After everyone was asleep, she let herself in, went to their daughter's bedroom, roused the little girl from sleep. It was Morgan who caught them as they were making their way back outside. Courtney had plane tickets in her possession; she'd somehow already gotten a passport for their girl. She planned to leave the country with their daughter. "Morgan wanted to fight for full custody. She didn't think Courtney was fit to parent."

The day at the memorial service comes

back to me.

My temper got the best of me.

I was angry.

You can't blame me for trying to take back what's mine.

I'm not sorry she's dead.

Were these words double-edged? Maybe not a confession to murder, but rather a reference to the night she tried to steal her own child.

"Taking a child away from her mother . . ." I say, letting my voice trail off. What that is — taking a child from her mother — is motive to kill. Except I don't say it like that. Instead I say, "If anyone ever got between me and my children, I'd be beside myself."

Jeffrey is resolute. "Courtney isn't a murderer," he says. "And the threats Morgan received were . . ." But he stops there, unable to put into words what exactly the threats were.

"What did the notes say?" I ask hesitantly. I'm not sure I want to know.

There were three notes, Jeffrey tells me. He doesn't know for certain when they arrived, but he has his assumptions on one. He had watched Morgan make her way to the mailbox one afternoon. It was a Saturday a month or so ago. He was home. He watched out the window as Morgan went down the drive.

"I had a habit of staring at her when she didn't know I was watching," he confesses. "It's because of how beautiful she was. It was easy to do. Morgan," he tells me, smiling nostalgically at the memory of his wife, "was easy on the eyes. Everyone thought so," and I remember what Officer Berg said about the men in town having eyes for her. About Will having eyes for her.

"Yes," I reply. "She was lovely," changing the way I think of him because I can see in his eyes just how much he loved Morgan.

That day Jeffrey says that he watched as she bent at the waist, as she stretched a hand into the box to retrieve the mail, as she made the long walk back up the driveway, thumbing through the mail as she went.

Halfway up the drive, Morgan came to a standstill. Her hand went to her mouth. By the time she made it inside, she was as white as a ghost. She brushed past Jeffrey in the doorway, shaking as she did so. He asked what was wrong, what she found in the mail that made her so upset. Morgan said only bills — that the insurance company hadn't covered a recent doctor appointment. The balance left for them to pay was highway robbery.

It should have been covered, she snapped,

marching up the stairs with the mail in her hand.

Where are you going? he called up the stairs after her.

To call the insurance company, she said, but she went into the bedroom and closed the door.

Everything about Morgan changed that day. The changes were subtle. Another person might not have noticed. There was a sudden propensity toward closing the curtains as soon as the sky turned dark. A restlessness about his wife that hadn't been there before.

The notes that the police found were all different, slipped in between the box spring and the mattress that Jeffrey and Morgan slept on. She'd intentionally hidden them from him.

I ask what they said, and he tells me.

You know nothing.

Tell anyone and die.

I'm watching you.

A chill runs up my spine. My eyes go to the windows of homes on the street.

Is someone watching us?

"Did Morgan and your ex-wife get along?" I ask, though even I can see these threats make no sense coming from an aggrieved ex-wife. These threats have nothing to do with a woman trying to reclaim the rights to her child. These threats have nothing to do with a husband hoping for a life insurance payout in the wake of his wife's death.

These threats are something else.

All this time, I've been wrong.

"I'm telling you," Jeffrey says, becoming agitated now. Gone is the man who stood smiling at his wife's memorial service. He's come undone. Jeffrey is unwavering now as he states emphatically, "Courtney had nothing to do with this. Someone else was threatening my wife. Someone else wanted her dead."

I see this now.

Sadie

"I used the last of the milk on the mac and cheese," Will tells me when he gets home, stepping into the house only minutes after me. Tate is with him. He skips merrily through the front door, tells Will to count to twenty and then come find him. He dashes off to hide as Will unpacks a handful of items from a grocery sack on the counter.

Will winks at me, admits, "I told him we'd play hide-and-seek if he went with me without a fuss." Will can turn any errand into an adventure.

In the Crock-Pot cooks Will's famous macaroni and cheese. The table is set for five, as if Will bullishly believes Imogen will be home. He carries the gallon of milk he's just brought home to the table, and fills the empty glasses in turn.

"Where's Otto?" I ask, and Will tells me, "Upstairs."

"He didn't go with you and Tate?"

Will shakes his head no. "It was only a quick trip for milk," he says.

Will turns to me, seeing me perhaps only then for the first time since he's arrived home.

"What's the matter, Sadie?" he asks, setting the milk on the edge of the table and coming to me. "You're shaking like a leaf."

He wraps his arms around me and I want to tell him about the discoveries of the day. I want to get it all off my chest, but for whatever reason, instead I say, "It's nothing," blaming low blood sugar for the reason I shake. I'll tell him later, when Tate isn't just in the next room waiting for Will to find him. "I didn't have time for lunch."

"You can't keep doing this to yourself, Sadie," Will tenderly reprimands.

Will reaches into the pantry and finds a cookie for me to eat. He hands it to me, saying, "Just don't tell the boys about this. No cookies before dinner. It'll ruin your appetite." He smiles as he says it and, even after everything we've been through, I can't help but smile back, because he's still there: the Will I fell in love with.

I stare at him awhile. My husband is handsome. His long hair is pulled back and all I can see is that chiseled jawline, the sharp angles of his cheeks, and those beguiling eyes.

But then I remember suddenly what Officer Berg said about Will having eyes for Morgan and I wonder if it's true. My own smile slips from my face and I feel regret begin to brew inside.

I can be cold, I know. Glacial even. I've been told this before. I often think that I was the one to push Will into the arms of another woman. If only I had been more affectionate, more sensitive, more vulnerable. More happy. But in my life, all I've known is an inherent sadness.

When I was twelve, my father complained about how moody I could be. High as a kite one day, sad the next. He blamed the imminence of my teenage years. I experimented with my clothing as kids that age tend to do. I was desperate to figure out who I was. He said there were days I screamed at him to stop calling me Sadie because I hated the name Sadie. I wanted to change my name, be someone else, anyone other than me. There were times I was snarky, times I was kind. Times I was outgoing, times I was shy. I could be the bully just as easily as be bullied.

Perhaps it was only teenage rebellion. The need for self-discovery. The surge of hormones. But my then-therapist didn't think so. She diagnosed me with bipolar disorder. I was on mood stabilizers, antidepressants, antipsychotics. None of it helped. The tipping point came later, after I'd met and married Will, after I'd started my family and my career.

Tate calls out from another room, "Come find me, Daddy!" and Will excuses himself, kissing me slowly before he leaves. I don't pull away. I let him this time. He cradles my face in his hands. As his soft lips brush over mine, I feel something I haven't felt in a long time. I want Will to keep kissing me.

But Tate calls for him again and Will leaves.

I head upstairs to change. Alone in the bedroom, I wonder if it's possible to dream about a place you've never been. I take my question to the internet. The answer isn't so easy to find about places. But it is about faces. The internet claims that all the faces we ever see in our dreams are faces we've seen in real life.

It's been over an hour, but Officer Berg still hasn't called me back.

I change into a pair of pajamas. I drop my clothes into the laundry basket. The basket itself overflows, and I think that after everything Will does for us, the least I can do is a single load of laundry. I'm too tired to do it now, but first thing tomorrow, before work, I'll throw in a load.

We eat dinner together. As expected, Imogen is a no-show. I pick at my food, hardly able to eat. "Penny for your thoughts," Will says toward the end of dinner, and only then do I realize I spent the entirety of our meal staring off into space.

I apologize to him and blame fatigue.

Will does the dishes. Tate disappears to watch TV. Otto plods out of the room and up the stairs. I hear his bedroom door close from this distance, and only then, when I'm certain they're both out of earshot, do I tell Will what Imogen said to me in the cemetery. I don't hesitate because, if I do, I might just lose the nerve. I'm not sure how Will is going to respond.

"I saw Imogen today," I begin. I fill him in on the details: how the school called, how I found her alone at the cemetery. How there were pills with her. I don't dance around the words.

"She was angry but unreserved. We got to talking. She told me, Will, that she yanked that stool out from Alice's feet the day she died," I tell him. "If it wasn't for Imogen, Alice might still be alive."

I feel like a snitch as I say it, but it's my

duty, my responsibility to tell Will. Imogen is a disturbed child. She needs help. Will needs to know what she has done so that we can get her the help she deserves.

Will goes stiff at first. He's at the sink with his back toward me. But his posture turns suddenly vertical. A dish slips from his wet hands, falls to the sink. It doesn't break, but the sound of a dinner plate hitting the sink is loud. I jump because of it. Will curses.

In the moments of silence that follow, I offer, "I'm sorry, Will. I'm so sorry," as I reach out to touch his shoulder.

He turns off the water and comes to face me, drying his hands on a towel. His eyebrows are lowered, his face flat. "She's messing with you," he says incontrovertibly. The denial is clear as day.

"How do you know?" I ask, though I know that what Imogen told me is true. I was there. I heard her.

"She wouldn't do that," he says, meaning that Imogen wouldn't help her mother die. But the truth of the matter, I think, is that Will doesn't want to believe she would.

"How can you be sure?" I ask, reminding him that we barely know this girl. That she's been a part of our life for only a few long weeks now. We have no idea who Imogen is.

"There's this animosity between you and

her," he says, as if this is something petty, something trivial, and not a matter of life and death. "Can't you see she's doing it intentionally because it gets a rise out of you?" he asks, and it's true that Imogen doesn't behave this way toward Will and the boys. But that doesn't change things. There's another side to Imogen that Will can't see.

My mind goes back to our conversation this morning about the photograph on Imogen's phone. "Were you able to recover the photos?" I ask, thinking that if he found the photo, there will be proof. He'll be able to see it the way that I do.

He shakes his head, tells me no. "If there was a photograph, it's gone," he says.

His carefully chosen words come as a punch to the gut. *If* there was a photograph. Unlike me, Will isn't sure there ever was.

"You don't believe me?" I ask, feeling bruised.

He doesn't answer right away. He thinks before he speaks.

In time he says, expression thoughtful, arms folded across his chest, "You don't like Imogen, Sadie. She scares you, you said. You didn't want to come here to Maine and now you want to leave. I think you're looking for a reason —" he begins, tiptoeing around the truth. His truth. That I'm manufacturing a reason to leave.

I hold up a hand and stop him there. I don't need to hear the rest of it.

Only one thing matters. He doesn't believe me.

I turn on my heels and leave.

SADIE

I spend another fitful night tossing and turning in bed. I give up the fight near five a.m., slipping quietly from bed. The dogs follow, eager for an early breakfast. On the way out the bedroom door, I reach for the basket of laundry I left for myself to clean, hoisting it onto my hip. I walk out into the hall and down the stairs.

I'm approaching the landing when my bare foot lands on something sharp. It pokes me in the arch of the foot. I sink to the steps to see what it is, resting the laundry basket on my lap. In the darkness, I feel blindly for the offending item, taking it into the light of the kitchen to see.

It's a small silver pendant on a rope chain, now coiled into a mound on my palm. It's broken, snipped in two, not at the clasp but in the center of the chain so that it can't go back together again. Such a shame, I think.

I clasp the pendant between my fingers,

seeing the one side is blank.

I turn it over. There on the other side is an *M*. Someone's initial. But whose?

Hers isn't the first name that comes to me. I think of Michelle and Mandy and Maggie first. But then the thought arrives, crashing into me, knocking the wind from my lungs.

M for Morgan.

In the kitchen, I suck in a sudden breath. Did this necklace belong to Morgan?

I can't say with certainty. But my gut thinks so.

What is this necklace doing in our home? There isn't one good reason why it would be here. Only reasons I'm too scared to consider.

I leave it on the countertop as I turn and make my way to the laundry room. My hands are shaking now, though I tell myself it's theoretical only. The necklace could just as well belong to a Michelle as it could to Morgan Baines. Perhaps Otto has a crush on some girl and planned to give this to her. A girl named Michelle.

I upend the basket and laundry comes tumbling out, onto the floor. I sort the laundry, separating the whites and colors into piles. I grab armfuls of it and begin thrusting it into the washing machine, too much for one load. But I want to get it done. I'm not thinking about any one thing in particular, but many things, though the thing that trumps all is how I can get my marriage, my family back on track. Because there was once a time when we were happy.

Maine was meant to be a new beginning, a fresh start. Instead it's had a detrimental effect on everything, Will's and my marriage, our family, our lives. It's time that we leave, go somewhere else. Not back to Chicago, but somewhere new. We'll sell the house, take Imogen with us. I think of the places we could go. So many possibilities. If only I could convince Will to leave.

My mind is elsewhere. Not on the laundry. I'm hardly paying attention to the laundry at all, other than this quick, forceful way I jam things into the machine, slamming the door. I reach for the detergent on a nearby shelf. Only then do I catch sight of a few items that sneaked out, escapees from the washing machine lying limp on the laundry room floor.

I bend at the waist to retrieve them, ready to open the door and toss them back in. It's as I stand, hunched over, scooping the items into my hand, that I see it. At first I blame the poor lighting in the laundry room for what it is I see. Blood, on a washcloth. A great deal of it, though I try to convince myself that it's not blood.

The stain is not as red as it is brown because of the way blood changes color as it dries. But still, it's blood. Undeniably blood.

It would be so easy to say that Will had cut himself shaving, or that Tate had a scraped knee or — worst-case scenario — Otto or Imogen had picked up a habit of cutting, save for the amount of blood on the washcloth. Not merely a dab or a trace, but the washcloth has been wet through with it and allowed to dry.

I turn it over in my hand. The blood has seeped to both sides.

I let the washcloth fall from my hand.

My heart is in my throat. I feel like I can't breathe. I've had the wind knocked out of me.

As I rise quickly to stand upright, gravity forces all the blood in me down to my trunk. There it pools, unable to make its way back up to my brain. I become dizzy. Everything before me begins to blur. Black specks dance before my eyes. I set my hand on the wall to balance myself before lowering slowly to the ground. There I sit beside the bloodstained washcloth, seeing only it, not touching it now because of all the DNA evidence that must be on that rag.

Morgan's blood, her murderer's fingerprints. And now mine.

I don't know how this bloody washcloth came to be inside our home. But someone put it here. The options are few.

I lose track of time. I sit on the laundry room floor long enough that I hear the sound of footsteps galloping around the house. Light, quick footsteps that belong to Tate, followed by heavier ones: Will.

I should be in the shower by now. I should be getting ready for work. Will calls out quietly for me, having noticed that I wasn't in bed. "Sadie?"

"Coming," I call breathlessly back, wanting to show Will the washcloth, but unable to when Tate is there in the kitchen with him. I hear Tate's voice asking for French toast. The washcloth will have to wait. I hide it for now in the laundry room, laying it flat beneath the washing machine where no one will find it. It's stiff with blood and easily slides under.

I rise from the floor reluctantly and creep back into the kitchen, overcome with the urge to vomit. There is a killer living in my home with me.

"Where've you been?" Will asks at seeing me, and all I can tell him is "Laundry." It comes out in one forced breath, and then again, the black specks appear, dancing before my eyes.

"Why?" he asks, and I tell him there was so much.

"You didn't need to do that. I would have done it," he says, reaching into the refrigerator for the milk and eggs. I know he would have done the laundry eventually. He always does.

"I was trying to help," I say.

"You don't look good," he tells me as my hand holds tightly to the crown molding of the door so that I don't fall. I want so much to tell him about the blood-soaked washcloth that someone left in the laundry basket. But I don't because of Tate.

I hear Tate, beside him, ask, "What's wrong with Mommy?"

"I don't feel good. Stomach flu," I force out. Will comes to me, presses a hand to my forehead. I'm not running a fever. But I feel hot and clammy nonetheless. "I need to go lie down," I say, clutching my stomach as I leave. On the way upstairs, the bile inside me begins to rise and I find myself rushing to the bathroom.

Mouse

Mouse froze. She waited for the sound of the bedroom door to open on the first floor, for Fake Mom to come for her. Mouse was scared, though it wasn't Mouse's fault she'd made noise. It's not like a person can stop themselves from sneezing.

Her legs shook in fear. Her teeth began to chatter, though Mouse wasn't cold.

How long she waited there on the stairs, Mouse didn't know. She counted to nearly three hundred in her head, except she lost count twice and had to start all over again.

When Fake Mom didn't come, Mouse thought maybe she hadn't heard her. Maybe Fake Mom had slept right through that sneeze. She didn't know how that was possible — the sneeze had been loud — but Mouse thanked her lucky stars if she had.

She continued on to her bedroom and climbed into bed. There, in her bed, she talked to her real mom, same as she always did. She told her what Fake Mom had done, how she had hurt Mouse and Mr. Bear. She told her real mom how she was scared and how she wanted her father to come home. She said it in her head. Mouse's father always told her that she could talk to her real mom whenever she wanted to. He told her that wherever she was, her mom was listening. And so Mouse did. She talked to her all the time.

Though sometimes Mouse took it a step further than that and imagined what her real mom said back. Sometimes she imagined her real mom was in the very same room as her and they were having a conversation, like the kind of conversations Mouse had with her father, the kind where he talked back. But that was only pretend. Because there was no way to know what her mother said back, but it made Mouse feel less alone.

For a while Mouse felt satisfied knowing her stomach had food, though three butter cookies was hardly the same thing as dinner. Mouse knew those cookies wouldn't hold her off for long. But for now, at least, she was content.

For now, she could sleep.

Sadie

"How are you feeling?" Will leans over me and asks.

"Not good," I tell him, still tasting vomit in my mouth.

He tells me to sleep in, that he'll call me in sick to work, and drive the boys to school. He sits on the edge of the bed, stroking my hair, and I want to tell him about the washcloth. But I can't say anything to Will when the kids are just down the hall getting ready for school. Through our open door, I see them move in and out of the bedrooms, the bathroom.

But then a moment comes when they're all in their bedrooms, out of earshot, and I think that I'll come right out and say it.

"Will," I say, the words on my lips, but then, just like that, Tate comes scampering into the bedroom, asking Will to help him find his favorite socks. Will grabs him by the hand, catches him before he has a

chance to jump on the bed.
"What?" Will asks, turning toward me.
I shake my head, tell him, "Never mind."
"You sure?" he asks.
"Yes," I say.
Together Will and Tate go to leave, to head to Tate's bedroom in search of the missing socks. Will glances over his shoulder as he leaves, tells me to sleep as long as I can. He pulls the door closed behind himself.
I'll tell Will later.
I hear Will, Otto, Tate and Imogen moving about in the house. From upstairs I hear ordinary, everyday conversations ensue about ham-and-cheese sandwiches and history tests. Their words come to me through the floor vents. Tate tosses out a riddle, and by God, it's Imogen who answers it, Imogen who knows that in the one-story blue house where everything is blue — blue walls, blue floor, blue desk and chairs — the stairs are not blue because there are no stairs.
"How did you know?" Tate asks her.
"I just knew."
"That's a good one, Tater Tot," Will declares, his nickname for Tate, as he tells him to find his backpack before they're late for school.
The wind outside is ferocious. It flogs the clapboard siding, threatening to tear it right

off the house. It's cold in the house now, the kind of cold that gets under the skin. I can't warm up.

"Let's get going, guys," Will calls, and I rise from the bed and stand at the door, listening as Tate noses around the coat closet for his hat and boots. I hear Imogen's voice in the foyer with them. She is riding along to the ferry with them, and I don't know why. Maybe it's only the weather's doing, but I can't help but notice the irony of it. She'll let Will drive her to the ferry, but not me.

Suddenly all I hear is feet, like the rush of animals, before the front door opens and then closes again, and the house is nearly still. The only sounds are the whistling of the furnace, the rush of water through pipes, the wind scourging the outside of our home.

It's only after they're gone that I rise from bed and leave the room. I've only just stepped into the hallway when something catches my eye. Two things actually, though it's the doll's marble-like eyes that get my attention first. It's the same doll of Tate's that I found in the foyer the other day, the one he carried roughly to his room at Will's request.

She's perched at the edge of the hallway

where the wooden floor meets the wall. She sits nicely on her bum, wearing floral leggings and a knit print. Her frizzy hair lies over her shoulders in two neat braids, hands set in her lap. Someone has found her missing shoe.

Beside the doll's feet is a pencil and paper. I go to it, reaching for the scrap of paper.

I brace myself, knowing what it is before I look. I turn the paper over in my hand, seeing exactly what I expected to see on the other side. The same crying, dismembered body as on the drawings I found in the attic. Beside the dismembered body, an angry woman clutches a knife. Charcoal blobs fill in the excess white space, tears or blood, though I don't know which. Maybe both.

I wonder if these were here early this morning when I carried the laundry down. But it was dark then; I wouldn't have seen if they were. And on the way back up, I was nauseous, running to the toilet, barely getting there in time. I wouldn't have noticed them then either.

I wonder if Will saw these things before he left. But the doll he'll have assumed was Tate's and the drawings were upside down. He wouldn't have seen the content.

These things terrify me, because I think that if they do belong to Otto, he is regressing. It's a defense mechanism, a way to cope. Taking on childish behavior to avoid facing a problem head-on. My own therapist used to say this about me, telling me I acted like a child at times when I didn't want to tackle adult issues in my life. Perhaps Otto is doing the very same thing. But why? On the surface he seems happy enough. But he's the quiet type; I never know what's going on inside his mind.

I think back on that therapist of mine. I was never very fond of her. I didn't like the way she made me feel silly and small, the way she denigrated me when I expressed my feelings. It wasn't just that. She also confused me with other patients.

Once I sank down into her leather swivel armchair and crossed my legs, took a sip of the water she always left on the table for me. She asked what had been happening lately, in that way she always did. *Tell me what's been happening.* Before I could reply, she began to counsel me on how to sever ties with some married man I was seeing, though I wasn't seeing a married man. I was married already. To Will.

I blanched in embarrassment for her other client, the one whose secrets she'd just shared.

There is no married man, I explained.

She asked, *No? You broke it off already? There was never a married man.*

I stopped seeing her soon after.

Otto had a therapist back in Chicago. We swore we'd pick up the therapy when we moved to Maine. We never did. But I think it's time we do.

I step past the doll. I go downstairs. I take the drawing with me.

A plate of French toast sits on the kitchen counter. That and a pot of coffee, keeping hot on the coffee maker's warming plate. I help myself to the coffee but I can't bring myself to eat a thing. As I lift the mug to my lips, my hands tremble, casting waves across the coffee.

Beside the plate of French toast is a note. *Feel better,* it reads, with Will's signature closing, the ever-present *XO.* He's set my pills out for me. I leave them where they are, not wanting to take them until I've gotten some food inside of me.

Out the kitchen window, I see the dogs. Will must have let them outside before he left, which is fine. They're snow dogs — huskies — in their element in weather like this. It'd be nearly impossible to get them back in before they're ready to come.

In the backyard, the wind beats through the naked trees, making their limbs bend.

It's snowing, a heavy snow. I hadn't expected so much. I'm surprised that school wasn't canceled today. But I'm also grateful for it because I need this time alone.

The snow doesn't fall vertically, because of the wind. It falls sideways instead, with abandon, forging snowdrifts across the yard. The sill of the kitchen window begins to collect with snow, burying me alive inside. I feel the weight of it on my chest. It's harder to breathe.

I take a careful sip of the coffee, noticing that the pendant necklace I left on the counter early this morning is gone. I search the floor, behind the canisters, the junk drawer where we keep random things. The necklace is nowhere. Someone has taken it. I picture it lying there how I left it, the dainty chain coiled into a mound with the *M* on top.

The fact that it's now missing only adds to my suspicion. This morning while I lay in bed, the four of them — Will, Otto, Tate and Imogen — were in the kitchen together. It would have been so easy for Imogen to slip that necklace from the countertop when no one was looking. I consider the threatening notes Morgan received. Would Imogen have sent those? Why, I wonder at first, and then just as quickly: Why not? I think of the way Imogen treats me. The way she scares me. If she could do this to me, she could just as easily do it to Morgan.

I leave the drawing where it is and carry my coffee to the laundry room. There I see that this morning, after I went back to bed, Will finished the laundry for me. The piles of clothes I left are gone. They've been replaced instead with an empty laundry basket and a clean tile floor.

I drop to my hands and knees beside the washing machine, looking beneath, grateful to find the bloodstained washcloth still there, and yet just as horrified as I was at seeing it for the first time. All the emotions come rushing back to me, and I know that I have to tell Will about this.

I leave the washcloth where it is. I go back to the kitchen to wait. I sit at the table. Otto's drawing sits six feet away, the eyes of the decapitated head staring at me. I can't stand to look at it.

I wait until nearly nine o'clock to call Will, knowing that by then he'll have taken Tate to school. He'll have dropped him off. He will be alone by now and we'll be able to speak in private.

When Will answers, he's on the ferry, heading to campus.

He asks how I'm feeling as he answers the

call. I tell him, "Not good." I hear the sound of the wind whipping around him, gusting into the handset. He's outside, standing on the outer deck of the ferry getting peppered with snow. Will could be inside in the nicely heated cabin, but he isn't. Instead he's relinquished his seat indoors for someone else, and I think that this is so classic Will, to be selfless.

"We need to talk, Will," I say, and though he tells me that it's loud on the ferry, that this isn't the best time, I say it again. "We need to talk."

"Can I call when I get to campus?" he asks. Will talks loudly through the phone, trying to counter the noise of the wind.

I say no. I tell him this is important. That this can't wait.

"What is it?" he asks, and I come outright and say that I think Imogen had something to do with Morgan's murder. His sigh is long, exasperated, but he humors me nonetheless, asking why I think this now.

"I found a bloody washcloth, Will. In the laundry. Completely saturated in blood."

From the other end of the line comes an earsplitting silence.

I go on, because he says nothing. I feel the words rattle in my throat. Before me, my hands have turned sweaty, though inside

I'm so cold I shake. I tell him how I discovered it as I was doing the laundry. How I found the washcloth and hid it beneath the washing machine because I didn't know what else to do with it.

"Where is this washcloth now?" he asks, concern in his voice.

"Still under the washing machine. The thing is, Will, I'm thinking about turning the washcloth over to Officer Berg."

"Whoa," he says. "Stop right there, Sadie. You're not making any sense. Are you sure it's blood?"

"I'm sure."

Will tries to make excuses. Maybe someone had wiped up a spill with it. Paint, mud, some mess the dogs made. "Maybe dog shit," he says, and it's so unlike Will to be crass like that. But perhaps, like me, he's scared. "Maybe one of the boys cut himself," he suggests, and he reminds me then of the time Otto was small and ran the pad of his thumb across the razor's sharp blade just to see what it would feel like, though he had been told before to never touch Daddy's razor. The razor sliced through his skin. There was a surge of blood that Otto tried to hide from us. He didn't want to get in trouble. We found bloodstained tissues packed in the garbage can, an infection festering days later on his thumb.

"This isn't the same thing as playing with razors," I tell Will. "This is far different than that. The washcloth, Will, was wet through with blood. Not a few drops of blood, but it was literally soaked. Imogen killed her," I say decisively. "She killed her and wiped herself clean with that washcloth."

"It isn't fair what you're doing to her, Sadie," he says, voice loud, and I don't know if he's yelling at me or yelling over the wind. But he's most definitely yelling. "This is a witch hunt," he says.

"Morgan's necklace was here, too," I go on. "I found it on the stairs. I stepped on it. I set it on the kitchen counter and now it's gone. Imogen took it to hide the evidence."

"Sadie," he says. "I know you don't like her. I know she hasn't taken kindly to you. But you can't keep blaming her for every little thing that goes wrong."

His choice of words strikes me as strange. *Every little thing.*

Murder is not an inconsequential thing.

"If not Imogen, then someone in this house killed her," I tell Will. "That's a given. Because how else can you explain her necklace on our floor, the bloody washcloth in the laundry. If not her, then who?" I ask, and at first the question is rhetorical. At first I ask it only to make him see that of course it was Imogen because no one else in the house is capable of murder. If she did it once — yanking that stool from beneath her mother's feet — she could do it again.

But then, in the silence that follows, my eyes come to land on Otto's angry drawing with the decapitated head and the blobs of blood. The fact that he's regressed to playing with dolls. And I think of the way my fourteen-year-old son carried a knife to school.

I draw in a sudden breath, wondering if Imogen isn't the only one in this house who is capable of murder. I don't mean for the thought to leave my head. And yet it does.

"Could it have been Otto?" I think aloud, wishing as soon as the words are out that I could take them back, put them back in my head where they belong.

"You can't be serious," Will says, and I don't want to be serious. I don't want to believe for a second that Otto could do this. But it isn't outside the realm of possibility. Because the same argument rings true: if he did it once, he could do it again.

"But what about Otto's history of violence?" I ask.

"Not a history of violence," Will insists. "Otto never hurt anyone, remember?"

"But how do you know he wouldn't have, if he hadn't been caught first? If that student hadn't turned him in, how do you know he wouldn't have hurt his classmates, Will?"

"We can't know what he would have done. But I'd like to believe our son isn't a killer," Will says. "Wouldn't you?"

Will is right. Otto never hurt any of those kids back at his old high school. But the intent was there. The motive. A weapon. He very intentionally took a knife to school. There's no telling what he might have done if his plan hadn't been thwarted in time. "How can you be so sure?"

"Because I want to believe only the best about our son. Because I won't let myself think Otto could take another life," he says, and I'm overcome with the strangest combination of fear and guilt that I don't know which prevails. Am I more scared that Otto has murdered a woman? Or do I feel more guilty for allowing myself to think this?

This is my son I'm speaking of. Is my son capable of murder?

"Don't you know that, Sadie? Do you really believe Otto could do this?" he asks, and it's my silence that gets the best of him. My unknowingness. My silent admission that, yes, I do think maybe Otto could have done this.

Will breathes out loudly, feathers ruffled. His words are clipped. "What Otto did, Sadie," Will says, words razor-sharp, "is a far cry from murder. He's fourteen, for God's sake. He's a kid. He acted in self-defense. He stood up for himself the only way he knew how. You're being irrational, Sadie."

"But what if I'm not?" I ask.

Will's response is immediate. "But you are," he says. "What Otto did was stand up for himself when no one else would."

He stops there but I know he wants to say more. He wants to tell me that Otto took matters into his own hands because of me. Because even though Otto told me about the harassment, I didn't intervene. Because I wasn't listening. There was a hotline at the school. A bullying hotline. I could have called and left an anonymous complaint. I could have called a teacher or the school principal and made a not-so-anonymous complaint. But instead I did nothing; I ignored him, even if unintentionally.

Will has yet to call me out on this. And yet I see it there in the unspoken words. Silently, he's castigating me. He thinks it's my fault Otto took that knife to school because I didn't offer a more reasonable alternative, a more appropriate alternative for our fourteen-year-old son.

Otto isn't a murderer. He would never have hurt those kids, I don't think.

He's a troubled boy, a scared boy.

There's a difference.

"I'm scared, Will," I admit, and he says, voice softening, "I know you are, Sadie. We both are."

"I have to turn the washcloth in to the police," I tell him, voice cracking, on the verge of tears, and only then does Will relent. Because of the tone of my voice. He knows as well as I that I've become discomposed. "It isn't right for us to keep it."

"All right, then," he says. "As soon as I get to campus I'll cancel my classes. Give me an hour, Sadie, and then I'll be home. Don't do anything with the washcloth until then," he pleads, before his voice takes on a different tone, a softer tone, and he says, "We'll go see Officer Berg together. Just wait until I get home and we'll speak to Officer Berg together."

I end the call and move into the living room to wait. I drop down onto the marigold sofa. I stretch my legs before me, thinking that if I close my eyes, I will sleep. The weight of worry and fatigue come bearing down on me, and suddenly I'm tired. My eyes sink shut.

Before I can fall asleep, they bolt open again.

The sound of the front door startles me. It shifts in its casing, getting jostled around.

It's only the wind blowing against it, agitating the door, I tell myself.

But then comes the sound of a key jiggling in the lock.

It's only been a few minutes since Will and I hung up the phone. No more than ten or fifteen. He would have scarcely reached the mainland by now, much less waited for passengers to disembark and then board the boat. He wouldn't have had time to make the twenty-minute commute back across the bay, or drive home from the ferry dock.

It's not Will.

Someone else is here.

I inch myself away from the door, searching for a place to hide. But before I've gone a step or two, the door presses violently open. It ricochets off the rubber stopper on the other side.

There, standing in the foyer, is Otto. His backpack is slung across a shoulder. His hair is covered with snow. It's white with it. His cheeks are rosy and red from the cold outside. The tip of his nose is also red. Everything else is pallid.

Otto slams the door shut.

"Otto," I breathe out midstride, pressing my hand to my chest. "What are you doing here?" I ask, and he says, "I'm sick." He does look peaked to me, yes. But I'm not certain he looks sick.

"The school didn't call," I tell him because this is the way it's supposed to happen. The school nurse is supposed to call and tell me my son is sick and then I go to the school and pick him up. But this isn't what happened.

"The nurse just sent you home?" I ask, feeling cross at her for allowing a child to walk off campus in the middle of the school day, but also scared. Because the look on Otto's face is alarming. He shouldn't be here. Why is he here?

His reply is off hand. He takes a step into the room. "I didn't ask," he says. "I just left."

"I see," I say, feeling my feet inch backward.

"What's that supposed to mean?" he asks. "I told you I was sick. You don't believe me?" It isn't like Otto to be antagonistic with me.

Otto stares at me with his jaw clenched, chin forward. He runs his fingers through his hair, then jams them into the pockets of his jeans.

"What doesn't feel good?" I ask, a lump forming in the pit of my stomach.

Otto moves another step closer and says, "My throat," though his voice isn't raspy. He doesn't clutch a hand to his throat as one does when it hurts.

But it's conceivable, of course. His throat could hurt. He could be telling the truth. Strep throat is going around, as is the flu.

"Your father is on his way home," I force out, though I don't know why.

"No, he's not," he says, voice chillingly composed. "Dad's at work."

"He canceled his classes," I say, shambling backward. "He's coming home. He should be here soon."

"Why?" Otto asks as, in my subtle retreat, I bump softly into the fireplace mantel.

I lie, telling Otto that Will also didn't feel well. "He was turning around just as soon as his ferry reached the mainland." I glance at the clock and say, "Any minute, he should be home."

"No, he won't," Otto says again. It's irrefutable the way that he says it.

I suck in a breath, release it slowly. "What do you mean?" I ask.

"Ferries are delayed 'cause of the storm," he tells me, thrusting that hair of his back again with a hand.

"How'd you get home?" I ask.

"Mine was the last to leave."

"Oh," I say, thinking of Otto and me trapped together in this house until ferry traffic resumes. How long will that take? I wonder why Will hasn't called to tell me about the ferries, though my phone is in the other room. I wouldn't have heard it if he did.

A gust of wind rattles the house just then, making the whole thing shake. As it does, the lamp on the end table flickers. I hold my breath, waiting for the room to go dark. There's a meager amount of light coming through the windows, but as they fill with snow it gets harder to see. The world outside turns a charcoal gray. The dogs bark.

"Do you want me to look at your throat?" I ask Otto. When he doesn't reply, I retrieve my penlight from my bag in the foyer and go to him. Standing beside Otto, I see how he's surpassed me in height nearly overnight. He looks down on me now. He isn't heavily built. Rather, he's lanky. He smells of teenage boy: all those hormones they secrete in their sweat during puberty. But he's handsome, the spitting image of Will, just younger and thinner.

I reach up and press my fingers to his

lymph nodes. They're enlarged. He might be sick.

"Open up," I tell him, and though he hesitates, he complies. Otto opens his mouth. It's lazy at best, just barely enough for me to see inside.

I shine my penlight in, seeing a red, irritated throat. I press the back of my hand to his forehead, feeling for a fever. As I do, I feel a sudden rush of nostalgia, bringing me back to a four- or a five-year-old Otto, sick as a dog with the flu. Instead of a hand, it used to be my lips, a far more accurate measure of temperature to me. One quick kiss and I could tell if my boys were febrile or not. That and the way they'd lie limp and helpless in my arms, wanting to be coddled. Those days are gone.

All at once Otto's strong hand latches down on my wrist and I jerk immediately back.

His grasp is strong. I can't free myself from his hold.

The penlight drops from my hand, batteries skidding across the floor.

"What are you doing, Otto? Let go of me," I cry out, trying desperately to wiggle free from his grasp. "You're hurting me," I tell him. His grip is tight.

I look up to find his eyes watching me.

They're more brown than blue today, more sad than mad. Otto speaks, his words nothing more than a whisper. "I'll never forgive you," he says, and I stop fighting.

"For what, Otto?" I breathe, still thinking about the washcloth and the necklace, as again the lights in the home flicker and I hold my breath, waiting for them to go out. My eyes move to a lamp, wishing I had something to protect myself with. The lamp has a beautiful glazed ceramic base, sturdy, solid enough to do damage but not so heavy that I can't pick it up. But it's six feet away now, out of reach, and I don't know that I'd have it in me anyway, to clutch the lamp by the neck and bash the heavy end into my own son's head. Even in self-defense. I don't know that I could.

Otto's Adam's apple bobs in his throat. "You know," he says, fighting back the urge to cry.

I shake my head and say, "I don't know," though I realize in the next moment that I do. He'll never forgive me for not standing up for him that day in the principal's office. For not complying with his lie.

"For lying," he hollers, composure waning, "about the knife."

"I never lied," I tell him. What I want to say is that he's the one who lied, but it doesn't seem a smart time to lay blame. Instead, "If only you'd have come to me. I could have helped you, Otto. We could have talked it through. We could have come up with a solution."

"I did," he interjects, voice quivering. "I did come to you. You're the only one I told," and I try not to imagine Otto opening up to me about what was happening at school and me giving him the brush-off. I struggle to remember it, as I have every day and night since it happened. What was I doing when Otto told me about the bullying? What was I so busy doing that I couldn't pay attention when he confessed to me that kids at school called him heinous names; that they shoved him into lockers, plunged his head into dirty toilet bowls?

"Otto," I say under my breath, full of shame for not being there when Otto needed me most. "If I wasn't listening. If I wasn't paying attention. I'm so sorry," I tell him, and I start to tell him how I was completely inundated with work in those days, tired and overwhelmed. But that's little consolation to a fourteen-year-old boy who needed his mother. I don't make excuses for my behavior. It wouldn't feel right.

Before I can say more, Otto is speaking,

and for the first time there are details I've never heard before. How we were outside when he told me about the bullying. How it was late at night. How Otto couldn't sleep. He came looking for me. He tells me he found me outside on our building's fire escape, just outside the kitchen window, dressed in all black, smoking a cigarette.

The details, they're ludicrous.

"I don't smoke, Otto," I tell him. "You know that. And heights." I shake my head, shuddering. I don't need to say more; he knows what I mean. I'm acrophobic. I've always been.

We lived on the sixth floor of our condo in Chicago, the top floor of a Printers Row midrise. I never took the elevator, only the stairs. I never stepped foot on the balcony where Will spent his mornings sipping coffee and enjoying the sweeping city views. *Come with me,* Will used to say, smiling mischievously while tugging on my hand. *I'll keep you safe. Don't I always keep you safe?* he asked. But I never went with him.

"But you were," Otto claims, and I ask, "How did you know I was there if it was the middle of the night? How did you see me?"

"The flame. From the cigarette lighter."

But I don't own a cigarette lighter. Because I don't smoke. But I go quiet anyway. I let him go on.

Otto says that he climbed out the window and sat beside me. It'd taken him weeks to work up the courage to come and tell me. Otto says I went ballistic when he told me what the kids were doing to him at school. That I was totally worked up.

"We plotted revenge. We made a list of the best ways."

"The best ways for what?" I ask.

He says it unambiguously, like it's the most obvious thing in the world. "The best way to kill them," he says.

"Who?"

"The kids at school," he tells me. Because even the kids that didn't mock him still laughed. And so, he and I decided that night that they all needed to go. I blanch. I humor him only because I think that this is cathartic somehow for Otto.

"And how were we going to do that?" I ask, not certain I want to know the ways he and I supposedly came up with to kill his classmates. Because they're Otto's ideas, every last one of them. And I want to believe that somewhere inside of him is still my son.

He shrugs his shoulders and says, "I dunno. A whole bunch of ways. We talked about starting the school on fire. Using lighter fluid or gasoline. You said I could poison the cafeteria food. We talked about that for a while. For a while that seemed like the way to go. Take out a whole bunch of them at once."

"How did we plan to do that?" I ask as he grows lax and his hand loses its grip on my wrist. I try to pull free, but just like that, he reengages, clinging tighter to me.

His answer is so sure. "Botox," he says with another shrug. "You said you could get it."

Botox. Botulinum toxin. Which we stocked at the hospital because it treats migraines, symptoms of Parkinson's disease, and a host of other conditions. But it can be fatal, too. It's one of the deadliest substances in the world.

"Or stabbing them all," he says, telling me how we'd decided that was the best way because he didn't have to wait for poison, and a knife was easier to hide in his backpack than bottles of lighter fluid. He could do it right away. The very next day.

"We went inside," Otto reminds me. "Remember, Mom? We climbed back in the window and went to look over all the knives, to see which would be best. You decided," he tells me, explaining how I chose the chef knife because of its size.

According to Otto, I then took out Will's whetstone and sharpened the knife. I said something canny about how a sharp knife is safer than a dull one, before smiling at him. Then I slipped it in his backpack in the soft laptop sleeve, behind all of his other belongings. As I zipped the backpack closed, I winked at him.

You don't have to worry about getting an organ, Otto says that I said. *Any old artery will do.*

My stomach roils at the thought of it. My free hand rises to my mouth as bile inches up my esophagus. I want to scream, *No!* That he's wrong. That I never said such a thing. That he's making this all up.

But before I can reply, Otto is telling me that before he went to bed that night I said to him, *Don't let anyone laugh at you. You shut them up if they do.*

That night Otto slept better than he had in a long time.

But the next morning, he had second thoughts about it. He was suddenly scared.

But I wasn't there to talk it through. I'd gone in to work for the day. He called me. That I remember, a voice mail on my phone that I didn't discover until later that night. *Mom,* he'd said. *It's me. I really need to talk to you.*

But by the time I heard the voice mail, it was done. Otto had taken that knife to school. By the grace of God, no one was hurt.

Listening to Otto speak, I realize one gut-wrenching truth. He doesn't think that he's made this story up. He believes it. In his mind, I *am* the one who packed the knife in his backpack; I am the one who lied.

I can't help myself. I reach up with my one free hand and trace his jawline. His body stiffens but he doesn't retreat. He lets me touch him. There is hair there, only a small patch of it that will one day grow to a beard. How did the little boy who once lacerated his thumb on the blade of Will's razor grow old enough to shave? His hair hangs in his eyes. I brush it back, seeing that his eyes lack all the hostility they usually have, but are instead drowning in pain.

"If I hurt you in any way," I whisper, "I'm sorry. I would never do anything to intentionally hurt you."

Only then does he acquiesce. He lets go of my wrist and I step quickly back.

"Why don't you go lie down in your room," I suggest. "I'll bring you toast."

"I'm not hungry," Otto grunts.

"How about juice, then?"

He ignores me.

I watch, grateful that he turns and lumbers up the stairs to his bedroom, backpack still clinging to his back.

I go to the first-floor study and close the door. I hurry to the computer on the desk and open the browser. I go to look up the website to the ferry company to search for news on delays. I'm anxious for Will to be home. I want to tell him about my conversation with Otto. I want to go to the police. I don't want to wait anymore to do these things.

If it wasn't for the weather, I'd leave. Tell Otto I'm running out on an errand and not come back until Will is here.

As I begin to type in the browser, a history of past internet searches greets me.

My breath leaves me. Because Erin Sabine's name is in the search history. Someone has been looking up Will's former fiancée. Will, I assume, feeling nostalgic on the twenty-year anniversary of her death.

I have no self-control. I click on the link.

Images greet me. An article, too, a report from twenty years ago on Erin's death. There are photographs included in the article. One is of a car being excavated from an icy pond. Emergency crews hover solemnly in the background while a wrecker truck lugs the car from the water. I read through the article. It's just as Will told me. Erin lost control of her car in a wicked winter storm like the one we're having today; she drowned.

The second image is of Erin with her family. There are four of them: a mother, a father, Erin and a younger sister who looks to me somewhere in between Otto's and Tate's ages. Ten, maybe eleven. The photograph is professional-looking. The family is in a street between an avenue of trees. The mother sits on a garish yellow chair that's been placed there for purposes of this photograph. Her family stands around her, the girls leaning into their mother indulgently.

It's the mother I can't take my eyes off of. There's something about her that nags at me, a round woman with shoulder-length brunette hair. Something strikes a chord, but I don't know what. Something that hovers just out of the periphery of my mind. Who is she?

The dogs begin to howl just then. I hear it all the way from here. They've finally had enough of this storm. They want to come inside.

I rise from the desk. I let myself out of the study, padding quickly to the kitchen, where I yank open the back door. I step outside, onto the deck, hissing to the dogs to come. But they don't come.

I move across the yard. The dogs are both frozen like statues in the corner. They've caught something, a rabbit or a squirrel. I have to stop them before they eat the poor thing, and in my mind's eye I see the white snow riddled with animal blood.

The yard is covered in snowdrifts. They rise a foot high in some spots, the grass barely flecked with snow in others. The wind tries hard to push me down as I trek through the yard, making my way out to the dogs. The property is large, and they're far away, pawing at something. I clap my hands and call to them again, but still they don't come. The snow blows sideways. It gusts up the leg of my pajama pants and into the neckline of my shirt. My feet, covered in slippers alone, ache from the bitter cold. I didn't think to put shoes on before I came outside.

It's hard to see much of anything. The trees, the houses, the horizon disappear in the snow. I find it hard to open my eyes. I think of the kids still in school. How will they get home?

Halfway to the dogs, I think about turning around. I don't know that I have it in me to make it all the way there. I clap again;

I call to them. They don't come. If Will was here, they would come.

I force myself to go on. It hurts to breathe; the air is so cold it burns my throat and lungs.

The dogs bark again and I run the last twenty feet to them. They look sheepishly at me as I come, and I expect to find a half-eaten cadaver lying between their feet.

I reach out, grabbing ahold of one of the girls' collars and pulling, saying, "Come on, let's go," not caring if there's a maimed squirrel there, but just needing to be back inside. But she just stands there, whining at me, refusing to come. She's much too big for me to lug all the way home. I try, but as I do I stagger from the weight of her, losing balance. I fall forward to my hands and knees where there, before me, between the dogs' paws, something sparkles in the snow. It's not a rabbit. It's not a squirrel. It's much too small to be a rabbit or a squirrel.

And then there's the shape of it, long and slender and sharp.

My heart races. My fingers tingle. The black specks return, dancing before my eyes. I feel like I could be sick. And then suddenly I am. On my hands and knees, I retch into the snow. My diaphragm contracts but it's a dry heave only. I've had nothing to eat but a few sips of coffee. My stomach is empty. There's nothing there to come back up.

One of the dogs nudges me with her nose. I latch on to her, steadying myself, seeing plainly that the object between the dogs' feet is a knife. The missing boning knife. The blood on it is what's piqued the dogs' interest. The blade of the knife is approximately six inches long, same as the one that killed Morgan Baines.

Beside the knife sits a hole that the dogs have carved into the earth.

The dogs dug up this knife. This knife was buried in our backyard. All this time, they've been digging into the backyard to unearth this knife.

I glance quickly back to the house. Though in reality I see nothing, just barely the softened periphery of the house itself, I imagine Otto standing at the kitchen window, watching me. I can't go home.

I leave the dogs where they are. I leave the knife where it is. I don't touch it. I limp across the yard. My feet tingle from the cold, losing feeling. It makes it hard for them to move. I lumber around the side of the house, missing my footing because of my frozen feet. I fall into snowdrifts and then force myself back up.

It's a quarter-mile hike to the bottom of our hill. That's where the town and the public safety building are located, where I'll find Officer Berg.

Will said to wait. But I can no longer wait.

There's no telling what time Will will be home, or what may happen to me by the time he is.

The street is barren and bleak. It's saturated in white. There's no one here but me. I shamble down the hill, nose oozing with snot. I wipe it away with a sleeve. I'm wearing only pajamas, not a coat or a hat. Not gloves. The pajamas do nothing to keep me warm, to protect me. My teeth chatter. I can barely keep my eyes open because of the wind. The snow blows from all ways simultaneously, constantly airborne, swirling in circles like the vortex of a tornado. My fingers freeze. They're blotchy and red. I can't feel my face.

Off in the distance, the blade of a shovel scrapes a sidewalk.

There's the littlest bit of hope that comes with it.

There is someone else on this island besides Otto and me.

I go on only because I have no choice but to go on.

Mouse

In the middle of the night, Mouse heard a noise she knew well.

It was the squeak of the stairs, which had no reason to be squeaking since Mouse was already in her bed. As Mouse knew, there was one bedroom on the second floor of the old house. At night, after she was in bed, there was no reason for anyone to be upstairs but her.

But someone was coming up the stairs. Fake Mom was coming upstairs, and the stairs themselves were calling out a warning for Mouse, telling her to run. Telling her to hide.

But Mouse didn't have a chance to run or hide.

Because it happened too fast and she was disoriented from sleep. Mouse barely had time to open her eyes before the bedroom door pressed open, and there Fake Mom stood, backlit by the hallway light.

Bert, in her cage on the bedroom floor, emitted a piercing screech. She rushed under her translucent dome for safety. There she held still like a statue, mistakenly believing no one would see her on the other side of the opaque plastic, so long as she didn't move.

In her bed, Mouse tried to hold real still, too.

But Fake Mom saw her there, just as she saw Bert.

Fake Mom flicked the bedroom light on. The brightness of it overpowered Mouse's tired, dilated eyes, so that at first she couldn't see. But she could hear. Fake Mom spoke, her voice composed in a way that startled Mouse even more than if it wasn't. Her steps were slow and deliberate as she let herself into the room, when Mouse wished she would come running in, screaming, and then leave. Because then it would be over and through.

What did I tell you about picking up after yourself, Mouse? Fake Mom asked, coming closer to the bed, stepping past Bert and her cage. She grabbed Mouse's bedspread by the edge and tugged, revealing Mouse in her unicorn pajamas beneath, the ones she put on without anyone having to tell her to put them on. Beside Mouse, in the bed, was

Mr. Bear. *Did you think that picking up after yourself didn't mean flushing a toilet or wiping up after you piss all over the seat, the same seat that I have to sit on?*

Mouse's blood ran cold. She didn't have to think about what Fake Mom was talking about. She knew. And she knew there was no point in explaining, though she tried anyway. Her voice trembled as she spoke. She told Fake Mom what happened. How she tried to be quiet. How she didn't want to wake Fake Mom up. How she didn't mean to pee on the seat. How she didn't flush the toilet because she knew it would be loud.

But Mouse was nervous when she spoke. She was scared. Her little voice shook so that her words came out unintelligibly. Fake Mom didn't like mumbling. She barked at Mouse, *Speak up!*

Then she rolled her eyes and said that Mouse wasn't nearly as smart as her father thought she was.

Mouse tried to explain again. To speak louder, to enunciate her words. But it didn't matter because Fake Mom didn't want an explanation, whether an audible or inaudible one. The question she'd asked, Mouse realized too late, was rhetorical, the kind of question that doesn't want an answer at all.

Do you know what happens when dogs have accidents inside the house? Fake Mom asked Mouse. Mouse didn't know for sure what happened. She'd never had a dog before, but what she thought was that someone cleaned the mess up, and that was that. It was done. Because that was the way it happened with Bert. Bert was forever pooping and peeing in Mouse's lap, and it was never a big deal. Mouse wiped it up, washed her hands and went back to playing with Bert.

But Fake Mom wouldn't have asked the question if it was as easy as that.

Mouse told her that she didn't know.

I'll show you what happens, Fake Mom said as she grabbed Mouse by the arm and pulled her from bed. Mouse didn't want to go where Fake Mom wanted her to go. But she didn't object because she knew it would hurt less if she just went with Fake Mom than allowing herself to be pulled from bed and dragged down the squeaky stairs. So that was what she did. Except that Fake Mom walked faster than Mouse could walk, and so she tripped. When she did, she fell all the way to the floor. It made Fake Mom angry. It made her scream, *Get up!*

Mouse did. They made their way down the steps. The house was mostly dark, but there was a hint of the night sky coming in through the windows.

Fake Mom brought Mouse into the living room. She brought her to the center of the room, turned her in a specific direction. There, in the corner of the room, was the empty dog crate, door open as it never was.

I used to have a dog once, Fake Mom said. *A springer spaniel. I named him Max, mostly because I couldn't think of a better name. He was a good dog. A dumb dog, but a good dog. We took walks together. Sometimes, when we'd watch TV, he'd sit by my side. But then Max went and made an accident in the corner of my house when I wasn't home, and that made Max bad,* she said.

She went on. *See, we can't have animals urinating and defecating inside our homes, where they're not supposed to go. It's dirty, Mouse. Do you understand that? The best way to teach a dog is by crate training. Because the dog doesn't want to have to sit with its own piss and shit for days. And so it learns to hold it. Same as you can,* Fake Mom said as she grabbed Mouse by the arm and yanked her the rest of the way across the living room for that open dog crate.

Mouse fought back, but Mouse was a child, only six years old. She weighed less than half of what Fake Mom weighed and she had nearly no strength at all.

Mouse had had no dinner. Only three Salerno Butter Cookies. She's just been woken from sleep. It was the middle of the night and she was tired. She wiggled and writhed, but that was the best she could do, and so she was easily manhandled by Fake Mom. She was forced into the dog crate, which was not even as tall as she was when she sat down. She couldn't even sit all the way up inside the cage, and so her head rubbed against the hard metal bars of the cage, her neck kinked. She couldn't lie down, couldn't stretch out her legs. She had to keep them pulled into her, so that they went numb.

Mouse was crying. She was begging to be let out. Promising to be good, to never pee on the toilet seat again.

But Fake Mom wasn't listening.

Because Fake Mom was making her way back upstairs.

Mouse didn't know why. She thought maybe Fake Mom was going back up to get her poor Mr. Bear.

But when Fake Mom returned she didn't have the bear.

She had Bert.

It made Mouse shriek, seeing her sweet guinea pig in Fake Mom's hands. Bert never did like to be held by anyone other than Mouse. She was kicking her tiny feet in Fake Mom's grasp, squealing her high-pitched squeal, louder than Mouse had ever heard her before. It wasn't the same squeal she made for carrots. It was a different kind of squeal. A terrified kind of squeal.

Mouse's heart was beating a million miles a minute.

She beat on the bars of that dog crate but couldn't get out.

She tried forcing the door open but it wouldn't budge because there was some sort of padlock on that door.

Did you know, Mouse, that a dull knife is more dangerous than a sharp one? she asked, holding one of her knives up in the air to examine the blade in the moonlight.

How many times, she asked, not waiting for an answer to the question she'd already asked, *do I have to tell you that I don't want one rodent in this house, let alone two?*

Mouse closed her eyes and pressed her hands to her ears so that she couldn't see or hear what came next.

It wasn't a week before Mouse's father had another work trip.

He stood in the doorway saying his good-byes as Fake Mom stood beside Mouse.

I'll only be gone for a few days. I'll be back before you can miss me, her father said as he stared into Mouse's sad eyes, promising her that when he got home they'd pick out a new guinea pig for her, one to replace Bert. Her father was of the opinion that Bert had merely run away, that she was getting her kicks somewhere in the voids of the house where they couldn't find her.

Mouse didn't want a new guinea pig. Not then, not ever. And only Mouse and Fake Mom knew the reason why.

Beside her, Fake Mom squeezed Mouse's shoulder. She stroked her mousy brown hair and said, *We're going to get along just fine. Aren't we, Mouse? Now say goodbye to your father so that he can go on his trip.*

Mouse tearfully said goodbye.

She and Fake Mom stood beside each other, watching as her father's car pulled from the drive and disappeared around the bend.

And then Fake Mom kicked the front door closed and turned on Mouse.

Sadie

The public safety building is a small brick building in the center of town. I'm grateful to find the door unlocked, a warm, yellow light glowing from the inside.

A woman sits behind the desk, pecking away on a keyboard as I let myself in. She startles, clutching her bosom when the door bursts open and I appear. On a day such as this, she hadn't expected anyone to be outside.

I trip over the door's threshold on the way in. I didn't see the one-inch rise. I fall to my hands and knees just inside the doorway, not having it in me to catch myself in time. The floor isn't as yielding as the snow; this fall hurts far more than the others.

"Oh dear," the woman says, rising quickly to her feet to come help me to mine. She nearly runs around the edge of the desk and reaches for me on the floor. Her mouth hangs open, her eyes wide with surprise.

She can't believe what she's seeing. The room around me is boxy and small. Yellow walls, carpeted floors, a double pedestal desk. The air is miraculously warm. A space heater stands in the corner, blowing heated air throughout the room.

I've no sooner found my feet than I go to the heater, dropping to my knees before the oscillating fan.

"Officer Berg," I just manage to say, lips sluggish from the cold. My back is to the woman. "Officer Berg, please."

"Yes," she says, "yes, of course," and before I know what's happening, she's screaming for him. She graciously reaches past me to turn the space heater to a higher speed, and I press my hands to it, burning from the cold.

"There's someone here to see you," she says uneasily, and I turn.

When he appears, Officer Berg says nothing. He walks quickly because of the screaming, because of the edge in his secretary's voice that warns him something is wrong. He takes in my pajamas as he moves past me for the coffeepot. He fills a disposable cup with coffee and extends it to me in an effort to warm me up. He helps me rise to my feet, pressing the cup into my hands. I don't drink it, but the heat off the cup feels good to touch. I feel grateful for it. The storm perseveres outside, the entirety of the little building shuddering at times. Lights flicker; the walls whine. He reaches for a coat on a coatrack and wraps me in it.

"I have to speak with you," I tell him, the desperation and fatigue in my voice palpable.

Officer Berg leads me down the hall. We sit side by side at a small expandable table. The room is bare.

"What are you doing here, Dr. Foust?" he asks me, his tone thoughtful and concerned, but also leery. "Heck of a day to be outside," he says.

I find myself shaking uncontrollably. For as much as I try, I can't warm up. My hands are wrapped around the cup of coffee. Officer Berg gives me a nudge and tells me to drink up.

But it's not the cold that makes me shake.

I start to tell him everything, but before I can, Officer Berg says, "I received a call from your husband a short while ago," and my words get stuck in my throat. I'm at a loss, wondering why Will called him after we'd agreed that we'd come see him together.

"You did?" I ask instead, sitting upright, because these aren't words I expected to hear. Officer Berg nods his head slowly. He has an uncanny way of maintaining eye contact. I struggle not to look away. I ask, "What did he want?" bracing myself for the officer's reply.

"He was worried about you," Officer Berg says, and I feel myself relax. Will called because he was worried about me.

"Of course," I say, softening in the chair. Perhaps he tried to call me first, and when I didn't answer the phone, he called Officer Berg. Perhaps he asked Officer Berg to check on me and see if I was all right. "The weather. And the ferry delay. I was upset the last time we spoke."

"Yes," he says. "Mr. Foust told me."

I start, again sitting upright.

"He told you I was upset?" I ask on the defense, because this is personal, not something Will needed to tell the police.

He nods. "He's worried about you. He said you were upset about some washcloth," and it's then that the conversation shifts, because it's patronizing the way he says it. As if I'm just some stupid ninny running off at the mouth about a washcloth.

"Oh," I say, and I leave it at that.

"I was getting ready to head to your house and check on you. You saved me a trip," he says. Officer Berg tells me the afternoon commute will be messy because the local schools weren't called off ahead of the storm. The only saving grace is that the snow is to slow in the hours to come.

And then Officer Berg begins to pry. "You want to tell me about this washcloth?"

"I found a washcloth," I tell him slowly, "covered in blood. In my laundry room." And then because I've said that much already, I go on. "I found the knife buried in my backyard."

He doesn't so much as blink. "The knife that was used to kill Mrs. Baines?" he asks.

"I believe so," I say. "Yes. It had blood on it."

"Where is the knife now, Doctor?"

"It's in my backyard."

"You left it there?"

"I did."

"Did you touch it?"

"No," I say.

"Whereabouts in your backyard?" he asks, and I try to describe it for him, though I imagine that by now the knife is engulfed in snow.

"And what about this washcloth? Where is that?"

"Under the washing machine. In the laundry room," I tell him. He asks if there's blood on that still, too, and I say yes. He excuses himself and leaves the room. For nearly thirty seconds he's gone, and when he comes back, he tells me that Officer Bisset is going to my home to retrieve the washcloth and knife. I say to him, "My son is home," but he assures me that's all right, that Officer Bisset will be in and out quickly. That he won't bother Otto.

"But I think, Officer," I start and then just as soon stop. I don't know how to say this. I pick at the rim of the disposable cup, pieces of foam coming with me, gathering in a pile on the tabletop like snow.

And then I come right out and say it. "I think maybe my son murdered Mrs. Baines," I say. "Or maybe Imogen did."

I expect more of a reaction. But instead he goes on, as if I didn't just say those words aloud.

"There's something you should know, Dr. Foust," he says, and I ask, "What's that?"

"Your husband . . ."

"Yes?"

"Will —"

I hate this way he beats around the bush. It's utterly maddening. "I know my husband's name," I snap, and for a moment he stares at me, saying nothing.

"Yes," he says in time. "I suppose you do."

A beat of silence passes by. All the while,

he stares at me. I shift in my seat.

"When he called, he retracted his earlier statement about the night Mrs. Baines was killed. About how the two of you were watching TV and then went straight to bed. According to your husband, that's not entirely true."

I'm taken aback. "It's not?"

"It's not. Not according to Mr. Foust."

"What did Mr. Foust say happened?" I churlishly ask as voices come through on the police scanner, loud but indistinct. Officer Berg goes to it, turning the volume down so that we can speak.

He returns to his chair. "He said that that night, after your program ended, you didn't go to bed like you said. He said you walked the dogs instead. You took the dogs for a walk while he went up to the bedroom to wash up. You were gone quite some time, your husband said."

I feel something inside of me start to shift. Someone is lying. But I don't know who.

"Is that right?" I ask.

"That's right," he says.

"But that's not true," I argue. I don't know why Will would say this. There's only one thing that I can think. That Will would do anything to protect Otto and Imogen. Anything at all. Even if it means throwing me to the wolves.

"He said you took the dogs for a walk, but as time went on and you didn't come home, he started to worry about you. Especially when he heard the dogs barking. He looked outside to see what was the matter. When he did, he found the dogs out there but not you. You left the dogs in the yard when you went over to the Baineses' home that night, didn't you?"

My stomach drops. There's the sensation of free-falling, of plummeting down the first hill of a roller coaster, organs shifting inside of me.

I say, enunciating each word at a time, "I didn't go to the Baineses' home that night."

But he ignores this. He goes on as if I didn't even speak. He starts speaking of Will on a first-name basis. He is Will and I am Dr. Foust.

Officer Berg has chosen sides. He isn't on mine.

"Will tried you on your cell phone. You didn't answer. He started thinking that something terrible had happened to you. He hurried to the bedroom to put his clothes on so he could go searching for you. But just as he was about to panic, you came home."

Officer Berg pauses for breath. "I have to

ask you again, Doctor. Where were you between the hours of ten and two on the night that Mrs. Baines was killed?"

I shake my head, saying nothing. There's nothing to say. I've told him where I was, but he no longer believes me.

Only now do I realize that Officer Berg has carried a large envelope into the room with him. All the while it's sat on the table, just out of reach. He stands and reaches for it now. He slips a finger beneath the flap to open it up. Berg begins to lay photographs on the table for me to see. They're truly heinous, growing more ghastly with each image he draws out. The images have been enlarged, eight by ten inches at least. Even when I avert my eyes I see them. There's a photograph of an open door — doorjamb and latch intact. Of sprays of blood trickling down the walls. The room is strikingly tidy, which makes me think there wasn't much of a scuffle. The only things out of place are an umbrella stand, which lies on its side, and a framed photograph, hanging cockeyed as if it got elbowed in the fracas.

At the center of it all lies Morgan. She's splayed in an uncomfortable position on an area rug, brown hair veiling her face, arms thrown up and over her head as if, in a last-ditch effort, she tried to protect her face from the blade of the knife. A leg looks broken from the fall, bent in a way it's not meant to go. Her pajamas are on, flannel pants and a thermal top, all of it red, so it's impossible to see where the blood ends and the pajamas begin. The left leg of her pants is hitched to the knee.

Small footprints are pressed into the puddles of blood. They lessen in density as they drift away from the body. I envision an officer's hands luring the little girl away from the dead woman's body.

"What I see here, Doctor," Officer Berg is telling me, "isn't a sign of a random crime. Whoever did this wanted Morgan to suffer. This was an act of anger and aggression."

I can't tear my eyes away from the photo. They drift over Morgan's body, the bloody footprints, back to the photograph mounted on the wall, the one that hangs cockeyed. I grab the photograph from the table and bring it to my eyes for a better look at that mounted picture frame, because I've seen it before and not so long ago. The way the trees line the street is familiar. There is a family of four. A mother, father and two daughters, roughly the ages of ten and twenty.

The woman, the mother, in a pretty green dress is set on a bright yellow chair in the center of it, while her family stands around her.

"Oh God," I gasp, hand going to my mouth, because this photograph — framed and mounted to Morgan Baines's wall — is the same as the one in the newspaper article about Erin's death. The one on my computer. The older girl, nearly twenty years old, is Will's former fiancée, Erin. It was likely taken just months before she died. The younger girl is her little sister.

I choke on my own saliva. Officer Berg pats my back, asks if I'm okay. I nod because I can't speak.

"It's not easy to look at, is it?" Officer Berg asks, thinking it's the dead woman's body that has me rattled like this.

I see it now, what I couldn't see before. Because the woman in the photograph — the mother perched on the chair — is older now. Her brown hair is now gray, and she's lost a significant amount of weight. Too much weight, in fact, so that she's gaunt.

It's utterly impossible. It's too hard to digest. This can't be.

The woman in this photograph is Morgan's mother. The woman I met at the memorial service. The woman who lost another child years ago and has never been the same since, according to her friends Karen and Susan.

But I don't understand it. If this is true, it means that Morgan was Erin's sister. That Morgan is the little girl in the photograph, the one who's about ten years old.

Why didn't Will tell me about this?

I think I know why. Because of my own insecurities. What would I have done if I'd learned Erin's sister was living in such close proximity to us? I realize Will and Morgan's friendship, their chumminess, it was real. It existed. Because of their shared affinity for the one woman Will loved more than me. Erin.

The room drifts in and out of focus. I blink hard, trying to get it to stop. Officer Berg teeters on the chair beside me. He doesn't move; it's my perception of him that makes him move. It's all in my head. The edges of his face begin to soften. The room suddenly expands in size, walls widen, moving out. When the officer speaks, his words are nearly extinguished by whatever is going on in my head. I see his lips move. His words are harder to make out.

The first time he says it, it's unintelligible.

"Pardon me?" I ask, speaking loudly.

"Will told us that you have a tendency toward being jealous and insecure."

"He did, did he?"

"Yes, Dr. Foust, he did. He said he never expected you to act on those feelings. But he also said that you've been having a hard time lately. That you're not quite yourself. He mentioned a panic attack, a forced resignation. You're not the violent type, not according to Will. But," he says, repeating his own words, "he says you haven't been yourself lately."

He asks, "Do you have anything to say to that?"

I say nothing. A headache begins just then, inching up the nape of my neck, stabbing me between the eyes. I clench my eyes shut tight, pressing my fingertips to my temples to dull the pain. I must experience a drop in blood pressure because all at once, it's hard to hear. Officer Berg is talking, asking if I'm okay. But the words are more muffled than they were before. I'm underwater.

A door opens and then closes. Officer Berg is speaking to someone else. They found nothing. But they're conducting a search of my home because Will has given them permission to do so.

"Dr. Foust? Dr. Foust?"

A hand shakes my shoulder.

When my eyes open up, some old guy's looking at me. He's practically drooling. I glance at the clock. I look down at my shirt.

A blue button-down pajama shirt buttoned all the way up, making me gag. I can barely breathe. She can be such a prig sometimes. I unbutton the top three buttons, let in a little air. "It's fucking hot in here," I say, fanning myself, seeing the way he looks at my clavicle.

"Everything all right?" he asks. He's got one of those looks on his face, like he's confused about what he sees. His eyebrows are all scrunched up. He digs the heels of his hands into his eye sockets, makes sure he isn't seeing things. He asks again if I'm all right. I think I should ask if he's all right — he seems to be in far more distress than me — but I don't so much care if he is. So I don't ask.

Instead I ask, "Why wouldn't everything be all right?"

"You seem, I don't know, disoriented somehow. You're feeling okay? I can fetch you some water, if you don't want your coffee."

I look at the cup before me. It's not mine.

He just looks at me, saying nothing, staring. I say, "Sure," about the water. I twirl a strand of hair around my finger, taking in the room around me. Cold, bland, a table, four walls. There's not much to it, nothing to look at, nothing to tell me where I am.

Nothing except for this guy before me, fully decked out in a uniform. Clearly a cop.

And then I see the pictures on the table beside me.

"Go on," I tell him. "Fetch me some water."

He goes and comes back again. He gives me the water, sets it on the table in front of me. "So tell me," he says. "Tell me what happened when you took the dogs for a walk."

"What dogs?" I ask. I've always liked dogs. People I hate, but I'm quite fond of dogs.

"Your dogs, Dr. Foust."

I get a great big belly laugh out of that. It's preposterous, ludicrous, him mistaking me for Sadie. It's insulting more than anything. We look nothing alike. Different-color hair, eyes, a heck of an age gap. Sadie is old. I'm not. Is he so blind he can't see that?

"Please," I say, tucking a strand of hair behind an ear. "Don't insult me."

He does a double take, asks, "Pardon me?"

"I said don't insult me."

"I'm sorry, Dr. Foust. I —" But I stop him there because I can't stand the way he keeps referring to me as *Sadie,* as *Dr. Foust.* Sadie would be lucky to be me. But Sadie is not me.

"Stop calling me that," I snap.

"You don't want me to call you Dr. Foust?"

"No," I tell him.

"Well, what should I call you, then?" he asks. "Would you prefer that I call you Sadie?"

"No!" I shake my head, insistent, indignant. I tell him, "You should call me by my name."

His eyes narrow, homing in on me. "I thought Sadie was your name. Sadie Foust."

"You thought wrong, then, didn't you?"

He looks at me, words slack as he asks, "If not Sadie, then who are you?"

I stick a hand out to him, tell him my name is Camille. His hand is cold when he shakes it, limp. He looks around the room as he does, asks where Sadie went.

I tell him, "Sadie isn't here right now. She had to go."

"But she was just here," he says.

"Yeah," I tell him, "but now she's not. Now it's just me."

"I'm sorry. I'm not following," he says, asking again if I'm feeling okay, if I'm all right, encouraging me to drink up the water.

"I'm feeling fine," I say, drinking the water in one big swig. I'm thirsty and hot.

"Dr. Foust —"

"Camille," I remind him, searching the room for a clock, to see what time it is, how much time I've missed.

He says, "Okay. Camille, then." He shows me one of the pictures from the tabletop, the one where she's covered in her own blood, eyes open, dead. "Do you know anything about this?"

I leave him hanging. Can't let the cat out of the bag just yet.

SADIE

I'm alone in a room, sitting in a chair that backs up to a wall. There isn't much to the room, just walls, two chairs, a door that's locked. I know because I've already tried leaving. I tried turning the knob but it didn't turn. I wound up knocking on the door, pounding on the door, calling out for help. But it was all in vain. Because no one came.

Now the door easily opens. A woman walks in, carrying a teacup in her hand. She comes to me. She sets a briefcase on the floor and helps herself to the other chair, sitting opposite me. She doesn't introduce herself but begins speaking as if we already know one another, as if we've already met.

She asks me questions. They're personal and invasive. I bristle in the chair, drawing away from them, wondering why she is asking about my mother, my father, my childhood, some woman named Camille whom I don't know. In my whole life, I've never known anyone named Camille. But she looks at me, disbelieving. She seems to think I do.

She tells me things that aren't true, about myself and my life. I get agitated, upset when she says them.

I ask how she can claim to know these things about me, when I don't even know them for myself. Officer Berg is responsible for this, for sending her to speak to me, because one minute he was interrogating me in his tiny room, and the next minute I'm here, though I have no idea what time it is, what day it is, and I can't remember anything that happened in between. How did I get here, into this chair, into this room? Did I walk here myself or did they drug and bring me here?

This woman tells me that she has reason to believe I suffer from dissociative identity disorder, that alternate personalities — alters, she calls them — control my thoughts, my behavior from time to time. She says that they control me.

I take a deep breath, gather myself. "That's impossible," I breathe out, "not to mention utterly ridiculous," I say, throwing my arms up in the air. "Did Officer Berg tell you that?" I ask, getting angry, losing my composure. Is there nothing Berg won't do to pin Morgan Baines's murder on me? "This is unprofessional, unethical, *illegal* even," I snap, asking who is in charge so that I can demand to speak to him or her.

She answers none of my questions, but instead asks, "Are you prone to periods of blackouts, Dr. Foust? Thirty minutes, an hour pass that you can't remember?"

I can't deny this, though I try. I tell her that's never happened.

But at the same time, I don't remember getting here.

There are no windows in this room. There's no way to get a sense of the time of day. But I see the face of the woman's watch. It's upside down, but I see it, the hands in the realm of two fifty, but whether that's a.m. or p.m. I don't know. Either way, it doesn't matter, because I know good and well it was ten, maybe eleven o'clock in the morning when I walked to the public safety building. Which conceivably means that four — or sixteen — hours have passed that I can't account for.

"Do you remember speaking to me earlier today?" she asks. The answer is no. I don't remember speaking to her. But I tell her I do anyway. I claim I remember that conversation quite well. But I've never been a good liar.

"This isn't the first time we've spoken," she tells me. I gathered as much from her line of questioning, though that doesn't mean I believe her. That doesn't mean she isn't making it all up. "But the last time I was here, I wasn't speaking to you, Doctor. I was speaking to a woman named Camille," she says, and then she goes on to describe for me a pushy, garrulous young woman named Camille who is living inside of me, along with a withdrawn child.

I've never heard anything as ridiculous in my whole life.

She tells me that the child doesn't say much but that she likes to draw. She says that the two of them, this woman and the child, drew pictures together today, which she shows me, plucking a sheet of paper from her briefcase and handing it to me.

And there it is, sketched with pencil on a sheet of notebook paper this time: the dismembered body, the woman, the knife, the blood. Otto's artwork, the same picture I've been finding around the house.

I tell her, "I didn't draw that. My son drew that."

But she says, "No."

She has a different theory about who drew

this picture. She claims that the child alter inside of me drew it. I laugh out loud at the absurdity of that, because if some *child alter* living inside of me drew it, then what she's saying is that I drew this picture. That I drew the pictures in the attic, in the hallway, and left them around the house for myself to find.

I did not draw this picture. I did not draw any of the pictures.

I'd remember if I did.

I tell her, "I didn't draw this picture."

"Of course you didn't," she said, and for a split second I think she believes me. Until she says, "Not you specifically. Not *Sadie Foust.* What happens with DID is that your personality gets fragmented. It gets split. Those fragments form distinct identities, with their very own name, appearance, gender, age, handwriting, speech patterns, more."

"What's her name, then?" I challenge. "If you spoke to her. If you drew pictures with her. Then what's her name?"

"I don't know. She's shy, Sadie. These things take time," she says.

"How old is she?" I ask.

"She's six years old."

She tells me that this child likes to color and draw. She likes to play with dolls. She has a game she likes to play, which this woman played with her in an effort to get her to open up. Play therapy, this woman tells me. In this very room, they held hands and spun in circles. When they were both as dizzy as could be, they stopped. They froze in place like statues.

"The statue game, she called it," this woman tells me, because they held still like statues until one of them finally toppled over.

I try to imagine what she's telling me. I picture this child spinning in circles with this woman, except the child alter — if I'm to believe her — is not a child. It's me.

It makes me blush to think of it. Me, a thirty-nine-year-old woman, holding hands and spinning around this room with another grown woman, freezing in place like statues.

The idea is absurd. I can't stand to entertain it.

Not until Tate's words come rushing back to me: *Statue game, statue game!* and it strikes a nerve.

Mommy is a liar! You do know what it is, you liar.

"On average, those with DID have around ten alters living within them," she tells me. "Sometimes more, sometimes less. Sometimes as many as one hundred."

"How many do I supposedly have?" I ask. Because I don't believe her. Because this is just some elaborate scam to besmirch my name, my character, making it easier for me to take the fall for Morgan's murder.

"So far I've met two," she says.

"So far?"

"There may be more." She goes on to say, "Dissociative identity disorder often begins with a history of abuse at a young age. The alternate personalities form as a coping mechanism. They serve different purposes, like protecting the host. Standing up, speaking up for the host. Harboring the painful memories."

As she says it, I think of myself, harboring parasites. I think of the oxpecker bird, who eats bugs off the backs of hippos. A symbiotic relationship, once thought, until scientists realized the oxpeckers were actually vampire birds, digging holes to drink the blood of the hippopotamuses.

Not so symbiotic after all.

She says, "Tell me about your childhood, Dr. Foust."

I tell her I can't remember much of my childhood, nearly nothing, in fact, until I was around eleven years old.

She just looks at me, saying nothing, waiting for me to put it together.

Are you prone to periods of blackouts, Dr. Foust?

But blackouts are temporary losses of time, caused by things like alcohol consumption, epileptic seizures, low blood sugar.

I didn't black out for the extent of my young childhood. I just don't remember.

"That's typical in cases of DID," she tells me after a while. "The dissociation is a way to disconnect from a traumatic experience. A coping mechanism," she says again, as if she didn't just say that moments ago.

"Tell me about this woman," I say. I'm trying to catch her in a lie. Certainly sooner or later she'll contradict herself. "This Camille woman."

She tells me there are different types of alters. Persecutor alters, protector alters, more. She has yet to ascertain which this young woman is. Because sometimes she stands up for me, but more often her portrayals of me are hate-filled. She's huffy, ticked off. Angry and aggressive. It's a love-hate relationship. She hates me. She also wants to be me.

The little girl doesn't know I exist.

"Officer Berg took the liberty of doing some research," she says. "Your mother died in childbirth, no?" she asks, and I say that yes, she did. Preeclampsia. My father never spoke of it, but by the way his eyes got glossy whenever her name came up, I knew it had been horrific for him. Losing her, raising me alone.

"When you were six, your father remarried," she says, but I object to this.

"No, he didn't," I say. "It was just my father and me."

"You said you don't remember your childhood, Doctor," she reminds me, but I tell her what I do remember: being eleven years old, my father and me living in the city, him taking the train to work, coming home fifteen, sixteen hours later, drunk.

"I remember," I say, though I don't remember what came before this, but I'd like to believe it was always the same.

She pulls paperwork from her briefcase, telling me that the year I was six years old, my father married a woman by the name of Charlotte Schneider. We lived in Hobart, Indiana, and my father worked as a sales rep for a small company. Three years later, when I was nine, my father and Charlotte divorced. Irreconcilable differences.

"What can you tell me about your stepmother?" she asks, and I tell her, "Nothing. You're mistaken. Officer Berg is mistaken. There was no stepmother. It was only my father and me."

She shows me a photograph. My father, me and some strange but beautiful woman standing before a home I don't know. The house is small, just one and a half stories tall. It's nearly engulfed in trees. In the drive is a car. I don't recognize it.

My father looks younger than I remember him, more handsome, more alive. He stares sideways at the woman, his eyes not meeting the camera lens. His smile is authentic, which strikes me as odd. My father was a man who didn't often smile. In the image, he has a full head of dark hair and is without all the saw-tooth lines that later took over his eyes and cheeks.

My father had a nickname for me when I was a girl. Mouse, he called me. Because I was one of those twitchy, tic-prone kids, always wrinkling my nose up, *like a mouse.*

"I showed this picture earlier today. It didn't sit well with the child alter, Sadie. It made her run to the corner of the room, begin scribbling furiously on paper. She drew this," she says, holding the drawing up, showing it to me again. The dismembered body, the blob of blood.

"Around the time you were ten years old, your father filed for an order of protection against your stepmother. He sold your home in Indiana, moved with you to Chicago. He started a new career, at a department store. Do you remember this?" she asks, but I don't. Not all of it, anyway.

"I need to get back to my family," I tell her instead. "They must be worried about me. They must wonder where I am," but she says that my family knows where I am.

I picture Will, Otto and Tate in our home without me. I wonder if the snow relented, if ferry traffic resumed, if Will made it home in time to pick Tate up from school.

I think of Otto at home when the police arrived to collect the washcloth, the knife.

"Is my son here? Is my son Otto here?" I ask, wondering if I'm even at the public safety building anymore or if they've taken me elsewhere.

I look around. I see a windowless room, a wall, two chairs, the floor.

There's no way to know where I am.

I ask the woman, "Where am I? When can I go home?"

"I just have a few more questions," she says. "If you'll bear with me, we'll get you out of here soon. When you arrived at the station, you told Officer Berg there was a bloody washcloth in your home, along with a knife."

"Yes," I tell her, "that's right."

"Officer Berg sent someone to your home. The property was thoroughly searched. Neither item was there."

"They're mistaken," I say, voice elevating, my blood pressure spiking as a headache forms between my eyes, a dull, achy pain, and I press on it, watching as the room around me begins to drift in and out of focus. "I saw them both. I know for certain they're there. The police didn't look hard enough," I insist because I know I'm right about this. The washcloth and the knife were there. I didn't imagine them.

"There's more, Dr. Foust," she tells me. "Your husband gave the police permission to search your home. They found Mrs. Baines's missing cell phone there. Can you tell us how it came to be in your home, or why you didn't turn it in to the police?"

"I didn't know it was there," I say defensively. I shrug my shoulders, tell her I can't explain. "Where did they find it?" I ask, feeling hopeful that the answers to Morgan's murder are there on her phone.

"They found it, oddly enough, charging on your fireplace mantel."

"What?" I ask, aghast. Then I remember the dead phone. The one I assumed was Alice's.

"We asked your husband. He said he

didn't put it there. Did you put the cell phone on the mantel, Dr. Foust?" she asks.

I tell her I did.

"What were you doing with Mrs. Baines's cell phone?" she asks, and this I can explain, though it sounds so unbelievable as I say it, telling her how I found Morgan's cell phone in my bed.

"You found Mrs. Baines's phone in your bed? Your husband told the police you're the jealous type. That you're mistrustful. That you're intolerant of him speaking to other women."

"That's not true," I snap, angry that Will would say these things of me. Every time I accused him of cheating, it was with good reason.

"Were you jealous of your husband's relationship with Mrs. Baines?"

"No," I say, but that's of course a lie. I was somewhat jealous. I was insecure. After Will's history, I had every right to be. I try to explain this to her. I tell her about Will's past, about his affairs.

"Did you think your husband and Mrs. Baines were having an affair?" she asks, and I did, truth be told, think that. For a time I did. But I never would have acted on it. And now I know that it wasn't an affair they were having, but something that went deeper than that. Will and Morgan had a bond, a connection, to his former fiancée. The one he claimed he didn't love any more than me. But somehow, I think he did.

I reach across the table, take ahold of her hands and say, "You have to believe me. I didn't do anything to hurt Morgan Baines." She pulls her hands away.

I feel disembodied then. I watch on as another me sits slumped in a chair, speaking to a woman. "I do believe you, Dr. Foust. I do. I don't think Sadie did this," the woman says, though her voice comes to me muffled as if I'm slipping away, drowning in water, before the room drops entirely from sight.

Will

They let me into the room. Sadie is there. She sits on a chair with her back to me. Her shoulders slump forward; her head is in her hands. From the back side, she looks to be about twelve years old. Her hair is matted down to her head; her pajamas are on.

I tread lightly. "Sadie?" I gently ask because maybe it is and maybe it isn't. Until I get a good look at her, I never know who she is. The physical characteristics don't change. There's always the brown hair and eyes, the same trim figure, the same complexion and nose. The change is in her demeanor, in her bearing. It's in her posture: in the way she stands and walks. It's in the way she talks, her word choice and pitch. It's in her actions. If she's aggressive or demure, a killjoy or crass, easy or highstrung. If she comes on to me or if she cowers in a corner, crying out like a little girl for her daddy every time I touch her.

My wife is a chameleon.

She looks at me. She's wrecked. She's got tears in her eyes, which is how I know she's either the kid or she's Sadie. Because Camille would never cry.

"They think I killed her, Will."

Sadie.

Sadie's voice is panicked when she speaks. She's being hypersensitive as always. She rises from the chair, comes to me, attaches herself to me. Arms around my neck, getting all clingy, which ordinarily Sadie doesn't do. But she's desperate now, thinking I'll do her bidding for her as I always do. But not this time.

"Oh, Sadie," I say, stroking her hair, being amenable as always. "You're shaking," I say, pulling away, keeping her at an arm's length.

I've got empathy down to a science. Eye contact, active listening. Ask questions, avoid judgment. I could do it in my sleep. It never hurts to cry a little, too.

"My God," I say. I let go of her hands long enough to reach for the tissue I put in my pocket before, the one with enough menthol to make myself cry. I dab it at my eyes, put it back in my pocket, let the waterworks begin. "Berg will rue the day he did this to you. I've never seen you so upset," I tell her, cupping her face in my hands, taking her in. "What did they do to you?" I ask.

Her voice is screechy when it comes. She's panicking. I see it in her eyes. "They think I killed Morgan. That I did it because I was jealous of you and her. I'm not a killer, Will," she says. "You know that. You have to tell them."

"Of course, Sadie. Of course I will," I lie, always her Johnny-on-the-spot. Always. It gets old. "I'll tell them," I say, though I won't. I'm not convinced of the need to commit obstruction of justice for her, though Sadie, herself, could never kill. That's where Camille comes in handy.

Truth be told, I like Camille more than Sadie. The first time she manifested herself for me, I thought Sadie was yanking my chain. But no. It was real. And almost too good to be true. Because I'd discovered a vivacious, untamable woman living inside my wife, one I was more smitten with than the woman I married. It was like discovering gold in a mine.

There's a whole metamorphosis that happens. I've been at this long enough that I know when it's happening. I just never know who I'll get when the mutation takes place, if I'll wind up with a butterfly or a frog.

"You have to believe me," she begs.

"I do believe you, Sadie."

"I think they're trying to frame me," she says. "But I have an alibi, Will. I was with you when she was killed. They're blaming me for something I didn't do!" she yells as I go to her, hold her pretty little head in my hands and tell her everything will be all right.

She recoils then, remembering something.

"Berg said you called him," she says. "He said you called him and took back what you said about that night. He says you said I wasn't with you after all. That I walked the dogs. That you didn't know where I'd gone. You lied, Will."

"Is that what they told you?" I ask, aghast. I let my mouth drop, my eyes go wide. I shake my head and say, "They're lying, Sadie. They're telling lies, trying to pit us against each other. It's a tactic. You can't believe anything they say."

"Why didn't you tell me Morgan was Erin's sister?" she asks, changing tack. "You kept that from me. I would have understood, Will. I would have understood your need to connect with someone Erin loved if only you'd have told me. I would have supported that," she says, and it's laughable, really. Because I thought Sadie was smarter than this. She hasn't put two and two together.

I didn't need to connect with Morgan. I needed to *disconnect.* I didn't know she lived on the island when we moved here. If I did, we wouldn't have come.

Imagine my surprise when I saw her for the first time in ten years. I could have let it go, too. But Morgan couldn't let sleeping dogs lie.

She threatened to snitch. To tell Sadie what I'd done. The picture of Erin she left for Sadie to find. I found it first, put it in the last place I expected Sadie to look. It was just my luck that she did.

Morgan was a stupid kid the night I took Erin's life. She heard us fighting because Erin had fallen for some dick when she was off at school. She came home to break the engagement off. She tried to give me the ring back. Erin had only been gone a couple of months, but by winter break she was high and mighty already. She thought she was better than me. A sorority girl while I was still living at home, going to community college.

Morgan tried to tattle, to tell everyone she heard us fighting the night before, but no one was going to believe a ten-year-old over me. And I played the role of the distraught boyfriend quite well. I was heartbroken as could be. And no one yet knew Erin had been seeing someone new. She only told that to me.

The evidence — the storm, the icy patches on the street, the lack of visibility — was also insurmountable that night. I'd taken precautions. When they found her, there were no external signs of violence. No signs of a struggle. Asphyxiation is extremely difficult to detect. They didn't do a tox screen either, on account of the weather conditions. No one considered that Erin might've died because of a shitload of Xanax in her system, because of hypoxia, because of a plastic bag strapped down over her head. The cops didn't. They didn't think once about the way I pulled the bag from her head when she was dead; how I moved Erin's body to the driver's seat, shifted the car into Drive, watched her corpse take a ride into the pond before I walked the rest of the way home, grateful for the snow that covered my tracks. No, they thought only of the icy road, of Erin's lead foot, of the indisputable fact that she swerved off the road and into the freezing water — which was quite disputable after all. Because that's not the way it happened.

Premeditated murder. It was almost too easy to do and get away with.

I moved on, met Sadie, fell in love, got

married. Enter Camille.

She took care of me in ways Sadie never could. I never imagined all that she'd do for me over the years. Morgan wasn't the first woman she killed for me. Because there was Carrie Laemmer, too, a student of mine who accused me of sexual harassment.

Again Sadie speaks. "They say I disassociate. That I'm only one of many parts. That there are people living inside of me," she says. "It's ludicrous. I mean, if you, my husband, didn't see it, how could they?"

"It's one of the many things I love about you. Your unpredictability. Different every day. I'll tell you this, Sadie — you were never boring. I just never came up with a diagnosis for your condition," I say, though it's a lie, of course. I've known for eons what I was dealing with. I learned how to turn it in my favor.

"You knew?" she asks, aghast.

"It's a good thing, Sadie. The silver lining. Don't you see? The police don't think that you killed Morgan. They believe that *Camille* did. You can plead not guilty by reason of insanity. You won't go to jail."

She gasps, coming undone. It's fun to watch. "But I'll be sent to a psychiatric institution, Will. I won't be able to go home."

"That's better than jail, isn't it, Sadie? Do you know what kind of things happen in jail?"

"But, Will," she tells me, desperate now. "I'm not insane."

I step away from her. I go to the door because I'm the only one of us with the freedom to leave. There's power in that. I turn and look at her, my face changing, becoming visibly apathetic because the sham-empathy is getting exhausting.

"I'm not insane," she tells me again.

I hold my tongue. It wouldn't be right to lie.

Sadie

Sometime after Will has gone, Officer Berg steps into the room with me. He leaves the door open.

I know my rights. I demand to see a lawyer.

But he just shrugs half-heartedly at me and says, "No need," because they're letting me go. They have no evidence to hold me on. The murder weapon and the washcloth that I said I saw were nowhere to be found. The going theory is that I made them both up in an effort to throw off the investigation. But they can't prove that either. They say I killed Morgan. That I transformed into some other version of me and killed her myself. But the police need probable cause before they can arrest me. They need something more than mere suspicion. Even Mr. Nilsson's statement isn't damning enough because it doesn't place me at the crime scene. The cell phone in my home also doesn't do that. These things are circumstantial.

It feels like some phantom thing. There are parts of my life I can't account for, including that night. It's in the realm of possibility that I murdered that poor woman — or some version of me did — though I don't know why. The pictures Officer Berg showed me come to mind and I stifle a cry.

"Would you like us to call your husband to come get you?" Officer Berg asks, but I say no. Truth be told, I'm a bit upset that Will left me at the police station alone. Though the weather outside is still inclement, I need to be alone with my thoughts. I need fresh air.

Officer Berg himself offers me a ride, but I say no to that, too. I need to get away from him.

I start to shrug off the coat Officer Berg gave me, but he stops me, saying I should keep it. He'll get it another time.

It's dark outside. The sun has set. The world is white, but for now the snow has stopped coming down. Traffic moves slowly. Headlights maneuver through snowbanks. Tires scrape against the packed-down snow. The streets are messy.

There are slippers on my feet, though they're a far cry from shoes. They're knit and a faux fur that only absorbs the moisture, making my feet wet, red, numb. My hair hasn't seen a comb today. I have no idea what I look like, though I'd venture to guess it's just a hairbreadth away from a madwoman.

As I walk the few blocks home, I piece together the last few hours of my life. I left Otto alone with the washcloth and the knife. The police came searching for these things. By the time they did, they were gone. Someone did something with the washcloth and the knife.

As I make my way toward our street, I put my head down and walk, my arms tied into a knot to stave off the night's fierce wind. The snow on the ground still blows about. There are icy patches on the street, which I slip on, falling once, twice, three times. Only on the third time does a Good Samaritan help me to my feet, taking me for a drunk. He asks if he can call someone to come pick me up, but by then I'm almost home. I just have our street to climb, and I do so gracelessly.

I see Will in the window when I arrive, sitting on the sofa, the fireplace red-hot. His legs are crossed and he's lost in thought. Tate dashes through the room, smiling merrily, and on his way past, Will tickles his belly and he laughs. Tate takes off, running up the stairs and away from Will, and then he's gone, to some other part of the house where I can no longer see him. Will returns to the sofa, laces his hands behind his head and leans back, seemingly content.

There are lights on in the upstairs windows, Otto's and Imogen's, which face the street, though the curtains are closed. I can't see anything but the glowing peripheries of the windows, though it surprises me that even Imogen is home. At this time in the evening, she isn't often home.

From the outside, the house looks perfectly idyllic as it did that first day we arrived. The rooftops, the trees are covered with snow. It covers the lawn, sparkling white. The snow clouds have cleared, the moon illuminating the picturesque scene. The fireplace spews smoke from the chimney, and though outside the world is freezing, inside it looks undeniably homey and warm.

There's nothing amiss with this scene, as if Will and the kids have moved on without me, no one noticing my absence.

But the very fact that nothing is amiss makes me feel instinctually that something is wrong.

WILL

The door bursts open. There she stands, all slovenly and windblown.

Nice of Berg to give me fair warning that she'd been let go.

I hide my surprise. I rise to my feet, go to her, cup her cold face in my hands. "Oh, thank God," I say, embracing her. I hold my breath. She smells putrid. "They finally came to their senses," I say, but Sadie's giving me the cold shoulder, pulling away, saying I left her there, that I abandoned her. It's all very dramatic.

"I did no such thing," I say, playing to her weakness, her penchant for losing time. Roughly a quarter of the conversations Sadie has, she doesn't remember having. Which has become unexceptional for me, but is quite the nuisance for coworkers and the like. It makes it difficult for Sadie to have friends because on the surface she's moody and aloof.

"I told you I'd be back just as soon as I made sure the kids were all right," I say. "Don't you remember? I love you, Sadie. I would never have abandoned you."

She shakes her head. She doesn't remember. Because it didn't happen.

"Where are the kids?" she asks, looking for them.

"In their rooms."

"When were you going to come back?"

"I've been making calls, trying to find someone to come stay with the kids. I didn't want to leave them alone all night."

"Why should I believe you?" she asks, a doubting Thomas. She wants to look at my phone, see whom I've called, and it's only because fortune smiles down on me that there are recent calls in the call log to numbers Sadie doesn't know. I assign them names. Andrea, a colleague, and Samantha, a graduate student.

"Why wouldn't you believe me?" I fire back, playing the victim.

We hear Tate upstairs jumping away on his bed. The house groans because of it.

She shakes her head, feeling spent, and says, "I don't know what to believe anymore." She rubs at her forehead, trying to figure it out. She's had a hell of a day. She can't understand how a knife and washcloth could just up and disappear. She asks me, her tone exasperated and contentious. She's looking for a fight.

I shrug my shoulders and ask back, "I don't know, Sadie. Are you sure you really saw them?" because a little gaslighting never hurts.

"I did!" she says, desperate to make me believe her.

This is turning into a bit of a shitstorm now that the police are involved, unlike last time when things went so smoothly. I'm usually so much tidier about such things. Take Carrie Laemmer, for example. All I had to do that time was wait for Camille to come, put the idea in her head. Camille is suggestible, as Sadie is easily suggestible. It's just that Sadie isn't the violent type. I could have done it myself. But why would I, when I had someone willing to do my bidding for me? I cried my eyes out, told her all about Carrie's threats, how she accused me of sexual harassment. I said I wished she would just go away and leave me alone. My career, my reputation would be gone if Carrie made good on her threats. They'd take me away from her; they'd put me in jail. I told her, *She's trying to ruin my life. She's trying to ruin* our *lives.*

I didn't specifically ask Camille to kill her.

And yet, nevertheless, a few days later Carrie was dead.

The way it happened was that one day, poor Carrie Laemmer went missing. There was a wide-scale search. Word had it that she'd been at a frat party the night before, boozing it up. She left the party alone, stumbled out of the house, drunk. She fell down the porch steps while fellow partygoers watched on.

Carrie's roommate didn't return home until the following morning. When she did, she found that Carrie's bed hadn't been slept in, that Carrie hadn't made it home the night before.

Security cameras across campus caught glimpses of Carrie staggering past the library, falling down in the middle of the quad. It was unlike Carrie, who could hold her liquor, or so said the students who saw the CCTV footage. As if it was brag-worthy, a high tolerance for alcohol. Her parents would be so proud to know what their fifty grand a year bought them.

There were lapses in the video surveillance. Black holes where the cameras didn't reach. I was at a faculty event that night. People saw me. Not that I was ever a suspect because no one was. Because that time, unlike this, things went swimmingly.

No pun intended.

Not far from campus was a polluted canal where the university's crew team rowed. The water was more than ten feet deep, contaminated with sewage, if the rumors were true. A wooded running path sat parallel to the canal, all of it shadowed by trees.

After three days missing, Carrie turned up there, in the canal. The police called her a *floater* because of the way she was found, most of her body parts bobbing buoyantly on the surface of the canal, while her heavy head dragged beneath.

Cause of death: accidental drowning. Everyone knew she'd been drunk, stumbling. Everyone saw. It was easy enough to assume, then, that she tumbled drunkenly into the canal all on her own.

The entirety of the student population mourned. Flowers were laid at the edge of the canal beneath a tree. Her parents traveled from Boston, left her childhood teddy bear there at the scene.

What Camille told me was that Carrie never thrashed about in the water. She never gasped and screamed for help. What happened instead was that she bobbed listlessly on the surface for a while. Her mouth sank beneath the water. It came back up, it went back down.

It went on this way for a while, head tossed back, eyes glassy and empty.

If she bothered to kick, Camille said, she couldn't tell.

She struggled that way for nearly a minute. Then she submerged, slipping silently beneath the water.

The way Camille described it for me, it sounded as undramatic as drowning gets. As anticlimactic. Boring, if you ask me.

This time, it was just unlucky that Sadie got to that laundry before me.

I've been careless. Because the night with Morgan, the transformation from Camille to Sadie happened too quickly, leaving me to clean up the mess. Her clothes I burned. The knife I buried. I just never counted on Sadie doing the laundry. Why would I? She never does. I also never knew that Camille had taken Morgan's necklace. Not until I saw it sitting on the countertop this morning.

Camille should have been more careful where she stood that night. She should have better anticipated the sprays of blood. It wasn't like it was her first rodeo. But she came home a bloody mess. It was up to me to wipe her clean, leaving my fingerprints on the knife and washcloth. I couldn't let the police find that.

Sadie rubs at her face and says again, "I just don't know what to believe."

"It's been a long day. A stressful day. And you haven't been taking your pills," I say. It dawns on her. She went to bed without taking her pills. She forgot about them this morning. I know because they're still where I left them.

That's why she feels this way, out of control as she always does when she doesn't have her pills. She reaches eagerly for them, swallows them down, knowing that in a short while she'll be back to feeling like herself.

I almost laugh out loud. The pills do nothing. It's only in Sadie's head that something happens. The placebo effect. Because she thinks popping a pill will naturally make her feel better. Have a headache, pop some Tylenol. A runny nose? Some Sudafed.

You'd think, as a doctor, Sadie would know better.

I bought the empty capsules online. I filled them with cornstarch, replaced the ones the doctor prescribed with these. Sadie took them like a good girl, but she'd whine about it at times, say the pills made her tired and fuzzy because that's what pills are supposed to do.

She can be so suggestible sometimes.

I make Sadie dinner. I pour her a glass of wine. I sit her down at the table and, as she eats, I rub her cold, dirty feet. They're mottled and gray.

She nods off at the table, so tired she sleeps upright.

But she sleeps for only a second at best, and when she awakes, she groggily asks, voice slurred with fatigue, "How did you get home in the storm? Otto said the ferries weren't running."

So many questions. So many fucking questions.

"Water taxi."

"What time was that?"

"I'm not sure. In time to get Tate."

She's coming to now, speaking clearly. "They kept the kids at school all day? Even with the storm?"

"They kept them there until parents could get to them."

"So you went straight to the elementary school? You didn't come home first?" she asks. I tell her no. She's cobbling together a timeline. I wonder why. I tell her I took the water taxi to the island, picked up Tate, came home. Then I went to the public safety building for her.

Only some of it is true.

"What was Otto doing when you came

home?" she asks.

I'll have to shut her up soon. Because her curiosity is the only thing standing between me and getting off scot-free.

Sadie

I stand in the bedroom, rummaging through my drawers, finding clean pajamas to replace the ones I have on. I need a shower. My feet are aching, my legs bruised. But these things are inconsequential when there are bigger worries on my mind. It's an out-of-body experience. What's happening can't possibly be happening to me.

I spin suddenly with the knowledge that I'm no longer alone. It's a metaphysical sensation, something that moves up my spine.

Otto comes into the bedroom unannounced. He's not there and then he is. His sudden arrival makes me leap, my hand going to my heart. I come to face him. The signs of his illness are now visible.

He wasn't lying. He's sick. He coughs into a hand, his eyes vacant and feverish.

I think of the last conversation I had with Otto, where he accused me of putting the knife in his backpack. If what that policewoman said is true, I didn't do it. But the part of me known as Camille did. The guilt is enormous. Otto isn't a murderer. Quite possibly, I am.

He says to me, "Where were you?" and then again he coughs, his voice scratchy like it wasn't before.

Will didn't tell the kids where I was. He didn't tell them I wasn't coming home. How long would he have waited to tell them? How would he have said it, what words would he have used to tell our children I'd been arrested by the police? And when they asked why, what would he have said? That their mother is a murderer?

"You just left," he said, and I see the child still in him. He was scared, I think, panicked that he couldn't find me.

I say vaguely, "I had something I needed to take care of."

"I thought you were here. I didn't know you were gone till I saw Dad outside."

"You saw him come home with Tate?" I assume. I picture Will's small sedan fighting its way through the snow. I can't imagine how the car made it.

But Otto tells me no, it was before Tate came home. He says that soon after we talked in the living room, he changed his mind. He was hungry. He wanted that toast after all.

Otto says he came down to find me. But I wasn't here. He looked for me, caught a glimpse of Will traipsing through the backyard in the snow.

But Otto is mistaken. It was me, not Will, he saw in the backyard in the snow.

"That was me," I tell him. "I was trying to get the dogs inside," I say. I don't tell him about the knife.

I realize now what must have really happened with the knife back in Chicago. Camille must have put it in Otto's backpack. The story he told me about the night, on the fire escape, when I convinced him to stab his classmates wasn't a pipe dream. From Otto's perspective, it happened just as he said it did. Because he saw me.

And the disturbing drawings, the strange dolls. That wasn't Otto. That was also me.

"It was Dad," he says, shaking his head.

I realize that my hands are shaking, my palms sweaty. I rub them against the thighs of my pajama pants, ask Otto again what he said.

"Dad was here," he repeats, "in the backyard. Shoveling."

"Are you sure it was your father?" I ask.

"Why wouldn't it be?" he asks, put off by

my questions now. "I know what Dad looks like," he says.

"Of course you do," I say, feeling lightheaded and breathless. "Are you sure it was in the backyard that you saw him?"

I'm grateful that he's speaking to me. After his disclosure this afternoon, I'm surprised that he would. I'm reminded of his words. *I'll never forgive you.* Why should he? I'll never forgive myself for what I've done.

Otto nods his head. He says out loud, "I'm sure."

Will was shoveling the lawn? Who in the world shovels grass?

I realize then that Will wasn't shoveling. He was digging through the snow for the knife.

But how would Will have known about the knife? I only told Officer Berg.

The answer comes to me, shaking me to my core.

The only way Will would know about that knife is if he was the one who put it there.

WILL

Sadie is quickly working out that my story is full of holes. She knows someone in this house killed Morgan. She knows it might be her. With a little sleuthing, she'll soon discover — if she hasn't already — that I'm the puppet master pulling the strings. And then she'll tell Berg.

I won't let that happen. I'll get rid of her first.

After she ate, Sadie went upstairs to wash up for bed. She's tired, but her nerves are frayed. Sleep won't come easily tonight.

While the pills she takes are placebos only, that doesn't mean that the pills I pick up at the pharmacy — those I save for a rainy day — aren't the genuine thing. Combine them with a little wine and, voilà, I have myself a deadly cocktail.

The best part of the plan is that Sadie's mental state is well documented before we came to Maine. Add to that the discoveries of the day and it wouldn't be such a stretch to think she might want to kill herself.

A murder meant to look like a suicide. Sadie's words, not mine.

I find the pills high above the kitchen cabinets. I use the mortar and pestle to crush them. I run the sink to lessen the sound. The pills aren't exactly easy to dissolve, but I have my ways. Sadie has never been averse to a glass of wine after her pills. Thought she should know better because such things don't mix well.

What I'm anticipating is some form of respiratory distress. But who really knows. There's a whole host of things that can go wrong with a lethal overdose.

I draft a suicide note in my mind. It will be easy enough to forge. *I can't live with myself. I can't go on this way. I've done a horrible, horrible thing.*

After Sadie is dead it will be just the boys, Imogen and me. This is quite the sacrifice I'm making for my family. Because as the breadwinner, Sadie is the one with the life insurance policy. There's a suicide clause in it, which says the company won't pay out if Sadie kills herself within two years of the policy going into effect. I don't know that she's had it two years. If she has, we're due a lump sum of five hundred grand. I feel a ripple of excitement at that prospect. What five hundred thousand dollars could buy me. I've always thought I'd like to live in a houseboat.

If she hasn't had the policy for two years, we'll get nothing.

But even then, I reassure myself, it's not as if Sadie's death will be for naught. There's still much value in it — most important, my freedom. There just won't be any financial gain.

Momentarily I stop crushing the pills. The thought of that saddens me. I think that perhaps it's best to shelve Sadie's suicide until I've looked into the policy. Because a half a million dollars is a lot to waste.

But then I reconsider. Silently I scold myself. I shouldn't be so greedy, so materialistic. There are more important things to consider.

After all that Sadie has done, I can't have my boys living with a monster.

Sadie

Why would Will bury a knife in the backyard? And what reason would he have to dig it up and hide it from the police?

If he took the knife, did he take the washcloth, too? The necklace?

Will lied to me. He told me he picked Tate up from school and then came home, but it happened the other way around. Will knew about my condition, this way I have of transforming into someone else, and he didn't tell me. If he knew there was a potentially violent side of me, why didn't he get me help? *You were never boring,* he said, such a glib thing to say in light of what I know now.

Will is hiding something. Will is hiding many things, I think.

I wonder where the knife is now. Where the washcloth and necklace are. If the police did a thorough search of our home, then they're not here. They're somewhere else.

Unless Will had these things on his own person while the police searched our home and he hid them afterward. In which case, they may be here.

But if I'm the one who killed Morgan, why would Will hide these things? Was he trying to protect me? I don't think so.

I consider what Officer Berg told me, that Will called him and retracted his alibi for me that night. Will said he wasn't with me when Morgan was killed.

Was Officer Berg lying, as Will said he was, trying to pit us against each other?

Or did it happen as Officer Berg said? Was Will incriminating me?

I consider what I know about Morgan's murder. The boning knife. The threatening notes. *You know nothing. Tell anyone and die. I'm watching you.* This is helpful, but unthinkable. Because I can't get the idea of Erin and Morgan as sisters out of my mind. It's the most damning evidence of all. Because they're both dead.

My mind gets lost on our wedding day, the days we welcomed our babies into the world. The idea that Will, that ever gentle and compassionate Will, whom everyone likes, whom I've known half my life, could be a killer cripples me. I begin to cry. But it's a silent cry because it has to be. I press my hand to my mouth, lean against the bedroom wall, my body nearly collapsing. I press hard, stifling the cry somewhere inside. My body convulses. The tears stream from my eyes.

I can't let the others hear me. I can't let them see me. I steady myself, tasting Will's dinner as it moves back up and into my esophagus. By the grace of God, it stays there.

I know now that Will had a hand in Morgan's murder because he was in on Erin's, too. Erin's murder, I think, and not a horrible unfortunate accident. But why kill Morgan? I go back to the threatening notes and decide: she knew something he didn't want the rest of the world to find out.

With Will downstairs, I begin to search our bedroom for the missing things: the knife, the washcloth, Morgan's necklace. Will is too smart to hide these things in obvious places, like under the mattress or in a dresser drawer.

I go to the closet. I search the inside of Will's clothing for secret pockets, finding none.

I drop to my hands and knees, crawling across the floorboards. It's a wide plank floor, which could conceivably house a secret compartment beneath. I feel with my fingers for loose boards. With my eyes, I scan for subtle differences in the height of the boards and in the wood grain. Nothing immediately catches my eye.

On my haunches, I think. I let my eyes wander around the room, wondering where else Will could hide something from me if he wanted to. I consider the furniture, the floor register, a smoke detector. My eyes move to the electrical sockets, where one is placed evenly in the center of each wall, totaling four.

I rise to my feet, foraging inside the dresser, under the bed, behind the curtain panels. And that's when a fifth electrical outlet catches my eye, tucked behind the heavy drapery.

This outlet is not evenly placed as the others are — in the dead center of each wall — but disproportionately placed in a way that doesn't make sense to me. It's mere feet to the left of another outlet and, on close examination, looks slightly different than the rest, though an unsuspecting person would never notice. Only someone who very much believed her husband had something to hide.

I let my gaze fall to the doorway. I listen, making sure Will isn't on his way up. The hallway is dark, empty, but it's not quiet.

Tate is wound up tonight.

I drop to my hands and knees. I don't have a screwdriver, and so I plunge a thumbnail into the head of the screw. I turn and turn, warping the nail, tearing it low enough that it makes my finger bleed. The screw comes out. Instead of peeling the outlet cover away from the wall, it opens, revealing a tiny safe behind. There is no knife, no washcloth, no necklace there. Instead there's a roll of cash, hundred-dollar bills mostly, which I quickly, ham-fistedly tally up, losing count, landing somewhere well into the thousands of dollars. My finger bleeds on the dollar bills. My heart races inside of me.

Why would Will be hiding this money in the wall?

Why would Will be hiding this money from me?

There's nothing else there.

I don't replace the contents of the safe. I hide that in my own dresser drawer. I drop the drapes back into place. I stand from the floor, press a hand to the wall to steady myself. Around me, the world spins.

When I get control of myself, I walk lightly from the bedroom and down the stairs. I hold my breath. I bite down hard on my lip as I descend the steps one at a time.

As I approach the bottom steps, I hear Will humming a happy tune. He's in the kitchen, washing dishes, I think. The sink water runs.

I don't go to the kitchen. I go to the office instead, turn the knob and softly close the door behind myself so there is no audible noise of the latch bolt retracting. I don't lock the door; it would rouse suspicion if Will found me in the office with the door locked.

I check the search history first. There's nothing there. It's all been wiped clean, even the earlier search I found on Erin's death. It's gone. Someone sat at this computer after me, got rid of the internet search just like the knife and the washcloth.

I open a search engine. I type in Erin's name for myself and see what I can find. But it's all the same as I saw before, detailed accounts of the storm and her accident. I see now that there was never an investigation into her death. It was ruled an accident based on the circumstances, namely the weather.

I do a search into our finances. I can't understand why Will would be hiding so much money in the walls of our home. Will pays the bills for us. I don't pay much attention to them unless he leaves a bill lying around on the counter for me to see. Otherwise the bills come and go without my knowledge.

I go to the bank website. The passwords for our accounts are all nearly the same, some variation on Otto's and Tate's names and birth dates. Our checking and savings accounts seem to be intact. I close the site and look into our retirement accounts, the kids' college savings, the credit card balance. These seem reasonable, too.

I hear Will call for me. Hear his footsteps go up and then down the stairs, looking for me. "I'm here," I call out, hoping he doesn't hear the tremor in my voice.

I don't minimize the screen. Instead I enter another search: dissociative identity disorder. When he comes into the room and asks, I tell him I'm trying to learn more about my disease. We haven't yet talked about how he knew and I didn't. It's just another thing he's been keeping from me.

But now that I know about it, there's a new worry: that I'll simply up and disappear at any moment and someone else will take my place.

"I poured you a glass of Malbec," he says, standing in the office doorway with it, carrying it in a stemless glass. He comes farther into the room, strokes my hair with his free hand. My skin crawls as he does and it takes everything in me not to pull away from his touch. "We were out of the cabernet," he says, which he knows is my favorite wine. Malbec is decidedly more bitter than I like, but it doesn't matter tonight. I'll drink anything.

He peers over my shoulder at the website I've landed on, a general medical site that lists symptoms and treatment. "I hope you aren't upset that I didn't tell you," he says by means of an apology. "You'd take it hard, I knew. And you were managing the condition quite well. I kept an eye on you, made sure you were fine. If I'd have ever thought things were turning problematic . . ."

He stops abruptly there. I glance up to face him.

"Thank you," I say, for the wine, as he sets the glass on the desktop and tells me, "After everything you've been through today, I thought maybe you could use a drink."

I could most certainly use a drink, something to calm and soothe me. I reach for the glass and angle it toward my lips, imagining the anesthetizing sensation as it slips down my throat and dulls my senses.

But my hand shakes as I do, and so I put the glass instantly back, not wanting Will to see how nervous I am because of him.

"Don't worry yourself over this," he says. With two free hands, he massages my shoulders, up my neck. His hands are warm and assertive. His fingers worm their way onto my scalp, through my hair, kneading the base of my skull where I'm prone to tension headaches.

"I've done some research myself," Will says. "Psychotherapy is the recommended treatment. There are no medications that treat this thing," as if it's cancer that I've got.

I wonder if he knows so much, why he never suggested psychotherapy before. Perhaps it's because I've seen therapists in the past. Perhaps it's because he mistakenly believed I was getting treatment.

Or perhaps it's because he never wanted me to get better.

"We'll come up with a plan in the morning," he says, "after you've had a good night's sleep."

He withdraws his hands from my head. He steps to the side of the chair, and with a soft spin, he turns the chair so that I'm looking at him.

I don't like the control he has over me.

Will waits a beat, and then he drops to his knees. He looks me in the eye. Says dotingly, “I know this has been a hell of a day. Tomorrow will be better, for both of us.”

“Are you sure?” I ask, and he tells me, “I am. I promise.”

And then he cups my face in his hands. He runs his lips over mine, softly, delicately, as if I’m easily broken. He tells me I mean the world to him. That he loves me more than words could ever say.

From upstairs, there’s a thump. Tate begins to scream. He’s fallen from bed.

Will draws back, eyes closed. In a moment, he rises up to standing.

He nods toward the glass of wine. “Just holler if you’d like more.”

He leaves, and only then do I catch my breath. I hear his footsteps on the stairs, his voice call out to Tate that he’s on his way.

Will

For as smart as Sadie is, she's also utterly clueless. There's a lot she doesn't know. Like how, if I log in to her Google account from another device — as I do from the bedroom now — I can see her search history.

She's been up to no good. Nosing around on the bank's website. Not that she'll find anything there.

But she found other things.

It was the blood that gave it away, as I first came into the bedroom a few minutes ago. Four stray drops of it on the floor, from the door to the curtains. I went to the bedroom curtains, looked behind, saw that the outlet cover hung lightly aslant. I opened the safe. The money was gone.

That avaricious hog, I thought. *What has she done with it?*

Now that she's found the money, it won't take long for Sadie to figure out I've been robbing Imogen's trust fund. The girl is a pest but she's worth keeping around just for that. I'm slowly creating my own little nest egg.

According to her search history, Sadie's also been looking into Erin and Morgan online. Connecting the dots.

Perhaps she's not as clueless as I thought.

I put Tate to bed. He's glum from the fall. I give him Benadryl, tell him it will help his little noggin feel better. I give a dab more than the recommended dose. I can't have him awake tonight.

I kiss the spot on Tate's head where it hurts, get him in bed. He asks for a bedtime story, and I oblige. I'm not worried. No matter what Sadie finds, it will be a moot point when she drinks her wine.

It's only a matter of time.

SADIE

I have to find a way to call Officer Berg and tell him what I've found. He won't believe me. But I have to tell him anyway. He'll be obligated to look into it.

I haven't seen my cell phone since the morning. The last time I saw it, it was in the kitchen, the same place our landline is. That's where I need to go.

But the idea of leaving the office scares me. Because if Will could kill Erin, he could kill me.

I take a series of deep breaths before I go. I try to act nonchalant. I carry my wine with me. I bring a letter opener just in case, with a sharp-enough blade. I slide it in the waistband of my pajama pants, worried it will fall.

On the other side of the office door, I'm vulnerable. The house is oddly quiet and dark. The kids are asleep. No one told me good-night.

A light glows in the kitchen. It's not bright. A stove light only, which I go to, like a moth to a porch light, trying hard to shake the feeling that Will is behind me, that Will is watching me, that Will is there.

If he killed Erin, how did he do it? Was it in a fit of rage, or was it premeditated? And what about Morgan? How, exactly, did she die?

I feel the letter opener slipping deeper into my pants. I hoist it up. My hands are trembling, unsteady, and so the wine spills as I do, the glass getting cocked too far to one side. I lick the rim of the glass to wipe it clean. I purse my lips, not liking the bitter taste of the Malbec. Regardless, I take another sip, force it down as tears prick my eyes.

A noise from behind startles me and I turn, seeing only the shadowy foyer, the indefinite dining room. I hold still, watching, waiting, for movements, for sound. This old home has so many dark corners, so many places where someone can hide.

"Will?" I say lightly, expecting him to reply, but he doesn't. No one does. No one's there, or at least I don't think someone is there. I hold my breath, listen for footsteps, for breathing. There's none. A blunt headache lingers, worsening in intensity as the moments go by, and I find myself becoming hot and bothered because of it. Under my armpits and between my legs, the skin is tacky. I take another sip of the wine, try to calm my nerves. The wine doesn't taste as bad this time. I'm getting used to the bitterness.

I see my phone on the table. I quickly cross the room and grab for it, stifling a cry when I turn it over to see that the battery is dead again. It will take a couple of minutes for the phone to charge well enough to use. There is another option, the landline, which is corded. The only way to use it is here in the kitchen. I'll have to be quick.

I walk back across the kitchen. I grab the landline, a dated thing. Officer Berg's business card is tucked in the letter holder on the counter, which I'm grateful for because, without my cell phone, I don't have my contacts. I dial the number on the card. I wait desperately for the police officer to answer, sipping nervously from the glass of Malbec as I do.

Will

I follow her as she goes from one room to the next. She looks for me. She doesn't know that I'm here, closer than she thinks.

She's monkeying around in the kitchen now. But when I hear the spin of a rotary dial I know it's time to intervene.

I come into the room. Sadie whirls around to face me, eyes wide. A deer in headlights is what she is, clutching the phone to her ear. She's scared shitless. Beads of sweat edge her hairline. Her skin is colorless, damp. Her breathing is uneven. I can practically see her heart thumping in her chest, like a scared little bird. It's reassuring to see that a third of the wine's been drunk.

I'm on to her. But does she know that I am?

"Who are you calling?" I ask calmly, just to see her grapple for a lie. But Sadie's never been a good liar, and so instead she's a deaf-mute. It's telling, isn't it? That's how I know that she knows that I know.

My tone shifts. I'm tired of this game.

"Put the phone down, Sadie."

She doesn't. I step closer, snatch the phone from her, set it back on the cradle. She tries to hold on to it, but Sadie lacks physical strength. The phone gives effortlessly.

"That," I tell her, "was not your brightest idea." Because now I'm mad.

I weigh my options. If she hasn't drunk enough, I may have to coerce her into finishing the wine. But gagging and vomiting would be counterintuitive. I think of another way. I hadn't been planning on disposing of a body, not tonight, but it'd be just the same to make Berg believe she ran away as it would to make it look like a suicide. A little more laborious than originally thought, but still doable.

Don't get me wrong, I love my wife. I love my family. I'm quite torn up about this.

But it's unavoidable, a necessary consequence of the can of worms that Sadie has opened. If only she'd have left well enough alone. It's her fault this is happening.

Sadie

I feel woozy. Disoriented. Panic-stricken. Because Will is angry, livid in a way that I've never seen him before. I don't know this man who stands before me, glaring intimidatingly at me. He looks vaguely like the man I married, and yet different. His words are clipped, his voice hostile. He jostles the phone from my hand, and that's how I know I wasn't imagining things. If I had any doubts about Will's part in Morgan's death, they're gone. Will did something.

I take a step back for each step he draws near, knowing that soon my back will be to the wall. I have to think quickly. But my mind is foggy, thick. Will goes out of focus before me, but I see his hands, coming at me, in slow motion.

I remember the letter opener just then, tucked away in the waistband of my pants. I grope for it, but my hands are trembling, careless; they get caught up in the pants' elastic, knocking the letter opener loose by mistake, sending it sliding down my pant leg, crashing to the floor.

Will's response time is far faster than mine. He hasn't been drinking. I feel drunk already, the alcohol hitting me harder than it usually does. Will leans down to the ground quicker than me, plucks the letter opener from the floor with nimble hands. He holds it up for me to see, asks, "What did you think you were going to do with this?"

The meager kitchen lighting glints off the end of the stainless-steel blade. He points it at me, dares me to flinch, and I do. His laugh is heinous, mocking me.

How well we think we know those closest to us.

And then, what a shock to the system it is to find out we don't know them at all.

In his anger, his rage, he no longer looks familiar.

I don't know this man.

"Did you think you were going to hurt me with this?" he asks, stabbing his palm with it, and I see that, though the edge is sharp, sharp enough to slice paper with, the point is dull. It does nothing but redden his palm. It leaves no other mark. "Did you think you were going to *kill* me with this?"

My tongue thickens inside of my mouth. It makes it harder to speak.

"What did you do to Morgan?" I ask. I won't answer his questions.

He tells me, still laughing, that it wasn't what he did to her, but what I did to her that matters. My eyes turn dry. I blink hard, a series of times. A nervous tic. I can't stop.

"You don't remember, do you?" he asks, reaching out to touch me. I draw swiftly back, thwacking my head on the cabinet. The pain radiates through my scalp, and I wince, a hand going involuntarily to it.

He says condescendingly, "Ouch. Looks like that hurt."

I drop my hand. I won't satisfy him with a reply.

I think of all the times he was so solicitous, so caring. How the Will I once knew would have run for ice when I hurt myself, would have helped me to a chair, pressed the ice to my aching head. Was that all in jest?

"It wasn't me who did something to Morgan, Sadie," he says. "It was you."

But I can't remember it. I'm of two minds about it, not knowing if I did or didn't kill Morgan. It's a terrible thing, not knowing if you took another's life. "You killed Erin," I say, the only thing I can think to say back.

"That I did," he says, and though I know it, hearing him admit to it makes it somehow worse. Tears well in my eyes, threaten to fall.

"You loved Erin," I say. "You were going to marry her."

"All true," he says. "The problem was, Erin didn't love me back. I don't take well to rejection."

"What did Morgan ever do to you?" I cry out, and he smiles wickedly and reminds me that I'm the one who killed Morgan.

"What did she ever do to *you*?" he quips, and I can only shake my head in reply.

He tells me. "I don't want to bore you with the details, but Morgan was Erin's kid sister, who made it her life's mission to blame me for Erin's death. While the rest of the world saw it as an unfortunate accident, Morgan did not. She wouldn't give it up. You took matters into your own hands, Sadie. Thanks to you, I've come through this thing unscathed."

"That didn't happen!" I scream.

He's the epitome of calm. His voice is even, not mercurial like mine. "But it did," he says. "There was this moment when you came back. You were so proud of what you'd accomplished. You had so much to say, Sadie. Like how she would never get between us again, because you took care of her."

"I didn't kill her," I assert.

His laugh is a giggle. "You did," he says. "And you did it for me. I don't think I've ever loved you as much as I did that night." He beams, claims, "All I did was tell the God's honest truth. I told you what would have become of me if Morgan made good on her threats. If she was able to prove to the police that I killed Erin, I would have gone to jail for a long, long time. Maybe forever. They would have taken me away from you, Sadie. I told you we wouldn't ever see each other, we wouldn't ever be together again. It would be all Morgan's fault if that happened. Morgan was the criminal, not me. I told you that and you understood. You believed me."

The look on his face is triumphant. "You never could live without me, could you?" he asks, looking quizzically at me, like a psychopath.

"What's the matter, Sadie?" he asks, when I say nothing. "Cat got your tongue?"

His words, his nonchalance make me see red. His laugh makes me enraged. It's the laugh, the awful, abominable laugh, that gets the better of me in the end. It's the self-satisfied look on Will's face, the way he stands there, head cocked at an angle. It's the complacent smile.

Will manipulated my condition. He made me do this. He put an idea in my head — in the part of me known as Camille — knowing this poor woman, this version of me, would have done anything in the whole wide world for him. Because she loved him so much. Because she wanted to be with him.

I feel saddened for her. And angry for me.

It comes from somewhere within. No thought comes with it.

I lunge at Will with all my might. I regret it as soon as I do. Because though he stumbles some, he is much larger than me. Much stronger, much more solid. And again, he hasn't been drinking. I shove him and he steps back. But he doesn't fall to the floor. He inches backward, latching down on a countertop to regain his balance. He laughs even more because of it, because of my paltry shove.

"That," he tells me, "was a bad idea."

I see the wooden block of knives on the countertop. He follows the gaze of my eyes.

I wonder which of us will get to it first.

Will

She's weak as a kitten. It's laughable, really.

But it's time to end this thing once and for all. No use putting it off any longer.

I come at her quickly, wrap my hands around that pretty little neck of hers and squeeze. Her airflow is restricted because of it. I watch on as panic sets in. I see it in her eyes first, the way they widen in fright. Her hands clamp down on mine, scratching her little kitten claws to get me to release.

This won't take long, only about ten seconds until she loses consciousness.

Sadie can't scream because of the pressure on her throat. Other than a few insubstantial gasps, all is quiet. Sadie never has been much of a conversationalist anyway.

Manual strangulation is an intimate thing. It's much different than other ways of killing. You have to be in close proximity to whoever it is you're killing. There's manual labor involved, unlike with a gun where you can fire off three rounds from the other side of the room and call it a day. But because of the work involved, there's a sense of pride that comes, too, of accomplishment, like painting a house or building a shed or chopping firewood.

The upside, of course, is there isn't much of a mess to clean.

"I can't tell you how sorry I am it's come to this," I say to Sadie as her arms and legs flail and she tries pathetically to fight back. She's tiring out. Her eyes roll back. Her blows are getting weaker. She tries to gouge my eyes out with her fingertips, but her thrust isn't strong or quick. I draw back, her efforts wasted. There's a pretty tinge to Sadie's skin.

I press harder, say, "You're too smart for your own good, Sadie. If only you'd have let it be, this wouldn't be happening. But I can't have you go around telling people what I did. I'm sure you understand. And since you can't keep your own mouth closed," I tell her, "it's up to me to shut you up for good."

Sadie

I deliberately collapse, my weight suspended only by his hands around my neck. It's a desperate attempt, a last-ditch effort. Because if I fail, I will die. As my vision blurs, fading in and out in those final moments, I see my children. I see Otto and Tate living here alone with Will.

I have to fight. For my children's sake, I cannot die. I cannot leave them with him.

I have to live.

The pain gets worse before it gets better. Because without the strength of my legs and my spine to hold me upright, his grip on my neck intensifies. He bears the weight of my entire body in his hands. There's a prickling sensation in my limbs. They go numb. The pain is excruciating, in my head and in my neck, and I think that I will die. I think that this is what it feels like to die.

In his arms, I am limp.

Thinking he's succeeded in his task, Will

loosens his hold. He eases my body to the floor. He's gentle at first, but then drops me the last couples of inches. He isn't trying to be gentle. He's trying to be quiet. My body falls, colliding with the cold tile. I try not to react, but the pain is almost too much to bear — not from the fall itself, but from what this man has already done to me. There's the greatest need to cough, to gasp, to throw my hands to my throat.

But if I want to live I have to suppress the need, to lie there motionless instead, unblinking and unbreathing.

Will turns his back on me. Only then do I steal a single short, shallow breath. I hear him. He starts making plans of how to get rid of my body. He's moving quickly because the kids are just upstairs and he knows he can't delay.

An unwanted thought comes to me and I fill with horror. If Otto or sweet little Tate were to come down now and see us, what would Will do? Would he kill them, too?

Will unlocks and pulls open the sliding glass door. He tugs open the screen. I don't watch. But I listen and hear him do these things.

He finds his keys on the counter. There's the sound of metal scraping against the Formica countertop. The keys jangle in his hand and then are quiet. I imagine he's forced them into his jeans pocket, making plans to drag me out the back door and into his car. But what then? I'm no match for Will. He can easily overpower me. There are things I can use in the kitchen to defend myself with. But outside, there is nothing. Only the dogs who love Will more than they love me.

If Will gets me through the doors, I don't stand a chance. I need to think, and I need to think quickly, before he's able to haul me out.

Still as a statue on the kitchen floor, I'm as good as dead to him.

He doesn't check for a pulse. His one and only mistake.

It's not lost on me, the fact that Will doesn't show remorse. He doesn't grieve. He isn't sad that I am gone.

Will is all business as he leans over my body. He quickly assesses the situation. I feel his nearness to me. I hold my breath. The buildup of carbon dioxide burns inside of me. It becomes more than I can bear. I think that I will involuntarily breathe. That, as Will watches on, I'll no longer be able to hold my breath. If I breathe, he will know. And if he discovers I'm alive as I'm lying flat on my back as I am, I'll have no capacity to fight back.

My heart beats hard and fast in fear. I wonder how he can't hear it, how he can't see the movement through the thin pajama shirt. Saliva collects inside my throat, all but gagging me, and I'm overwhelmed by the greatest need to swallow. To breathe.

He tugs on my arms before reconsidering. He grabs me by the ankles instead and pulls roughly. The tile floor is hard against my back and it takes everything in me not to grimace from the abrading pain, but to be limp instead, dead weight.

I don't know how far away from the door I am. I don't know how much farther we have to go. Will grunts as he moves, his breath wheezy. I'm heavier than he thought.

Think, Sadie, think.

He pulls me a handful of feet. Then he stops to gather his breath. My legs drop to the floor; he gets a better grip on my ankles. He tugs gruffly in short bursts. I slide, inches at a time, knowing the time to save myself is running out.

I'm nearing the back door. The cold air is closer than it was before.

It takes great willpower to get myself to fight back. To let Will know that I'm alive. Because if I don't succeed, I will die. But I have to fight back. Because I'll die either way if I don't.

Will lets go of my feet again. He takes a breath. He helps himself to a sip of water straight from the tap. I hear the water run. I hear his tongue lap at it like a dog. The water turns off. He swallows hard, comes back to me.

When he leans down to gather my ankles back into his hands, I use every bit of strength I have to sit suddenly upright. I brace myself and smash my head into his. I try to use his growing fatigue to my advantage, his state of imbalance. His equilibrium is thrown off because he's hunched over my body, pulling. For this one second, I have the upper hand.

His hands go to his head. He staggers suddenly backward, losing balance, falling to the floor. I waste no time. I press on the ground and force myself to my feet.

But as the blood rushes down, the world around me spins. My vision fades to black. I nearly collapse before the adrenaline rushes in and only then can I see.

I feel his hands on my ankle. He's on the floor, trying to pull me down with him. He calls me names as he does, no longer worried about being quiet. "You bitch. You stupid, stupid bitch," he says, this man I married, who vowed to love me till death do us part.

My knees buckle and I collapse to the floor beside him, falling fast. I land face-down, my nose hitting the floor so that it begins to bleed. The blood is profuse, turning my hands red.

I get quickly to my hands and knees. Will comes at me from behind, attempting to reach over me for my neck as I struggle to crawl away from him. I kick backward. I have to get away from him.

My hands reach desperately for the countertop. They latch on, trying to pull me upward, but just as soon lose their grip. My hands are sweaty, my hold weak. Everywhere there is blood. It comes from my nose, my mouth. I can't hold on to the countertop. I slip away, falling back to the floor.

The wooden block of knives sits just out of reach, mocking me.

I try again. Will grapples again for my ankle. He takes me by the lower leg and pulls. I kick hard, but it isn't enough. The blows only leave him momentarily dazed but I'm growing tired, my efforts weakening. I fall facedown again on the floor, biting my tongue. I can't keep doing this. The adrenaline in my body has slowed, the wine, the lethargy taking over.

I don't know that I have it in me to go on.

But then I think of Otto, of Tate, and I know that I must go on.

I'm on the floor facedown as Will mounts my back. All two hundred pounds of him bear down on me, forcing me face-first into the kitchen floor. I couldn't scream if I wanted to. I can barely suck in a breath. My arms are pinned beneath me, getting crushed by Will's weight and mine.

I feel his hands in my hair, massaging my scalp. It's oddly gentle. Sensuous. I feel his satisfaction at having me in this position.

Time slows down. I try to press up against the weight of him, but go nowhere. I can't find my arms.

Will runs his fingers through my hair. Breathlessly he says my name. "Oh, Sadie," he exhales. He enjoys that I'm pinned to the ground as I am, in a powerless position, a slave to my master. "My lovely wife," he says.

He leans in close enough that I feel his breath on my neck. He runs his lips the length of it. He bites gently on my earlobe. I let him. I can't make him stop.

He whispers into my ear, "If only you would have left it alone."

And then he clutches a handful of my hair in his tacky hand, hoists my face inches from the floor and smashes it back down to the tile.

I've never felt such pain in my life. If my nose wasn't broken before, it is now.

He does it again.

Whether it's enough to eventually kill me, I don't know. But soon it will render me unconscious. And there's no telling what he will do then.

This is it, I tell myself. This is where I will die.

But then something happens.

It's Will, not me, who makes a sound, some strange, inarticulate scream of pain. I feel suddenly weightless, not knowing what's happened.

A breath later I realize that the reason for the weightlessness is that he's fallen from my body. He's perched inches to my side, struggling to get to his feet, though his hands are at his head and he, like me, is bleeding. His blood comes from his head, where there is a sudden laceration that wasn't there before.

I crane my aching neck to see. I follow the gaze of his eyes — now shrouded in fear — to see Imogen standing in the kitchen doorway. The fireplace poker is in her steady hands, and it's raised over her head. She blurs in and out before me, until I'm not certain she's real or a result of a head injury. Her face is deadpan. There is no emotion. No anger, no fear. She comes forward and I brace myself for the debilitating pain of the fireplace poker as it strikes me. I clench my eyes, my jaw, knowing the end is near. Imogen will kill me. She will kill the both of us. She never wanted us here.

I grind my teeth. But the pain doesn't come.

I hear Will grunt instead. I open my eyes to see him stumble and fall to the ground, calling Imogen names. I look to her. Our eyes meet and I know.

Imogen is not here to kill me. She's come to save me.

I see the determination in her eye as she raises the weapon for a third time.

But one death on Imogen's conscience is enough. I can't let her do this for me.

I spring to my unsteady feet. It's not easy. Every part of me aches. The blood is abundant, in my eyes so that I can hardly see.

I lunge forward. I throw myself at the wooden knife block, getting in between Will and Imogen. I take the chef knife into my grasp; there's no feeling, no awareness of the handle in my hand.

I barely register this man's face, his eyes as he rises to standing and, at the same time, I turn to face him.

I see the movement of his mouth. His lips move. But there's a ringing in my ears. I can't stand it. I think that it will never stop.

But then it does stop. And I hear something.

I hear that heinous laugh as he says to me, "You'd never do it, you stupid cunt."

He comes at me, attempts to grab the knife from my hands. He gets ahold of it for a minute, and I think, in my weakness, that I will lose the knife to him. That when I do he will use it to kill both Imogen and me.

I pull violently back, regaining full possession of the knife.

He comes at me again.

I don't think this time. I just do. I react.

I plunge the knife into his chest, feeling nothing as the tip of the chef knife cuts right through him. I watch it happen. Imogen, behind me, watches, too.

The blood comes next, spraying and oozing from his body as all two hundred pounds of him collapses to the floor with a dull thud.

I hesitate at first, watching the blood pool beside him. His eyes are open. He's alive, though the life is quickly leaving his body. He looks to me, a beseeching glance as if he thinks I might just do something to help him survive.

An arm rises, reaches enfeebled for me. But he can't reach me.

He won't ever touch me again.

I am in the business of saving lives, not taking them. But there are exceptions to every rule. "You don't deserve to live," I say, feeling empowered because there's no tremor, no shaking in my voice as I say it. My voice is as still as death.

He blinks once, twice, and then it stops, the movement of his eyes coming to a stop, as do the heaving movements of his chest. He stops breathing.

I fall to my hands and knees beside him. I check for a pulse.

It's only then, when Will is dead, that I rise and turn to Imogen, folding her into my arms, and together we cry.

Sadie

One Year Later . . .

I stand on the beach, staring out at the ocean. The shoreline is rocky, creating tide pools that Tate splashes barefoot in. The day is cool, midfifties, but unseasonably warm for this time of year, compared to what we're used to. It's January. January is often bitterly cold, thick with snow. But here it's not, and I'm grateful for it as I'm grateful for all the ways in which this life is different from our life before.

Otto and Imogen have gone ahead to climb rock formations that extend out into the sea. The dogs are with them, tethered to leashes, eager as always to climb. I stay behind with Tate, watch as he plays. As he does, I sit on my heels, examine the rocky beach with my hands.

It's been a year now since we threw into a hat the names of the places we wanted to go. A decision like that shouldn't be taken lightly. And yet we had no family to speak of, no connections, no ties. The world was our oyster. Imogen was the one to reach into the hat and pick, and before we knew it, we were California-bound.

I've never been one to sugarcoat or to lie. Otto and Tate know now that their father isn't the man he led us to believe he was. They don't know all the details of it.

Self-defense, it was decided in the days after Will's death, though I don't know if Officer Berg would have believed it if Imogen, hiding just on the other side of the kitchen door that night, hadn't managed to record Will's confession on her phone.

She also managed to save my life.

Hours after Will was dead, Imogen played the recording for Officer Berg. I was in the hospital, receiving treatment for my wounds. I didn't know about it until later.

You're too smart for your own good, Sadie. If only you'd have let it be, this wouldn't be happening. But I can't have you go around telling people what I did. I'm sure you understand. And since you can't keep your own mouth closed, it's up to me to shut you up for good.

Imogen and I never talked about how she hadn't recorded the entire conversation that night, the parts where Will made it clear I was the one to physically carry out Morgan's murder. Only she and I would ever know the whole truth. No evidence of my involvement in Morgan's murder was found. I was exonerated. Will was charged with both women's deaths.

But that wasn't the end of it. Months of therapy followed, with much more to come. My therapist is a woman named Beverly whose purple-dyed hair seems incongruous with her fifty-eight years. And yet it's perfectly suited to *her.* She has tattoos, a British accent. One goal of our time together is to locate and identify my alters and reunite them into one functioning whole. Another is to face head-on the memories my mind has hidden from me, those of my stepmother and her abuse. We're slowly succeeding.

The kids and I have a family therapist. His name is Bob, which delights Tate. It makes him think of SpongeBob. Imogen has her own therapist, too.

Otto goes to a private art academy, finally finding a world where he feels he fits in. Getting him there is a sacrifice. The tuition is steep and the commute long. But there is no one in the world who deserves this happiness more than Otto.

I watch as ocean waves pound the shoreline. The spray of the waves splashes Tate and he giggles with glee.

This beach was once the site of a city trash dump. Long ago, residents tossed their trash over the cliffs and into the Pacific Ocean. In the decades that followed, the ocean smoothed and polished that trash. It spit it back out onto the shoreline. Except that by then, time and nature had repurposed the trash into something extraordinary. It was no longer refuse but now beautiful beach glass that people come from all over the state to collect.

I gaze at Otto and Imogen at the peak of a rock formation, sitting beside one another, talking. Otto smiles, and Imogen laughs as the wind blows through her long hair. I see Tate splashing sublimely in the tide pool with a grin. There's a little boy beside him now; he's made a friend. I feel light because of it, buoyant. I close my eyes and stare up at the sun. It warms me through.

Will stole many years from my life. He stole my happiness and made me do reprehensible things. It's taken time, but I'm finding ways to forgive myself for all that I have done. Will broke me at first. But in the process of healing, I've become a stronger, more confident version of myself than I used to be. In the aftermath of Will's exploitation and his abuse, I've discovered the woman I was always meant to be, a woman I can be proud of, a woman my children can look up to and admire.

I now know what true happiness is. I experience it every day.

I step from a pair of sneakers and sink my bare feet into the sea, thinking of beach glass.

If time can turn something so undesired into something so loved, the same can happen to all of us. The same can happen to me.

It's happening already.

AUTHOR'S NOTE

Mental illness affects over forty-six million Americans each year. It is an issue of critical importance to our society, and to me personally, as I have experienced the impacts that the disease can have on a family. In *The Other Mrs.*, Sadie is a victim of cruel manipulation by those seeking to take advantage of her illness, and in the end, she is empowered to seize control and ultimately to seek the help she needs. It is my hope that we, as a society, will continue to bring awareness to this important issue and that in the future, we will place greater emphasis on ensuring that those in need have access to proper care and treatment. For more information about mental health or dissociative identity disorder, visit the National Institute of Mental Health (NIMH) and the Cleveland Clinic.

ACKNOWLEDGMENTS

Thank you to my editor, Erika Imranyi, for helping steer me in the right direction, for your diligence and dedication to this book and your patience with me. Thank you to my agent, Rachael Dillon Fried, for offering insight and endless encouragement during the writing and revision process. I'm so proud of what we've accomplished here and look forward to many more books to come. Thank you to Loriana Sacilotto, Margaret Marbury, Natalie Hallak and so many others at HarperCollins for providing indispensable editorial feedback.

Thank you to the wonderful people at HarperCollins, Park Row Books and Sanford Greenburger Associates. I'm so grateful to be a part of such committed, hardworking teams. Thank you to my publicists, Emer Flounders and Kathleen Carter; to Sean Kapitain and crew for another fabulous cover design; to Jennifer Stimson for the copy edits; to sales and marketing; and to the proofreaders, booksellers, librarians, bloggers, bookstagrammers and everyone else who has a hand in getting my words out to readers. This wouldn't be possible without you. And a huge thanks to my Hollywood dream team, Shari Smiley and Scott Schwimer, for your hard work and enthusiasm.

Thank you, as always, to my family for the emotional support; to my children for allowing me to terrify you while I plotted ideas aloud; and to those incredible people who willingly and eagerly dropped everything to read a draft of this novel and provide essential feedback: Karen Horton, Janelle Kolosh, Pete Kyrychenko, Marissa Lukas, Doug Nelson, Vicky Nelson, Donna Rehs, Kelly Reinhardt, Corey Worden and Nicki Worden. This book wouldn't be what it is without your insight and eagle eyes.

ABOUT THE AUTHOR

Mary Kubica is the *New York Times* and *USA Today* bestselling author of *The Good Girl* and *Pretty Baby.* She holds a Bachelor of Arts degree from Miami University in Oxford, Ohio, in history and American literature. She lives outside of Chicago with her husband and two children and enjoys photography, gardening, and caring for the animals at a local shelter.

The employees of Thorndike Press hope you have enjoyed this Large Print book. All our Thorndike, Wheeler, and Kennebec Large Print titles are designed for easy reading, and all our books are made to last. Other Thorndike Press Large Print books are available at your library, through selected bookstores, or directly from us.

For information about titles, please call:
(800) 223-1244

or visit our website at:
gale.com/thorndike

To share your comments, please write:
Publisher
Thorndike Press
10 Water St., Suite 310
Waterville, ME 04901